Praise for
Scoop

"Scoop is a hilarious, smart look at life inside the evening news. Gutteridge's characterization is, as always, spot on and full of wisdom. I loved this book. Rene is one of the few authors who can make me laugh out loud."

——KRISTIN BILLERBECK, author of *What a Girl Wants* and
A Girl's Best Friend

"The scoop on *Scoop*—a fun, irresistible read that also provides a thoughtful look at our culture's emphasis on youth, beauty, and the allure of bad news."

——MEREDITH EFKEN, speaker and author of *SAHM I Am*

"The opening obituary in *Scoop* got my attention. The first page of chapter 1 made me laugh. And then Rene Gutteridge's writing talents sublimely piqued my curiosity. Not one of those uncontrollable responses waned until the end—when a new impulse arrived, one to yell, 'No! Not the end!'"

——CHARLENE ANN BAUMBICH, author of the Dearest Dorothy series

"A full line-up of fun, *Scoop* offers a hilarious, suspenseful show with a cast of enjoyable characters to love from sign-on to sign-off. Tune in to Rene Gutteridge's latest today!"

——LISA SAMSON, author of *The Church Ladies*, *Straight Up*,
and *Apples of Gold: A Parable of Purity*

scoop

OTHER NOVELS
BY RENE GUTTERIDGE

Boo
Boo Who
Boo Hiss
My Life as a Doormat
The Splitting Storm
Storm Gathering
Storm Surge

scoop

a novel

Rene Gutteridge

WATERBROOK
PRESS

SCOOP
PUBLISHED BY WATERBROOK PRESS
12265 Oracle Boulevard, Suite 200
Colorado Springs, Colorado 80921
A division of Random House Inc.

The characters and events in this book are fictional, and any resemblance to actual persons or events is coincidental.

Scripture quotations and paraphrases are taken from the Holy Bible, New International Version®. NIV®. Copyright © 1973, 1978, 1984 by International Bible Society. Used by permission of Zondervan Publishing House. All rights reserved.

10-Digit ISBN 1-4000-7157-7
13-Digit ISBN 978-1-4000-7157-9

Published in association with the literary agency of Janet Kobobel Grant, Books and Such, 4788 Carissa Avenue, Santa Rosa, CA 95405.

Library of Congress Cataloging-in-Publication Data
Gutteridge, Rene.
    Scoop : a novel / Rene Gutteridge. — 1st ed.
      p. cm.
    ISBN-13: 978-1-4000-7157-9
    ISBN-10: 1-4000-7157-7
  1. Television journalists—Fiction. 2. Television news anchors—Fiction. I. Title.
    PS3557.U887S35 2006
    813'.6—dc22

                              2006019168

Printed in the United States of America
2006—First Edition

10 9 8 7 6 5 4 3 2 1

For Susanna Aughtmon, my dear friend
and the funniest woman I know!

HAZARD

PERCY MITCHELL HAZARD was born January 7, 1940, in Dallas, Texas, and passed away June 8 at the age of 65. He was born to Gordon and Ethel Hazard and raised in Austin, Texas. He was baptized at the age of fourteen at Christ the Lord Church. He married Lucy Boyd in 1962, and shortly thereafter moved to Plano. He worked as the manager of a feed store for two years before becoming a computer manager at the unemployment office. A dedicated and hard worker, he spent twenty-eight years of his life there until he was replaced by a computer and became unemployed. Determined to provide for his family, he and Lucy started their own successful clown business, The Hazard Clowns, entertaining children and adults alike. Many people knew him only as Hobo, but his family and friends knew him as a loving and kind man, full of wisdom and laughter. He is survived by his children: Mitchell, 26, married to Claire; Cassie, 24; Hank, 23; Mackenzie, 22; Hayden, 20; Avery, 18; Holt, 16. He will be greatly missed, but is now safely in the hands of his loving Father in heaven. Funeral services will be at Chapel Christian Church on Tuesday at 10:00 a.m.

HAZARD

LUCILLE "LUCY" MARGARET BOYD HAZARD was born February 15, 1945, in St. Louis, Missouri, to Gilbert Boyd, a pastor, and Wanda, a homemaker. She was raised in Louisville, Kentucky, where she spent most of her life until her family moved to Austin, Texas, where she met and married her husband, Percy. She had a long and distinguished career as Inspector 49 at Hanes until 1992, when the company was forced to downsize to 42 inspectors. As her husband lost his job three weeks earlier, they decided to start a clown business. Along with running The Hazard Clowns, this special woman homeschooled all seven of her beloved children. She went to be with her Lord on June 8. She is survived by her children: Mitchell, 26, married to Claire; Cassie, 24; Hank, 23; Mackenzie, 22; Hayden, 20; Avery, 18; Holt, 16. She died happily alongside her husband and will be laid to rest next to him at Resurrection Cemetery. She will be greatly missed by her family who adored and loved her. Funeral services are Tuesday at 10:00 a.m. at Chapel Christian Church.

Chapter 1

Y our parents died with smiles on their faces," the coroner had told the
  Hazard siblings.

Hayden couldn't help but replay his words as she watched the crowded
grave-side service start to disperse. Her oldest brother, Mitch, looked like
their father today, his wise, confident eyes greeting every person who
wanted to shake his hand and console him.

Hayden didn't want anyone consoling her, except her sister Mack.
And Mack was busy distracting those curious minds who wanted to know
exactly how their parents had died. Hayden still wasn't sure she could
explain it. And none of the Hazards were used to being around large
groups of people without their clown makeup and costumes on.

"You just don't see that often," the coroner told the family when they
all stood in a small, stale room. "Smiling, I mean. A lot of people die in
hot tubs. You'd be surprised. Well, I mean, *you* wouldn't, but the average
person who'd never had someone die in a hot tub would be surprised.
Anyway, people don't die with smiles on their faces. Sure, there are some
embalming tricks you can use, but rarely do you actually find people smiling upon death."

Apparently, the smiling was quite a find for the young coroner, who
didn't look a day over Hayden's twenty years, but the fact that her parents
were smiling upon death had brought Hayden no comfort.

A longtime client of their family business, Mr. Stewart, made his way
across the lush grass toward her. He was a bossy old man, and nosy too,
but he did like clowns. And the Hazard Clowns made an appearance at
every one of his company parties, not to mention all the birthdays of his

grandchildren and his great-grandchildren. He even surprised his wife once on their anniversary with clowns, and what a surprise it was. Mrs. Stewart wasn't impressed, the Hazards exited promptly, leaving Mr. Stewart trying to explain why clowns were romantic.

"Hayden, I don't know what to say."

Hayden politely shook his hand. It was strange having a conversation with Mr. Stewart. Normally he was gooing and gushing and attempting to calm the children who were afraid of clowns. To Hayden, the high-pitched cadence he used when speaking with children always seemed as terrifying as the clowns themselves.

Mr. Stewart's sharp eyes narrowed, and he looked around before saying, "How, exactly, did your parents die?" He didn't pause long. "There's a lot of speculation, and I understand your need for privacy, but when you hide something like this, it only causes rumors to grow."

What had grown, Hayden noticed, was the rather large mole on the tip of his long nose. She tried to keep direct eye contact, just like her parents had taught her. But it was inches from her face, as was his breath, which had actually made a woman at a barbecue pass out once.

Hayden didn't know what to say to make him go away. The family had agreed not to divulge the details about how their parents had died, but she couldn't afford to offend Mr. Stewart either. He was one of their biggest clients.

"Well, Mr. Stewart, there's nothing to hide. It was an accident. They were on vacation—"

"You see, that's the strange thing," Mr. Stewart said. "I've known your parents twenty years, and I've never known them to go on vacation before."

Hayden nodded. It was true. Their first...and last...vacation. Percy and Lucy Hazard decided to go while their youngest two children were away at clown school. Hayden, the third youngest, worked double-time to keep up with the office work while they were gone. Just an hour or so before the accident, they'd even called to say what a good time they were having. "Gotta go!" Dad had said. "Mom wants to go down to that heart-shaped hot tub again!"

"So?" Mr. Stewart urged, his beady eyes fierce while he held her hand like it was a baby bird.

Hayden glanced around. Nobody else who could help seemed to be nearby. Hank, her quiet older brother, loitered alone by a tree. Her sister Cassie was making a scene by the coffin, blotting tears and hugging anyone's neck that would let her. The youngest Hazards, Avery and Holt, looked like small children, wide-eyed and clinging to Mitch's wife, Claire. Where was Mack? Hayden wondered.

"I'm a trusted friend," Mr. Stewart said, in a not-so-friendly voice.

"I know." She just wanted Mr. Stewart to go and the service to end so she could be back at home, curled up in her bed, crying.

"Hayden," he said, his voice rising to that terrifying cadence that unsettled her nerves along with every kid under six. "You know I can be discreet. Your parents were good friends, that's all."

Hayden couldn't stand it anymore. Everything was about to spill out when she felt a hand on her shoulder. Right beside her, out of nowhere, Mack was there. "Mr. Stewart," Mack said, "I'm sorry, but we have to go. We're having a family meeting."

"A family meeting?" Hayden asked. "About what?"

Mack glanced at Mr. Stewart and then said, "I'll tell you on the way."

Their abrupt departure bewildered Mr. Stewart, who trailed behind them as they made their way to the car. "What's going on? What's the meeting about? Who's running this meeting?" His questions continued all the way to the car, where Mack opened the door for Hayden, who quickly climbed in.

"Mackenzie," Mr. Stewart said sternly, "I am one of your company's best clients. I demand to know what's going on. First of all, were your parents murdered?"

Hayden watched as Mack kept an even expression. "Why would you think they were murdered?"

"The rumor is they went to Las Vegas for their vacation, and we all know what kind of city that is."

Mack sighed, looking exhausted. "Mr. Stewart, they were not murdered. It was just an unfortunate incident."

"Incident? Accident? What?"

Mack glanced at Hayden. She looked desperate for relief, and Hayden smiled a little, hoping to assure her.

"Well?" Mr. Stewart asked.

"Look, we don't really understand it ourselves," Mack finally said, "but it boils down to an overly ambitious serenading guitar player, a hundred-foot extension cord, and a rack of mood lighting." Mack shook Mr. Stewart's hand while his jaw dropped a little. "We'll talk soon."

A lump formed in Hayden's throat. Her father used to say that all the time. *"We'll talk soon."*

Hayden shut the passenger door while Mack went to the driver's side. Unfortunately, Hayden's window was rolled down and the next thing she knew, that mole stared her down.

"What's this meeting about? The business? What's going to happen?"

As Mack pulled the car away from the curb, Hayden said, "Mr. Stewart, please don't worry. It's our family's business, and we're still a family. I can assure you, nothing is going to happen to the business."

"The family business is no more."

All the Hazard siblings sat clustered in their parents' living room, talking among themselves, wondering why their eldest brother had called the meeting, when Mitch made the pronouncement. Claire stood beside

Mitch, and by the expression on her face, it was clear that Mitch had planned to say something else.

Mitch cleared his throat and loosened his tie, but he couldn't look at any of them, which struck Hayden as very odd, since Mitch was by far the most confident Hazard sibling.

Finally, he gathered himself. "I'm sorry. I didn't intend to begin like that. There's more to say. I haven't even called the meeting to order," Mitch said, a tight grin stretching across his startled expression.

Their father had always started the day with prayer, and then a formal call to begin the meeting. Hayden once asked her mother why he did that, since it seemed silly to her. Her mother said it helped distinguish the family from the business.

"But the family is the business and the business is the family," Hayden exclaimed.

Her mother replied, "There must be a distinction." Hayden had never really understood that statement. And now she was not understanding what Mitch was trying to say.

He attempted to call the meeting to order when Mack popped up from her chair. She was never any good at raising her hand like they were supposed to.

"What are you talking about?" Mack asked.

Mitch held up his hands. "Let me try this again. Some of you are too young to remember, but Mom and Dad started the family business to put food on the table. The two of them had both lost their jobs, and the business made money but allowed Mom to stay home and school us."

Cassie's hand shot into the air, but she didn't bother to wait to be called on. "What do you *mean* the family business is no more? I happen to know that the business is doing just fine!"

"If you'll let me explain," Mitch looked sad and exhausted. He glanced at Claire and then said, "I have other dreams. Bigger dreams…and you all should too. I love our business. I love our family, but I don't want to be a clown for the rest of my life."

Hayden squeezed Mack's hand until Mack's knuckles popped, causing Holt and Avery to glance over with large round eyes. Mitch lowered his voice and came closer to the rest of them. "This world is bigger than our little slice of the universe. There's so much more to see and do. Mom and Dad loved us, and that's why they sheltered us. But everything they've taught us has equipped us to go out into the world. We have everything we need to survive, and not only survive, but thrive."

"What are you saying?" Everyone turned to stare at Hank. Nobody could believe he'd spoken. Most of the time in family meetings, he fashioned artwork from foam cups. Now, apparently, he spoke for them all.

"I've sold the company."

Complete silence fell, and then Cassie squeaked, "You sold *us*?"

Everyone's eyes shifted from Cassie to Mitch, except Cassie's eyes, which shifted from Mitch to a nearby mirror, where she blotted away the mascara she wasn't supposed to be wearing. Mitch smiled a little. "I sold ownership. We're incorporated, which means we have clients, supplies, equipment, venues."

Nobody could contain themselves, and Hayden began to cry. She clutched Mack's arm, while Mack just looked mad.

Mitch tried to settle everyone down.

"Please, just listen. I know this is a shock, but I also know, deep down inside, that we're not supposed to be clowns for the rest of our lives. Mom and Dad are gone, and now it's time for us to go out into the world and make something of ourselves."

"How could you do this to us?" Cassie wailed.

"Because I know all of you," Mitch said, his soothing confidence returning. He made eye contact with each of them. "I know what you're made of, what you're capable of. Each one of you has an extraordinary chance to make your life count. What are you going to do with it?"

The room grew quiet again as he paused. Then Mitch continued. "The company sold to Clowns Inc. for a lot of money, and it will be divided equally among all of us. Believe it or not, with the life insurance and Mom and Dad's savings, there's enough for each of you to go to college, if you wish, plus have enough money left over to start a new life."

Hayden's voice trembled. "Without each other?"

"We'll always have each other. Nothing will change that. No matter how far apart we are, we'll always have each other. It's going to be a magnificent journey for each of you. You're going to discover things about yourself you never knew, things about the world you never knew. You're going to be a light in this world."

He beckoned to Claire, the only other person in the room who looked excited about the prospect of magnificent journeys. "There's one more thing you should know," Mitch said, wrapping an arm around Claire's shoulder. "You all are going to be aunts and uncles!"

Ordinarily, that kind of thing would've caused great applause among the Hazard family. But nobody could clap. Or even smile. It was just another reminder of how sad and tragic their parents' death was. They would never get to see their grandchildren. And the business they'd built from the ground up was now gone.

Mitch said, "Brothers. Sisters. Trust me. It'll all be okay. It's a new chapter in your life, but it's not the end of the world."

Hayden stood, walked out of the house and into the backyard. How could Mitch have done this? How? This was all she knew! She'd been born in the farmhouse, raised there, schooled there. Her only friends were her siblings. The farthest she'd ever been from home was on trips to county fairs with their clown act. Where would she live? How could she possibly know what she was supposed to do with her life? Her life was her family.

She stood against the tree she'd once climbed as a child and cried into her hands. She'd grieved for her parents, but now she grieved over a life that was no longer there. It wasn't possible! No other occupation suited her.

A hand pressed against her back. She turned to find Mack, who embraced her and let her cry for a long time. Mack led her to a nearby bench and sat her down.

"I hate Mitch right now," Hayden said, gasping as the words flowed out of her mouth. Her parents had always taught her not to hate anyone.

Mack nodded, but then she said, "You know, I've always wanted to be a police officer."

Hayden blinked through her tears. "You have?"

Mack shrugged. "It was just a dream, though, you know? I never thought I'd actually have a chance to do it."

"You never told me that."

"I know. I hid it down deep. I thought it was silly."

Hayden smiled through her tears. "Well, you did play eight different law-enforcement characters."

Mack hugged her. "Hayden, Mitch is right. Mom and Dad built this company to put food on the table. And then it grew into this big thing that we all became involved in. But when I was five, Dad and I were lying in the backyard under the stars one night, and he asked me if I could do anything in the world, what would it be?"

"What did you say?"

"I don't remember," she laughed, "but I do remember him telling me that whatever I put my mind to, I could do. At five, Dad had big dreams for me." She sighed. "I think Mom and Dad saw an ugly world out there, and after they both lost their jobs, they were determined to protect us from it."

Hayden stared into the evening sky, the tiny stars twinkling above. "I never had any dreams. I never thought I'd do anything except what I was doing." She looked down. "And truthfully, I didn't do it all that well."

"Hayden, it's not your fault you were coulrophobic. Besides, you were great at the administrative stuff. The business really needed that. Mom couldn't handle it by herself anymore."

Hayden sighed. In the last year, since she'd finally admitted she was deathly afraid of clowns, she'd felt so guilty, but thankful to be included.

Mack squeezed her hand. "You'll find your purpose. I guarantee it. God won't let you down."

With a collective sigh, they both leaned back into the bench and took in the expansive night sky that could only be seen from outside the city limits. Mack chuckled. "So you want to know what Mitch is going to do?"

"He told you?"

"He told us after you left the room. He's working for a company called Ditch Witch."

"Ditch Witch? That sounds weird. Mitch at Ditch Witch."

"He'll be one of their managers."

Hayden sighed and folded her arms across her chest. "So that's the secret to finding your life purpose. It has to rhyme with your first name." She leaned her head on Mack's shoulder. "This family is safe. I don't want to leave it."

Mack stroked her hair. "I know. It's scary to think about. If we could all have Mitch's confidence, right?"

"What in the world am I going to do out there, Mack? What kind of difference can I make?"

"Mitch is right. Mom and Dad equipped us. We just have to remember what we were taught, and we'll be just fine."

Hayden didn't know the world beyond children's birthday parties and company picnics. She'd seen only glimpses, and that had been fine with her.

Mack laughed. "Remember what Dad used to say any time we complained about change? 'Blessed are the flexible, for they shall not be bent out of shape.'"

Chapter 2

Five years later

H ugo Talley had told his doctor that he was fairly sure the antianxiety medication he was on was not working anymore. "My body has
gotten used to it," he complained. The doctor, a woman who looked better suited for the fashion industry, explained that was not possible. When
Hugo replied, "Well, it's not working," the doctor had the audacity to
suggest that the stress in his life had increased.

"I'm in the news business." Hugo wanted to shout it, but he didn't.
That was how he knew the Blue Pill wasn't working well anymore. He was
a few insults away from screaming at a woman half his age. "If people
would stop drinking and driving, stealing cars, abusing their spouses, and
being, in general, regular idiots, I wouldn't have to take this at all."

The doctor sent him home with orders to get his stress under control.

Now, sitting at his desk, Hugo popped the pill in his mouth and
waited. And waited. Nothing. No difference. He'd seen the commercials
on television. Being in the television business himself, he knew about all
the smoke and mirrors. He'd still fallen prey to idea that he, too, could be
smiling and bike riding, and holding the hand of a gray-haired woman
with the face of a thirty-year-old, enjoying life with no sexual side effects
and only a slight risk of a seizure, stroke, or death. His job was more likely
to kill him than this little Blue Pill.

"Come on, kick in," he muttered. He looked at the shiny brass name
plate on his desk—facing him, not the door. It read "Hugo Talley, Executive Producer." *Executive.* What he wouldn't give to be a good, old-fashioned, everyday news producer again. But with the pay he had now.

He wondered why he had an office at all. It was a square box with a fake wooden door and an all-glass wall that served no purpose at all. The former executive producer, who'd died of a heart attack last January, thought a glass wall was a good idea so he could keep an eye on everything. But in reality, it served only to keep a hundred pairs of eyes on him.

He guzzled more water, hoping to get that tiny pill dissolved. That was the other mystery, why the color of the pill was so important in the commercial. "Are you on the Blue Pill yet?" it asked. Maybe he should be on the Red Pill. Or the Purple Pill.

Hugo hunched over his desk, trying to look like he was too busy to be disturbed. He'd learned long ago in this all-seeing office that if he looked even the least bit unoccupied, one person behind a pair of those hundreds of eyes would feel the need to come in and occupy him.

It had not been a good afternoon. The news meeting had gone poorly, and Chad Arbus, Hugo's boss and the station news director, had made sure everyone knew how unhappy he was about it. But Chad was unhappy in general, and there were times that Hugo had actually thought about slipping one of his Blue Pills into Chad's coffee.

But anxiety wasn't really young Chad's problem. The problem with Chad was that he was a jerk. He was probably born a jerk. He probably soiled his diapers at all the worst places and times, just to see his mother have to try to clean it all up. That was the kind of man Chad was, and Chad was half the reason Hugo needed the Blue Pill.

The other half was Gilda Braun. Gilda was an icon. She'd been doing the news for thirty-five years. There was even a statue of her at the airport. Gilda was the reason that every nursing home within the station's viewing area watched News Channel 7. Channel 7 couldn't boast about much, but it could boast that it was the most-watched news channel among the geriatric population. Unfortunately, even their voice-over guy couldn't make that sound favorable.

Instead, they boasted about their hard work. "News Channel 7...

Working Around the Clock to Bring You the News." Their logo was a clock, an indication that any time the news was appropriate, they would have the news. So there was the morning show, which lasted two hours, until the national morning show came on. Then there was an hourlong noon show, a four-thirty, a five, a six, a six-thirty, and the Big Daddy, the "tenner" as they called it.

And that was where Gilda came in. She'd been the ten o'clock news anchor since Hugo was a teenager and before Chad was even born. And she had a lot of clout.

Hugo's thoughts were interrupted by a voice on his speaker phone. "Hugo, in my office now." Chad hung up, and Hugo could only assume Chad knew he was in his office because he could see him. Hugo sighed and slouched toward his door and into the hallway. It irritated him that Chad continued to call him Hugo. Maybe Hugo was old-fashioned, but there were things that he expected. He called superiors and co-workers Mr. and Ms., and expected to be called the same. And he dressed up for work, complete with a tie and pressed slacks. Chad, on the other hand, was on a first-name basis with everyone and thought buttoning two of the four buttons on his polo was dressing up. Hugo had even witnessed him wear a cotton shirt tucked in only at the belt buckle to a board meeting before. It was hideous.

Hugo held his ground on it, though, and continued to dress in a way that suited his idealism. And as much as it wounded him on every occasion that it occurred, Hugo addressed his thirty-three-year-old boss as Mr. Arbus. It was just the way things were supposed to be done, even if he was the only one doing it. That's what his father had taught him, and his father, with great pride, had been a live truck operator for fifteen years. His father was dedicated and loyal and apparently a dying breed. Live truck operators these days stayed around for about three months.

Never once did Hugo see his father leave the house without a tie on. He knew what to expect as he came closer to Chad's corner office, which had a glass wall too, except with a view of the city, not the newsroom. It was too big to call a window, Hugo thought. Ten pictures of Chad with various celebrities hung neatly on one wall.

Hugo knew Chad was going to rant. It was what Chad liked to do. He never really had any suggestions or solutions, but he certainly loved to point out one problem after another.

He was a man of small stature, barely over five foot three, but his demeanor was fierce, and when he grimaced and bared his teeth, his face turned blood red and the premature bald spot on the peak of his scalp turned white. He also liked to pound his fist a lot, and Hugo once thought that perhaps he learned all of his leadership techniques from a comic strip, because that's what he looked like most of the time…a cartoon. His big, googly eyes, tiny ears, casual polos, and slicked-back ponytail didn't help matters. Hugo hated that ponytail.

Not that Chad Arbus was a complete monster. He was also a shrewd businessman. He knew the important times when his googly eyes should take on a more wise and astute nature. But Hugo would bet an entire bottle of the Blue Pill that he would not see anything wise or astute now.

Opening the door to Chad's office, Hugo greeted the younger man with a taut smile and took a seat that wasn't offered. Chad turned away and looked out his window, the sun highlighting his pale skin.

"Hugo," he said, "I am not going to settle for another disastrous sweeps week." He turned, stuffing his hands in his pockets. "We can't fall into last place. Not again."

"We've got a lot of things lined up for sweeps week. We've planned a segment on five ways to reduce your risk of choking while dining out. And a week-long series on the ten deadliest backyard dangers, plus—"

Chad held up his hands. "Hugo," he said mildly, his big eyelids drooping a bit like he was about to tell an inside joke, "we both know what the problem is." He turned back to the window again. "*Who* the problem is."

Hugo didn't know what else to do, so he rose, went to the door, and shut it. The click seemed to be Chad's cue to talk freely. "She's ruining us!"

Biting his lip, Hugo couldn't think of a thing to say for or against Gilda. Everyone at Channel 7 knew that Gilda's departure was long over-due—everyone but Gilda—yet there were so many complexities to the matter that there didn't seem to be a plausible solution. Channel 7 owned about seventy percent of the market in the sixty-five and over crowd. The problem was, they owned about nineteen percent in the twenty-five to thirty-four crowd. And even less in the other demographics. The only way to get the younger crowd to tune in was to bring in younger talent, which they'd done by hiring Tate Franklin, who looked like Tom Cruise's better-looking brother, as coanchor. Though Tate came with a lot of nearly unbearable idiosyncrasies, he was still a young-looking face. The trouble was the two anchors were so mismatched, you almost expected Gilda to call Tate "dear" on air occasionally. She'd actually patted his hand once.

Hugo decided to get comfortable. The Blue Pill was kicking in. *Finally.* And he figured if he sat really still for about fifteen minutes, Chad would rant and then let him get back to work.

Chad, in completely predictable fashion, pulled out two eight-by-ten glossy photos from a folder, holding them up in each hand for Hugo to look at, which he did, pretending interest, as if he hadn't seen them a thousand times.

The left photo showed Grace Johnson and Robert Kelly from Channel 3 News. They looked like they could be twins—both had dark brown hair, olive skin, and dark eyes. They were a striking news duo that Channel 3 hired about four years ago and paid big bucks to keep. That's why Channel 3 was number one.

In his right hand Chad held a photo of Channel 10's Jennifer Wallace and Patrick Buckley, or Barbie and Ken, as Hugo liked to refer to them. Jennifer, a striking blonde whose teeth glowed white enough to rival a solar flare, landed the job two years ago. Soon after, they hired Patrick, whose news-do (hair specifically cut to part and feather backward, signaling a conservative maturity) had propelled him farther than his ability to anchor. Yet these two continued to climb the ratings ladder and were giving Channel 3 a run for its money.

Chad dropped the photos to his desk. "I've given this woman every opportunity to retire with dignity. The problem is, she's completely out of touch with the reality of a midlevel market. It's not about experience and tenure. It's about hot-looking anchors and cutting-edge, breaking news feeds." Chad fell into his plush leather chair and shook his head. "There's only one solution I can think of, and you're the man to carry it out."

"Me, sir?" This caught Hugo's attention because Chad was not one for offering solutions or handing out compliments. Hugo sat a little taller in his chair. It wasn't really a logical question, since he hadn't even heard the proposed solution, but something about it made him feel uncomfortable.

"Hugo, you're a very calm person. Unnaturally calm, really. That's one thing I've noticed about you. And it takes a supremely calm person to be the executive producer of a news station and the ten o'clock producer. I've never doubted you for a single day."

"Oh," Hugo said. "Uh, thank you, Mr. Arbus."

"And it's going to take someone with nerves of steel to solve this problem." Chad leaned forward, placing his short arms on his desk and folding his petite fingers together.

Hugo felt himself tremble a little.

"Wh—? Uh, what are you suggesting I do?"

"You are going to have to convince Gilda she needs Botox."

Pre–Blue Pill days, this would've made his heart flutter. And even though his heart was not fluttering, his head knew his heart should be, which caused him to panic, but with no real physical signs to confirm it.

"Excuse me?"

"Botox. I hear it works wonders. If she gives you grief about it, tell her it's that or the knife."

Hugo wasn't completely sure if Chad was referring to a cosmetic surgeon's knife or a hit man's.

Chad growled as he studied Hugo's expression, whatever it was. "Well, tell her we'll pay for it. But it's coming out of her wardrobe allowance."

"Sir, how can I convince Gilda she needs Botox? We can't even get her to change the way she wears her makeup." The only time Gilda's concoction of blue eye shadow, fake eyelashes, bright pink blush, and red lipstick had changed was when her husband died twelve years earlier. She stopped wearing red lipstick, saying she'd worn it for Charles all those years because that was his favorite. She'd moved on to mauve, and occasionally she'd wear a peach color that clashed with every piece of clothing she owned. But it was part of what made Gilda. In the seventies and eighties she was saucy, sassy, and audacious. Now she was just overdone.

Besides that, Gilda had been adamant about avoiding cosmetic procedures to make herself look younger. She felt women should grow old gracefully. She swore she didn't even color her hair, blaming the strange purple sheen that reflected off the top of her auburn hair on the harsh studio lighting. As she'd grown older in front of the camera over the years, she made reference to her age now and then, joking about it and making lighthearted remarks about the upsides of aging in a way that warmed every senior citizen's heart. It was a constant reminder to everyone that "their day was coming."

So while Jennifer Wallace might jump in line for Botox and teeth bleaching, Gilda Braun would just as quickly punch out Hugo just for suggesting it.

Chad said, "Look, Hugo, you're savvy enough to figure this out. Women love compliments. Say something like, 'You're really good-looking for your age. It's just that we don't want you to look your age anymore.'" Chad waved his hand in the air as he verbalized the worst thought any woman-fearing man could think. There was a reason Chad Arbus had never married, and it wasn't that he was married to his job. Even a job like this couldn't find him attractive.

"Go on," Chad said, shooing him with hands so small Hugo thought if he squeezed hard enough during a handshake one might just break right off.

"Sir, with all due respect, I'm not certain I'll be able to convince Gilda of the Botox idea. And you know how she can hold a grudge."

Chad's expression reflected that he knew firsthand.

"You're our last hope."

"Our last hope before what?"

"Just get it done, Hugo." Chad's tone turned deep and serious. "And Hugo? You should be aware that I've ordered an independent evaluation of the station. A company is assessing our situation and finding the weak links. I should have the report in a few days. Just thought you should know."

Hugo stood and walked back to his office. The Blue Pill was so strange. Physically, he was having none of the symptoms one should have when told a confrontation with Gilda Braun was inevitable. Yet his mind knew that this was a situation that could—and most likely would— ensure bodily harm. His body was numb to the idea, at the moment, and was carrying along like any other day. Maybe the numbness would last through his face-off with Gilda.

He'd begun taking the Blue Pill fifteen months ago, after he rushed himself to the emergency room with chest pains. Two thousand dollars worth of tests had shown it was just stress.

His doctor, whom he'd known since the day she graduated from medical school, said he wasn't really a good candidate for anxiety medication, as meant for people who had chemical imbalances resulting in uncontrollable anxiety. Hugo explained he was indeed chemically imbalanced, and had been since 1987 when he stopped smoking.

Hugo went on and on about his need for it. He knew to do this because the ten o'clock had just run a news story about doctors who over-prescribe to patients who insist on it.

The doctor relented, but said she would allow it on a temporary basis only, during which time Hugo should work to manage the stress in his life.

That's when he was promoted to executive producer.

Back in his office, Hugo sat down in his chair, grabbed a pencil, hunched over his desk, and pondered how he would tell Gilda that the deep crease in her brow was causing hundreds of thousands of viewers to change the channel. Was it really true? Was it Gilda's aging face?

"Good morning," sang a voice as his door opened and his assistant walked in. He couldn't remember her name, couldn't even remember if she was a temp or an intern. She'd been around about four weeks, ever since his supposedly permanent assistant, Judith, went on maternity leave for the fifth time in six years. Hugo had to wonder who was working harder, her or her ovaries, but wondering that out loud would probably mean a lawsuit, so he just shut up, sent baby gifts, and tried to cope with each new assistant who replaced her.

This particular one, a quiet but sunny young woman with white blonde hair and morning-person eyes, hadn't been half bad. She'd caught on quickly to the tasks Hugo needed performed and hardly ever ran late or forgot to complete something. She did, however, seem to lack a few basic social skills, but Hugo could manage personality disorders as long as they didn't interfere with his job or show up on camera.

She handed him his coffee, doctored to perfection. That was one thing that was really growing on him: she seemed to want to serve him in every way. She was old-fashioned in that sense, didn't seem to have the women's lib thing going on. Plus, she managed a smile every day, which was nothing short of miraculous in this business, especially without the presence of a red glowing light atop three cameras.

Hayden Hazard. That was her name.

"Good morning, Ms. Hazard," he said, stirring his coffee. He watched as she went straight to the out-box that held all of her morning duties. As she was gathering the folders and papers, Hugo Talley suddenly had a good idea. A great idea. Quite possibly the best idea of his career. It could solve what he previously thought was an unsolvable problem. How small of him to think there were problems that couldn't be solved. All problems had a solution, if you just thought hard enough and didn't mind getting your hands a little dirty now and then.

He watched the young woman shuffle papers as the plan grew inside his head, detail by detail.

Gilda Braun sat on her stool in front of a mirror with so much glaring light it made her makeup lady squint. Gilda was used to light. She'd been in front of lights for thirty-five years.

And even after all that time, sweeps week was still a thrill. She loved the challenge. It was one week away, and she could already feel the buzz in the newsroom. The news team was at the top of its game, and she was the leader. She'd taught the infant Tate Franklin how to turn it up a notch for sweeps week. Before his contract update prevented him from doing anything that threatened to mess up his face, Tate used to be into extreme sports, so Gilda used words such as "rush" and "free fall" to talk on his level. The guy never knew he could be so charming. And she also let him in on her little secret: there was nothing wrong with using a little bit of sex appeal to get people to watch. That's how she'd done it all these years. Nothing over the top, nothing you could really put your finger on or stare at. It was a subtle flirtation with the camera—the way she joked with the weatherman about how she hated to water her petunias, the way she begged the sportscaster for good news about her alma mater—these were the things that gave her lasting power. It wasn't a plunging neckline. It was a familiarity, a calmness, a sense of wisdom *and* whimsy, all wrapped up in small, highly scrutinized sound bites.

A tap on her door caused her to spin on her stool. "Come in, Tate." Tate liked to check in with her every day, the poor lad. She'd never met a man more insecure. And he had reason to be. He had some nasty little idiosyncrasies that would shame him if they ever came to light. But Gilda would never let that happen. She was seasoned enough to handle him, and she couldn't deny that it made her feel powerful. Something about the idea that he was unable to anchor alone appealed to her. Hugo had found this out by mistake when Gilda was sent on special assignment. Tate fell apart on air, his eyes bouncing all over the place, his words streaming out like nonsense. During a psychological evaluation the next morning, he confessed that his mother had abandoned him as a child and that he now had codependency issues. *That was putting it mildly,* Gilda thought. But whatever the case, Hugo didn't allow Tate to anchor by himself anymore. This was the first of several strange tics that Tate Franklin, with his pretty brown eyes and his fancy smile, began to reveal. Gilda couldn't help revel in the idea that "young and sexy" had come back to bite Chad Arbus on the butt. And that made Gilda feel very, very powerful.

The door opened and a young woman entered. Hugo's new assistant. Gilda had seen her flitting around the newsroom with gust and glee. There were few times Gilda felt compelled to smile. This was not one of them.

"What is it?"

"Um, Ms. Braun," the girl said, fumbling several attempts to state her reason for coming into her dressing room. Gilda Braun was the only anchor who actually had her own dressing room, but then again, nobody else had been there thirty-five years.

"What's your name again?" Gilda asked.

"Hayden. Hayden Hazard."

"Hayden Hazard. Odd name."

The young woman blinked and smiled feebly.

"Okay, we've got that much out. Now, what are you here for? You're Hugo's assistant. Does he have you running little errands for him?"

The girl took a deep breath and stared at the carpet for a moment, shaking her head and mumbling to herself. Gilda grew a little nervous.

"Are you okay?" Gilda finally asked. She slid her hand next to the phone on her vanity, just in case she had to call security.

Hayden finally looked up at her with a worried, no, sad expression on her face. "May I sit?"

Gilda glanced at the stool her makeup lady usually used and nodded, but the young lady didn't seem to notice that it was with a great deal of apprehension. Instead, Hayden seemed caught up in the conversation she was having with either herself or some imaginary friend. Either way, it was disconcerting.

Finally, she looked directly at Gilda with a smile more confident than anyone should wear who has just been talking to oneself.

"I'm having a little bit of an internal conflict," Hayden said.

Gilda replied, "Well, it should probably stay right there inside yourself then."

"It involves you."

Gilda raised an eyebrow.

"There's a party. And you're invited."

"A party?"

"Yes but, Ms. Braun, I'm going to have to tell you that I'm not g[o] and I don't think you should either. You see, I feel compelled to t[e] the truth. There's a lie going around this country about women an[d] and it has to stop. The only way a lie stops is to smack it down wi[th] truth." She slapped a hand against her knee. "That's what my dad use[d] say, anyway."

Gilda felt her lip quiver…her top lip, in a weird Elvis sort of way. It

hadn't twitched that way since she lost her voice on air eight years ago. In
a moment of unexpected honesty, she wasn't sure she wanted to hear this
imminent truth. Maybe she should just take the lie and deal with the consequences later.

But it was too late. The truth came tumbling out.

Chapter 3

T he chill against Ray Duffey's cheeks could be felt all the way through his skin and into his teeth. He walked briskly along the dark, wet street, Doug Beaker, his cameraman, a few steps behind him growling about how they were probably going to get shot.

"Shut up about it, Beaker."

"Your buddy Roarke says the police won't even go down this street without backup."

"Well, Roarke knows too much and lives for the thrill of telling people like you about streets like this." Ray knew Roarke had a lot of fun playing on Beaker's fears.

"It screams murder. How many murders do you think took place on this street last year?"

Ray kept walking. Hoover Street was quiet under a bright, clear sky. Beaker was annoying at times, with a chip on his shoulder that left little room for the camera that was supposed to be there. But in this case he was right. They weren't in the safest of neighborhoods. They'd been in worse, but those were crime scenes lit up by police cars' strobing red and blue lights.

Only three times in his career as a reporter had Ray refused to carry out an assignment for fear of mortal danger. He didn't really fear for his own life. His dream was to be an investigative reporter for a national network, and in that line of work, you're going to make a few enemies. But he felt a certain responsibility for his crew.

Ray made his way up a crumbling sidewalk toward a dilapidated house. The screen door hung on one hinge, and a couch sat on the porch. A dog barked next door, causing Beaker to scuttle closer to Ray.

These were the days he hated, the assignments he hated. He told himself it was a means to an end, that he had to serve his time doing this in order to get the experience to do what he really wanted to do.

But it just made his stomach sick. And it wasn't even the nonsense of it all. He had real internal conflicts at times. Maybe the internal conflict came from the fact that he'd gotten so good at it.

Behind Ray, Beaker said, "I'd sue my neighbors if they ever let their houses get like this!" The cameraman was an enigma. Among the delicate balance of Beaker's personas was a lawsuit-happy one. He had sued a major fast-food chain because his burger didn't resemble the burger in the restaurant's advertising. He won the lawsuit, and ever since then, suing had been like a gambling addiction. He'd lost most of the money he won in the settlement paying court costs for his new lawsuits.

But he swore up and down he was going to get rich off of it. And then, "I won't have to do this dangerous job anymore." Ray figured the guy had a better chance of being shot by someone he sued than being a videographer, but he kept his thoughts to himself.

Ray knocked and waited for the face that would soon greet him with bewilderment or anger. As he stood there, his mind wandered back to the face of Janet Bixby. Janet's son had killed another driver. He was seventeen, coming home from a party, and driving drunk. He was also the star quarterback at his school. Hugo had sent Ray out to the Bixby home to try to get them to make a statement on camera. It was gritty, disgusting work, but it was what people wanted to see, and so he went.

At first Mrs. Bixby refused the interview, begging for privacy so the family could deal with the tragedy.

"But ma'am," Ray had said, in his most polite, trustworthy voice, "others could learn from your experience. You could save someone else from this horror."

The woman's face, puffy with distress and drawn downward from grief, looked up at him, and tears pooled in her eyes. She believed him.

She believed that telling her story on the news might keep some other teenager from drinking and driving.

Ray wanted to bury himself alive. It was the lowest moment of his career.

It wasn't that he didn't believe that Janet's story might make a difference. Maybe it could. But he had crossed a line to get what he wanted.

Their show had gotten the highest ratings of that night because he had landed the only interview with the grieving family of the drunk teenage driver. Ray couldn't even remember what she'd said on camera, and probably nobody else could either. What was permanently branded into his and everyone else's mind was the image of this grief-stricken mother trying to make sense of a senseless tragedy.

Over the years Ray had learned to read body language as well as the basic needs of people. A lot of them were easy. Very rarely would the station have to go to the trouble of shadowing somebody's face, because most everyone in the world wanted his moment of importance. "This is your fifteen minutes of fame" brought out the kinds of confessions that a priest would envy. "Don't you want to tell your side of the story?" was usually a sure bet for people involved in some kind of dispute. In more difficult circumstances, he would play to someone's personality. If he was in a rough crowd, he'd lose his manners and try to blend in. If he wanted a quote from a politician, he'd put on a tie and even a jacket, throw out a compliment about the job he or she was doing, and in the same breath, tag on a question that somehow related. Once, when he was trying to break a story about cockfighting, he'd actually put on cowboy boots and a fake Hank Williams Jr. tattoo when he interviewed the men who believed cockfighting should be legal. When he interviewed the lawmakers who were trying to ban it, he donned regular shoes, a starched white shirt, and plenty of knowledge about the repercussions of the practice.

Now standing on this porch, Ray could hear a television and a few words of conversation as someone passed by the front door on the other side. Cold calls like this one were the worst. He hated knocking on the door of someone's home. And to make matters worse, this was a ridiculous story. He'd said so in the afternoon meeting.

"Aren't there more important issues we should be covering?" Ray had asked. Trent Baker, a newbie reporter, had agreed. Of course Trent would agree. He had to cover worse stories than Ray. Last week, he was given the splendid task of following the story of a man whose "gut-wrenching" decision involved participating in clinical studies for an alternative to hair plugs. Yet it looked as if the weeklong report would have a happy ending; the man said he was seeing "favorable results." It was horrific to watch Trent try to report this as if nobody at home was snickering. No one could look past the fact that Trent's own hairline was receding like the shores of a drought-stricken lake.

"What are you waiting for? A gang to show up?" Beaker asked, tilting his head away from the camera to look at Ray. "Knock again."

Ray sighed and knocked on the door. Footsteps shuffled closer, and the door cracked open slightly, a safety chain taut in front of the eyes and nose of the person looking out.

"Mrs. Elva Jones?"

"Who wants to know?"

"I'm Ray Duffey from News Channel 7."

The woman's eyes narrowed with scrutiny. "From the tube?"

"Yes ma'am. From News Channel 7. May I talk to you about your pet pigs?"

"I watch Channel 10."

"Yes ma'am, but I just wanted to talk to you about your pigs."

"The police already done that."

"We wondered if you had anything to say about the law regarding pet pigs on private property? Would you mind coming out to speak with us for a moment?"

She turned her attention to Beaker. Ray assumed he was smiling pleasantly behind him, like he should be, and trying his best not to draw attention to the large camera on his shoulder. In tough interviews, Beaker would often carry the camera at waist level until the person was ready to be interviewed.

"Whaddya want me to say 'bout it?"

"Just your side of the story, ma'am. We want to report the whole story, and that includes what you have to say about it."

She released the chain, pulled open the door, and pushed open the lopsided screen door. She didn't seem to notice or care that she wasn't exactly dressed for the camera. She was wearing a housecoat of some sort, and her hair was wound up tightly in curlers.

Ray hoped Beaker already had the camera rolling. Mrs. Jones looked around and then gave an angry nod toward her neighbor's house. "Petey over there turned me in, and I know it. He's been complaining about the smell for a year now."

"The smell doesn't bother you, ma'am?"

"They're pigs. 'Course they're going to smell."

"So you understand why your neighbors complained?"

"No. I don't complain about Petey's mailbox leaning to the left, do I? Or the fact that he's always screaming at his dog. I mind my own business, and Petey should mind his."

"Do you agree with the law?"

"That you shouldn't kill your neighbor?"

Ray bit his tongue and kept a straight face. "Uh, no ma'am, the law about owning farm animals on city property designated for homes."

"What good is it to own your own home if you can't do with it what you want? This land was passed down from my daddy to me. And we were here long before all these other houses came around. What we want to do with it is our business. We rightfully own it, and my daddy paid good money for it. This is America. If I want a pig in my yard, I should be able to have a pig in my yard!" She gathered her housecoat and said,

"Now I gotta get inside because *Wheel of Fortune* is 'bout to start."

"Thank you for your time," Ray said. He and Beaker turned and walked back toward the news truck. Beaker was suppressing one chuckle after another.

"'I don't complain about Petey's mailbox leaning to the left, do I?'" Beaker let out a laugh. "It was all I could do to hold the camera steady."

Ray opened the van door. "Don't you find that the least bit sad?"

Beaker loaded his equipment into the van. "What?"

"That. Back there I mean, she does have a point."

"A point? She's got a literal pigsty in the middle of her backyard, Ray. The smell about knocked me over, and we were on her front porch."

"She really believed in her right to own her property. There's something to that. Maybe there's no common sense in raising pigs in the middle of a neighborhood, but it's the principle of it."

"So you'd want to live next door to her? I'm sure Petey would sell you his house." Beaker rolled his eyes as he wrapped the cords around one arm. "She's an old woman who doesn't have a clue about the real world, Ray."

Ray sighed and Beaker crawled into the van's compact editing bay.

Jim, the live truck operator, glanced back and said, "They want this live from in front of the house."

"Why doesn't that surprise me," Ray groaned. He checked his watch. He had thirty-five minutes to edit and memorize his notes.

Chapter 4

In a quiet corner of the control room, with everyone abuzz, Hugo reviewed the anchors' script for smirk pitfalls. Nobody quite understood how important this task was, but then again, nobody knew Tate Franklin like he did. Chad had believed that Hugo had scored big by landing this playboy-looking anchor at a busboy price. But the other price he was paying for the good looks and the charming smile was probably going to send Hugo to an early grave.

Tate looked the part and certainly practiced all the skills of a well-established anchor. Hugo had never seen anyone perform the eye-bounce as well as Tate. While many people didn't see how this detail mattered for an anchor, Tate understood. He never cut his eyes sideways to his coanchor or to another camera. He always looked down, then looked up and focused on whatever it was he was supposed to look at. Anything other than that makes an anchor look awkward, even shifty.

There was also a lot to be said for Tate's intelligence. Not just a talking head, Tate seemed to understand what he was reporting. If he were given the chance, Hugo knew the young man could add some insight into certain topics. If only he didn't have that smirk. That one, uncontrollable little smirk. Hugo wasn't sure if he would hire Tate again, knowing what he knew now. Of course, desperate times called for desperate measures, so he supposed he didn't have much of a choice in the matter. But still, in all his years in the news business, he had never gone to such extremes to make a show work.

The smirk first appeared on Tate's fourth broadcast. Gilda took a four-car accident story, because it was a more recent event and involved a lot of detail. When it came time for a plane-crash story, Tate read the prompter like a pro. The script ended with, "And tonight, two families grieve the loss of two extraordinary men who were simply out for a nice day in the sky."

And then he smirked. Hugo had not noticed it until that story.

Tate's smirk was unbelievably detrimental to any kind of tragic news story. Hugo had spent hours with the kid, trying to help him realize that he smirked after his segments. But no matter how much they worked, the smirk always appeared. Tate tried his best to frown, to look serious, to capture the tragic moment in his expression, yet it was useless. The smirk always followed, and Hugo knew it made for a disastrous perception. Hugo would've even settled for feigned empathy. But nothing Tate tried could get past that uncontrollable expression on his face.

So Hugo decided there was only one thing *he* could do, and it worked out so well that he had celebrated by buying himself a new pair of shoes. Hugo wasn't one for rewarding himself much.

Now they gave all the lighthearted stories to Tate and all the sad or tragic stories to Gilda. As far as Hugo knew, nobody had caught on to the formula, but it had worked out beautifully. Thanks to the deep vertical crease between Gilda's eyebrows, she could carry any tragic story and look completely serious and saddened by it even if she wasn't.

Of course, he'd told Gilda she was more experienced at those kinds of stories and that he needed her for that purpose. But in reality, it came down to an uncontrollable smirk and an unmentionable wrinkle.

It was pure magic. But it also kept Hugo on his toes, because he had to review every TelePrompTer script with unfailing accuracy, or things could come undone very quickly. It was especially tricky when breaking news was involved.

As if the smirk weren't enough, Tate also had a laugh that sounded like a wheeze. It was the most awful thing Hugo had ever heard. Even a slight chuckle from Tate sounded like someone needed to run for an inhaler. So everyone knew, including the weatherman, Sam Leege, and the sportscaster, Leon Black, that they were never to crack a joke if Tate was going to be on camera. Everyone had gotten used to this. Leon and Gilda always shared space before the sports segment, so that was the best time to get a few jokes in. And occasionally Sam, who was very witty, made jokes during his segment. At such times, Tate's microphone was always turned down, so it just looked like he was smiling. Or smirking.

Tate had a few superstitions that Hugo chose to accommodate, but the most serious was Tate's belief that he could not anchor a show on his own. He'd told Hugo this in his first interview, and Hugo had brushed it off as inexperience. But that one night when Gilda was out on assignment, Tate made a believer out of Hugo. In fact, it wasn't a superstition. Tate simply couldn't do the news alone. So Hugo lived with it, which really hadn't been a problem, because Gilda wasn't going anywhere. She'd once done the news while fighting off pneumonia, so there was a slim-to-none chance that Tate would ever have to go it alone.

Hugo glanced at one of the monitors, where Gilda was getting situated at the news desk. He checked his watch. She was out there a little early. He'd been trying to avoid her for most of the late afternoon because he wasn't sure what the fallout was going to be from her talk with his assistant. Hayden had told him it went well. "Sometimes the truth is hard to take, but it's always the best," she'd said.

He'd taken that to mean that Gilda had finally seen the light concerning her dark spots and wrinkles. Really, his plan was absolutely perfect. He told Hayden to tell Gilda that some of the girls were going to a Botox party that coming weekend. Hugo knew that Gilda would feel less threatened if everyone was doing it. Now, of course, he was going to have to arrange a Botox party and spread the word about it to the other women at the station, but that was tomorrow's problem. Tonight, he just needed to get through the newscast.

Roarke Keegan, the director of the assignment desk, rushed in with breaking news. "A tanker truck's overturned, and traffic is backed up for three miles on the interstate. Ed's already up in the chopper and is going to cover it."

"Thanks, Roarke. Keep me posted." Hugo went to work on adding it to the script.

Ed Klawski was a godsend. He was a retired air force pilot who just wanted something to do with his day. So even though they couldn't afford a real helicopter reporter, Ed did a fairly nice job of covering breaking news from the sky. But he had a bad tendency to shout out the report like he was back in Danang.

Hugo continued to flip through the agenda. Ray would cover an escalating dispute over pigs on private property, Jill was assigned to report on a controversial execution at the prison, and Trent was doing a report on the efficacy of the over-the-counter drug Beano. As the sound tech was attaching her microphone, Hugo noticed Gilda wasn't her normal chatterbox self. Her face looked more drawn than usual, and she was staring off as if she were alone in a quiet room. He watched Tate ask her something, concern in his eyes, and she mumbled something back, nodded, and then looked away.

Hayden opened the door to the control room. Hugo beckoned her over.

"Hayden, you said that you thought it went well today with Gilda."

"Yes."

"So she didn't seem upset?"

"I think she took it well."

"I thought you said it went fine. Something about the truth is hard to take, you said, but she seemed okay."

"We had a real heart to heart, which seems like something Gilda doesn't get to do very often."

Hugo shifted his weight, trying not to lose his patience. He checked his watch. "Why don't you tell me exactly what happened?"

"Well, you told me to tell her about the Botox party that some of the girls were going to."

"Yes? And?"

"We started talking about age and beauty and what real beauty is."

Hugo swallowed. "What do you mean?"

"You know, just girl talk." Hayden winked.

"I don't girl talk much, so you're going to have to fill me in." He leaned toward her, feeling his eyes widen, which made her eyes widen.

She hesitated, took a little breath, and then said, "Well, Mr. Talley, I just felt that I needed to share the truth with Gilda."

"Th-the truth? What truth? The truth about what?"

Hayden shrugged. "About what beauty really is. It comes from the inside, you know. We all age, and this world wants us to think that it's all about what we look like on the outside, but what really matters is the heart."

Hugo felt himself smiling. He didn't know why. Possibly because, in theory, yes, the heart matters. But this wasn't reality. This was the news business. What was she thinking?

"Mr. Talley, are you okay?"

He tried to focus on her. "What?"

"Your hands are shaking."

He looked down and balled them into fists behind his back. "I'm fine. I'm...I'm just..." He sighed. "So is she going to the Botox party or not?"

"Well, I don't know. She asked if I received an invitation, and then she asked Jill, and of course none of us really had received anything official."

Hugo's face dampened with sweat in a half a second. "She...she was asking around?"

"I assured her not to worry, Mr. Talley, and that if the worst of her problems was that she got invited to exclusive parties that others didn't, then she's living the good life."

Hugo slapped his forehead. This was one party that you didn't want to be exclusive. "Hayden!" he barked.

She jumped backward. "What?"

"You were supposed to… It's just that… You shouldn't have…" Hugo wanted to scream. All she had to do was tell Gilda about a Botox party. How could it have gotten all screwed up like this? It was a foolproof plan!

He looked at her alarmed face. "You didn't happen to mention my name in all of this, did you?"

Hayden looked like she didn't want to speak, so he tried to soften his expression and smile, as if it was just a casual afterthought with no frightful consequences.

She grinned. "Oh, Mr. Talley, I am so good at keeping secrets, especially about surprise parties. I figured you'd want to tell all the girls yourself."

Hugo wiped his hand across his forehead and managed a relieved, if not genuine smile. "Oh. Good." At least he couldn't be implicated. "All right, get back to work. We have a news show to run." Hugo looked out at Gilda. She wasn't smiling. She wasn't even focused.

Neither was he.

Chapter 5

R ay shivered inside his lightweight jacket. With the microphone in his grip and his arms wrapped around himself, he studied his notes. There were several points he wanted to make. Through his voice-over, he told the basic story. First, he knew people would immediately identify with Petey Green, the neighbor who had to live with the stench, sound, and stigma of five next-door pigs. So he wanted to make sure to state the city ordinances concerning farm animals on private residential property. But he thought Elva Jones had a point too. After all, she and her family had lived there long before the rest of the neighborhood had moved in. Some research earlier in the day revealed that ten years ago she lost a small farm when the city zoned it commercial, and she was forced to sell it.

Trying to force out of his head the thought of how cold he was, Ray read his notes over and over. That was one talent he'd perfected early in his career. He could rattle off an entire litany without ever glancing down, even amid distraction. A kid once pelted him with pebbles during a live shot, yet he managed to get through it without even a hint of hesitation. The delivery was all about concentration and focus. The story was about research and investigation.

Ray was disappointed they weren't going to be first up. He didn't like the location from which they were shooting, and he would be glad to get out of there. Beaker stood by his mounted camera and signaled that the newscast was about to begin.

Ray kept looking over his notes, hoping to bring out the real human story behind what, at the end of the day, was really a sideshow. It's what people wanted to see. They loved a good conflict, especially with people like Elva Jones and Petey Green…people who didn't understand in the least that they were being exploited for what was essentially entertainment. Sure, the pig law had news value, but without Ray's help, it would have very little. People wanted to see what a woman living with a pigsty might look like and the man's reaction to it next door.

Ray couldn't stop feeling a little disgusted. Ben James, a reporter who had been with the station twenty years before retiring, once told him that eventually he would get over it. "You think you're going to change the world," Ben had said. "But the world always changes you, Ray. After a few years, I realized that this business was always going to be what it was. So I took the sensationalism and everything that came with it, I accepted it, and I did the best reporting I could. And you know, over the years, I think there were a few stories that at least made a small difference. I really believe that. And the rest? Well, you gotta do something to bring home a paycheck." Ray had spent a sleepless night pondering Ben's words…and the news story that they were covering at the time. A child had disappeared from a playground, and the probable outcome was looking more and more grim. Ray felt sick to his stomach every time they relentlessly used the story to hook the viewer.

"News Channel 7 has uncovered shocking new details in the disappearance of David Blare."

"New at ten, learn what police are saying about a man who was seen near the park."

"After the break, learn why David's parents are taking their anger out on police."

He hated every moment of it. He'd felt so ashamed when he arrived at the prayer vigil, feeling like he was intruding on a private moment for David's friends and family. His producer had wanted quotes. How could you grab a sound bite from a person's living nightmare?

Ray and Beaker had wandered around looking for anyone who seemed willing to talk about it. The willing people had only known David distantly.

Afterward, as Ray and Beaker were loading their equipment into the truck, he felt someone touch his shoulder. It was David Blare's mother. Ray wasn't sure whether to grab his microphone or embrace the woman and tell her how sorry he was for what she was going through.

She had a stern look on her face, so he stared at the ground. "Mrs. Blare, I'm sorry, we're just trying to cover this story. I tried to stay out of the way and—"

She held up her hand. Then she placed it on his arm. "I want to thank you."

"Thank me?"

"For keeping this story out in front of the public. It's our best shot at getting David back." Tears welled in her eyes, then she patted him on the arm and walked away. Ray felt the shame melt away, and he realized he was doing something important, even if he hadn't known it or felt it at the time.

He'd covered the story with all his energy for the next four days, working closely with the police and eyewitnesses to uncover clues while keeping the public alert for any signs of the boy.

Then, one afternoon, Hugo had decided they wouldn't cover it that day. Ray couldn't believe it.

"Mr. Talley, every day that we keep this in front of viewers may be the day someone comes forward with a clue or spots the car."

"I wish we could, Ray," Hugo had said, "but we've got a packed lineup today. There's just too much to cover. We might be able to squeeze it into the six o'clock, but there's no room in the ten o'clock."

"But sir, I just think—"

Chad Arbus swiveled his chair toward Ray. "It's a dying story, Ray. Pure and simple. The public has lost interest. We move on. Period."

Ray's hands were tied. Yet he couldn't shake the feeling that he'd personally let down Mrs. Blare.

"Three minutes," Beaker said, and Ray snapped back into the reality of the cold night and his upcoming pigsty segment.

Then, from the corner of his eye, he saw something. He glanced up to see a man standing about twenty-five feet away, his face darkened by the shadow of a tree. He stood perfectly still, his arms crossed, his feet spread apart like he was ready for something to happen.

Ray was used to people stopping to watch, but this was a dark, quiet street, and nobody was out watching anything.

Except this man.

Beaker noticed too. "Is that Mr. Green?" he whispered.

"I don't know. I don't think so. We've been knocking on his door all day and evening. Nobody was home." Ray tried not to let the man distract him, but something about his body language was making him nervous.

"Are you Mr. Green?" Ray called.

The man didn't answer, so Ray decided to take that as a yes.

"We've been trying to contact you, sir. We wanted to get your side of the story on the pig incident with your neighbor. Would you like to comment on camera?" Ray asked, unsure if this man was "live interview" material.

The man still didn't answer.

Ray glanced at Beaker, who looked like a ball of nerves.

Ray concentrated on his notes again. Or tried to. It would've been easier had a crowd been staring at him. There was something disconcerting about just one man standing there in the dark.

Beaker walked to the other side of his tripod-mounted camera and whispered, "I told you Roarke was right about this street."

"News Channel 7, working around the clock to bring you the news." The show opening rolled, and the familiar ten o'clock music filled the control room. Hugo stepped back to watch. The director of the ten o'clock show, Willis Hill, called out his directions with precision and calmness. Everything looked to be on track. The only thing making Hugo nervous was Gilda. It was subtle, but he could tell something was not right about her. She kept doing a really odd little number with her finger. She would place it above her eyebrow and lift. And then she'd move it over to her temple and pull. Tate had the tics, not Gilda. He couldn't imagine what she was doing, but he just prayed her wandering fingers would find their way to the news desk and stay put.

"And...camera two," Willis said.

On the monitor, Hugo watched Gilda carefully. Thankfully, she turned it on at the last second. "Good evening," she said in her authoritative voice, her fingers laced together on top of the desk. "I'm Gilda Braun."

"And I'm Tate Franklin," Tate added.

"We have breaking news tonight," Gilda said. "Word of a tanker-truck explosion on I-35, just south of Clayeton. Ed Klawski is there with Chopper 7 covering it. Ed, some amazing pictures you're capturing."

"Go to video," Willis said.

A ball of fire exploded onto the screen, lighting up the night sky. It was quite a picture. A small box in the upper-right-hand corner showed a still shot of Ed's face, and Ed started shouting out his report.

"That's right, Gilda! We're flying right above the scene! I've never seen anything like this! People are scrambling everywhere! We're hearing that the trucker may still be trapped in the cab, but we cannot confirm that at this time!"

"Lower his audio," Willis instructed.

"Police tell us that the highway is closed both north and south at this time! Take an alternate route! As soon as we get word on the trucker, we will get back to you!"

The camera cut to Gilda's grim expression. "Ed, that is a horrible scene. Any word on what caused the accident?"

"Eyewitnesses say they believe the trucker fell asleep at the wheel, but that has not been confirmed!"

"All right," Gilda said solemnly. "Thank you, Ed. We know you'll keep us updated. What an amazing view from Chopper 7 and Ed Klawski. And I'll tell you one thing, Ed sure doesn't look sixty-seven, does he?"

Tate's smirk couldn't cover his surprise at the comment, but he said, "We appreciate the amazing job he does." Then Tate turned to camera one. "Good news tonight from Yates, where a blind man's Seeing Eye dog has been returned…"

"Mr. Talley," Hayden said from the back of the control room, holding a phone up. "It's Beaker."

"Beaker? What does he want?"

"I'm not sure. He sounds panicked and wants to talk to you."

Willis glanced up worriedly at Hugo, who rushed to the phone. "Beaker, what is it?"

"There's a man standing here, staring at us. Mr. Green."

"Who is Mr. Green?"

"The man who has been complaining about the pigs."

"So what's the problem?"

"I think he's dangerous."

Hugo sighed. Loudly. He'd never seen a cameraman more scared of the dark. If Beaker weren't his best cameraman, Hugo would switch him to the afternoon. But he'd probably get sued.

"Beaker, unless he's aiming a gun at you, I don't have time for this. And if he is aiming a gun at you, get it on video, for crying out loud."

He could hear Ray's whisper-like voice in the background. "Beaker, it's fine. C'mon. You're totally freaking on me."

"Yeah, you're totally freaking." Hugo rolled his eyes. He was way too old to use the word *freaking*. "You have a job to do, so do it."

He could hear Beaker grumbling something about life insurance and meeting his Maker, but he finally hung up. Hugo stepped back beside Willis, who said, "Are we still on for Ray's segment?"

"Yes, we're good."

Hugo focused on the monitor, where Tate was finishing his Seeing Eye dog story and pitching it back to Gilda. "Now let's go live to the prison, where Jill Clark is standing by with a report on the controversial death-row case of Frederick Bills."

"That's right, Gilda. Twenty-eight-year-old Bills is scheduled to die tonight by lethal injection…"

As Jill gave her report, Hugo leaned forward and watched Gilda in the monitor. She looked like she was watching pigeons at the park. Willis was too busy to notice, and Tate was looking over his notes for his next segment. "Willis, ask Gilda if she's okay."

Willis looked at her on the monitor. "Why? Is she having technical problems? Roll footage."

As the footage rolled for Jill's segment, Hugo said, "No, but just make sure she's all right."

Willis spoke to her through her IFB, which fit snugly inside her ear. "Gilda?"

Gilda didn't even blink.

Willis tried again. "Gilda? Can you hear me?" Willis looked at his audio director. "We've got audio problems with Gilda's IFB. Tate, can you hear me?"

Tate looked up and nodded.

"That's strange," Willis said.

Hugo stepped forward. "There's nothing wrong with the audio. Gilda's fazing out."

"What?" The entire control room stared at Gilda as Jill finished up her report.

"Officials here at the prison aren't commenting on this particular case, but they said they intend to follow usual protocol. Gilda, back to you."

Heads turned from Jill on the monitor to Gilda, who sat staring just to the left of the camera she was supposed to be looking at.

The two-box, which showed their pictures side by side with Jill's picture on the left and Gilda's on the right, framed an awkward moment as Jill stared forward, waiting for a response as Gilda simply stared forward.

Jill put her finger to her ear and said again, "Gilda, back to you."

Willis grabbed his mike, hit a button, and said, "Tate, take this!" Off mike he said, "Camera three!"

The two-box shifted pictures, now displaying Jill and Tate. Tate looked disoriented but tried to recover. "Uh…yes, thank you, Jill. We appreciate that report." He then turned to the TelePrompTer, but the next story was Gilda's. Tate's eyes widened.

"Everything's falling apart!" Hugo cried. Willis scrambled, trying to choose between two anchors who looked like deer in somebody's headlights. "Should we cut to commercial?"

Hugo was about to say yes when Gilda suddenly snapped back to reality, sitting up straight and transforming right in front of them. Willis went to camera two, and now Gilda and Jill both shared the screen.

"Jill," Gilda said, "have Mr. Bills's parents been vocal about their son's imminent execution?"

Jill recovered quickly and professionally. "They haven't commented at all to the press, though a neighbor tells us that they're devastated that it comes to an end tonight. Back to you."

"Thank you," Gilda said. "That was Jill Clark reporting from outside the prison this evening. Thank you, Jill. And might I say what a flattering suit you're wearing. You look radiant."

Jill's eyes popped wide and her mouth opened a little. Willis switched to camera one, displaying both Tate and Gilda.

"What is she doing?" Willis grumbled. "This isn't a fashion show!"

Hugo's forehead was nearly touching the monitor as he waited for what Gilda would do next. All she had to do was introduce Ray's piece. He held his breath and glanced at Ray, who stood looking cold and shifting his eyes sideways every few seconds.

"And now," Gilda said, as if nothing peculiar had just happened, "we go live to Ray Duffey, who is covering a dispute between two neighbors and a pig. Is that right, Ray?"

"Go to Ray," Willis said.

Ray's picture filled the screen. "That's right, Gilda. These two neighbors have been tangled up in quite a dispute, and at the end of the day, it comes down to the smell."

"Roll the tape," Willis said.

As the video rolled, Hugo fell into a nearby chair. "What is wrong with her?"

Willis shook his head. "I've never seen her like this."

"Let me talk to her." Hugo leaned into the microphone. "Gilda, what's going on out there?"

Gilda looked into camera one and stared at him through the monitor. "Hugo, is that you?"

"Yes, it's me. And I want to know what's going on. You're missing cues and acting like you've got your head in the clouds!"

Gilda's eyes narrowed, and Hugo realized he'd overstepped his bounds. Willis's surprised expression confirmed that.

"I mean, I'm wondering if you're having some technical difficulties out there," Hugo added quickly.

"I can hear you fine," Tate said.

"And I, too, heard you loud and clear, Hugo," Gilda purred. Hugo's hair stood on end. Something was up. Gilda was onto him, and maybe this was her way of punishing him.

"Look, everyone, let's get back on top of our game and get through this," Willis said. "We're almost back to Ray, and then Tate, you'll pitch to the weather teaser."

"Ten seconds," the VTR operator called out, indicating the video for Ray's segment was almost finished.

"Please don't let anything else go wrong," Hugo mumbled, resisting the urge to cover his eyes so he wouldn't have to see the rest of the show.

"Three...two...one..."

"Go to Ray."

Ray's picture came back up, but this time Ray wasn't holding the microphone. He was clutching it.

"We, uh...we were hoping to get comments from Mr. Green, but we were unable to make contact with him at—ahhhh! AHHH!"

"What the—?" Willis shouted. Something had flown across the screen and tackled Ray. Hugo lunged toward the monitor. The camera now showed a steady picture of nothing but a dark, lifeless background. Plenty of noise, however, indicated something was happening even though the camera didn't show it.

A blur flew across the screen again, and this time it was Beaker, who'd never been seen this side of the camera.

Chaos erupted around Hugo, but everyone was helpless to do anything. Then a skinny-looking man filled the screen. He stood up, straightened his shirt, and yelled, "I hate Channel 7! I hate you!" He pointed straight to the camera and then stomped off.

"Ray! Ray? Beaker?" Willis said, "Jim? Jim, can you here me?" Not even the live truck operator was answering.

Suddenly Beaker was back on, speaking through Ray's microphone. The camera captured part of his face and shoulder as he stooped. "Willis...can you hear me?" He sounded out of breath.

"I'm here. What happened?"

"Ray was attacked."

"Is he okay?"

"I don't know. He's got a gash on his head, and he's bleeding."

Willis switched his attention quickly to Gilda and Tate. "Gilda, I'm cutting to you. You're going to have to carry this for fifteen seconds, and then we're going to commercial. Three…two…one…"

"As you can see, something terrible has happened. One of our reporters was attacked while giving us a live report. As soon as we know anything more, we will let you know. For now, let's all say a prayer for Ray Duffey, and we'll be back after this short commercial break."

"Go to commercial."

Hugo leaned into the microphone. "Beaker, can you hear me?"

"Yeah. I'm okay. I'm calling an ambulance."

"Beaker, make sure you get all this on video."

He could see Beaker move and take out his cell phone to call. Hugo stepped back, realizing he was starting to hyperventilate. In all his years in the news business, he'd never seen anything like that. He felt completely helpless. He turned and noticed Hayden was the only one not running around the control room like a headless chicken. And she was taking Gilda's remarks to heart.

She was praying.

Chapter 6

With a quick snap of her arms, the nurse jerked back the curtain in Ray's hospital-room window. Ray shielded his eyes from the bright light. She rolled a breakfast cart toward his bed and swung it over his legs. "The doctor will be in to release you this morning," she said. "How are you feeling?"

"I've got a headache," Ray said, touching the bandage on his forehead.

"I'll bring you some Tylenol. See if you can eat something."

Ray looked down. He was starving, but not for watery eggs and cardboard bacon. He touched his head again. Eight stitches, right across his hairline. The entire thing had been caught on live television, including the humiliation of the police questioning him as he was being loaded into the back of the ambulance. He really didn't think he needed to go by ambulance, but Hugo insisted, citing something about insurance policies. And somehow Hugo had talked the doctors into admitting him.

Ray peeled back the foil on his orange juice cup and was about to take a sip when the door flew open and Hugo walked in.

"How are you?" he asked, his arms flung out like he was hosting a variety show.

"Hugo, I'm fine. I didn't need to stay in the hospital, for crying out loud."

"It was just a precaution." Hugo smiled a little. "It's all the buzz this morning."

"I bet."

"The other news stations are forced to cover it, or they know they'll lose viewers who want to see the footage."

Ray rolled his eyes. "Great."

"Ray, you're a hero!"

"A hero? I got clobbered by a very skinny man who hates my news channel."

"But our ratings are soaring, and we haven't even entered sweeps week yet, my friend. I can hardly believe our luck. All from a story about pigs." Hugo minded his manners and pulled back from the glory he was apparently imagining. "So you're feeling okay?"

"Yeah. I mean, it could've been a lot worse. I'm a little sore and my head is—"

"That will be perfect."

"What?"

"The bandage. The cut's right at your hairline, so you can't really see it, but the bandage will make quite a statement on camera."

"What camera?"

Just then the door opened again and Beaker came in, hauling his equipment, followed by Trent. Ray groaned. "Hugo, please. Don't do this."

"Don't do this? Ray, this is the biggest news story of the day. You're asking me not to cover it?"

"I don't want to *be* the news, Hugo. I want to report it."

"This business is about sacrifice. You know that, Ray. You were attacked by the man we were ultimately defending. If that's not a news story, I don't know what is." Hugo sighed. "Look, just let Trent interview you, and I'll give you the rest of the day off, okay? You can go home and relax."

Ray tugged at his hospital robe. "Go home and relax? Yeah, right. Knowing I'm being plastered all over television in a hospital gown."

Trent stepped up. "This is an important story, Ray. We saw an act of violence right in front of our eyes."

Ray pinched his nose. Of course this would feel important to a man whose last story was an exclusive on Beano. Ray looked at Beaker, who seemed to feel his pain but had every intention of hitting the record button. Hugo had the most desperate look on his face, like he thought his entire world might come crashing down if Ray didn't do this.

And he knew the truth. Their ratings would soar.

He leaned back into his pillow and groaned. His best friend, Roarke Keegan, would never let this die, nor would his church, his family, or the lady who sold him his Slurpees at 7-Eleven every night after the show. This would be his fifteen minutes of unwanted fame. He'd been beaten up by a redneck who likes Channel 3 instead.

Ray opened his eyes and asked, "Can we at least spin this so people realize I was holding a microphone and was taken completely by surprise?"

Beaker laughed. "Believe me, the 'taken completely by surprise' part won't be a problem. The freeze-frame of your face is absolutely hilarious."

Hugo shot Beaker a look and said, "Ray, I promise. You'll come out of this looking like a hero."

"I'll just settle for not looking like a pansy, okay?"

Gilda woke at precisely 10:00 a.m. every morning. So as she rolled over in bed to see four red numbers indicating 10:47 a.m., it startled her heart into near cardiac arrest.

She yanked the covers back and stumbled across her bedroom floor toward the bathroom, freeing herself of the sleep mask that was entangled in her hair. She turned on the water at the sink and drank from the faucet to try to get her tongue unstuck from the roof of her mouth.

It was like a hangover without the benefit of the high.

She wasn't exactly sure what had happened last night, but if she were being diplomatic about it, she would probably guess it was some sort of breakdown. Having never had a breakdown before, she couldn't be sure, but uncontrollable crying, screaming at the top of one's lungs, and cursing people she thought should die a slow and painful death were probably all signs that something wasn't quite right.

She splashed water onto her face, dried it with a towel, and looked at herself carefully in the mirror. "You're a good person. People like you because of who you are on the inside, not the outside." She stared hard into her own eyes. That's what that intern Hayden had told her. It sounded so ridiculously naive at the time, like a bad self-help tape.

"Believe it. You must believe it." She shook her head. But today her heart wouldn't believe it. Not after what had happened yesterday. There had been hints over the years, all of which Gilda had pretended to ignore. But the hints were becoming more and more obvious, and yesterday was the worst. *To stage some sort of Botox party... How moronic.* Chad was a cruel dictator and Hugo was simply a spineless weenie. To send his intern in to do his dirty work was hardly fathomable.

Gilda fluffed her hair and applied her two favorite antiwrinkle creams before heading to the kitchen for breakfast. Prior to opening the refrigerator, Gilda touched the handwritten note that hung by a magnet on her freezer door. She'd written it down five years ago, and the quote was attributed to Barbara Walters. It said, "Women in television don't get older, they get blonder." She was no blonde, but she appreciated the sentiment of it anyway. The fact was, women could age gracefully in front of the camera if society wasn't so determined to fight the inevitable stages of aging.

Over the years, she'd taken a few nonradical steps to try to look as young as she possible could. She'd allowed special lights to be set up in front of the news desk to create a white, illuminating glow around her neck, to supposedly hide the fact that her neck looked like it was sliding down itself.

She'd also gone to using a heavy base makeup, so thick-feeling she swore she was wearing a second face. It did make a difference. For a couple of years.

She was getting older. No amount of wrinkle cream or special light-ing was going to change that. Yet she seemed to be the only one at peace with it.

Opening the fridge, she took out the orange juice and two eggs. Whisking the eggs in a bowl, she poured them into a skillet and walked to the front door. It was Tuesday. And Tuesday almost always brought a welcomed surprise. She'd not told anyone about it for fear that it might go away or that it was just a figment of her imagination.

Slowly, she opened the door. And there it was. A rose. Next to her newspaper. She stooped to pick it up, her knees cracking as she bent. Attached to the rose was a note held on by a neatly tied string. *"Dearest Gilda, you deserve to be loved in the very best way."*

She smiled and closed her fingers over the note. These little treasures (flowers, chocolates, trinkets, and more) had been coming for several months now. Lately they'd been coming more frequently. At first she thought she was being stalked. But if that was the case, the stalker was so delightfully charming, she was willing to let her fear of death slide for now.

She took the rose inside, placed the newspaper on the table, and fin-ished cooking her eggs. Back at the table, she opened the paper up to find Ray Duffey as the front-page headline: "Reporter Attacked." Hugo would be ecstatic. Maybe this was the boost they needed right before sweeps week.

Stroking the petals of the rose, Gilda couldn't help but wonder why her secret admirer had been admiring from a distance for so long. After several months, wouldn't he at least want to go to the next stage by now?

She lost her appetite and shoved her breakfast away. Grabbing her orange juice, she made her way back to the bathroom where she applied a skin smoother and an eye gel. With one finger, she traced the deep crease that started midforehead and ended up between her two eyebrows. This. This was the one that had done it. All the other lines were noticeable but not irreverent, like somehow she had better control of how she aged since she was on television. This line, though, was practically offensive. Yet she knew what made this line—years of hard work, concentrating, taking seriously the job she loved so much.

And what thanks did she get for it?

A showcase wrinkle and a Botox offer.

With a deep and determined breath, Gilda placed her hands on the bathroom counter, leaned toward the mirror, and said, "Honey, you've fought the good fight. You really have. I'm so proud of you."

With drapes drawn, Ray sat on the couch in his apartment and watched *The Price Is Right.* A large bouquet of flowers, his only company, sat next to him on the table. Hugo sent them with a card that read, "You are brave and courageous." Ray knew the truth. He was neither brave nor courageous. He just happened to be at the wrong place at the right time—or at the right place at the wrong time, depending on your perspective. Either way, he scored big for the team and scored a nice scar by which to remember it all.

He'd tried his best to take the interview seriously and answer the questions Trent threw his way.

"Did Mr. Green say anything to you?"

"When did you first notice Mr. Green?"

"What did he do after he knocked you to the ground and kicked you?"

"How did you respond?"

"Well, I didn't have much time to respond," Ray had said. *"Obviously my attention was on doing the report, and had I seen him coming, obviously I would've responded in an appropriate way. Obviously, Mr. Green has some issues that go beyond his obvious anger with the pigs."*

He'd used the word "obvious" in some form four times. He prayed they'd reduce his rambling to a sound bite. "Mr. Green has some issues" would be great. Or "My attention was on doing the report." Something that didn't make him sound like the obvious idiot that he was.

Part of the problem was Trent's intense shakedown. Ray tried to be polite and realize that Trent hadn't had a real story to report since coming to the news station. But if the microphone had been shoved any closer to Ray's face, he could've eaten it for breakfast.

Ray decided to stop thinking about the last twelve hours' events. He watched Bob Barker and noticed how annoyed Bob seemed to be. How many years had the man been doing this? Did he really love his job or was he just pulling in a paycheck these days? Bob snapped at a woman jumping up and down at the prospect of winning a new camper, telling her to stand still if she wanted to hear how to play the game. Was that what he would be reduced to later in life? Snapping at people? Plastering a smile on his face and going through the motions? Ray sank into the couch. Would what happened to him last night be the kind of story he'd tell his uninterested grandchildren? "I was nearly killed by man who weighed a hundred and ten pounds."

Ray fell over sideways into the cushions and groaned. Someone knocked on his door, and he flew upright and stood still. Surely there weren't reporters outside. Did the rival news stations really think they were going to get a quote from him? Ha! Not a chance. As humiliating as this was, it was Channel 7's story, and only one station would get an exclusive.

Knock, knock.

Ray held his breath. He wasn't about to open the door and have a camera shoved in his face. Already one too many "surprised Ray" videos were floating around.

"Ray? Open up. I know you're in there."

Ray opened the door and Roarke stood there with a large pizza box in his hand. "Figured you'd want some company and something to drown your sorrows in." He held up a Coca-Cola bottle. "Don't ask me where I found hot pizza at this time of morning."

"You have no idea how glad I am to see you," Ray said, opening the door wider and ushering Roarke in. Huffing and puffing, Roarke's three-hundred-eighty-pound frame made it to the kitchen table where he set the pizza down. Ray grabbed glasses and ice, and then they both took slices to the couch where they settled in.

Ray had known Roarke for five years, and they'd hit it off from the beginning. Their relationship had survived a lot, including Roarke's obsessive need to forward every e-mail that came across his computer and Ray's impulsive use of the word *voilà*. Nevertheless, they'd made it five years. Roarke was the kind of person who was hard not to like. He had a huge heart, a genuine personality, and an admirable determination to better himself.

The amazing thing about Roarke was that he never let his obesity affect him negatively. He had a sense of who he was, pounds or no pounds, and nothing ever changed that.

They both kicked their feet up and started shoving in the pizza. Roarke glanced at him. "I thought it'd be a lot worse."

"Eight stitches."

"Yeah, but the way your feet flew up into the air, you could've really been hurt, dude."

Ray sighed. "The man weighs less than my right leg. He just took me by surprise. The gash came from my head hitting the sidewalk."

"Still." Roarke shook his head. "I can't tell you how freaked I was. I watched the whole thing unfold."

"I know. You and who knows how many other people." Ray sighed. "I don't want to talk about it. It makes me ill."

"You shouldn't be so hard on yourself. It could've happened to anyone, and that Green fellow's a real loser for doing it. Everyone can see that. By the way, he posted bail this morning."

"Terrific."

"You might want to get a restraining order."

"I am not getting a restraining order. If Mr. Green wants to come around again, bring it on. But this time, I won't be holding a microphone and looking the other way."

Roarke smiled. "Having some masculinity issues, are we?"

Ray shoved more pizza in his mouth and turned his attention to the game show, staring at a box of Tide priced somewhere over four dollars. Most of the time, Roarke and Ray would get together either after the newscast or the next morning to watch one of the many crime dramas that Roarke recorded on his ancient VCR or to play video games. But they tried not to play games all the time. They didn't want to dumb themselves down. Instead, they made sure they watched at least one crime drama a week, just to keep their brains sharp.

"Dude, you are taking this way too hard. You need a date."

"What?"

"A date. Heard of it?"

"What makes you think I need a date?"

"So you got clobbered on television. Is it the end of the world?"

Ray frowned and stared forward. "You don't understand what it's like to be humiliated like that, Roarke."

"Try having to ask the station to order you a double-wide, reinforced steel chair to sit in because the other one can't hold you anymore."

Ray lowered his eyes. Humiliation was a part of Roarke's everyday life. He seemed to handle it fine, so why was Ray having such a hard time?

As Roarke got up for more pizza, Ray said, "So all my problems will be solved with a date?"

Roarke laid another slice in his hand. "Not necessarily, but it might lighten you up a little. Besides," he said, making his way back to the couch, "I've seen how you've been watching her."

"Who?"

"Don't give me that. I am, after all, the assigner. It's my job to know everything, and I know you've got the hots for the new intern." In his role, Roarke did know what was going on everywhere, but he also had an uncanny ability to know everything that didn't relate to the news day too. He could tell you where to get "buy one get one free" Vienna sausages. He could tell you who was having an office affair. He could tell you when the copier paper was about to run out.

Ray tried an expression to indicate he didn't have any idea what Roarke was talking about, but those wise eyes weren't fooled.

"Don't worry, it's not obvious," Roarke said. "I've just noticed you noticing her. And she is hot. A little weird though."

"You think so?" Ray asked.

Roarke shrugged. "I can definitely see her being your type, but the way she goes around talking about God and the Bible and all that seems a little, I don't know...like she might belong to a cult."

"She's not in a cult. She was homeschooled."

"I'm just saying, you don't see that kind of thing often, where a person talks openly about religion. So much. All the time. All I'm saying is that if she offers you Kool-Aid, you might want to think twice about drinking it."

"She *is* very...passionate...about the subject."

"But hey, man, you're all into that too."

"Not like that," Ray said. "I mean, not so...you know, verbal about it."

"She invited me to church." Roarke smiled. "I told her I'd see her at Christmas and Easter. She did think that was funny. She has a nice sense of humor."

"You think anyone who laughs at your jokes has a nice sense of humor."

"That's because they do. She said, 'Lucky for you, God sees you year round.' But she also told me that she was going to keep asking me until I said yes. And then she told me God loves me."

Ray gnawed on his crust. She was cute. And she did seem to have a nice personality. But there was no getting around the fact that she made no bones about her religious views. Yet she did it with such a sweet voice, it was hard to get mad. Everyone seemed to sort of smile and make an excuse to walk away.

And she was certainly forthright. The first time they'd met, when Ray had introduced himself, she had politely introduced herself as well. He'd expected some light chitchat, but she just came right out and asked if he knew the Lord.

It was a socially awkward moment, to say the least.

He didn't know why, but he had only nodded feebly. He was a Christian after all. But it wasn't what he was expecting from a new co-worker as he reached for a doughnut.

Yet he had to admit there was something really attractive about her. Social skills aside, he found himself wanting to be around her. Why, he didn't know. He didn't need an invitation to church. He already went. He didn't need the gospel message. He already knew it. So what, exactly, was so appealing about her?

Maybe it was that she didn't have normal inhibitions.

"Okay, man, I'm going to say it," Roarke said, jolting Ray back to the present.

Ray looked at him. "Say what?"

Roarke paused, pressing his lips together and shaking his head.

"Maybe you shouldn't say it," Ray offered.

"No, I think I should."

Ray braced himself. Whatever it was, he was pretty sure he didn't want to hear it. But then Roarke said, "There's somebody I dig."

Ray's mouth would have fallen open had it not been stuffed with pizza.

Roarke glanced at him. "I know, I know. It's crazy. But this lady…she does something to me."

"Someone at work?" Ray asked, swallowing his bite whole.

"Yeah. This lady, Ray, well, let's just say she puts the lace in workplace."

Ray tried to imagine who Roarke could be talking about. There were plenty of women around the station, but none of them seemed to be Roarke's type…or particularly fond of lace. Of course, Ray didn't really know Roarke's type, because as long as he had known Roarke, he'd never dated anyone.

"I think that's great, Roarke," Ray said. "Who is it?"

"I'm not ready to say."

"Why?"

"This lady…she's way out of my league."

"Roarke, as a general rule, I think all women are out of our league."

"True. So what do we have to lose, right?"

"Just promise me you won't use the 'lace in workplace' line on her."

"That's just man-to-man talk. I know how to treat a woman. If this woman would give me a chance, I know I could make her happy."

"Any woman would be lucky to have you, Roarke."

"You mean that, dude?"

"Every word."

Roarke sighed and set down his unfinished slice of pizza. "Maybe I'll do it. Maybe I'll ask her out." He turned to Ray. "I'll do it if you will."

"Whoa," Ray said. "I'm not even sure Hayden is the right kind of woman for me. Like you said, she's kind of kooky."

"Well, whatever. I still think I might go for it. Why not, right? You're living proof that life is fragile."

Ray must have been feeling better, because moments before the word *fragile* would've propelled him back into self-loathing. "I say you should go for it."

"Yep. It's time to burp the Tupperware." That was a term Roarke coined for "sealing the deal." According to Roarke, his mother sold the stuff for years, and people actually "burped" the lids to get them sealed.

Ray went to the table for more pizza. "I'm glad you came by. You put a lot into perspective for me."

Roarke waved his hand. "Don't worry about last night. I mean, it's not like the whole world knows."

The phone rang, and Ray picked it up. "Hello?"

"Ray Duffey?"

"Yes?"

"My name is Karen Shore. I'm a producer with *Late Show with David Letterman.* We've seen the footage from your report last night, and we're wondering if you would be willing to do the Top Ten List for our show tomorrow?"

Chapter 7

H ugo couldn't stop smiling. It shouldn't be, but it felt like the best day of his life. People were noticing him smile, so he dialed it down a notch, but it was hardly containable.

He'd called Ray three times to see how he was doing and update him on the fact that this was indeed the big story not only of the day but of the week. Even Chad seemed caught up in the excitement.

They'd been working the story from every angle since sunrise, including capturing pictures of Petey Green walking out of the front of the jail and cursing at the reporters as he made his way to a taxi.

He never came home, unfortunately. Probably his best move, since a horde of reporters stood waiting outside his front door.

Ray even said *The Late Show* had called.

"I'm glad you turned them down," Hugo had told him. "This is a serious news story. That's the spin we're putting on it."

The footage from the hospital was priceless. The large bandage on Ray's forehead was almost the only thing you noticed. They'd put some nice string music in the background and slowed the footage down to capture a touching moment when Ray looked down, remembering the frightful incident. Blinking slowly, you could see the pain flashing through his eyes.

Rumors were flying that the footage might even be aired on the national news, and Chad had been working the phones all morning. It had been a long time since the newsroom buzzed with this much fervor.

Hayden arrived with Hugo's afternoon coffee. "Have you heard from Ray? Is he okay?"

"He's doing fine. He might even come in later." Hugo shut the door behind her and actually did a little jig as he made his way around his desk. "I'm just about to explode! This is amazing. And right before sweeps week. I can hardly believe our luck."

"I know," she breathed. "Ray could've been seriously hurt or even killed."

Hugo cleared his throat. "Exactly. So glad it wasn't worse." He stopped jigging and said, "Gilda's usually in by now. Have you heard from her?"

"No. She hasn't called, and I haven't seen her."

"Okay. Well, alert me as soon as she's here. She didn't seem herself yesterday, and I want to make sure she's okay."

"I think she's struggling with the issue of outward beauty."

Hugo tried to smile. "Aren't we all."

"I tried to tell her it's all about who she is on the inside. I'm not sure she listened."

One could only hope.

Chad walked into Hugo's office and said, "We couldn't have staged this any better!"

Hugo cut his eyes to Hayden. "Thanks for the coffee."

She took her cue and left. Chad fell into a chair. "This is beautiful."

"The police department is going to give a statement this afternoon. We'll cut into programming to air it."

"Perfect."

"We ran a preview of Ray's interview on the noon newscast, and a small part of it at five, six, and six-thirty, and we'll run the entire package at ten. By then we'll have all the other interviews gathered and edited. It should be quite a punch."

Chad stood. "All right. Let's make sure we're all at the top of our game."

"We'll be ready."

Chad left and Hugo quietly closed his door. Checking his watch, he went to his desk and took out his pill bottle. One Blue Pill left. Why hadn't he gone by the pharmacy? He was pouring the last pill into his hand when his door flew open. Pulling out his drawer, he dropped the pill into the drawer and shoved it closed. He looked up with a nonchalant expression. Hayden stood there.

"Are you okay?" she asked.

"Fine. What's the matter?"

"Gilda called. She said she's running late, but she'll be here."

"Thank you."

"Need more coffee?"

"No. Thanks."

"Okay." She shut the door and Hugo yanked open the drawer, but as he peered into the pill bottle, the single pill was not there. Carefully, he took out his stapler, scissors, tape, sticky notes, letter opener, and all the other items in the drawer, until nothing was left but a lonely paperclip. Scooting his chair back, he reached his hand all the way back into its dark corners, but his fingers just came out dusty. He looked on the ground, underneath his desk, on top of his desk, and in his chair, but the pill was not to be found. He went to his door, turned so his back was against it, and quickly unbuttoned his shirt to see if it had fallen in, but there was no Blue Pill.

Hugo felt the need to guzzle something, but all he had was hot coffee, so he drank it in short sips, fanning his lips with one hand. What was he going to do? His mother had always warned him about procrastination. And now, here he was, down to one misplaced pill. Where could it have gone?

After one more visual sweep of his desk, he put all the contents back in the drawer and slowly closed it. Something very interesting was happening. He couldn't explain it, or immediately identify it, but it was a strange feeling of empowerment.

"I don't need it," he whispered to himself as he held the empty bottle in his hand. He already knew this was going to be a good day, an exciting day. Did he really want to be calm and collected? That's what everyone expected of him, but truthfully, he was an excitable guy when the circumstances were right. And how could the circumstances get any better? This was going to be a groundbreaking day for the news department. Did he really want to miss it because his emotions were perfectly aligned with the planets?

Hugo screwed the top on the medicine bottle and, with a flick of his wrist, threw it into the trash. A strange sense of liberation came over him. This would be his best day.

Ray decided to go with Roarke to the station. If he stayed at home to "recuperate," he would probably drive himself mad. At least at work he would have some control over what was going on.

Plus—he couldn't kid himself—he wanted to see Hayden. It shocked him when Roarke had called him out about it, because he wasn't sure if he even knew it himself. But here he was at work, hoping to run into her in the break room.

Yet nobody was hanging out in the break room because everyone was preparing for tonight's newscast, so Ray decided to go to his desk and work. Work on what, he wasn't sure. He'd watched the newscast from the police department, which was an utter joke. The police captain, an opportunist who could suck fifteen minutes of fame out of a running vacuum, exploited the incident to make the police look good, using phrases like "apprehended this violent man before he could continue his rampage." The captain failed to mention Petey Green's only weapons were a disproportionate temper and well-placed left hook.

Not that Petey Green was a saint. But had it not happened on camera, to a reporter, this wouldn't have made the news.

Ray looked up just in time to see Hayden walking directly toward him, studying a piece of paper in her hand. She had the most beautiful hair he'd ever seen—white-blonde and silky, cut just below the shoulders. And her eyes were bright blue, like the sky in the peak of the afternoon. Her skin had a slight olive tone to it, making her look tan without the help of a booth or a lotion. A sweet innocence showed itself every time she smiled.

She was only twenty feet away now, and Ray felt his heart pound a little. He stood up, wanting to catch her attention but unsure of what he could say that wouldn't sound like a ridiculous excuse to catch her eye. Maybe the bandage would do the talking.

He opened his mouth, but another voice replaced his.

The weatherman (or meteorologist, as Sam Leege liked to be called) had stepped into Hayden's path.

"Hey, Hayden."

"Hi, Sam," she said.

"How are you doing?"

"Pretty good. Just running around like crazy, trying to get ready for our big night."

"Yeah," Sam said. "I thought I'd play a little trick on Hugo and tell him severe weather's moving in. Possible tornadoes."

"I don't think he could handle a joke today. He's pretty focused."

"My weather segment's been cut by three minutes, and it was only four to begin with." He shrugged. "But we're looking at temps in the fifties all week, no chance of rain, so I guess I don't have much to say. At least about the weather."

He'd gotten that right. Sam had an uncanny knack for making the weather dramatic. He hooked viewers regularly with lines like, "Stay tuned. Big weather changes ahead." If you did stay tuned, you would find out the big weather changes were for Canada. When severe weather struck, move over, because the rest of the news immediately became inconsequential. Ray longed for the day when weathermen just reported the weather and tried to make you smile with a few off-the-cuff jokes. But these days, weathermen—meteorologists—were like local heroes.

With Doppler radar, satellite tracking, and a gaggle of computers, they could nearly predict a tornado outbreak five days ahead of time. Yet there was no predicting how obnoxious Sam could be on any given day. To his credit, he could make even the dullest things—like the allergy index—seem interesting.

Ray knew he held a little grudge. More than once, one of Ray's reports had been scratched because Sam insisted he needed to break into the newscast, commercials, and anything else that got in his way to keep viewers abreast of potentially life-threatening weather situations. And Ray suspected that the computer modules Sam was always quoting were programmed toward doomsday scenarios on purpose. More than once, Sam had stood in front of the camera and said, "Our computers are indicating softball-sized hail is now moving into the metro area."

Ray had actually stepped outside once to see if he could find anything that resembled a softball. Nothing more than marbles fell from the sky.

Ray complained about it to Hugo once, telling him he thought the weather reports were a little overblown. Hugo had agreed but said that weather watching in this part of the country was practically a pastime.

"I wanted to compliment you on your shoes," Sam said to Hayden. They both looked down.

"My shoes?" Hayden looked baffled.

Ray couldn't see her shoes from where he was standing. Only Sam would notice a woman's shoes. Realizing he was standing there, gawking at the two of them, Ray slowly sat down, but it was impossible not to eavesdrop. He could hear every word they were saying.

"Well, Sam, I better get back to work."

"Um, wait. Hayden, there's something I need—I want—to ask you."

"What is it?" she asked.

"I wondered if you might want to accompany me this weekend to view a sunset that I guarantee will be the most spectacular thing you've ever seen."

Ray made a gagging noise that he couldn't begin to control, but he managed to keep from looking suspicious. That was so Sam. He couldn't just ask the lady out. It had to be the equivalent of a Category-5 pickup line.

Glancing up, Ray hoped to catch Hayden's expression, but she was now fully blocked by Sam.

"I love sunsets," she said.

Ray shook his head and squeezed his eyes shut. Unbelievable. He was too late. The story of his life.

"You are so kind to think of me," she continued.

"Well," Sam replied, "the truth of the matter is that I think of you a lot."

Surely Hayden was blushing, because Ray sure was. This was painful on so many levels.

He looked up again. Hayden had shifted her weight, and now he could see half of her face. She looked a little shocked. Ray prayed she would see Sam for the Don Juan impressionist that he was.

"I think we could have fun together. I don't date much, though."

"Why?" Sam asked, true shock in his voice. Ray had to admit, he was curious too.

"Well, we both have to ask ourselves, could we be equally yoked?"

Ray was in a full-blown stare now, but neither Sam nor Hayden noticed. He wished he could see Sam's expression.

"I love yolks. I eat eggs every morning."

"No," Hayden laughed gently. "By equally yoked, I mean spiritual equals."

Ray wanted to jump up and announce that he understood Hayden, but Sam was doing a fine job of digging his own hole.

"What does being spiritual have to do with a date?"

"It's important because then both people know that their guide to the marriage comes from biblical principles."

"Whoa now," Sam said, holding up his hands. "Who said anything about marriage? I just wanted to ask you out."

Ray could see Hayden smile, that confident, self-assured smile that made her seem so oblivious to her social shortcomings. "Well, if you're the kind of man I want to date, then you would only ask a woman on a date if you felt she might have the potential to be your wife and you wanted to get to know her better."

Ooh. Zinger. Ray smiled and waited for Sam's reply.

Sam held up his hands and said, "You've already lost me. I'm not big into the Bible."

"Then even if we did go out, we might not have a lot to talk about. But thanks for asking, Sam. I appreciate your thoughtfulness." Hayden turned and walked off. Ray could hardly contain himself as he watched her go.

But the next thing he knew, Sam was staring at him. The smile fell off Ray's face like an after-lunch crumb.

Sam slowly walked toward Ray, a strange sneer on his face. "You're hot for her, aren't you?"

Ray looked down at his keyboard. "I don't know what you're talking about. Hot for whom?" *Great.* He'd used proper grammar. A sure guilt indicator.

Sam laughed. "Give me a break. I saw you watching her. *Us.*"

Ray looked up. "Doesn't look like there's going to be an *us.*"

Sam's tongue appeared to trace his inner cheek. Then he said, "You should ask her out. You really should."

Ray avoided Sam's eyes again. He didn't know what to say, how much to admit. Sam wasn't making this statement as a friend. It was almost a taunt.

"You might want to brush up on your Torah though," Sam said.

"I don't need to. I read it regularly."

"No kidding," Sam said, feigning surprise. "Well, good for you. Say hello to Moses for me."

"I will. As soon as I'm finished watching the sunset. I hear the cirrus clouds are going to be perfect this weekend."

"I don't give up that easy."

Ray tried to ease up a little. He didn't want a fight brewing over Hayden. "Look, Sam, it's not you. She just wants someone who is interested in the same things she is."

"I'm not going to let some old fogy with a special talent for parting bodies of water stand between me and a beautiful woman." Sam grinned. "I'm a fast learner. It won't be long before I'll be dishing out some impressive Bible quotes."

"Good luck finding the CliffsNotes."

Sam didn't look amused but luckily must have decided the conversation wasn't worth the effort and left. Ray blew out a relieved sigh. He'd held a good poker face, but the fact of the matter was that he was in real need of brushing up on his Torah and everything else in the Bible. He attended church regularly but rarely cracked open his Bible. Luckily for him, as a child, his parents dragged him to church every Sunday, so he had a basic understanding of it. He could even name the books of the Bible...if he could sing the little jingle that went along with it.

Ray left his desk and went to find Roarke. He was at the assignment desk, monitoring all the scanners and radios. "This is great," Roarke said. "Some old lady is giving fits to this police officer for pulling her over. You should hear the chatter. I am cracking up. The officer is asking for backup. The lady is ninety-four years old!"

Ray leaned on the counter that encircled Roarke. "I've got a problem."

"What?"

"Sam just asked Hayden out."

"Leege? Are you kidding me? She doesn't seem his type."

"She's not. But Sam isn't going to take no for an answer."

"She turned the metrosexual down?"

Ray laughed. "In a big, bad way. She basically told him he wasn't spiritual enough."

"Whoa. Never heard that one before, but that's gotta sting. Especially since it can't be purchased at Bloomingdale's."

"You know how competitive Sam is. He's apparently going to memorize Scripture passages to romance her."

Roarke shook his head. "What happened to the old days when a rosebud and a hot fudge sundae were enough?" He sighed. "I don't know what to tell you, dude. I've got my own woman problems."

"Really? What's wrong?"

Roarke turned down the volume on a couple of his scanners. "Something weird's happened to her."

Ray looked around, trying to figure out who was Roarke's crush.

"She's the same, but different. I can't put my finger on it, dude."

"What could've changed?"

"I don't know. But there's something off. I won't lie. I'm worried about her."

"Look, Roarke, I told you my crush, now you need to tell me yours."

"Dude, people don't use the word 'crush' anymore."

Ray couldn't argue with that. But "hot for her" sounded a little awkward after discussing the spiritual standards he would have to rise to.

Roarke waved his hand. "Doesn't matter. Whatever. She won't give me the time of day anyway. It's a pipe dream. I'll never get a date with this lady."

"Don't give up that easy." Ray sighed. "At least you don't have homework."

Chapter 8

T hings were getting better and better as the day went on. It started at about six, when Gilda finally made her way into work. There were whispers, then rumors, and then it was the topic of conversation on everyone's lips. Hugo had tried to remain neutrally uninterested, showing little emotion as each tidbit of information came to him. But inside, he was wiggling with astonishment. His plan had actually worked. At least in reverse. Or something. He wasn't exactly sure how it all came together, but the important thing was that it had.

Or at least that's what he'd heard. He had yet to verify the rumors, which in the news business was one of three sins. Deadly ones, anyway.

He could see Gilda's dressing-room door from his glass-encased office, and he had watched her walk in there forty-five minutes ago. From what he could tell, she'd been alone for fifteen minutes now. It was time to see for himself.

His legs felt a little wobbly as he left his office and circled the newsroom, heading toward her dressing room. Too many people had claimed to see the evidence for it to be just a rumor.

At her dressing-room door, he took a deep breath before knocking. He didn't want to seem too enthusiastic, but he also wanted to be complimentary and supportive. This was going to take finesse.

"Enter," he heard. Slowly, he opened the door. He could see the back of her hair and a little of her face, but her dressing-room lights were so bright, he was nearly squinting at the reflection in the mirror.

"Hugo," she said and turned on her stool.

Without the glaring lights now, Hugo got a good look at her, and as best he could, he suspended the steadiest, most even-keeled smile on his face. His eyes desperately wanted to widen, but he commanded them to freeze in place. This was better than he could've expected. She looked ten, no, fifteen years younger. Instantly. It was like he'd traveled back in time.

And for the first time in years she looked genuinely happy. Really, really happy.

"Hi," Hugo said.

She drew her hands up to her face. "Satisfied?"

Hugo played it cool. "With?"

"Let's not play games here, Hugo. I know this is what you wanted. What you've wanted for a long time."

"It's not what you want?" he asked.

Gilda seemed to ponder the question. "No. But"—she glanced at herself in the mirror—"I do look good."

Hugo cracked a smile. "Gilda, you look amazing. Not that you didn't before, but I mean…" He was truly speechless and gestured with his hands to try to find a word that meant the impossible had become possible in the most superficial way imaginable.

Gilda didn't seem to share the excitement quite as much. She was smiling. At least her mouth was. And there did seem to be a satisfied shimmer within her eyes. But she was not ecstatic like Hugo was trying not to be.

"We've got a big night tonight," Hugo said. The timing couldn't have been better. "Ray's attack is all over the news. They even covered it briefly on the national news. This is our chance, Gilda. It's our chance to prove that we've got what it takes to be the number one news station."

Gilda's expression didn't change, but she nodded as if she understood. "How is Ray?" she asked.

"He's fine. He's here. Did a great interview with us this morning. It's going to be a hit. We're ready to roll, and you're going to be the star who gets us there. Tate doesn't have the experience to carry this like you do, Gilda."

"I won't let you down, Hugo. I never have."

And it was true. Gilda always came through during tough situations. She was highly dependable and always at her best—which would've carried her even farther had she been able to hold her collagen.

Nearly overwhelmed with emotion, Hugo stuck out his hand for Gilda to shake. She looked at it like she'd just witnessed the Nessie emerge from the loch. Hugo knew people weren't used to seeing him emote, but sometimes in life, there's cause for celebration.

Gilda shook his hand gingerly, as if she were afraid he might lunge forward for a hug. But he minded himself and stepped toward the door.

"We'll have the script for you in an hour or so," he said.

"Okay."

Hugo opened the door, and she said, "Good luck, Hugo. I know this is a big night for you."

"For all of us. We're going to do great."

He stepped outside, and for the first time in months and months, Hugo Talley felt hopeful.

Gilda couldn't stop touching the space between her eyebrows. She had yet to feel anything except numbness, but she could hardly believe that deep line that refused to leave, even when she smiled, had vanished. In its place was smooth, supple skin. Even the lines around her eyes were gone, and the two creases on either side of her nose. The doctor explained she could experience some swelling and redness, but so far none of that had happened.

She'd been studying the script for the evening carefully, though it wasn't in its final draft. Still, there was a lot to this story, and Gilda wanted the transitions to be smooth and her delivery to be perfect. She decided to take a break and get some coffee, despite the warning about it after her teeth-bleaching session this afternoon. She couldn't live without coffee, even if it meant her teeth looked a little dull.

In the break room, she was delighted to discover a fresh pot in the coffeemaker. She poured it into her favorite lipstick-stained mug and was stirring in cream when the door flew open and Tate bolted in.

"I'm nervous," he said. "At first I thought I was coming down with the flu, but I think it's nerves." He looked genuinely baffled. "I've only felt like this one other time, when a bungee rope got tangled around my neck."

Gilda reached for his hand. "Dear, you'll do fine. I'm here with you. It's just like riding a bike. Or in your case, a snowboard off a cliff."

"Hugo keeps saying, 'Don't mess this up,' and I'm going to mess it up."

Gilda set her mug down and cupped his shoulder. "You're not going to mess it up. You must think about it like any other news day."

"Skydiving is easier than this. There's a rip cord you pull to open your chute. If that doesn't work, you pull another one. If that doesn't work, well, you're dead. But you've pretty much done all you can do." Tate shook his head. "There's so much to keep track of here."

Gilda realized it was a lot for Tate to process. He wasn't really the multifaceted type, at least as far as his mind was concerned.

Although she felt the pressure, too, she had a hard time understanding why someone who could jump out of an airplane was feeling nervous about reading from a TelePrompTer, but she tried to remain encouraging. "That's what being an anchor is all about. You have to keep your cool under pressure. Sure, most nights you're trying to make news out of the most mundane of things. But there are those shining moments in your career when real news happens, Tate. And that's what you've been practicing for. All those nights that you've stared into that camera lens, faithfully reporting the day's events, have prepared you for this moment."

Tate stared at his feet. "You're amazing." He glanced at her. "I don't know how you do it. In the middle of such a stressful situation, you stand there so calm, smiling even."

She was smiling? She hadn't thought she was smiling. Huh. Botox really was miraculous.

"You look great by the way," he added.

"Thanks, honey. You're kind to say so. Now, the best way to shine, and not in the oily pore sort of way, is to be prepared. Have you been studying your script?"

"Yes. I throw it to commercial, and I welcome everyone back, I pitch the weather and the sports, but…well, most of the lines are yours."

"Hey, who would Penn be without Teller, right? Sometimes the silent guy does the talking without ever saying a word."

Tate nodded and left in a contemplative mood. Gilda followed him into the newsroom, stirring her coffee. As people looked her way, a few gave a thumbs-up. Others simply pretended nothing unusual was going on, even though they were staring like she'd grown a third eye. Well, if she had, she was sure there was some sort of injection for that too.

Hayden happened by, and before Gilda knew it, she'd reached out and taken her by the arm, pulling the girl beside her.

"Yes?" Hayden asked.

"Look, I know we had that little heart-to-heart about aging and all of that, but you have to understand the position I am in. Truthfully, you could never really understand my position. But I did this of my own accord. I've been pressured for years. *Years.* This was my decision, and my decision alone. Nobody made me do this."

"Ms. Braun, it's really none of my business."

"None of your business? What about all that beauty-is-on-the-inside talk?"

"Well," Hayden said, with a preemptive sweetness, "some people prefer to wear their beauty on the outside, I guess."

"Sure. Why not, right?" Gilda lifted her coffee mug in the air in a toasting gesture.

"It's just that on the inside, it can't be damaged by UVB rays." Hayden gave her a knowing wink and walked off. Gilda sighed and wished her the best, and a few premature sunspots to go along with it.

She was walking toward her dressing room when she saw Hugo rush out of his office, holding a piece of paper in his hand. He was gathering everyone to the center of the newsroom. He looked frantic, or excited. She couldn't really tell what was wrong with him, but she wasn't used to seeing Hugo this emotional.

"Hurry up," he beckoned, and pretty soon everyone was hushed and huddled.

"What's going on?" Gilda asked.

"I just received this fax," Hugo said, holding the piece of paper up in the air. "It's a threat."

"A threat?" someone asked.

"From Petey Green."

Mumbling ensued, and Hugo didn't try hard to hush them. Instead, he talked over them. "It says: 'To Whoever It Concerns. I hate your news station. You are all a bunch of biased pig lovers. I hated your station before you ever came to my street. But I can tell you one thing, I ain't gonna let you on my street again. You step on my street and you are gonna wish you never met me.'" Hugo paused. "It's signed by Mr. Green."

"What are we going to do?" someone asked.

"I've called the police, and they're on their way. In the meantime, folks, we're going to have to cover this angle as well. We've got every reporter already assigned to different parts of this story, so this is going to have to be from the anchor's desk." Hugo looked at Gilda. "You're going to read it live."

Gilda felt her heart flutter. "No problem," she replied. "We'll make it happen. When?"

"We're going to have to set up the story first, or the threat will make little sense, so I think we'll end the first segment with you reading it on air. Someone get a camera set up outside. I want a shot of the police arriving at the station. Everyone else, let's put the finishing touches on the show. We've got one hour." Hugo slapped his hands together, startling everyone. "Let's move, people!"

The crowd dispersed, and Gilda watched Hugo buzz around the room like a seven-year-old on a sugar high. This wasn't like him. Last year they'd thrown him a surprise birthday party, and when they jumped out of the dark and yelled, "Surprise!" all he managed was a mild smile and soft, "Thank you." Gilda thought maybe it was because Hugo's wife, Jane, was such a talker that Hugo never had anything left to say. Or had much practice talking. But whatever the case, Hugo was the most even-tempered person she'd ever met, and the fact that this whole scenario was getting to him made her wonder if she ought to be more nervous than she was.

Walking back to her dressing room, she thought, *What can go wrong? You're a pro. You've been doing this for years. You've covered every kind of news story there is.* She carefully sipped her coffee and let the rest of the crew go stir crazy. She was going to keep her cool. That was going to be the key to success. Keep cool.

She walked into her dressing room and to her vanity. Her makeup lady would be here soon, and what a surprise she was going to be in for! Gilda could hardly wait. This lady would save a ton on concealer.

And then she noticed something.

It was a small box, tied with a red ribbon, sitting right next to her hairbrush. She sat down on her stool and could hardly manage to reach out to read the card attached. Could this be from her secret admirer? It had all the familiar characteristics: the neat and tidy bow, the simple presentation, like it had just leaped out of the last century. She'd never received a box from her admirer at work. Did this mean she worked with him? There had been subtle hints…

She turned, almost feeling like someone was in the room, watching her, but she was alone. She looked back at the box and opened the note.

It simply said, "You make my heart stand still." She placed her hand on her chest; her heart was definitely not standing still. Pulling the string to the box, it fell to the side, and she lifted its top. There, in the middle, were four exquisitely decorated chocolates.

Gilda glanced up at her reflection in the mirror, about to smile. But to her delightful surprise, she was already smiling.

This admirer was a co-worker, and he'd just made a new move to make himself known. She hoped he wouldn't hide behind his gifts forever.

Chapter 9

H ugo still couldn't stop smiling. Finally, it was his turn to experience good luck or karma or divine blessing or whatever you wanted to call it. He'd watched it happen to other people for years. Now it was his turn. Something was going his way; something that he didn't have to work an eighty-hour week for.

They had twenty minutes until the news started, and to his surprise, everything looked exactly in place. The control-room personnel were focused but not stressed. Tate and Gilda looked ready to take the bull by the horns, and all the reporters were standing by for their segments. So far, they hadn't had a single glitch. Even Chad, who normally left at 6:30 p.m., was hanging around. And Hugo had heard from a few sources that the other news stations were carrying Ray's incident as their lead story.

Hugo was in such a good mood that he decided to call his wife. Normally, he didn't talk to Jane during work. They'd tried it a few times when he landed his first producer's job, but it never worked out well.

Jane hadn't always worked. She stayed home when their daughter was young, but Hugo didn't earn enough at his previous job to make ends meet, so Jane went to work. And to both their surprise, she loved it. Ever since then she worked. Because of it, they left more messages than they did actual talking, so they'd agreed to just e-mail each other if there was something important going on. He knew she'd be up because she always watched the news until the sports came on.

"Hello?"

"Hey, honey. It's me."

"What's wrong?"

"Nothing. I just wanted to say hello."

"Aren't you getting ready to start the news?"

"In a few minutes. It's just been a good day, and I wanted to share it with you. How was your day?"

"Oh, crazy. I had three meetings at work, and then the school called and wanted me to volunteer at the cupcake bake-off. You're going to have to make a batch in the morning. Plus, I had to take Kaylin to a special dance rehearsal tonight. We just got home thirty minutes ago."

"Is she in bed yet?"

"Yeah."

"Well, give her a hug for me anyway."

"I've left a list of a few other things I need you to do before work tomorrow. And your dinner is in the fridge."

"Okay. Well, I better run. I'll talk to you sometime tomorrow."

"Don't forget, I've got that corporate meeting until eight."

"Okay."

"Love you."

"Love you too."

Hugo hung up the phone and turned to find Hayden standing near him. "You must really miss your wife."

Hugo nodded, a little embarrassed that he'd been caught talking to his wife at work.

"My parents were really lucky. They worked in a business together for years, so they were with each other all the time."

Hugo couldn't quite imagine that, though he did long for a little more time with Jane. When he arrived home after work, she was already in bed, and by the time he got up, she was already gone. The only thing that worked out really well was Kaylin's schedule. Their twelve-year-old had a parent present for nearly every activity.

"We make the most of our weekends," Hugo said. "Now, is everything set? Are we sure we've got all our ducks in a row?"

"Yes sir. Everyone is ready to go."

"All right." Hugo checked his watch. Fifteen minutes. So this was what euphoria felt like.

Ray had tried several times to maneuver his way next to Hayden through-out the evening. He had little to do at work other than meander around and answer one question after another about the incident. His head was throbbing a little, but that didn't deter his mind from plotting how he intended to ask out Hayden. He was going to have to be really smooth about it since he'd witnessed Sam Leege crash and burn. He didn't want that to happen. But he also didn't want to give Sam an opportunity before he got his chance.

Nothing was panning out. Every time he got close to her, something happened to thwart him.

Time was ticking by. Soon the news would be over and his chance would be gone. Perhaps he was rushing things, but he knew the look in Sam's eye. It was a look that told him Sam wasn't going to go home to study the weather tonight.

Ray had to get in while he still had a chance. Sam would be back, and there was something about meteorologists in this part of the country that made women swoon. Maybe they knew something about the barometric pressure that other men didn't.

Ray stood at his desk and scanned the newsroom for her to no avail. She was probably in the control room with Hugo, and there was no way he was going to try his moves inside a dark box with a crowd and a bunch of open mikes.

He decided to get a cup of coffee. He hated coffee, but it was a nice excuse to leave his desk for a few minutes. He'd been taking coffee breaks for years and had yet to actually drink the stuff. As he turned toward the break room, he almost ran over Hayden, who was about to place a piece of paper on his desk.

"Hi," Ray said. "Sorry. Didn't know you were there."

"My fault," she said, grinning. "I should've made some noise or something."

Ray was already disgruntled at his inability to sense the woman of his dreams nearby. Even the smallest animal could smell the opposite sex from yards, sometimes miles, away. What was wrong with him?

And now he was caught off guard. He'd had so many lines prepared, so many openers, and now he was just staring at her. She started to look uncomfortable, as she should, because he was making a perfectly awkward moment worse.

So he started to say something about how beautiful she looked. He'd hoped to go for a more creative angle, but at the moment, nothing else was coming to him. He figured, *What woman doesn't like to hear how beautiful she is?*

She looked down, shaking her head. "Is it that obvious?"

Not only could he not sense her presence, but now he couldn't follow the conversation. This was the reason he was single and probably would be for the rest of his life. He was stuck between nodding and shaking his head, and it was making him dizzy.

"I know, I know. It's making me so upset. I'm trying to hide it, but it's just getting to me."

Ray tried his best to follow. "I…well, I would be upset too."

"You would? Really?"

"Sure," Ray smiled. "Wouldn't everyone?"

She frowned. "I don't think so. I mean, this sort of thing is accepted as the norm. But it's so sad. I'm really sad for her."

Ray followed her gaze as she looked toward… "Gilda?"

Hayden turned to him. "Who did you think I was talking about?"

Swallowing, Ray tried to play it cool again. He wished he had a cup of coffee to pretend to sip. "No, yeah. Of course, Gilda."

"I really tried to talk to her about beauty, what it means to be beautiful. How beauty comes from the inside. But at the end of the day, the lies of Satan won out." Hayden's shoulders slumped.

Ray wasn't exactly sure how to turn "lies of Satan" into a lead in to ask her out. *Speaking of lies… Speaking of Satan…* Nothing was working here. And *Speaking of beauty* wasn't going to fly, since it was obvious that Hayden wasn't concerned with outward beauty. *Speaking of beauty on the inside…* That sounded like he was getting ready to compliment her kidneys.

But he had to do something. She was standing right here. This was his chance, and he was blowing it, big time.

Hayden was about to walk off, so it was going to have to be a desperate move on his part, but at least it was a move. He was going to look like a fool. Maybe he'd end up being a fool in love. He reached out to take her arm, but suddenly Roarke came rushing by as fast as Roarke could actually rush. With a piece of paper in each hand, huffing and puffing straight for the control room, Roarke mumbled over and over, "Oh no. Oh no. Oh no."

With ten minutes to go in the newscast, Hugo decided to do something unprecedented. In all his years as a news producer, he had never done anything like this. But in all his years as a news producer, nothing like this had ever happened. Sure, he'd covered big stories, locally and nationally. But he'd never had the edge like he had today.

He'd instructed Willis to open up everyone's IFBs. He called the control room and all the reporters standing by to attention.

"Good evening, everyone," Hugo said. "I know you're all wondering why I've called this meeting." Hugo snickered at his own joke. Everyone in the control room managed at least a small smile. "In all seriousness, I just want to tell you how proud I am of every one of you. We've worked hard over the years to try to get to this place, and here we are. Maybe we got here with the help of a little dumb luck, and the fact that Ray's never taken a self-defense class, but we're here. We're prepared for it. Every one of us is prepared. Take in this moment." He sucked air through his nostrils, causing Willis to give him a strange look. "Really take it in. This doesn't happen often." Hugo closed his eyes. He didn't want to lose this feeling. It had been so long since he felt this good, this satisfied with life, without the help of a pill, which was by far cheaper than the fancy sports cars other men needed.

Suddenly, the door to the control room slammed open, jolting Hugo out of his meditative state. Roarke stood in the doorway, gasping for breath, eyes wide. Trying to catch his breath, he finally managed to say, "I've got breaking news."

Chapter 10

T he stunned silence in the control room was the first indication that what was happening was real. At first Hugo thought it must be a hallucination or some out-of-body experience or maybe he'd fainted and was dreaming. But as he looked around the small room, everyone stared back at him.

"The *what* exploded?" someone asked from behind him. Hugo was moving his mouth, he realized, but nothing was coming out.

Roarke looked down, like it was the hardest thing he'd ever had to say. "The…the, um, the wastewater treatment plant."

Hugo still couldn't speak. It was like his mind was playing in slow motion.

Someone else asked, "Do you mean the *sewage plant?*"

Roarke said, "Uh, yeah. Except it's more acceptable to say wastewater treatment plant. Ed's on his way…can be there in eight minutes with live pictures. Jill's less than two miles away, but the traffic is tied up with a stalled car. The chatter is that there's a huge fireball, and everyone nearby is being evacuated." Roarke's sad eyes made Hugo realize there was really no choice to be made. This was the story they had to cover.

And before Hugo knew what was happening, he was slapping his hand against the desk and yelling obscenities the likes of which he had never uttered, *ever,* in front of another human being.

"How could this happen?" he cried, his hands out, pleading with the room. "A sewage plant! That's what's going to undo us? A sewage plant?!" There was such a disturbing metaphor there that he could hardly get his mind to wrap around how real this was. They were back to a typical news day. They no longer had the exclusive story.

While still ranting, he glanced to the back of the room and saw Hayden standing there with her eyes closed and a single hand in the air, praying.

Hugo must've stopped, because there was silence all around him again. Then Willis asked, "What do you want to do? We've got three minutes until we're on."

A sheet of sweat poured down Hugo's face, and inside, he knew he was going to have to pull himself together. He berated himself for having held his expectations so high. Then he said, "We're going to roll with it. Get pictures up as soon as possible. Send Jill and Trent over there now. Roarke, get me the facts *now.* Someone get online and pull down information on the plant. Gilda, you're opening with what we know, and you're going to have to keep talking until Ed can get those pictures and we can get Jill out there live."

"All right, Hugo," Gilda said. Roarke was already out the door to gather the facts. Hugo watched the screen as the two anchors shifted notes and watched the computer monitor embedded in the desk for new information as it came available. It seemed like an eternity, but Roarke finally sent word that Jill was on the scene.

"She's saying it's quite a sight," Willis said. "A lot of people running."

"Any other stations there?"

Willis looked up at him. "Channel 10. We're on in a minute and a half."

Hugo's heart pounded frantically. He took a step back to gather himself, he was still in shock that he'd lost his composure. Then he grabbed the microphone to talk to Gilda. "Gilda?"

"Yes?"

"Gilda, I need you to stay calm, give the viewers the facts as you get them, and do what you do best. Just stay calm, okay?"

Hugo looked at the monitor and saw her smiling at him. "Don't worry, Hugo. We'll be fine. I'm calm."

"Okay…" Hugo stepped back and let Willis prepare as much as he could in the short time he had. Ed was feeding back the live pictures, and Jill was getting into place in front of the plant, which lit up the dark sky. Trent wasn't there yet, but he'd been assigned the task of trying to get interviews.

As Willis began the official countdown to airtime, Hugo felt a lump form in his throat. Nobody noticed; everyone's attention was elsewhere. Hayden was still praying in the back, and it started to make Hugo angry. He almost marched back there to tell her to knock it off when Willis gave the ten-second cue.

Hugo leaned forward and watched the monitor carefully. Something didn't seem right with Gilda, but he couldn't put his finger on it. She didn't look ready. In fact, she looked…amused? Why would she—?

"Cue opening," Willis said. Their opening music played, and then the zippy sound effect that indicated breaking news.

"Good evening," Gilda said, still looking amused. "I'm Gilda Braun, and we have breaking news tonight. There has been an explosion at the wastewater treatment plant. We are at the scene live, still gathering information about this dramatic situation that is unfolding even as we speak." Hugo blinked. What was wrong with Gilda? Was that a smile? Was she actually smiling?

"Cut to Ed," Willis said.

Gilda was still talking, rambling off what little facts they knew.

"What is wrong with her?" Hugo asked.

"Gilda?" Willis asked.

"Is it me, or is she smiling? Tell her she needs to be more serious."

"Gilda, we need a more serious tone," Willis said as Gilda paused for a moment. "Cut back to Gilda," Willis instructed. Now Gilda's face was back on the monitor, but again, she was looking like she might start singing show tunes. "Pitch it to Jill when you're ready," Willis said into Gilda's IFB.

"We're going to go live now to Jill Clark, the first reporter to arrive on the scene. Jill, what can you tell us?"

The picture cut to Jill, who stood in front of…the Channel 10 news truck? Was that the only picture she could get?

"Well, Gilda, we don't know much at this time. Firefighters are still assessing the situation and determining whether anyone is still inside. They are trying to account for all employees, who raced out of the building as soon as they heard the explosion. Right now, there are only two fire trucks at the scene, but we can hear sirens in the distance."

Channel 10 is playing dirty, Hugo thought. Blocking the view with their truck. Hugo studied Gilda, who still looked like she was about to crack a joke.

"Let me talk to Gilda," Hugo said. Willis patched him through. "Gilda!"

"What?" Gilda asked, looking up into the camera.

"What are you doing? This is a huge news story. There could be tons of people dead!"

"I know that. Why are you telling me that?"

"Because you're smiling. You were smiling all the way through the first piece."

"I am not!" Gilda said.

"Jill's pitching it back to Gilda," Willis announced.

Gilda sat up straight and looked into the camera, "Thank you for that report, Jill. We're now going to go to Ed Klawski, who is bringing us some amazing pictures from Chopper 7."

Willis quickly cut to the pictures. Hugo felt like his chest was about to explode. He'd take Tate's smirk right now. Maybe Gilda was high or drunk or—

"All right, Ed's pitching it over to Trent, who is trying to speak with someone who has come out of the plant," Willis said.

"This is an amazing scene," Trent said into the camera. He had a better angle than Jill, but the flames were barely visible over Trent's shoulder. Suddenly Trent looked to his left. "Sir...sir, please, can you speak with us about what you saw?" Trent reached out for someone as the camera zoomed out for a wider shot. The man Trent wanted to interview looked sweaty and frantic. He also looked like he didn't want to talk.

"Come on, Trent! Give it all you've got! Don't take no for an answer!" Hugo coached.

"Sir, what can you tell us?"

"I don't really...um..." The man looked around and tried to step away, but Trent took his arm.

"Please, sir. I understand you've been through quite an ordeal, but can you give us some idea what it's like in there?"

The man was shaking his head and glancing nervously at the camera.

"Come on, Trent! Pull it out of him!" Hugo yelled.

"Were you in the building?" Trent asked.

"Uh...yeah," the man replied.

"Good!" Hugo said. "Keep the questions coming!"

"Can you give us an idea of what's going on?"

The man paused, shaking his head. "There's just a lot of smoke and people running around screaming." The man wiped the sweat off his forehead.

"Are there any people trapped?"

"That's what we're trying to find out."

"What part of the plant do you work in, sir?"

"Great question! Keep 'em rolling!" Hugo said to the monitor. But he noticed the man looked confused by the question.

"Sir," Trent said in a calm voice Hugo had never heard before, "I understand your apprehension. But there are many people sitting at home right now, wondering if their friends or relatives are okay. You can give them some information. What part of the plant do you work in?"

"I don't work for the plant."

"You don't? Do you work in a building nearby? How did you get in the building?"

Again, the man looked unsure that he should answer. But Trent jabbed the microphone in his face and finally the man said, "I'm the live truck operator for Channel 10. Our cameraman got inside the building and nearly got us both killed, but the pictures are breathtaking."

Hugo's mouth dropped open just like Trent's. Trent slowly turned toward the camera as he mumbled, "Uh…thank you. Back to you, Gilda."

Hugo slapped his hand against his forehead. He could practically hear people grabbing their remotes and switching to Channel 10 for those "breathtaking" pictures. Hugo fell into the chair he hoped was still behind him.

"Let's run Ray's piece," Hugo said.

Willis said, "Gilda, tell everyone we'll be back to the scene as soon as we get more information. Pitch Ray's piece."

Hugo furiously rubbed his temples. He watched Gilda smile her way through the pitch, but he couldn't manage to watch Ray's segment, the one he'd been so excited about just a few minutes before.

As Ray's segment rolled, Gilda's voice came booming through to the control room. "This is your fault!" she screeched. "Hugo Talley, this is all your fault!"

"What is my fault?" Hugo blurted as Willis was careful to make sure all the mikes at the anchors' desk were closed.

Gilda raised a finger like she was about to make a point, then pointed straight to her forehead, where it came to rest between her eyebrows. *"I can't frown!"*

Gilda, though suddenly crying, still looked perfectly dreamy. *"I can't frown!"* she shouted again. "My face, I can't frown. I can hardly move my cheeks and my mouth feels numb…" Gilda was now hysterical, and her mascara was running as fast as her mouth. She was gesturing and wailing.

Next to her, Tate looked like a pale statue. Ray's segment finished, and Willis had no choice but to cut to Ed, who was doing his best to continue pointing out that the sewage plant was burning.

"Get Gilda out of there," Willis instructed one of the grips, who quickly made it to the anchor's desk and escorted her away. Willis turned his attention to Tate. "Tate, snap out of it. In a few seconds, we're going to cut from Ed. You've got to pitch it to commercial."

Tate blinked.

Hugo grabbed the mike. "Tate, listen to me. We cannot go down in smoke, do you understand me? This is important. We've got to do this flawlessly. You've got to end this segment before commercial in a way that makes the viewer not want to change the channel. You have got to hook them, okay? Stay calm and poised. This is a serious story, but don't look panicked. Look like you're in control of the entire situation. Make your final comments before commercial *count* for something, okay? You can do this, Tate. I know you can. And try your best not to smirk, okay? No smirking. Frown but don't scowl. Okay? Am I making sense? Are we clear here? You've got about ten seconds. Think about what you're going to say. Think about that hook that will leave the viewer pondering the situation."

Tate nodded through it all, his eyes wide enough to see white all the way around the iris.

Willis directed, "Ed, pitch it back to Tate."

"And that's the view from up here. Tate, back to you."

Tate turned toward the camera, and for a moment, he paused. It seemed like an eternity, but he suddenly found the exact right expression. His eyes bounced from his notes to camera one. He leaned forward and said, "Thank you, Ed. Amazing pictures from the sky. From the beginning of this breaking news story, Ed was there and you can see the result. Live pictures that are nearly beyond words."

Hugo stepped back to breathe. Tate was handling it. He was doing it.

It was a minor triumph, but at this point, he was going to take what he could get.

But before Hugo could take another deep breath, Tate said, "And folks, this begs the question, will my toilet flush when I get home? Stay tuned."

And then he smirked.

Chapter 11

Y ou're going to have to up my dosage. It's not working anymore. I might as well be taking a placebo. Maybe it is a placebo. Is it a placebo?" Hugo sat in the exam room of his doctor's office fully clothed yet feeling like he was wearing a hospital gown backward. He had yet to discover whether his vulnerability was willingly on display or not, but nevertheless, he figured it was the only way he was going to get through to Dr. Hoffman.

"Look, Hugo—"

Hugo held up his hands. "I know you think I'm overreacting, but you weren't there. You didn't see me. I completely lost my mind. It was some sort of nervous breakdown. I mentally snapped." Hugo twirled his finger around his ear. "Went totally bonkers. All because I didn't take my pill. Now listen, I've done my fair share of Internet research on my disability, and I know that the little pill can sometimes stop working at certain dosages—"

"Hugo, you don't have a disability."

"Then what do you call last night? What was that?"

"A stressful situation, from everything you've told me about it."

"Look, the fact of the matter is that I think I need to change antianxiety medication. Switch up brands, you know? Why not try that Purple Pill with the green monster? You know the one. Says something about the monster attacking any hope for peace in your life, and the monster walks around making irritating comments to illustrate what it feels like to live with generalized anxiety disorder. I don't really want to be on the one with the triangle character. He looks kind of dopey."

Dr. Hoffman crossed her arms as she leaned against the cabinets behind her. "Hugo, do you want to know what I think?"

"No."

"I think you're depressed."

"Depressed? I am not depressed! I haven't cried since the day I stopped smoking."

"You don't have to cry to be depressed."

"I am not depressed. And if I were depressed, it's because you won't diagnose me as anxious."

Dr. Hoffman sat down on a stool and rolled closer to Hugo, who was sitting on the examination table. "Hugo, tell me about your home life. How is your home life?"

"My home life is fine."

"Are you happy with your situation at home?"

"Sure." He stopped her next question. "Look, let's keep on track with the subject matter here. Last night was a disaster, and I was not able to handle it. I have to be able to handle stressful situations. I don't have the luxury of removing stress from my life, so the only other option is to be able to face it calmly with a clear and medicated head."

"Well, let's put some things in perspective first. You say things went badly last night, and you didn't handle yourself in the best manner. What's the worst that could happen? You get fired? People get fired every day and bounce back."

Hugo squeezed the bridge of his nose with his forefinger and thumb.

"Seriously, Hugo, let's name the fallout from this."

"For one, I will probably, for the rest of my life, have an aversion to toilets flushing." He resisted the urge to stand and pace the room. "Dr. Hoffman, I once watched a three-hour show on the Discovery Channel where doctors removed a two-hundred-pound tumor from a woman, and you're trying to tell me there's nothing you can do to fix me?"

"I don't have any magic pills."

"I'm not asking for a magic pill. I'm asking for the two-milligram version of what I'm on."

She shook her head. "I'm sorry, Hugo. I don't take things like this lightly. My advice to you is that you take a long look at your life and figure out what's causing you to feel this way."

Nearby, Hugo heard a toilet flush.

Throughout most of the night and into the early morning hours, Gilda Braun had stood in front of her mirror at home, trying to work her brows into a furrow. At precisely 3:00 a.m., they folded inward slightly, enough to make her face take on a more serious expression. She'd finally collapsed into bed, hoping that by morning she would be able to do more than look perpetually surprised.

Apparently all the Botox in the world couldn't keep her eyes from looking puffy, so she rubbed on some cream and wandered into her kitchen for coffee. Her appetite was shot, and she certainly didn't want to watch the show again. Since the VCR was invented, Gilda had always recorded the ten o'clock news to watch the next morning, trying to refine her skill. But last night was nothing she wanted to see again. She didn't have to imagine. Staring back at her in her rearview mirror on the way home was a very sad, dejected woman who looked like she'd just won the lottery.

Over the decades, Gilda had certainly seen her share of mishaps. In the few years that she was a reporter, she'd stumbled over lines, misquoted people, and even got her station sued by forgetting the word "allegedly" while reporting a story about a bank robber.

And in the anchor's chair, she'd pronounced world leaders' names wrong once or twice, had a sneezing fit, and had hiccupped herself all the way through a segment after returning from the company Christmas party. But that comes with the territory, and her cultivated talent made up for the few blunders she'd experienced.

Last night was at an entirely new level, and she was not sure she could recover from it. Never in her life had she been more humiliated. And no matter how hard she'd tried to make it right, she made it worse. Hours before, she'd had such a confidence in her new appearance.

Before Gilda knew what was happening to her, she was weeping at her breakfast table. And even that was a task, because as much as she wanted her face to assume an expression of grief, it would only move mere millimeters.

Then her phone rang. Gilda's head rose off the table and she stared at the phone, which lit up like a Christmas tree perched inside its stand. Wiping her nose, something told her not to answer it. She didn't know why. Maybe it was because she knew whatever—whoever—was on the other end would not be delivering good news. She felt compelled to let it go to voice mail, but yet, maybe…just maybe…

Rushing to the phone, she snatched it up, praying something good would be on the other end.

Roarke and Ray sat on the couch together, each with a bowl of buttered popcorn. Roarke was holding up the remote, fast-forwarding through the commercials.

"You should really get TiVo," Ray said.

"I've had the VCR for twelve years and it's never failed me." Roarke threw a handful of popcorn into his mouth. "And dude, please, never ever forget the M&M's again, okay? This is killing me." Ray had forgotten M&M's for the first time ever. Roarke always provided the popcorn, and Ray brought M&M's. They would mix them up, each take a bowl, and watch their favorite show that Roarke had taped the night before. The show varied from season to season. This year, Roarke had gotten him hooked on ultimate fighting.

A few minutes into the match, Roarke glanced over at Ray. "You okay?"

"Why?"

"You're totally not watching this."

Ray gestured at the television. "I'm looking right at the screen."

"But you're not into it."

Ray blinked. It was true. He wasn't really concentrating. He was having a hard time leaving last night behind. All of it. From his disastrous attempt to ask Hayden out to the loss of the news story that would have propelled them into the top rank, to the station's disappointing coverage of breaking news, he wasn't sure anything else could've gone wrong. The only thing that went right for him personally was the fact that the exploding sewage plant trumped his dreadful and embarrassing incident with the pig-hater. He felt guilty about that, so he couldn't really celebrate since the explosion had left two workers injured and the station very possibly mortally wounded.

To top it all off, two of the most even-tempered people he'd ever met had gone through what could only be described as nervous breakdowns, nearly at the same time. Gilda Braun was escorted away from the anchor's desk during what was probably the worst broadcast in the station's history. Hugo also lost it, and that was putting it politely. Ray wasn't sure he could describe exactly what it was like to see a man of such self-control implode, but as the ten o'clock news ended, so, it seemed, did Hugo's sanity. The man was cussing and ranting and at one point actually had to be physically restrained.

"He*llo*?"

Ray glanced at Roarke. "Sorry. I was just thinking about last night."

"Why?"

Roarke seemed nearly incapable of worry about anything outside the very small world he created. If it didn't affect him directly, he didn't worry about it. And if it did affect him directly, he worried in what could only be described as a healthy manner. Roarke certainly wasn't oblivious to the world's problems. His entire job revolved around listening to the tragedies of the outside world and reporting on which one was most newsworthy. Maybe that was why Roarke was so good at what he did, because he could turn it on and off and never bring it home with him.

Ray, on the other hand, was capable of bringing truckloads of frustration, depression, anger, and guilt, among other things, home with him every night, as if he were so bored with life that all he wanted to do was mull things over. And no matter how hard he tried, he just couldn't find the off switch.

Whenever Ray would bring up the fact that he struggled with his sensation-dependent job, Roarke would say, "Then don't do it." It was that simple for him. But for Ray, there were days when he felt like he was really making a difference. It's what kept him doing it.

This was a means to an end, to a greater good that would make up for all the guilt he felt. He wished so badly that he could feel no sense of moral responsibility, that he could exploit the daylights out of any story, knowing it was just part of his job.

Once Ray had come up with the idea of doing a segment called, "The Bright Side of Life," in which he would report on something good that was taking place around the city. It aired three times before it was cut because they actually got hate mail about it.

Roarke had commented, "Ray, people watch the news to see if their neighbor's being arrested for indecent exposure, or if their boss slammed his car into a house while drunk. If people want to watch the good side of life, they can tune into *Barney and Friends*."

Roarke paused the tape. "It was pretty wild last night, I have to admit."

There wasn't much that Roarke hadn't seen or heard, so it confirmed to Ray that last night was extraordinary.

"What do you think is going to happen?" Ray asked, turning toward him. "I mean, is Gilda going to get fired? Is Hugo?"

"I don't know," Roarke said. "Anything could happen at this point. But Sam Leege certainly had his moment in the spotlight, didn't he?"

That he did. The newscast was in such chaos that Hugo's only option was to run an extra-long weather segment to try to get Tate under control and everything back on track. Sam took advantage of every second, actually tracking the smoke plume from the explosion by radar. It was mostly an attempt to impress Hayden, who he'd recruited at the last minute to help him prepare.

Sam had always had an enormous ego, but it inflated to near capacity three years ago when Sam was credited for saving people's lives when he predicted a tornado would turn to the north, which it did, while all the other meteorologists around town predicted it would stay on an easterly course.

The problem with Sam was that he could never admit he was wrong. Not once in their five years of working together had Sam ever referred to a botched seven-day forecast or even tried to make a joke out of it. He could miss the temperature by twenty degrees and go on as if nothing had happened.

It irritated Ray, mostly because he couldn't make that big of a blunder and not address it. Any misrepresented fact had to be corrected. It was true for the anchors, the sportscasters, and the reporters. It just wasn't true for Sam the weatherman.

And this particularly irritating side of Sam trickled into his personality as well. Sam would never say he was wrong, never apologize, and certainly never correct himself. He'd once tripped and spilled coffee all over Ray, then blamed the slick floor.

But Sam was a charmer. Of all the ten o'clock personalities, Sam seemed to be the one with the most staying power. And his lineage didn't hurt. His father, Leroy Leege, stood in front of the green screen at the same station as Sam before retiring ten years ago and handing his legacy over to Sam.

Sam even had his own plug. The catch phrase "A Leege of His Own" preempted the description of Sam as a hero. Ray always wondered what was heroic about standing in front of a green screen and reading computer data while the storm chasers were out in the middle of all the chaos.

But there was nothing he could do. Ray had learned a long time ago that life wasn't fair. It wasn't that he liked it, but he accepted it. He didn't, however, have to accept Sam and Hayden. There was plenty of room in this world for Ray and Hayden. And their names practically rhymed.

"She's worth it," Ray mumbled, trying to get a mental fix on the fact that he was going to be doing battle with a man who thought he could do no wrong.

"Of course she's worth it, but why did she have to go do that to herself!" Roarke roared, making Ray jump. Roarke's popcorn spilled to the floor. Ray's jaw literally hung on its hinges. He'd never, not once, seen Roarke explode like that.

"I...I was talking about Hayden," Ray said softly.

"I knew that," Roarke snapped, his cheeks flushing a bright red color. He kept his eyes averted and said, "I thought you were reading my mind, man."

Ray stooped to pick up the popcorn. "When are you going to tell me who this is?"

Roarke glanced at him. "You don't know?"

"I swear I don't."

Roarke fell back into the couch. "I can't stop thinking about her."

"Who?"

"It's crazy. It's totally insane to think I could get a woman like that. Besides, she's not who I thought she was."

"She's not?"

"I think it's over," Roarke said, shaking his head. "I just don't think we were made for each other." With a hefty shove, he got himself off the couch and went to the TV, turning it off. "I don't think I'm in the mood for ultimate fighting, okay? I'm just going to take a nap or something. I'll see you at work later on."

Roarke padded down the small hallway of his apartment toward his bedroom. "Push the lock before you close the door," he said and disappeared.

Ray threw up his hands, though no one was around to see him look utterly confused. Who *was* Roarke's dream woman? The one woman he'd almost landed a date with three years ago was right out of college, a strawberry blonde with freckles. After that, Roarke hadn't seemed interested in anybody else.

Ray listened to see if he might change his mind and come out, but the apartment was silent, so Ray took the popcorn to the kitchen, dumped it in the trash, and left.

Chapter 12

Hugo didn't really need to get into work early. He couldn't do anything to salvage last night by arriving early today, but it was a good excuse to get out of bra shopping with his daughter.

Somewhere in some stupid parenting magazine, Jane had read that fathers and daughters can bond by doing things that mothers usually do with their daughters. Over the years, Hugo participated in tea parties, Barbie games, nail-polish fun, and more recently, hair salon trips. But bra shopping was an entirely new level of gender mixing that Hugo was not at all comfortable with.

Not that anybody would ever ask him, but Hugo was a little tired of all the gender mixing he had to do. He couldn't actually say it out loud. To anybody. But sometimes he longed for the day when women were secretaries and housewives and men were breadwinners and, well, men. It wasn't that Hugo minded running the sweeper every once in a while or that he minded the idea of a woman boss much. He'd worked for them over the years. It was just that everything seemed to be getting so mixed up.

Jane was hardly home anymore, and though he certainly supported her work endeavors, he sometimes dreamed of a day when she would be waiting for him to come home from work and they could have dinner together. A roast. A homemade apple pie. He wondered what it would be like to dole out fatherly advice to his young daughter rather than paint his toenails to show he adored her. Hugo never thought of himself as a terribly smart man, but he did have good instincts. Something told him that the world might be halfway to right again if he wasn't forced to take his daughter shopping for bras.

So after his doctor's appointment, he'd arranged for Kaylin to go to a friend's house since it was an in-service day for teachers at school, and he'd explained to Jane his need for getting in to work to put out fires. Jane understood. She'd seen the previous night's broadcast.

But there weren't any fires to put out. Nothing to do but sit at his desk and hope for the best.

At some point last night Chad had left. When the monumental broadcast had fizzled, Chad was no where to be seen. And the nine-to-six man wasn't in his office yet today either. Hugo could only imagine he was meeting with the GM to decide who would be the next executive producer.

Hugo glanced up and since he could see that Hayden was about to knock at his door, he waved her in. In one hand she held a cup of coffee; in the other, some papers.

"Here you are, Mr. Talley," she said in her cheerful voice.

"Is Mr. Arbus in yet?

"No, not yet. I've gathered the information you requested."

"What did you find out?"

"Well, nothing too definitive. There's no way to know exactly when Gilda's face will return to normal—"

"We don't want normal. We want the capability of serious expression without the furrow."

Hayden glanced at her notes. "Doesn't furrow, by definition, mean there's going to be a crease between the brows?"

"Yes. But it doesn't have to stay." Hugo sighed. "So what's the bottom line?"

"The bottom line is that there's really no way of knowing how long the paralysis will last. It's possible that the doctor injected too much Botox and that Gilda will stay that way for several weeks."

Hugo dropped his head into his hands.

"Also, I have several letters, e-mails, and faxes complaining about the show last night."

Hugo didn't look up. "I can only imagine what they say."

"You don't have to, sir. I'll leave them here on your desk to review."

A foul mood began to simmer inside Hugo. He glanced up at Hayden, who looked as if trouble didn't exist in the world.

"What else can I do for you, Mr. Talley?" she asked.

"I'd like to discuss one more thing with you. Why don't you take a seat?"

She sat like she was being invited to have lunch on the terrace. That kind of phrase would strike fear in most people, but Hayden seemed oblivious to Hugo's tone. Hugo pushed his eyebrows together and lowered his chin to make sure she knew this was serious.

"I want to talk to you about last night. We were in the middle of quite a crisis when I noticed you praying in the back of the control room. Now, I realize that you don't often see the side of me that you saw last night, but there's not often a circumstance like we saw last night either. And Ms. Hazard, I won't lie to you. Your praying made me uncomfortable. I realize that there were certainly many different ways I could've conducted myself, but the fact of the matter is that I had to react to the situation, and sometimes there's no time to stop and think or to formulate a response. Not that I couldn't have used some divine intervention. I am certainly no atheist, and I happen to have gone to church as a kid. I'm simply saying there seem to be appropriate times for prayer and, more specifically, appropriate days. Like Sundays. Do you understand?"

As he spoke, Hayden looked like she was trying to follow every word he was saying with great interest. When he finished, he sighed and waved her toward the door. She got up and was about to leave, when Hugo said, "Hayden, wait." He didn't want her feeling badly. She was a nice person, a rarity these days.

"Yes, Mr. Talley?"

"Look, you're welcome to pray for me, okay? Just not in public." Now she looked embarrassed. Great. He'd sufficiently made a complete donkey's behind of himself.

She lowered her voice. "I'm sorry, Mr. Talley. I wasn't praying for you. I was praying for them."

"Them?"

"The people at the sewage plant. I was praying they'd all be okay."

Hugo offered a terribly awkward smile, one drenched with grievance for the fact that the words "donkey's behind" did not come close to describing him.

"Right. Of course. Well, um—"

"But I will be very happy to pray for you, Mr. Talley."

What kind of beast would he look like now if he declined? He'd had his fill of feeling like the rear ends of animals.

"Thank you," he said meekly.

She smiled and left.

Hugo could feel the tremors of fear running through his body as the minutes ticked by. The afternoon meeting would be dreadful, at best. He pulled out his desk drawer and stared at his new bottle of Blue Pills. If he took an extra one, he would be short a pill at the end of the month, and who knew what kind of day the thirtieth would be. He slowly closed his drawer and picked up a pen, hovering it over a folder on his desk, secretly hoping that Hayden Hazard was some kind of saint and her prayers for him would be answered.

In the conference room, the afternoon meeting was about to begin. Gilda rarely made an appearance at the meetings. Still, he wanted some assurances that this evening's broadcast might resemble normalcy. He just wanted to see Gilda frown. That wasn't asking too much, was it?

Chad Arbus sauntered in, a look of disapproval smeared across a face already crowded with superiority. He eyed everyone as he took his seat and the room grew quiet. Hugo bit his lip and tried to prepare himself. He wanted to come across as a professional. They'd had a bad night. It happens. Of course, in the history of broadcasting it had never happened this bad, but nevertheless, they weren't going to bounce back if Hugo looked as desperate as he felt.

Hugo called the meeting to order, which seemed a little stupid since everyone was already staring at him. He folded his hands together and stretched a smile across his face.

"All right, everyone. I think we all understand what kind of position we're in. We've got to do better tonight, and we can't afford any mistakes." Hugo remembered to breathe. "I believe in everyone in this room. I know what we're capable of. So it's time to rise to my highest expectations of you. Let's ponder what—"

Chad stood. "Hugo, stop the namby-pamby string of manure that's running from your mouth. There's a word for what happened last night. Do you know that? I had to leave. I couldn't even watch it! We are the laughingstock of local news now!" Chad's voice rose and his face glowed red. "You want to hear my expectations? My expectations are that if you don't show me something extraordinary tonight, you're all fired!" He slapped his hand down on the table, causing everyone to jump except Hugo. Thanks to the Blue Pill, he was incapable of being startled.

Hugo cleared his throat. "All right. Let's get to business. Obviously our top story is the sewage plant. So Roarke, what's the update?"

"One man remains hospitalized, though they're not releasing his condition at this time. Right now, the only information we have about what caused the explosion is that it…well, it was caused by one of the chemicals that's used to purify our…you know, sewage."

Hugo said, "Okay. Jill, what do you have?"

"I've got two eyewitnesses ready to talk on camera about what they saw. One lives nearby and was driving home, and the other works at the sewage plant."

"Wastewater treatment plant," Roarke corrected.

"Anyway," Jill said, rolling her eyes, "both will be good angles. I've already confirmed with them that they'll do interviews today."

"Good," Hugo said.

"The deputy director of the plant is giving a press conference at 6:00 p.m. tonight," Roarke added.

"Good. Trent, why don't you cover the press conference?"

Trent looked relieved. He'd spent an hour in Hugo's office earlier apologizing profusely for last night. "Thank you, sir."

"What about me?" Ray suddenly said. "What am I going to cover?"

Roarke said, "We have footage of Mr. Green leaving jail, and apparently he's been making some pretty bold verbal threats against our station."

Hugo thought for a moment. They could bring this story back to life with some careful maneuvering. Petey Green was making sure it didn't just slip away.

"Ray, I want you covering the Green story."

"Me?" Ray asked. "I thought I was the story. How can I cover a story about myself? Have Trent cover the Green story. I'll do the sewage plant."

Hugo shook his head. "I think there's something to be said for a reporter who is facing the man who nearly beat him to death."

"He didn't nearly beat me to death," Ray protested. "He shoved me, and I hit my head. There's a big difference. Won't it seem a little awkward to talk about myself in the story? I mean, do I refer to myself in the first or third person? It doesn't work."

"I think it works great," Jill said, avoiding Ray's intense eyes. "It gives a real personal side to the story that this story wouldn't have otherwise. Plus, it shows that Ray isn't scared of Green."

Ray sighed loudly, but Hugo noticed Jill smiling at Ray like they were best buddies. "All I'm saying," Ray said, "is that we might seem a little more objective if someone else covered it. Like Trent."

Hugo held up his hands as everyone started to chime in an opinion. "Folks, we're going to have to see how this Green story plays out. If he's still making threats to the station, then we've got to cover it. And Ray, you standing there with that bandage on your head will be a grim reminder to all our viewers of what a dangerous job reporters have."

"Are you saying you want that to be the angle? That our jobs are dangerous?" Ray asked.

Hugo shrugged. "I kind of like it. People don't think about what you do as being dangerous."

"It's not dangerous," Ray said.

But Beaker disagreed. "They take for granted that we go out onto a dark street in a rough neighborhood to cover a story they're itching to see. These pictures don't just shoot themselves."

Ray said, "I just don't think it's a good idea. Why not switch me and Trent? Trent is perfectly capable of handling this story."

"I'm perfectly capable of handling the wastewater treatment plant story too. I was there yesterday. You were recovering from being beaten up, remember?"

"I didn't interview a rival station's employee!" Ray's temper quieted the room. "You want the best tonight, right? Then you want your best reporters on the top story."

Hugo wavered. Ray was one of his best and he tended to get the interviews the others couldn't. But Jill seemed on top of this one. There was a fire in her eyes that Hugo hadn't seen before. It was as if everyone had always accepted that Ray was the top reporter, and now they were seeing that they might have a chance to slide into that position. It wasn't really true, but if they thought it was true, maybe Jill and Trent would give a hundred and ten percent.

"Look," Hugo said, interrupting his own thoughts, "we're going to have to do something to really spice up tonight's broadcast. I want you to add the word 'controversial' to your report, Ray."

"Controversial?" Ray asked. "What's controversial about it?"

Hugo said, "It involves a news station, right? By promoting this as controversial, we'll have two hooks for tonight and an edge on the rest of the stations."

Ray fell silent. Hugo looked at Chad for any signs of approval. But Chad just stared at the table, lost in deep thought. Hugo continued. "Also, tonight, we're going to be continuing our segment 'Five Diseases You Can Catch from Your Toothbrush.'"

"What's the kicker?" Chad asked, referring to the lighthearted story they scheduled for every broadcast.

"We're doing a piece on the reopening of the downtown library."

Chad nodded his approval.

"So," Hugo said, "I want a lot of images, I want a lot of sound bites. Let's really paint a picture of how devastating this explosion could have been, okay?"

Suddenly Hayden raised her hand. Everyone looked at her, which was the only reason Hugo noticed she had done so. She normally stood quietly in the corner and took notes.

"Yes?" Hugo asked. Chad looked like he'd never seen her before.

"Why don't we report on how many people made it out alive? It's amazing that only one person was seriously injured."

Hugo tried not to be reactive. In a considerate tone, he said, "We will have one of the anchors mention that when we close out the segment."

"But," Hayden said, as Hugo was about to go on to other business, "surely there are plenty of miraculous stories to fill up an entire news segment."

"Lady, we'll let that TBN station handle the miraculous stories, okay?" Chad stood. "Now, I've got to go put out some fires. I trust you all will deliver tonight." He grabbed his notebook and walked out the door. Hugo glanced at Hayden, who looked disappointed. But what could he do? Sooner or later she was going to have to figure out what kind of business they were running, and it wasn't the "good news" business.

"All right," Hugo said, "let's get out there and do our thing. Remember, dive deep, folks. I want every angle covered. Leave no stone unturned. I want to know everything there is to know and more. Got it?"

The crowd dispersed, and Hugo Talley sat alone in the conference room, wondering if this was his last night at work.

Chapter 13

R ay stood with his cup of coffee and watched Jill gab it up with their co-workers. He'd blown enough heavy sighs to cool off the coffee he would never drink, which was unfortunate because the only thing a cup of coffee was good for in his world was to warm his hands and give him an excuse to wander around.

It had been an hour since the production meeting, and Ray was as furious as if it had just happened. Proof that he should be covering the sewage story was the fact that Jill was still hanging around the station. Ray would've been out the door immediately, digging up as much information as he could.

That was the difference between a good reporter and a great reporter. A good reporter gets the facts. Great reporters get the facts *and* the truth. As far as Ray was concerned, that was a big difference.

He'd known Jill for about two years, since she left Channel 10 to come work for more pay and less prestige. She'd been a weekend reporter there and felt she could climb the ranks at Channel 7, which she had.

She was tough competition for Ray. She had beauty, brains, and quite a bit of poise in front of the camera. And like Ray, she had no ambitions to be an anchor. She'd once told him it would be "beneath her." Ray never thought it would be beneath him—it was higher pay for a whole lot less work. Many reporters worked their whole careers for the anchor desk. But Ray liked the thrill of going out to find the clues, like a detective. He'd caught politicians lying on camera. He'd once gotten a criminal to confess, and later the confession was used to put the guy behind bars.

Jill, on the other hand, had her two "eyewitnesses" and wasn't worried about finding anything else. Her delivery of the news was near perfect, but she never worked hard to get "beneath" the facts, where the real story was almost always found. There were so many unanswered questions to this catastrophe, and Hugo wanted to leave the reporting up to Jill and Trent?

"Sorry about today," said a voice. Ray looked up to see Jill walking toward him. She smiled and, as she came to a stop, tossed her hair over her shoulder. "It's not personal."

"I didn't take it personally," Ray lied.

Her eyes narrowed a bit. "Sometimes, Ray, you have to fight for what you want."

"Uh...I did fight," he pointed out.

"I'm talking about things you *really* want." She touched his shoulder and walked off.

"Okay..." Ray said, shaking his head. He watched Trent race by with notes in his hand.

The kid had heart but not a lot of poise or self-confidence. He normally stumbled through his reports, glancing down several times at his notes. When Trent looked into the camera, he appeared frightened that his next word might be the beginning of the end for him.

Ray dumped his coffee and headed back to his desk. Why was he still hanging around? After all, he had a story to cover. Maybe he should set up a camera and shoot himself at his desk, rubbing the wound on his forehead and looking pathetic.

He noticed Roarke at the assignment desk, headphones on, listening to whatever he listened to all day. Ray was worried about him. Roarke had been quiet all afternoon, and though he acknowledged Ray, he wasn't himself. But Ray knew work wasn't the place to talk about it. Things could wait.

Then he saw her. She headed toward him. Ray's heart beat like it weighed more than he did, and strangely, his limbs felt numb.

She smiled while several feet away and made direct eye contact with him as she approached.

"Hi, Ray," she said.

"Hi…hi there, Hayden." Ray tried to casually stick his hand in the pocket of his pants, but missed and ended up stabbing his buttock. He slid his hands behind his back and clasped them there for safekeeping. "How are you?"

"Fine. Busy. It's kind of exciting, though, you know? Sweeps week and all that. I've never been in this kind of environment before. It's pretty fun."

Ray had never heard one of Hugo's assistants describe her job as fun.

"Hugo wanted me to tell you that whatever you do, he does not want you interviewing Mr. Green. He said there are plenty of angles to this story, and he suggested interviewing the police captain."

Ray groaned. He hated the police captain. Captain Wynn's obvious use of teeth whiteners did little to enhance his image of a man tough on crime. How could he be out chasing criminals when he was always available for the camera?

"What?" Hayden asked.

Ray glanced at her. "Nothing. It's just going to be a long day."

"I know what you mean. My feet already hurt!"

Feet…feet, think quick on your feet, man! With his hands still clasped behind his back, Ray said, "Well, you probably need a break."

"Oh, I wish I had time. Hugo's got me running all over the place."

"Yes, but it's been scientifically proven that workers are more productive if they take at least two fifteen-minute breaks a day. So you're really doing Hugo a favor."

Hayden grinned. "I didn't know that."

"What do you say we…get some coffee?"

"Sure. But I don't really drink coffee."

"Me either—" Ray stopped. "I mean, I do. Sometimes. I sip it, just a little, for the flavor but not the effect, you know?"

Hayden didn't look like she knew.

He gestured toward the break room. The precision of that gesture was remarkable, too, considering that his body was shaking so badly it felt like he was being electrocuted.

He followed closely—not so closely as to look like a stalker but close enough to keep her moving in the right direction. The last thing he needed was to run into Sam. He knew he wouldn't be able to hide his intentions behind a guilt-free expression.

Hayden opened the door to the break room. Out came Sam, holding his gigantic mug of steaming coffee and looking at the two of them like they were some sort of meteorological phenomenon.

"Well, hello," he said, his eyelids drooping with menace. He made a point to look at Ray and grin like he held Ray's darkest secret between his perfectly straight teeth.

"Hi, Sam," Hayden said. "We're just going on break. You want to join us?"

Sam stared at Ray a second longer, just to make some idiotic point, then looked at Hayden. "I would love to, but we have a blizzard moving into the northwest. People's lives depend on the accuracy of my report."

Ray let out a laugh, and Hayden glanced at him as if he were being rude. Ray stopped smiling. "Well then you'd better go," Ray said. Sam moved past him, and Ray couldn't stop himself. Wasn't the war already started? "And Sam, remember what Hugo said about drinking that much coffee before a broadcast."

"Does it make you jittery?" Hayden asked Sam.

Sam cut his eyes to Ray, daring him. And Ray accepted the dare. "Actually, one time Sam drank so much coffee before a broadcast that he had to cut his segment short so he could make it to the rest room on time."

Sam's lips pressed together as he tried to hold on to his cool expression. "Ray isn't really telling the whole story. I happened to have a bladder infection at the time, unbeknownst to me."

Ray smiled. Sam had actually said "bladder," "infection," and "unbeknownst" all in one sentence. Hayden looked grossed out. Ray wanted to pump his arm with satisfaction, but instead he simply let Sam's words hang in the air for everyone to carefully dissect.

"Well," Ray said, after letting at least five seconds of awkward silence pass, "as much as we'd love to hear more about that, I think we're going to go on break."

Sam turned without another word, and Ray followed Hayden into the break room.

"You do drink coffee?" Hayden asked.

"Uh…well, yeah. Sometimes. It's complicated."

"Do you want some now?"

Ray's fingers were fumbling all over themselves suddenly, so he figured it would give him something to do. "Sure." He went over to the pot while Hayden sat at one of the break tables. "So you're enjoying working here?"

"I am," she said. "Though I do worry about Hugo. He really is a ball of stress, isn't he?"

Ray poured his coffee, careful not to spill it. "It's interesting you would say that. Most people think of Hugo as one of the calmest people they know. I mean, he had a little episode yesterday, but normally he's very serene."

Hayden pointed to her eyes. "It's all here. He may seem serene, but on the inside, I don't think he is. I'm going to start praying for him."

Ray shook a cream packet and ripped it open. "So where do you go to church?"

"A little church on Eighth Street called Christ Our Lord."

"I've never heard of it."

"It was difficult finding a church when my parents passed away. Our whole family had gone to the same church for generations. But when we all moved away, we had to find a new place. It was like trying to find a new family."

"I'm sorry your parents died. How long ago was that?"

"A few years. It was the saddest day of my life. But God has taken me to places I never thought I'd go. I once worked at Kinko's. It's a copy shop."

"I know it," Ray smiled.

"That was an amazing lesson in customer service. I never knew how difficult making copies could be. I also worked as a waitress. And before that, as a candy striper, just for the experience. I really liked that job. I graduated from college with a business degree but had trouble finding a job. Was endlessly employed before, then graduated and couldn't find work!" She laughed. "My sister thought I should sign up for a temp agency, and that's how I landed this job, which isn't unlike the job I did for my parent's business. Out of all my jobs, I've felt the most comfortable here."

"I'm glad," Ray said, sitting down. "I hope we've all made you feel comfortable." He grinned, hoping she knew that by "all" he meant *him.*

"Sure. Everyone here is really nice. How about you? How do you like working here?"

Ray leaned back in his chair, not wanting to burst her bubble about how great the station was, but he wasn't even sure if he could fake it.

"What?" she urged. "You're not happy?"

"I'm not miserable. I'm just…I don't know. It's complex."

"How?"

"I love reporting. I feel like I'm doing something really important for the community. It's how people get their news, and having information is priceless in this world. But…" He glanced up at her. She was completely engaged. "There's this other side to it, you know? People don't always want information for what it can do to help them. Sometimes they want to see the gore and the dysfunction in other people's lives while they sit inside their homes, safe in their living rooms. And the more people want it, the more we report it."

"Maybe it's the other way around. Maybe the more you report it, the more people want it."

Ray nodded. He didn't know which came first, but he did know that one monster fed the other.

"Anyway," Ray said, "there doesn't seem to be a solution on the horizon."

She leaned forward. "I can tell this really bothers you."

"Well, I have a lot on my mind. I can't believe Hugo let Jill have that story and put me on the pig story. The pig story is yesterday's news, and Hugo's just trying to light a fire on damp wood, you know? If I could get the sewage plant story, I know I could…" Ray couldn't help but notice those innocent eyes staring back at him. Could she possibly understand office politics? Competition?

"Do better?" she asked.

Ray slumped. Okay, she was much savvier than he was giving her credit for.

"Do I sound arrogant?"

"Bitter." Suddenly she reached out and grabbed his arm.

A strange tingling sensation worked its way up to his scalp, where his hair stood on end. He felt a goofy smile emerge. Maybe he was bitter, but right now he was in heaven.

Hayden's expression turned serious. "Let me pray for you."

Ray laughed the kind of laugh that comes when you think someone has made a wry joke.

But Hayden wasn't laughing. "Ray, you can't let bitterness grow in you. It has long, tangled roots that you can't unearth with a simple tug."

His smile faded. How'd he go from warm and fuzzy feelings to talk of horticulture? He swallowed and tried to focus. Did she mean she actually wanted to pray for him—now?

"What's wrong?" Hayden asked, withdrawing her hand.

Ray looked down at his now lonely arm and realized he was going to have to do something quick if he was going to keep the chemistry going.

"Uh, nothing. Nothing at all."

Her arm reached toward him again. "We have to pray for each other, Ray. It's the only way we can survive in this world. Do you know what I mean?"

Ray couldn't help but self-consciously glance at the break-room door. He was a Christian and everything, but praying in the break room? That was kind of over the top. Ray desperately wanted to make a good impression. He also knew there were a number of ways Hayden could interpret even the most sensitive decline.

"Sure," he said softly.

And so he squeezed his eyes shut and prayed on his own—that nobody would walk through that door. He wasn't embarrassed by his religion. Most everyone at the station knew Ray was a Christian. That was half the reason he longed for the day when he could stand up and report good news—or at least relevant news. But praying in the break room…well, if he didn't like Hayden so much, he might call her a fanatic. But he did like her. He liked her honesty, her innocence, the way she went through each day like it was her first time to experience life. And when she called him bitter, it wasn't in a judgmental sense, like his mother used to do. She seemed deeply concerned about his roots' inability to be unearthed or something like that.

"Amen."

Ray opened his eyes and was surprised to find himself smiling. She was smiling back at him.

"Thank you," he said.

"You're welcome."

And then came the awkward silence, and more than anything, Ray hated awkward silence. Silence on air was deadly. Even two seconds of silence during a broadcast made everyone look bad.

Ray thought about pretending to sip his coffee, but instead he found himself offering to return the favor, and even as the words came out of his mouth, he tried to draw them back in by finishing with, "But you probably don't need any prayer."

Hayden laughed. It was as gorgeous as laughs came. It was slightly deep but feminine, and as she laughed, her nostrils flared. *Adorable.* "Ray, how can you say that?"

Ray was thinking the same thing, and was about to apologize for being a complete moron when she said, "Of course I need prayer. Everyone needs prayer."

"Of course," Ray feebly replied. Now what had he gotten himself into? He was going to have to pray for her? How was he going to do that? And what in the world was he going to pray for? That she'd go out with him?

Ray looked at her, and she tilted her head to the side as if he was embarrassing himself in some noteworthy way.

"What, um, what can I pray for you for?" Ray ignored his horrific sentence structure and tried to copy her serene expression.

"Ray, you're a Christian. What is the Spirit leading you to pray?"

Ray wanted to confess that the Spirit had probably fled a while back and he was pretty much on his own, but that wasn't going to help his cause. And his cause, he realized, was still out there waiting to be conquered. How was he going to turn this hour of power into anything that resembled a pickup line?

Ray bit his lip and decided he might as well reach out and hold her arm, since that was the sort of thing that made her comfortable. She closed her eyes and waited. As hard as Ray was thinking, he couldn't come up with a thing to say. Maybe he could just move his lips a little and pretend to be praying silently. But he did, after all, have a conscience, and didn't want to give Sam an edge by opening himself up to being struck by lightning because he pretended to pray for a woman just so he could ask her out.

Before Ray could decide exactly how he was going to get out of this situation, the door flew open, banging against the wall, and there stood Roarke, gasping, his arms stretched from one side of the door frame to the other. Ray shot up from the table, kicking his chair backward. It slammed against the floor, making a terrible racket. Hayden looked frightened at the sudden commotion.

Roarke eyed Ray, then Hayden. "Hayden, have you seen Gilda?"

She stood. "No. What's wrong?"

"Hugo can't find her anywhere. She was supposed to be here an hour ago to tape the teaser for tonight's broadcast."

Ray's face burned like he'd pressed his cheek up against a heat lamp. He tried to say casually, "Well, she's not in here."

Roarke sighed. "Hugo needs Hayden to track her down."

"Sure. Right away." She rushed out of the break room as Roarke moved aside. He studied Ray with skeptical eyes.

"What, um, what should I do?" Ray asked.

"Maybe you should spend some time reviewing the sexual harassment manual."

Chapter 14

C had's secretary insisted for the fifth time that he was meeting with the station's lawyers. She didn't say about what. But twenty minutes ago Chad had sent word by e-mail that he did not want Ray to interview Petey Green. Chad said that Green claimed the station provoked him. They would probably have a legal battle on their hands.

But Hugo had far more pressing issues to think about. Gilda had not come in yet, and they were now a full hour behind schedule. She was supposed to tape a teaser for sweeps week, "Five Ways to Escape a Burning or Sinking Car if Your Seatbelt Gets Stuck and There's Nobody Around with a Knife to Cut You Out." They were scheduled to start running the teasers that evening. So where was Gilda? In hiding? Was her face still not cooperating?

Hugo wanted to scream. Really loud. Just scream at the top of his lungs. But everyone was still shocked from last night's episode, and screaming like that would produce no good results. He tried some deep breathing instead.

He told himself to think. To get it together. This was simply a problem that needed to be solved, and he could solve it. There was a solution.

He buzzed Hayden in. When she appeared in the doorway, Hugo said, "Let's get Julia Richter in here."

Julia was the weekend anchor. She was one of the worst anchors Hugo had ever known, and she didn't seem to be improving since landing the job eight months ago. Their previous weekend anchor quit because her ambitions were to move to prime time, and she could see that Gilda was going nowhere fast. Channel 7 had other reporters who had anchored before, but they were all out on assignment for sweeps week. The reporter he would normally call as backup was out of the state following a local Olympic hopeful's quest to land a spot on the American team. And the late afternoon–early evening anchors both had clauses in their contracts that wouldn't allow them to work more than five broadcasts a day—at least at their current pay. And since they were on at 4:00, 4:30, 5:00, 6:00, and 6:30, he had no choice. He had to call Julia.

Hugo sighed. Everything had been in place to grab sweeps week by the horns, but the horns were doing a good job of impaling the situation.

He was already second-guessing his decision to use Julia when Hayden said, "I have bad news."

Hugo couldn't get himself to ask.

"Julia just called in. She slipped on the ice and knocked out her two front teeth."

Hugo took each word and analyzed it, yet after careful consideration, nothing made sense. Hayden waited patiently on him, so he took another stab at it, but his brain simply wouldn't process what she said.

"Mr. Talley?" she asked. "Are you okay?"

He held up one finger. He wasn't really sure. Finally he said, "What ice?"

Hayden shook her head like she didn't know.

So Hugo stood, left his office, and walked out the front door of the station. It had rained, apparently, and now the leftover moisture had turned to ice. The temperature seemed to drop in the few seconds Hugo stood there. Then, to his surprise, it began to snow. Hugo turned, walked back inside, and headed for the weather center, a separate studio crammed with expensive computers, a large green screen, maps, and satellite equipment. Somehow, it still had room for Sam's ego. Hugo found his weatherman doing a crossword puzzle at his desk.

"Sam, you said today would be cool but clear."

"Uh-huh. What's a three-letter word for pretentious?"

"Sam, it's not clear. Looks to be a bad storm coming."

"Like I said last night, it's going to stay in the northwest corner of the state."

Hugo folded his arms. "That's interesting. Because I just walked outside, and it's snowing. Plus there's ice."

Sam laughed. "Hugo, give me a break." He pointed to the computer. "Look, the temperature right now is thirty-eight degrees, and"—he pointed to another computer—"as you can clearly see on radar, the storm is about fifty miles to our north."

"I just saw snow." Hugo pointed toward the front of the station.

Sam looked at him like he'd lost his mind. "Are you okay?"

"I'm fine, Sam. But it's snowing outside, and that means employees are going to have a hard time getting to work."

"Hugo, there's no snow. Look!" He gestured to the computer screen again.

Hugo had not assaulted another human being since the seventh grade, when Albert Wong made fun of his glasses, but he grabbed Sam by the collar and hustled him to the front door. He didn't take Sam all the way outside, for fear of one of them meeting the same fate as Julia Richter.

"Snow," Hugo said plainly and pointed. It was falling heavily now.

Sam's face turned red. "I'm going to fire that little jerk."

"Who?"

"Arnie!"

"Your computer tech?"

"I've been telling him for months there's a bug in our program!"

"Well, next time, maybe you can step outside."

"Ha ha. Always easy to make fun of the weatherman."

"I'm not making fun of you. I'm just saying you might want to look outside next time."

Sam glared at him. "So this is my fault?"

"You're the meteorologist, Sam. Whose fault would it be?"

"Look, I'm not wrong here. Our computers malfunctioned. I'm only as capable as my best computer."

"I thought you had certain innate instincts about weather. Don't all weathermen? I hear their secret is to look up." Hugo pointed to the sky.

"I know I make weather predicting look easy, but it's not, Hugo. It happens to be a science, in case you haven't noticed."

"What's so scientific about it? Out of your seven-day forecast, you usually only get two days right." Hugo wondered why, in the midst of all his problems, he wanted to stand here and make Sam feel small. "If I had known a blizzard was coming, I would've paged everyone to come in early. Now what do I do?"

"Don't blame me for your problems," Sam said, throwing up his hands. "I'm not God. I can't control the weather." He stomped off.

Hugo thought, for good mental health, he should stay outside for a few minutes and observe the snow, which on any other day would've been gorgeous. He wondered why this kind of snow never fell at Christmas. He'd always wanted a white Christmas, where he could stand by the fire, drink hot cocoa, and watch the snow fall. But it never snowed on Christmas, no matter how many times Sam claimed it would.

He turned to see Hayden walking toward him. "Mr. Talley, there's a problem. None of the backup anchors can come in." By none, Hayden must have meant the only other female anchor available besides Julia, which was Michelle the Shell, nicknamed for exactly what she was. A shell. She looked beautiful but wasn't capable of thinking on her feet. She was their early morning anchor, and the one time they'd tried her for the tenner, she'd yawned her way through it. She stated simply, "I have a strict seven o'clock bedtime. No exceptions."

Hugo thought for a moment. Maybe they could get away with two male anchors tonight. It always looked very awkward, but for Tate's sake, they had to have somebody sitting next to him.

"Call Ronny," Hugo said. Ronny Bode was the male backup anchor they used frequently on the weekends. Ronny had a promising career ahead of him until his hairline started receding seemingly overnight. Within three months, he was half bald and in all the wrong places. His tufts of hair made the strangest patterns, and though he worked hard in cooperation with his hair gel, it was still obvious he was going bald at an alarming rate. Without hair gel, he almost looked like he had mange. Yet despite his hair problems, Ronny was a capable anchor, and his most appealing asset, his dark blue, intense eyes, managed to steer the focus off his hair. "Yes. Call Ronny. And keep trying to get ahold of Gilda."

"Calm down," he said.

"How can I calm down?" Gilda whispered.

"If you would just stop to think, you would understand this is what must be done."

Gilda shook her head, tears streaming down her face. "How could it all come to this?"

"Don't you understand that I'm trying to help you?"

She glared through the dark room. "You're trying to help yourself."

"I'm trying to help both of us."

Gilda wiped her tears and tried to regain her composure.

"Take it," he said, and walked toward her, his arm outstretched, holding an overstuffed white envelope.

"Why didn't you ever tell me his name? You knew and didn't tell me."

"Because, Gilda, you wanted answers. I wanted to keep everything afloat. And at the time, it just wasn't a story that was going to keep us from sinking."

"But it had the potential to be an important story!"

"You had all the information I had. You didn't find his name. What can I say? You should stick to anchoring."

"Do you know how many years I've worked in this business?" Gilda asked, refusing to reach for the envelope. "Do you know how hard I've worked to get where I am?"

"Nobody is disputing that. You have a chance to make things right."

"I didn't make anything wrong! You did!"

"Gilda, it's just an unfortunate circumstance. It's nobody's fault. Unless you want to blame God. I suppose he has some responsibility in the matter." He shoved the envelope into her hand. "There's no other way. I'm done with this conversation."

"You'll pay for this!" Gilda yelled at him.

He turned, his eyes fierce. "As far as I can tell, Gilda, I already have."

Ray sat at the police station, flipping through a few notes he jotted down. Beaker was setting up the camera for an interview with Captain Wynn. Ray told Beaker that he needed some time to figure out how he wanted the interview to go.

But in reality, he just had to get out of there. Even Beaker, who normally was oblivious to anybody's troubles but his own, noticed Ray was out of sorts. Ray said he would be back in about ten minutes, when the captain was ready for his interview.

In the hallway near the bathrooms, Ray tried to gain his composure. He couldn't remember feeling so frustrated. He tried telling himself this wasn't the end of the world, but it definitely felt like the end of his career. It was as if Hugo had lost confidence in him, yet everything that had happened was completely out of his control.

Ray told himself to do his best on this story. There was a day when this business was a thrill, and every story marked a new and exciting adventure. What had changed? All he wanted now was to move ahead, to be the best, to take another step up the career ladder.

To make matters worse, he still hadn't asked Hayden out. He kept wondering what it was about her that made it so important. The truth was she made him feel uncomfortable. So what kept drawing him back to her?

"Ray?"

Ray looked up to find Tanya Secrist standing above him. He stood. "Hi."

"What are you doing here?" she asked.

Ray pitched a thumb toward the captain's office. "Interviewing Wynn about the Green incident."

She noticed his forehead. "I saw that on the news. Are you okay?"

"Fine."

She looked around then said, "I need to talk to you." She steered him around a corner to a long hallway, which led, as far as Ray remembered, to the mechanical room and some janitor closets. Tanya had been Ray's source at the police department for two years. They'd dated briefly and broken up somewhat amicably, but Tanya still enjoyed leaking information to Ray now and then. He thought it was sort of a power-play thing, but nevertheless, it was how he got some of his best information. "It's about the sewage plant."

Ray glanced over his shoulder. "I'm…I'm not covering the story."

Tanya frowned. "Why not? It's the biggest story in town."

"Hugo thought this was…you know, a big story too."

Tanya frowned again. "Okay…"

Ray bit his lip. Tanya always had good information. How could he let this opportunity pass him by?

"Tell me," he said.

Tanya hesitated. "I don't want to waste good information."

"It won't be wasted."

Tanya didn't look convinced, but she leaned closer and said, "The director of the plant is a man named Howard Crumm. He has a criminal record. He was charged with embezzlement sixteen years ago."

Ray jotted down the information.

"I have to go. Don't let this go to waste. You know I've got other options." By other options, Tanya meant she could go to other news stations. She'd threatened Ray with this before, but he knew she just liked to see him squirm. So he tried to look worried.

She touched his arm. "But I know I can count on you." She walked away, and he leaned against the wall. He had the information. Now what was he supposed to do with it? He pressed his fingers against his forehead, trying to figure this all out when he heard his name being called.

When he rounded the corner, Beaker was headed in the opposite direction.

"Over here," Ray said.

Beaker spun around and threw up his hands. "I've been looking everywhere for you."

"Just, um, going for some coffee."

"Well, the captain's ready."

"Okay." Ray's head pounded. Never in his life had he felt so conflicted. The thing he knew he should do was the thing he least wanted to do in the whole world.

"What's the problem?" Beaker asked.

Ray glanced at his watch. "Give me a minute, okay?"

"We need to shoot this now. The captain's waiting."

Ray walked back to Beaker and in a low voice said, "You and I both know that he will wait around to see his mug on television. I just need a minute, okay?"

"For what?"

"Coffee."

Ray found a side exit and walked out. It was very cold and he noticed snowflakes falling, which was odd. He didn't remember that in the forecast. Glancing around to make sure he was alone, he called Jill's cell.

"Hello?"

"Jill, it's Ray."

"Hi, Ray. How are you?"

"Fine."

"And to what do I owe this unexpected pleasure?"

Ray paused. Jill was acting a little strangely.

"It's about the sewage plant story. One of my sources has given me some information about the director of the plant."

Jill was silent for a moment. Then she started laughing. "So this is it, huh? I knew you would somehow try to ambush me. You're going to have me chasing rabbits, aren't you?"

"Jill, for crying out loud, of course I'm not trying to ambush you." He sighed. They'd been rivals for a long time, but it surprised him that Jill was this suspicious of him. "I'm trying to *help* you."

"Why would you want to do that?"

Ray held the phone close to his ear, trying to figure out what to say. It wasn't really in his nature to be argumentative with people. It wasn't that he couldn't be. He'd done plenty of investigative stories through the years where he had to shove a microphone in someone's face and demand answers. But at the end of the day, he wasn't one to go out looking for a boat to rock.

"Jill, my source here tells me that Mr. Crumm has a criminal record and has been charged with embezzlement but never convicted."

"Who is your source? *The National Enquirer?*"

Ray suddenly realized what was so attractive about Hayden. She was the exact opposite of Jill.

"I have to go," he said.

"Good, because as far as I can tell, you have your own story to cover."

Ray ended the call. Both cheeks were stinging now, and though he had willed it in his heart to do the right thing concerning Jill, the unsettled angst swirling inside his heart afterward was glad he didn't have a third cheek to offer.

He headed back inside the police station, fighting with Jill inside his head. Why did she always want to stay on the surface of a story? She was so content to do the fluff interviews. She was the queen of interviewing every person who could offer a wide-eyed account of something, but she never dug deeper, where the real story was.

By the time Ray was inside, he was marching straight toward the captain's office. Beaker met him at the door with a not-so-subtle expression of weariness. "Wynn's irritated," he whispered. Ray stopped and looked over Beaker's shoulder at Wynn, who sat behind his desk, dusting dandruff off his shoulder and rubbing his teeth with his forefinger.

"Pack up the stuff," Ray said. "We're leaving."

"What?!" Beaker cried.

Captain Wynn looked up, as did another officer who stood in his office.

Ray kept his voice low. "The story isn't here."

"What are you talking about? Have you lost your mind?"

"I'm thinking very clearly, Beaker. Hugo wants a human drama out of this, does he not?"

Beaker's mouth was half open.

"Then let's get the real story. Let's dig deep." He patted the cameraman's arm. "Trust me. I know what I'm doing."

Beaker groaned. "Fine. But you're handling Wynn."

Ray nodded and looked at the police captain, who was now combing his hair to the side.

Chapter 15

R onny Bode stood in Hugo's office, his hands folded outward in his perpetual state of explanation. But it wasn't Ronny's hands that Hugo couldn't stop looking at. In fact, it was the red, oozing sores all over the top of his head.

"I wasn't supposed to be on air until Sunday," Ronny said. "They told me I just needed a day to heal. But it's been, well, a couple or three days now…"

Hugo had never seen anything like it. It was worse than a toupee.

"Ronny," Hugo said, his voice cracking like he was about to cry, which maybe he was. "Hair plugs?"

Ronny's embarrassment was evident. "Hair *inserts*. We ran that segment, you know? The one Trent did? And, well, it looked like a viable option for me. I mean, it's no secret what's been happening to my hairline."

"But…but…," Hugo stammered as vivid memories flashed through his mind. Ten years ago they'd had a fiftyish sportscaster, Monty Parker, who had worn a toupee since his midthirties. During some kind of midlife crisis, Monty decided that he was no longer going to wear his toupee and that he was going to face the world "as the man he really was." There had been a big uproar about it because, without his toupee, Monty was completely bald. Monty said that he would lay his career on the line, but that he was tired of hiding behind his wig.

With great trepidation, management decided to let him do it. It was a jaw-dropping moment for everyone, because to Monty's credit, his toupee looked very much like real hair. The glare on his scalp was so intense they had to put special filters on the lights. And for the next two weeks, they had to assure viewers that Monty wasn't ill or insane. Six weeks later, Monty resigned. Last Hugo had heard, he was selling cars somewhere north of town. Ever since then, they'd included a clause in the anchors' contracts that they could not drastically change their hair or appearance without written consent from the station.

"I thought this would be a good thing," Ronny said meekly. "I know it bothers everyone that I've been losing my hair. It bothers me too. I thought I'd just get a few pieces, then add some here and there, real subtle."

"Didn't you think even a few pieces would've been noticeable?"

"If it hadn't gotten infected, nobody would've noticed it. They might've thought something looked slightly different about me, but nobody would've guessed it was my hair."

Hugo looked down at his desk, trying to find some kind of compassion for the man. "Well, um, do they have you on antibiotics?"

Ronny nodded. "A ten-day round."

"It looks painful."

Ronny put on a brave face. "Oh, it's not too bad. It itches like crazy and feels like someone's sewn grass through my scalp, but I'm sure that's going to go away with time."

"Well," Hugo said, trying to smile, "I'm sure it will look…uh, more natural…once the antibiotics kick in."

"I did it for the station, Mr. Talley. I don't want to be the weekend anchor forever. I know Tate's young and good-looking, but I've got good attributes too, *and* I can anchor alone."

Hugo nodded. "Why don't you go home and get some rest."

Ronny looked like he was about to burst into tears. He quickly left the office. Hugo ran his fingers through his own thinning hair, gray thanks to years in the news business. He decided, against his better judgment, to see how Tate was doing taping the teaser. Since Gilda had yet to arrive, they had to do something, and Tate was really their only option.

As he headed toward editing bay one, he noticed Hayden walking briskly toward him. His chest constricted. It didn't look to be good news.

"What's wrong?" he asked while she was a good ways away.

"Mr. Talley, must something always be wrong?" she said with a grin.

"Nothing's wrong?"

"Yeah, something's wrong. But you shouldn't always assume something's wrong. It's not good for your health."

Hugo groaned. "What is it now?"

"Well, it's—"

"Wait."

"What?"

"Hayden, you seem to be in good with God. Tell me, does God hate me?"

"Mr. Talley, of course God doesn't hate you."

"You don't know that for sure. Have you asked? Specifically about me?"

Hayden folded her arms together and her angelic face suddenly turned stern. "Mr. Talley, are you saying you haven't been praying?"

Hugo couldn't help be amused by the fact that she looked exactly like his personal fitness trainer used to look when she'd ask if he'd been doing push-ups.

"It's been awhile," Hugo confessed.

"Well no wonder you're uptight all the time."

"I'm not uptight, Hayden. I'm focused."

"Focused on everything that could go wrong."

"In case you haven't noticed, everything is going wrong. Which is why I'd like to know if God has it in for me."

"Well, did you do something wrong?"

Hugo put his hands on his hips. "I'm no expert on the evangelical faith, but isn't this the part where you're supposed to assure me that God loves me no matter what I've done?"

"Yes, God loves you and forgives you. But if you're not working for God, then you're working for the devil."

Hugo cackled. "I've heard Chad called a lot of things, but I've never been so bold as to call him the devil."

"I'm talking about the real devil."

"Oh." Hugo stopped smiling. "Look, forget I said anything."

"Hugo, it's nothing to be embarrassed about. It's not that your life will get any better when you serve God. Sometimes it gets harder. But God will carry you through and make you stronger for it."

Hugo was smiling again, because he tended to smile at absurd things. "Are you for real? I mean, do you hear yourself? You're like a walking Sunday-morning pulpit."

"I'm just telling you the truth, Mr. Talley."

"It's just that you and Ray are so different."

"We are?"

"I've known Ray for years, and I happen to know that he goes to church every Sunday. The reason I know that is because he will not, under any circumstance, work on Sundays. I completely respect that. I also happened to notice the cross on his key chain. But not once has Ray ever told me I'm serving the devil."

Instead of looking even the slightest bit insulted, Hayden patted Hugo's arm. "God will never give up on you. And neither will I."

"Let me guess, you've been praying for me."

"Well, isn't it obvious? Now," she said, taking his arm and guiding him toward the editing bay, "we have matters to discuss. Tate is—well, he's struggling."

"What does that mean?"

"Maybe you should see for yourself."

Hugo walked into the editing bay as Tate sat on the editing desk with monitors behind him to serve as a backdrop. As soon as he saw Hugo, he jumped up, his lavaliere microphone ripping from his shirt. "Did you find her?"

"Gilda?" Hugo asked.

"Of course Gilda."

"No, Tate. Nobody can find her." Hugo sighed.

"I can't do this!" Tate said, flinging his arms in the air.

"Do what? The teaser?"

"It's just not working. I don't know. Maybe it's the...the...wording." Tate glanced around the small room. "Or the way the walls feel like they're closing in on me."

Hayden stepped up. "I've been trying to help Tate relax. He's feeling pretty uptight about having to do the news alone tonight."

"Don't focus on that right now. Gilda will show up. She's never missed a newscast, and she's well aware that we're closing in on sweeps week. She wouldn't dare ditch us." Hugo's emphasis on the word *dare* caused the room to grow still. Who was he trying to kid? He was as uptight as Tate. "It's just that—Tate, we really need this teaser, okay? We've got to start running this tonight."

But Tate shook his head like a schoolboy about to get beaten. Hugo had seen Tate nervous before, but he had never seen actual fear in his eyes.

"I'm just not feeling it," Tate said, his voice climbing into a falsetto.

Hugo's fists clenched. He would have to slap some sense into this kid without leaving a mark on him. But before he could do anything irrational, he felt a calm hand on his arm. Hayden was beside him.

"Mr. Talley, if you don't mind, I think I see the problem here."

Hugo could only hope Hayden wasn't going to lay hands on everyone and pray the devil out of the room. Though if that helped, at this point he was open to anything.

"I think, Tate," Hayden said, "that you're forgetting the basics. There's so much pressure right now that you're wanting to ride the bike but you're forgetting to pedal it."

Tate didn't look like he was following. Hugo couldn't say he was either. Hayden sat next to Tate on the editing desk and pointed toward the camera. "What are you trying to convey here?"

Tate blinked. "I…um…that your car could catch on fire and th-that you could get trapped and die…"

"You're trying to convey that in a desperate situation, there's a way out if you only stop and think. Right?"

Hugo's eyes shifted to Tate. Tate nodded. Hugo nodded too.

"You're really telling the viewers not to panic, to look around and use what is available to get themselves out of the situation."

Tate took a breath. "Yeah, I guess."

"So you've got to forget the script for a minute. Look right into that camera lens." She pointed and looked toward it. "Now, you're not talking to a piece of camera equipment. You're talking to my sister. Okay? Talk to my sister." Hayden focused and said, "You're in a burning car, and there's nobody to help. How will you get out?"

If only Tate could be that smooth. Hugo watched Tate take a deep breath and try it. "You're in a burning car, and there's nobody to help. How will you get out? Starting Monday we will have a week-long series on…how to save your life in a-a-a life-threatening—"

Hayden held up her hands. "Let's forget the script for a moment. Just look at my sister and talk as if you have important information that could save her life."

"What does your sister look like?" Tate asked.

Hugo wanted to moan. Was Tate missing the point here? What *was* the point exactly?

"Good question. She looks a lot like me, except she's a little taller with shorter hair. Her name is Mackenzie, but we call her Mack."

"Mack. Okay." Tate took a deep breath and looked at the camera.

"What if you were inside a burning car and there was no one to help? What if your car plunged into the river and you had to get yourself out? What if your car stalled on a road in the middle of a blizzard and you were alone? How would you survive? What would you do? Next week we'll show you ways you can survive life-threatening situations by being resourceful. It starts Monday."

"Good!" Hugo said, slapping his hands together. "That's what we want, Tate. Do you think you can do that when the tape is rolling?"

Tate looked down. "I don't know. My nerves are rattled. If someone could just assure me that Gilda would be here tonight."

Hayden laughed and everyone looked at her. "Guess what, gentlemen? We did get it on tape. I gave Ted over there a little wink and he recorded the whole thing."

A little wink? Hugo looked at Ted, who could only smile and nod. "So...we got it?"

Ted nodded again.

Hugo sighed with relief. "Great. Get that edited and ready to roll." He walked back toward his office, wondering how Tate was going to make it through the broadcast tonight. What were they going to do?

"Look around you and use what is at your disposal to get yourself out of the situation..." Hayden's words whispered through the storm inside Hugo's mind. He stopped, looking back toward the door of the editing bay.

"No...No." He shook his head, mumbling at the absurdity of the thought. "Maybe..." Hugo's heart thumped to the beat of fear. It would be a tremendous gamble, and if he failed, his career would be permanently over. But at the moment, he was banking everything on Tate's ability to get a grip, which wasn't likely, considering he couldn't even tape a teaser.

"Talley, you've lost your head." And headless he went, back to the editing bay.

Chapter 16

B eaker was stomping around like a scorned woman, and Ray had to will himself not to smile.

"You are unbelievable!" Beaker continued to say as he went from one side of the van to the other, gathering his equipment. Ray leaned against the side of the vehicle and studied his notepad, trying to ignore Beaker's ranting. "Plus, in case you haven't noticed, it's snowing! I hate snow!"

Maybe this was crazy. Maybe? It *was* crazy. He was getting ready to confront the man who had assaulted him…the man who'd just gotten out of jail for it. But the story was here, not in some police captain's office. There were a lot of unanswered questions. Why would Petey Green assault him, especially when the station was going to present his side of the story in the more favorable light? After all, who couldn't relate to a man disgruntled about pigs next door?

In Ray's heart, he knew he'd just scratched the surface of this story. There was something else going on, and he would get to the bottom of it. There was no reason he couldn't make *this* story the lead story. With the right information, it could slide into the top spot.

"You about ready?" Ray called.

He heard Beaker growl before he finally came around the van with the camera equipment. "At least we're here in daylight, though I can't say that brings me a whole lot of comfort. What are you going to do when he opens the door and pokes a shotgun in your face?"

"Hope that you've got the camera rolling."

"Funny. I only hope he's so distracted by you that he doesn't see me. But you and I both know they always go after the camera guy. The reporter is standing there asking all these obnoxious questions and poking a microphone in the guy's face, and what does he do? He shoves the cameraman."

"Well, Beaker, lucky for you—and I'm talking from experience here—Mr. Green seems more focused on me."

"You should've told me we were coming here. I would've packed a heat."

The edges of Ray's mouth trembled with restrained laughter at Beaker's misuse of Hollywood cop lingo. Ray had never known someone who watched more cop shows and movies. Beaker watched every version of *CSI* and *Law and Order,* plus he would rent two or three cop movies every weekend. Yet no matter how hard he tried, he could never get the jargon quite right. Once he'd gone through the day trying impressions of Mel Gibson's Martin Riggs character in *Lethal Weapon.* Somebody had recognized it from the movie, which prompted Beaker to grow out his hair for two years to try to look like the character. Ray never understood why Beaker couldn't at least feign a little bit more courage outside his imaginary world.

"We're going to be fine," Ray said. "Let's just both be on guard."

Ray couldn't deny the apprehension that built with every step he took toward Petey Green's house. The cut on his forehead even started to throb again.

He noticed that Beaker trailed a good distance behind him, pretending to fiddle with his camera in order to lose ground. He didn't let that deter him, but his feet felt heavy as he stepped up to the porch.

Petey Green's house was not unlike Elva Jones's house, with a screen door that looked barely attached and windows covered with sheets. Ray noticed two peepholes and wondered if the homeowner was staring through one of them at this moment.

Captain Wynn's quiet office suddenly didn't look so unappealing. Here Ray was, out in the action where he wanted to be, but his hands shook enough to make him realize that perhaps he hadn't made the wisest choice. Plus Hugo had specifically instructed him *not* to interview Petey Green, so now he was putting his life *and* his career on the line.

Ray knocked anyway.

Besides Beaker's heavy breathing behind him, the only things he heard were the pigs snorting next door. The smell was horrendous.

Ray knocked again.

"Nobody's home," Beaker said. "Great. Now we don't have an interview from the captain or any other footage. Maybe I could just get a closeup shot of your wound there, and if we're real quiet, and don't scare it, maybe it will give us a quote."

Suddenly the front door flew open, causing Ray to spin around and drop the microphone.

Obviously, they'd woken up Petey Green. That, or he was coming off a very bad hangover. Either way, this wasn't starting out well.

Green blinked at the dull daylight and scowled, looking as if he was trying to get his bearings. Ray used that moment to scoop up the mike.

"Mr. Green," Ray said, and to his horror, his voice cracked.

"Nice," Beaker whispered.

Ray kept his focus on Petey Green. "I'm Ray Duffey from News Channel 7."

Green's harsh, narrow eyes widened.

"I wanted to talk to you about the situation next door and give you a chance to tell your side of the story."

Green stumbled forward and out the front door. Ray backed up a little. "Ain't you the one that trespassed on my property before?"

"Sir, we just want your side of the story concerning the pigs. What about the pigs makes it difficult to live near them?"

Green was rubbing his left cheek for no apparent reason and pulling on his pants with the other hand. "I thought I told you to get outta here. I already went to jail once for *making* you get out of here, and here you are again. Ain't you learned your lesson?"

"Sir," Ray said, "I'm not here to harass you. I just want the truth."

"The truth is that I hate News Channel 7, and if you don't get yourself off my property, I'm going to call the police, who I know won't get here fast enough. So then I'm going to have to take matters into my own hands again."

Ray turned to Beaker and said, "Turn the camera off."

"What?"

"Turn it off."

"Why?" Beaker asked.

"Just do it."

The cameraman sighed and switched it off.

"I have the camera off now," Ray said.

"So?" Green said. "I ain't afraid of no camera."

"Mr. Green, I believe there's more to this story than we're seeing on the surface. And what better way to get the truth out than to tell it yourself?"

Petey Green walked toward Ray, who had backed down the porch steps until he stood in the middle of the man's front yard. "You're not here about the truth. You don't care nothin' about the truth."

"That's not true, sir. That is indeed why I am here. I just can't see why you would risk going to jail over a news station covering your neighbor's pigs."

"How 'bout the fact that I just don't like you?"

"You don't even know me, so I'm not buying that either."

A string of expletives tumbled out of Green's mouth. Ray tried to sort through them to find exactly what was making the man so angry.

In the middle of two words Ray would never use—in public anyway—he heard *Gilda Braun*.

"What did you say?" Ray asked, interrupting his rant.

Green stopped. "You want me to repeat all that?"

"Did you say 'Gilda Braun'?"

"Yeah, that's what I said."

"What about her?"

Green's eyes glared, and with a sneer he said, "Maybe you should ask her."

Chad Arbus walked into the station, his unbuttoned trench coat breezing behind him due to his quick stride. He pulled off his gloves in order to put his hair back into place. He looked around, trying to spot Hugo. He could see that he wasn't in his office.

Then he heard Hugo's voice at the anchor's desk. What was he doing there? It was hours before the broadcast, but the set was lit up like they were about to begin. Maybe there was breaking news.

And then he noticed a peculiar sight. That girl. What was her name? Hugo's new assistant. He'd had a couple of run-ins with Religious Rhonda and was perfectly content staying a good twenty-five yards away from her. The first time he'd met her, she'd thanked him for "blessing her" with her job. "I'm not a priest," he'd replied and then walked off.

Chad took a few steps forward for a better view but made sure he was out of her line of sight. He watched, half hidden behind a beam, as Hugo talked to her. What was he doing? Why was she sitting behind the anchor's desk? He sighed and settled in, watching Hugo's masterful technique. One of the most talented men Chad had ever known, Hugo had this amazing ability to pull out the best in people and remain calm under pressure. Hugo had created a wonderful sense of respect around the station. People called their bosses "Mr." and "Mrs." It was odd to hear people twice his age calling him Mr. Arbus, but the idea quickly grew on him. The rest of Hugo's old-school ways went out the window, though, when Chad arrived. He hated the dress code and wasn't about to wear a tie to work every day. He even told the anchors to dress only from the waist up. Everyone thought that was pretty funny, the anchors sitting behind the desk in shorts and a suit jacket. He knew it bothered Hugo, who felt the way a person dressed set the tone for his or her professional attitude. That was a bunch of bunk. The professional attitude was set by whether or not Chad treated them like they were worth his time.

Chad was hired to shake up the station and bring in some new blood, and the only way to do that was to demand respect. So far that hadn't been a problem. He'd ensured that no matter what his job was going to be done. And right now was no exception.

Chad removed his coat and draped it over his arm. He straightened his polo, and then, with as long a stride as his short legs would allow, he headed for Hugo. As soon as Hugo saw him, he stopped what he was doing and met him halfway.

"Mr. Arbus," Hugo said. "I've been trying to get ahold of you."

"I've had some important things to take care of."

"Mr. Green is going to sue?"

"It's a little more complicated than that." He gestured toward Hugo's assistant. "What's going on here?"

"This is going to sound crazy..."

"What?"

"We can't find Gilda. She's nowhere. I even had someone go by her house, and she's not there."

"So what's the big deal? We've got other options besides Gilda."

"I'm afraid something bad has happened to her."

"A bad case of Botox," Chad growled. "Maybe she's finally realized she's not anchor material anymore."

"As you know, our afternoon anchors have contract stipulations. And our other two options for anchors are..."

"Where? Everyone knows there's no vacation right before or during sweeps week."

"They're not on vacation. They're, um…"

"What?"

"Cosmetically unavailable."

"Another Botox mishap?"

"No."

Chad's eyes shifted to the girl, who noticed him and stood to wave. "Hello, Mr. Arbus. Good to see you again."

Chad looked at Hugo and pitched a thumb at her. "Why's she kissing my butt?"

"She's not, sir. Hayden's just nice."

Chad gave Hugo an unimpressed look. "So why is she behind the anchor's desk next to Tate? With a microphone on her shirt?"

Hugo was gesturing, but no words were coming out.

"What?" Chad demanded. "Speak up."

"I think she can do it."

"Do what?"

"Anchor the ten o'clock."

"You've lost your mind."

"You have to see her. She's got natural talent. She's very calm and together."

"Yeah, until the live broadcast. Then what?"

"Then…we're going to have to have faith."

"Faith?" Chad snorted. "This industry isn't built on faith, Hugo. It's built on cold, hard facts. Guarantees."

"Bringing in a new, young, pretty anchor is going to get us some attention."

Chad cut his eyes back to the girl. Strangely, she did have the right look. Cute but intelligent. Blonde hair that looked natural. With a little hair and makeup work, they could add a couple of years to her.

"She's our only option?" Chad asked.

"I'm not one to gamble, sir. But tonight, I'm afraid we're going to have to."

Chad studied Hayden as she spoke with Tate. They were a good visual match and seemed at ease with one another. Though Hugo didn't look anxious, he did look desperate, which wasn't making Chad feel any better about the situation.

"It's your call," Chad finally said. "But it better be the right one."

"Yes sir," Hugo said.

Chad turned and walked toward his office. He trusted no one more than Hugo, but things could change.

"Why are we back here?" Beaker complained. "We have nothing, Ray. Do you realize that? I don't have one minute of footage."

"We're following the story, Beaker," Ray replied as they walked into the news station.

"The story's going to be that you get fired if you don't come up with something. And quick."

"We'll have something. I don't know what, but we'll have something."

"What if we don't?"

"We will."

"How can you be so sure?"

Ray turned to Beaker, who almost ran into him. "Because there's a story here. Can't you see that?"

"I see a really ticked-off guy who doesn't want us anywhere near him."

"But why? Why does he hate us so much?"

"The public loves the news but hates newspeople. Everybody knows that."

"No, there's something more."

"And how do you plan on finding that 'something more'?"

"Easy. I just have to talk to Gilda."

Roarke slipped into Gilda's dressing room, which was still dark. He didn't turn on the light but could still see it, wrapped in red paper and neatly tied in a bow. His heart sank. He'd finally taken the next step. Inside the box was a note declaring his feelings, and at the end, he'd signed his name. It hardly looked like his signature because his hand had been shaking so badly.

Where was Gilda? With all that was at stake tonight, she should've been in two hours ago. His note had encouraged her, told her that he believed she was the most beautiful woman he'd ever known and that she didn't need to be "fixed."

Suddenly the door to her dressing room opened, and Roarke spun around, feeling he'd been caught red-handed. But he did sign his name. Maybe he could just tell her himself. It was time she knew. His heart told him so. No more hiding behind little gifts and poems. This was the woman he loved, and she had to—

"Ray?" Roarke squeaked as the lights came on.

"What are you doing?" Ray asked.

"Nothing."

"You look like you're doing something."

"I'm standing here."

"Doing what?"

"Nothing. Just standing here."

"In the dark. In Gilda's dressing room."

"So?" Roarke knew his face was flushing. He could feel his neck growing warm. "What are you doing here?"

"Looking for Gilda. What else?"

"Well, as you can see, she's not here."

"But why are you here?" Ray glanced behind Roarke. By Ray's expression, Roarke knew he had spotted the gift on her vanity. "No way…"

Roarke groaned and rolled his eyes.

"Gilda?" Ray nearly shouted. Roarke waved his hands and shushed him. "You're in love with Gilda?"

"You don't know her like I do," Roarke said.

"We both know her exactly the same."

"You don't see what I see."

Roarke could tell his friend was trying hard not to judge, nodding like he understood. But his eyes looked dazed and perplexed.

"I'm really in love with her, dude," Roarke said. "I wrote her a note telling her." He gestured toward the red box.

Ray stepped forward and put his hand on Roarke's shoulder. "I'm happy for you. And Gilda would be lucky to have a man like you. How, um, how does she feel about you?"

"I don't know yet. She apparently hasn't read the note."

"That's what you were doing? Leaving a note?"

Roarke sighed. "I left the note hours ago. I figured she'd be in by now. But she's not."

"She's not?"

"Weird, huh?"

Ray looked distressed. "I've got to talk to her."

"Why?"

"I went to interview Petey Green today."

"You what?"

"I know, I know."

"Hugo told you specifically not to interview him, didn't he?"

"Roarke, I'm telling you, something weird is going on here. Green mentioned Gilda, that I should ask Gilda why he hates us so much."

"You know people, Ray. They prefer one station over another because of an anchor's hairstyle or choice of tie."

"I don't know. This seems a little different."

"Yeah, well, everything around here seems a little different if you ask me. Gilda's not here and your lady's in the anchor chair."

"What are you talking about?"

"Hugo's been working with Hayden to fill in for Gilda if Gilda doesn't show up or shows up but can't frown."

"Hayden? Why Hayden? She has no experience in front of a camera. What about Julia…or Michelle? Why couldn't he use Ronny?"

"Rumor has it that Michelle can't stay up past seven, Julia knocked out her two front teeth, and Ronny's hair plugs are infected. All I know is that Hayden's been out there practicing all afternoon. She even taped a promo."

Ray shook his head. Roarke added, "You should probably ask her out soon."

"Why?"

"Because, dude, she's about to become famous."

Chapter 17

A t four o'clock in the afternoon, Gilda still hadn't shown, and Ray had nothing for his story except a few vague facts and a shot of Petey Green opening his front door. He felt such panic that he was actually drinking coffee. It tasted nasty, but he'd chewed off all his fingernails and he needed some other oral fixation. Sucking his thumb was out of the question.

He didn't dare tell Hugo what he'd done. Not yet, anyway. He still had time, if he could just get some information from Gilda. And if not from Gilda, then maybe from Gilda's computer.

"Roarke, I need your help."

Roarke took off his headphones. "I'm kind of busy. There's a wreck on the interstate."

"I need to get on Gilda's computer."

"Why?"

"I just want to see if there's anything there that connects her to Petey Green."

"Are you out of your mind?"

"You *can* get on Gilda's computer, right?"

"Me?"

"You're the assignment editor. With Gilda not here, you have reason to look for what stories she was working on to reassign them."

"That's Hugo's job."

"And Hugo is obviously busy trying to find a new anchor, so he doesn't have time." Ray paused. "And there's always the chance you could happen upon an e-mail from a male friend. It might be nice to know if she's seeing anybody else."

"I'm not promising anything." Roarke bit his lip and looked around. "But I'll see what I can do."

Ray looked up and saw Hugo waving him into his office. "Uh-oh," Ray muttered and walked to Hugo's office.

"This is the worst day of my life," Hugo announced.

Ray waited, unsure if Hugo was actually talking to him.

"How could so much bad luck happen all at once?" Hugo asked. "Could it be possible that Hayden Hazard, of all people, will be able to pull this off? She has the exact look, for sure, and apparently nerves of steel, because she doesn't look the least bit nervous. She keeps saying, 'Hugo, I just want to help. Whatever I can do to help.' Like she wants to bring over a casserole after knee surgery or something. It's like it doesn't occur to her that she should be nervous, that lots of people's jobs, including her own, rest on her ability to appear professional."

Ray could offer only a nod.

"So I should just act like I want the casserole?" Hugo asked, locking eyes with Ray, waiting for an answer. "Maybe Hayden has a special recipe that can make you forget about your knee pain, at least temporarily." Ray wasn't sure he was following the metaphor very well.

Hugo sighed. "Anyway, I called you in here because I need you to call in a favor to Captain Wynn."

"A favor?"

"You've always been tight with him, and he seems to like you a lot—"

"What do you need Captain Wynn for?"

"To help us find Gilda."

"Right. Sure. I'm on it."

Much to his dismay, Ray realized he was going to have to apologize profusely for earlier, then ask the captain to send an officer over to Gilda's. He was probably going to have to beg for another interview, which at this point could be the only piece of Ray's story.

Things were not looking good.

He walked out of the station, where Beaker was loading equipment into the truck and not looking very happy about it. At least the snow had stopped, almost at the exact time Sam had broken into the regular programming to alert the public that it was snowing.

"Hi."

Ray whirled around and saw Hayden. She was leaning against the brick wall, her arms wrapped around herself.

"What are you doing out here? It's freezing!"

"I just stepped out for a moment. I needed some fresh air."

"Hugo told me you're anchoring tonight."

"Looks like it," she grinned. "Tate couldn't do it alone, and Hugo was out of options."

"But you've never been in front of a camera, have you?"

"I did a lot of performing with my parents' clown company before we figured out I was afraid of clowns. People always had their video cameras out, taping us. I learned to memorize lines and things like that. This is easier. I don't have to memorize the lines because they're right there in that...what's it called?"

"TelePrompTer."

"Yeah. And plus, I'm terrified of clowns, so if I can hold it together around a clown, I figure this will be a breeze."

Ray wondered if Hayden had any idea what an extraordinary event this was. She didn't look like she did. He glanced toward the van and saw that Beaker was still busy. This was his chance. He had to ask her out now, or the weekend would be upon them, and he would lose a perfectly good opportunity to get to know her. Plus, he knew that somewhere inside Sam was studying the Torah.

"Let's go!" Beaker called to him and hopped inside the truck.

"Guess you better get going," Hayden said, smiling at him. Ray felt his knees go weak. That smile was the cutest thing he'd ever seen.

"Would you like to go out with me?" Ray could feel his eyes enlarge with each word until he imagined he looked dumbfounded. He tried to accompany it with a small smile.

"I'd love to. I always thought it would be fun to go out in the field, see what it's like to be a reporter. But I think Hugo's got plenty for me to do here. Looks like Beaker's ready to go, though."

Ray closed his eyes. She'd missed it completely, which meant she wasn't at all expecting it—which meant, quite possibly, she wasn't interested.

"Ray!" Beaker shouted, waving his hand as if Ray were too deaf to hear his name being called.

"Oh, right." Ray smiled, but then he stopped smiling. No, he wasn't going to give up this easy. "I meant, um, I meant on a date. Would it be okay if you asked me out... I mean, if I asked you out. On a date."

Hayden's hand found her mouth and she giggled. *Okay, giggling is a good sign,* he thought. "I'm sorry, Ray," she laughed. "I didn't realize that's what you meant."

"I should've been a little clearer," he said, though he'd never once had to reword that phrase before. "So what do you say? Would you like to go out this weekend?"

"I'm sorry, Ray. I already have plans for the weekend."

"Ray! Come on!"

"Hold on a second!" Ray shouted back, and Hayden covered her ears.

"Sorry," Ray smiled meekly. "So...plans. Surely not the whole weekend?" Ray tried to pose the question in a nondesperate way.

"Yeah. The whole weekend."

"Oh." Ray's gaze fell to his feet. "Cool. Well, have fun, then."

"Thanks. And thanks for the offer."

Offer. Great. No problem. Maybe next time he could offer to wash her car. He turned and barreled toward the van as fast as he could, considering there were patches of ice everywhere. The truck started rolling before Ray could close the door.

Beaker snickered. "Crashed and burned, did you?"

"Shut up, Beaker."

"She's kind of out of your league, isn't she?"

"What's that supposed to mean? How is she out of my league?"

"Hello? She's like an anchor now."

"She's not an anchor. She's filling in."

"Everybody knows anchors don't date reporters."

Ray glared out the windshield. Sam had gotten to her first. Apparently, so had fame.

"Yes, Mr. Talley?" Hayden asked as she walked into his office.

"Come on in, Ms. Hazard. Please, shut the door." He gestured toward the only chair in his office. "Have a seat."

The suit they'd taken from Gilda's wardrobe closet fit Hayden like it was tailored for her. She looked transformed in an instant, from lowly and humble assistant to hot, superstar anchor. But Hugo knew looks could be deceiving. There were no guarantees she could pull it off, and his only hope was that the police would be able to find Gilda soon.

In the meantime, he wanted to know Hayden's dirty little secret. "I know, you know," he said, giving her a wicked wink.

"Know, sir?"

"I recognize it."

"Recognize what, Mr. Talley?"

"Oh, now, come on. Don't be so discreet. And there's nothing to be embarrassed about. To tell you the truth, I'm a little jealous. That's why I wanted to talk to you."

"I'm sorry, sir, I don't understand what you're talking about."

A wide smile couldn't hide Hugo's embarrassment, but he wasn't going to take no for an answer. He was just going to have to prod a little more.

"Look, Hayden," he said, warming his tone, "I've been telling my doctor for a while now that I needed a stronger dosage, but maybe what I need is a completely different pill, you know? They're making such strides in medicine these days, finding all kinds of things out about the human body. So 'fess up, will you? I know you're on something."

"Sir, I—"

"Don't you think I recognize unnatural calmness when I see it? You're getting ready to anchor the ten o'clock for the first time, and if I didn't know better, I'd think you were about to embark on an all-expenses-paid vacation. Come on, now. Just tell me what you're on. Nobody in this room is going to judge you."

"You're the only other person in this room."

"Exactly. That's what I'm saying. We'll keep this between us, okay?"

"Mr. Talley, you're going to have to spell this out for me, because I'm clueless as to what you're talking about."

Hugo blinked. She really did look clueless. But then again, Hayden was turning out to be full of surprises. Maybe she was also a good actress. "Antianxiety medication."

Hayden shook her head. "I'm not on any medication."

"Hayden, come on. Don't make me pull it out of you. It's not obvious to everyone, okay? So don't go getting paranoid on me. If anyone understands, it's me. I just happen to think your pill is working better than mine. You're on the purple one, aren't you? I told my doctor the purple one was better, but she—"

Hayden held up her hands and leaned forward, looking Hugo directly in the eye. *There.* Now they were finally getting somewhere. "Mr. Talley," she said softly, "what in the world are you on antianxiety medication for?"

Hugo felt his chest tighten. "Because I'm anxious."

"No, you're not."

"That's because I'm on medication."

"You're saying you have an anxiety disorder?"

Hugo sighed. "I haven't been officially diagnosed, if that's what you mean, but that doesn't—"

"Mr. Talley, with all due respect, do you know where anxiety comes from?"

Hugo paused. Was this a trick question?

"From not trusting God, Mr. Talley. We're all going to be anxious if we think we're in control of our lives, because we're constantly making mistakes. Do you know what I mean? We've got to trust our Father in heaven to take care of us, even when we mess up. Or when others mess things up for us."

Hugo's mouth was still hanging open, and for the life of him, he couldn't shut it.

"Look," she said, very matter-of-factly, "you're a capable man, Mr. Talley. You show it day in and day out, and it's not because of medication. The only thing that's missing is trust. Trust in God. When you give God your life, and trust him to take care of you, what in the world do you have to be fearful of?"

"I'm not fearful, I'm anxious," Hugo replied.

"They're twins, Mr. Talley. One feeds the other." Hayden stood from leaning against his desk. "I challenge you to stop depending on that pill and start depending on God." Her finger pointed to the ceiling.

Hugo had no idea what to do, so he looked up. He'd been hit on, cursed at, lied to, but never preached at. Normally she looked so serene, but now she had some kind of fire in her eyes. He'd once had an aunt who liked to slay people in the Spirit. He wasn't exactly sure what was about to happen now, so he stared at the ceiling and hoped someone might glance in and notice something awry.

"See?" she said plainly. "You look anxious again."

"Listen," he said, tearing his eyes off the ceiling. "I'm not judging you, but you're making me very uncomfortable."

"That's because you're not trusting God. Mr. Talley, believe me when

I say that there simply is no other way to live. Don't you know that at any moment any part of your life could be gone in an instant? What would you do then? How do you cope when you don't have any guarantees?"

Hugo felt himself growing a little angry. What was she guaranteeing him? Some anxiety-free life if he repented and turned from his wicked ways?

"Look, if you want to talk about sin, go preach to Chad Arbus. He knows a thing or two about it."

Hayden frowned. "Who said anything about sin?"

Hugo paused, realizing she had not, in fact, mentioned sin. So why had he felt compelled to bring it up? He looked at her, embarrassed by the feeling that he needed to hold his ground. "Sorry, I'm not buying the fact that your religion is the reason you seem to have no fear."

"I have plenty of fear, Mr. Talley."

"Then why not about tonight? I can't think of anything more frightening than getting up in front of a camera to speak to a million or so people." Great. Now he was exaggerating viewing numbers.

She smiled. "You know, one of the best things I ever learned was to never take myself too seriously. That way you're never embarrassed when you're made to look like a fool."

Maybe that was a homeschool thing, because nobody had ever taught him that.

"It's going to be fine tonight. It may not be perfect, but we'll get through it. I promise." She smiled, gave him a friendly wink, and said, "And think about getting off that pill. I know you can do it."

Hugo led her out the door, went back into his office, closed the door, and tried not to think of his little blue friend.

Chapter 18

It was certainly an uncomfortable moment. In the patrol car, Ray sat next to Captain Wynn, whose face looked particularly stern. Ray had never noticed what a forceful profile he had, probably because the captain nearly always faced whichever way the camera was pointed.

Ray had decided it would be best to talk to the captain in person, to explain the situation…and the favor Ray was asking. He figured there wasn't any chance that he could work this without groveling, which he assumed would work with personality types like the captain.

It had. Sort of.

The captain had agreed to help find Gilda. But what Ray hadn't counted on was the fact that the captain would be personally involved…like driving his own car to her house and asking Ray to accompany him and Beaker to follow behind in the van. So the question lingering in the air was, "Don't you understand how busy I am and how much time it takes out of my day to do an interview?"

Obviously, Ray needed the groveling equivalent to an answer. But sometimes he just wanted to put the captain in his place. The man was so arrogant and in need of so much attention. Ray wanted to tell the captain how obvious it was that he was always looking for a chance to be in the spotlight. He wanted to ask why he had a department spokeswoman if he planned to do all the speaking. He wanted to assure the captain that he was capable of constructing a news story without one of his lame quotes.

The captain glared at Ray, his brows cutting deep into his bridge of his nose. "Well?"

"Yes, of course, Captain Wynn," Ray said. "I apologize." How many times had he said that? When was it going to be enough?

The captain focused his attention ahead again. Ray still had no idea why he needed to ride to Gilda's house with the captain, except maybe to issue another hundred apologies.

"So," the captain said, keeping his eyes forward, "this could be a big story."

Ray eyed him. Did he know something about Petey Green that Ray didn't?

"The more I find out, the more interested I become," Ray answered. "Know anything of interest about Mr. Green?"

The captain looked at him. "Green? I'm not talking about that loser. I'm talking about Gilda's disappearance."

"Gilda?"

"A well-known local newswoman disappears without notice—"

"We can't say she's disappeared. She just hasn't shown up for work."

"And why would she do that?" the captain asked, delight trickling out from underneath his feigned concern.

"This isn't a story," Ray said. "Mr. Talley simply wanted it investigated. We're worried. I'm sure we'll get there and find a perfectly reasonable explanation."

"You've already had someone go to her home to knock. No answer. Got an explanation for that?"

"Look," Ray said, "Hugo didn't send me out here to cover this as a news story."

"Then why did he send you?"

Ray hesitated, and the captain noticed. If he hedged any more, his expression would tell the whole story. "Mr. Talley knows that we have a good professional relationship, and he was hoping to call in a favor."

The captain chuckled. "Let's see what we can find at Ms. Braun's home."

Ray wasn't sure, but he thought that a burning sensation in both ears meant your blood pressure was on the rise. He didn't need his ears to tell him. His heart was doing a good job of beating out of control.

Despite Captain Wynn's thorough "on-camera" investigation of Gilda's condo, they found nothing to indicate she had been there recently or was taken against her will. The condo was simply quiet.

What should've taken ten minutes took an hour because of Captain Wynn's need to be sure he was captured from every angle. It was some sort of weird punishment, Ray could only guess, but the captain insisted it all be "caught on tape."

"I think this is going to be big," he kept saying. Ray tried not to roll his eyes. He just assumed Gilda had gone back for more Botox or a Botox reversal, if there was such a thing. Surely she would turn up.

The thought crossed his mind that perhaps Petey Green was involved in her disappearance, but that seemed a little far-fetched. Green had been in jail, and why would he mention Gilda's name if had done something to her?

He kept quiet and waited for Captain Wynn to finish. They left as quickly as they could.

Back at the station, the 6:30 news was wrapping up. Ray found Roarke at the assignment desk. "Did you get to her computer?" he whispered.

"Yeah. I didn't find anything."

"What do you mean you didn't find anything?"

Roarke raised an eyebrow. "You seem a little on edge."

"It has *not* been a good day."

"What's going on?"

"More than I can possibly explain, but as of right now, all I've got for my story is Green coming out of his house angry and Captain Wynn looking as if I bribed him for a quote."

"Did you?"

"Long story. Are you sure you looked in all the folders?"

"Dude, I had to work fast, okay? But I didn't find anything. And as I suspected, she's not dating anyone either." He smiled a little.

"Did you look for anything besides evidence of her love life?"

Roarke's smile faded. "You need to chill."

"I asked Hayden out." Ray folded his hands together and rested his forehead against them.

"You burped the Tupperware?"

"She's got plans this weekend."

"And...?"

"And what?"

"Well, she didn't say no. She just said she's got plans."

"For the whole weekend?"

Ray glanced around and added, "Sam must have gotten to her first."

"Oh, man. That stinks."

"Yeah. Big time." Ray looked up and noticed Sam walking from the weather desk toward the break room. "I'm going to give him a piece of my mind."

Roarke stood. "Ray, seriously, man, I think you should chill out for a little bit. I mean, what good is that going to do except make you look like an idiot? Or worse."

"What's worse?"

"A desperate idiot."

"Sam's asking her out for all the wrong reasons. Hayden's too naive to see that."

"Ray, wait..."

But Ray couldn't. His blood was boiling. He'd hit a dead end with the Green case, been manipulated by the police, and duped by Sam "A League of His Own" Leege. Something had to give.

Marching straight toward the break room, Ray tried to think of any way that he could come across as composed and cool about the situation. Nothing came to mind.

Pushing open the door, he was surprised to find Sam hanging over the sink with the water running. He didn't seem to notice anyone else in the room.

"Sam," Ray said harshly, but the weatherman continued to hang over the sink. Then he grabbed two paper towels, wet them, and rubbed them all over his face. "*Sam!*" Ray tried again. Sam looked up like the paper-towel dispenser had just spoken to him. "Over here," Ray said, and Sam turned his head. Then he squinted, like Ray was a beaming light.

"Ray?" he asked.

"What's wrong with you?" Ray asked, stepping forward, out of whatever light seemed to be blinding Sam.

Sam stood upright and took three attempts to turn off the water. He was trying to blot his face dry, but the paper towel was sopping wet. "Nothing. Why?"

Was he sick? He sounded different. Maybe he had a cold. *Good.* He was sick and going to get a tongue-lashing. Exactly what he deserved.

Ray was about to open his mouth when he noticed Sam's shirt was buttoned wrong. And then he noticed his tie, barely hanging by its knot, clashed with his shirt, which was odd since Sam was a certified metrosexual.

"Are you sure you're okay?"

"Did I stut—"

"What?" Ray asked.

"—ter?" Sam finished. "What are you doing in here anyway? Don't you have...have something to...do?"

Sam's eyes looked wild and unfocused. Ray began to wonder if maybe it was the flu and he should find a bottle of disinfectant really quickly. All of this was making it very difficult to be hard core. Sam's eyes, puffy and red, didn't seem the least bit interested in what Ray had to say.

"What are you, a...a...?"

"You need to sit down," Ray said, grabbing his arm. Sam yanked it away.

"A...nurse or something?"

"You don't look good, man," Ray said.

"I'm fine. I just need to step outside for a...thirty-two degrees."

"Huh?"

Sam's eyes suddenly turned shiny. "I'm a failure, Ray."

"What are you talking about?" Ray realized he should be agreeing with him in order to make his point, but something was very wrong here.

"I'm horrible at my job. My dad—now that man, he could stand outside, lick his finger, and tell you what it was going to do on Sunday. I've got"—he paused for what sounded like a hiccup—"these fancy computers and assistants and...I can't even tell you what it's doing outside now."

Ray ran his fingers through his hair. Sam had taken the wind out of his sails. This was not going well. Ray pulled up a chair. "Look, Sam, everyone makes mistakes—"

"You don't."

"Of course I do."

"No. You're...you're one of a kind, Ray. I've never told you this before," he said, leaning forward and stretching out his hand like Ray might grab it. He didn't. "But I look up to you, man. I do. You're really good at this...this...news stuff. I'm just your everyday hack. I mean, yeah, I can flirt on air and charm the daylights out of a camera lens, but at the end of the..." He paused. "What time is it?"

"Almost seven."

"At the end of the night, I'm nothing, Ray. Nothing." Sam laughed. As he did, Ray got a whiff of... Was Sam drunk?

"Sam, are you sure you're, uh, you're—"

"What? A loser. Yeah. I'm just really bad at this. I am in a league of my own. The league of losers." Every fourth word slurred. He blinked slowly and smiled at awkward times. "You have nothing to worry about, Ray. You'll always be on top. I talk but I don't walk, you know." For the first time, Ray noticed the coffee sitting in front of Sam. Sam gulped it suddenly, and Ray realized that coffee wasn't the only thing in that mug. Which surprised him as he tended to envision Sam as more of a martini-sipping type.

"Sam, you've got to stop this."

"Stop what?"

"You're dru—"

The door flew open, and Hugo walked in, his eyes wide like he was expecting something bad to happen.

"What are you two doing?" Hugo asked.

"Just...sit..." Sam's long blinks between words made Ray stand and address Hugo.

"What do you need, Mr. Talley?"

"I need to know that tonight's newscast is going to go off without a hitch." Hugo glanced at Sam, then at Ray.

Ray also glanced at Sam, who looked like he could pass out at any moment. Hugo was starting to notice too, so Ray took Hugo by the arm and said, "I need to talk to you for a second." He guided him out of the break room.

"What's wrong?"

"Look, I've put off telling you this because I wasn't sure what I could find. My story about Green is...a little weak. I don't have much."

"How can you not have much?" Hugo said, his voice tight with restraint. "You *are* the story."

"Well, sir, that's what I've been trying to avoid. But I found some-thing really interesting. It's a lead I'm following that—"

"What exactly do you have, Ray? For tonight?"

"I have a quote from the police captain...and a shot of Green com-ing out of his house."

Hugo's eyes lit. "What?"

"I know, I know. You told me not to go interview him. But I couldn't build a story around Captain Wynn's take on things. Something is telling me that there is more to this story. Why does Green hate our station so much? Why does—"

"He's saying we provoked him! And now you've gone to his house? To provoke him more?"

"Mr. Talley, listen for a minute. When I was there, Green said Gilda's name, and I think there may be something more to this story than just the pigs—"

Hugo's nostrils flared with each word Ray spoke. Then he held up his hands. "You don't show a second of that footage you have of Green. Do you understand me?"

"But…but all I have is Captain Wynn, and it's like a five-second quote."

"Then you better figure something out. You've got a three-minute segment. Are we clear?"

Ray nodded.

"We still haven't found Gilda. This is going to be a nightmare." He squeezed the bridge of his nose. "Everything else has to be perfect tonight. Perfect. No exceptions. I have no idea what's going to happen with Hayden, so nothing else can go wrong." Hugo glanced toward the break-room door. "Is he okay?"

"Sam? Oh…yeah, he's…he's just…you know. He's fine."

Hugo eyed Ray carefully then walked off. As soon as Hugo rounded the corner, Ray slipped back into the break room, only to find Sam passed out at the table. "Sam!"

Sam jerked up and with his right hand pointed to something and said, "Winds from the north, making for a chilly morning, but it'll warm up by noon—"

Ray rushed to him. "Sam! You've got to get a grip. You've got to get ahold of yourself before the newscast."

Sam's hand dropped and he eyed Ray. "Why do you care? You hate me, Ray. Everyone knows it."

Ray tried to keep his tone even though he really felt like shouting. "I don't hate you, Sam, but you've got to pull yourself together."

"Because you care so much about me?" Sam laughed. "Right. There's nothing you'd like to see more than me crash and burn."

Not tonight. "Sam, please. Let's just put all that aside. Hugo needs us to be at our best."

Sam sank in his chair. "Sorry, Ray. I'm not buying into your sudden concern for me."

"Look, Sam, the truth is that I was going to come in and confront you about asking Hayden out. It made me mad. She's a good and decent person, and she shouldn't be the object of a competition. I felt like you were asking her out just to get at me, to prove you could win. So you won…fine. Let's put that aside and—"

"Wait a minute," Sam said, finishing off the contents of the mug.

"What?"

"What do you mean I won?"

"You asked Hayden out. She's going out with you this weekend."

Sam's unfocused eyes managed to look amused. "I asked her out. But she said she couldn't." A sloppy smile spread across Sam's face. "A few minutes later, I heard her talking to Trent, asking him what he was doing this weekend."

"You're lying," Ray said.

Sam threw up his hands. "Now I'm a drunk and a liar. And I was beginning to think you cared." Sam stood, cradling the mug in his hands.

"Where are you going?"

"Why do you care?" Sam sneered.

Ray grabbed his arm as he tried to pass. "Sam, you cannot screw this up. You've got to…to…de-drunk yourself."

Sam laughed heartily. "De-drunk. Good one, Ray." And he stumbled out the door.

Chapter 19

H ugo wasn't sure why, but a strange and very real calmness swept over his body in waves. Between the waves, he experienced moments of sheer panic, but then the calm would come again. Maybe his Blue Pill was working again, though he couldn't imagine why, since he knew his level of anxiety this evening was twice what it normally was.

He watched Hayden in the monitor. She looked really good on camera. That engaging grin came through the lens. Her eyes sparkled underneath the lights. They'd been rehearsing like crazy, and now, with only a few minutes until time to go on air, she actually looked relaxed. She studied her script intently, talking a little with Tate, who didn't look all that uptight either.

It was so hard for Hugo to get his hopes up, though. Sure, he wanted to believe he'd witnessed a minor miracle with Gilda disappearing and Hayden Hazard, of all people, stepping in with near flawlessness. But he just wasn't sure he had enough faith, because deep in his heart he knew good things hardly ever happened. He'd been in the news business long enough to know that. That's what made the news a business.

Something about Hayden, though, made him want to believe. Either she was certifiable, or she really believed she could do this. Either way, she made him believe, at least a little, because there she sat in the anchor's chair. Even her name had an anchor's ring to it. Hayden Hazard. So, with all the horrible bad luck he'd witnessed in the last forty-eight hours, was it possible that things might turn around for him tonight?

Chad wasn't happy. He'd called Hugo a lunatic and made it clear that if this didn't work, Hugo was out of a job. But Chad couldn't deny that

Hayden had the look they'd been searching for. "Now let's just hope she doesn't make us look like idiots," he'd quipped before returning to his office.

"Yes, let's hope," Hugo said aloud, causing a few people to turn to look at him. He ignored them, realizing how much he wished Hayden could also be in the room, standing near the back wall like she normally did, offering words of encouragement.

Suddenly, her voice came crackling through the speaker. "Mr. Talley, how are you doing in there?"

Hugo smiled and leaned into the microphone. "Fine, Hayden. We're on in about two minutes. You ready?"

"Ready!"

"How about you, Tate?"

"I'm ready too, sir."

"Okay. Just remember, look for the floor director's hand signals. We're going to keep this very simple tonight, but if you get confused he'll be pointing to the correct camera. He'll also be giving you the countdown and will be letting you know when it's time to—"

"Mr. Talley," Hayden smiled, "you've told me this a hundred times."

Hugo found himself laughing. He didn't know why. Maybe because this was all so absurd. But now it was time for him to step back and release it all. There was nothing more he could do but watch himself either become a hero or unemployed. He decided to stand against the back wall, where Hayden normally stood.

He could hear the director counting down, and everything seemed to slow to a crawl. Except his mind. Thoughts raced through it like one bullet train after another. It seemed an odd time to be contemplating his life, but there he stood, wondering what exactly he was missing, because no matter how hard he tried, he couldn't be happy. Even when good things happened, he was fearful about when it would all go away. He'd never thought much about his soul or spirit or being or whatever you wanted to call it. But if he honestly thought about it, he pictured it huddled in a dark corner of himself, trembling and wide-eyed.

"On in ten, nine, eight, seven..." Each number Willis announced hung in air, and Hugo felt breathless as he watched the monitors. Hayden's hands were moving across the stack of papers on the desk, and she wasn't looking up at the camera.

"Look up, look up!" Hugo whispered.

"...three, two, one, roll intro..."

The News Channel 7 logo appeared with the music. And then it cut to Hayden and Tate. Tate was looking up at the camera, greeting it with his usual smile. Hayden was still looking down at her notes. Hugo clasped his hands together, begging whatever powers that be.

"Good evening. I'm Tate Franklin."

Hayden paused, looked up a little, then lifted her chin. She opened her mouth, but nothing came out. Tate glanced at her, worry flashing across his face.

"Come on!" Hugo shouted, causing everyone in the control room to jump.

Then she smiled. "And I'm Hayden Hazard. Thank you for joining us this evening."

Hugo let out a whimper, but he didn't care. She'd spoken.

"Tonight, we begin with coverage of the wastewater treatment plant explosion. For that, we go to Jill Clark, who is standing by live at the plant. Jill, what have you learned?" Hayden asked.

Hugo watched Jill give her report. The calmness he'd known just moments before returned. He didn't even listen to Jill's report but instead kept his eyes focused on Tate and Hayden.

"Back to you," Jill said.

"Thank you, Jill," Hayden said. "We're glad to hear there weren't more casualties. It could have been much worse."

The calmness washed away. Hayden wasn't sticking to the script. She was given no extra commentary, just the bare bones. But she looked at Tate, indicating he was up, and he went on to his part.

Hugo was afraid he might distract her if he whispered into her IFB, so he just let it go. She'd done a good job so far, though a little stilted. She was warming up fast.

"She's good," Willis said.

Hugo nodded. Something told him this was going to be a very, very good newscast.

"Sam? Sam!" Ray had gone looking for Sam after a grip had remarked that the weatherman had taken off his microphone and disappeared a few minutes into the newscast. Ray's segment was to air right before the weather, so he knew they both had at least ten minutes.

He'd been watching Hayden, who was doing amazingly well for her first time in front of the camera. The mistakes she made were minor, and Tate had been able to cover for her. They seemed to be working well as a team.

Now, though, Sam had the potential to undo the entire newscast. Ray had elected not to tell Hugo about Sam, because when he'd found Sam a couple of hours after their initial meeting, he seemed to be coming off his buzz.

Ray hadn't been able to get over the enormous disappointment he felt knowing that not only had Hayden turned him down for a date, but that she'd actually asked Trent out. Trent, of all people? It had ruined his entire night, and he was having a hard time caring about anything but himself.

But now, realizing they might not have a weather segment and thus, ten minutes to fill, Ray knew he was going to have to do something—and quick.

Although he looked everywhere, including the men's room, he came up empty. What were they going to do? The assistant director was heading for Ray, his arms thrown up. "We're four minutes until commercial!" he ranted. "Where is he?"

Ray sighed. "I don't know. I can't find him."

"I'm going to have to tell Mr. Talley." He rushed off. Ray just stood there, almost feeling paralyzed. Then he heard something. It sounded like an animal dying.

He turned, trying to identify the sound's location. He stood very still, and then he heard it again. It was right next to him. He looked...and it was coming from the women's room.

Without thinking of the potential embarrassing fallout, Ray pushed open the door and rushed in. Under the third stall's door he could see two feet, obviously belonging to a man.

"Sam?"

A moan answered.

Ray pushed open the door and found Sam in the stall, leaning against one of the walls, holding his stomach and looking pasty, his chin shiny with drool.

"Sam? Are you okay?"

Sam shook his head, hardly able to open his eyes.

Ray grabbed his shoulders. "Sam, you're on in eight minutes!"

Sam opened his eyes. "I am?"

"Yes!"

"I thought I had more time..." He groaned.

"Sam, you've got to snap out of it."

"No, I'm fine," he said, waving his hand and attempting to smile. "I just need a little more time."

"You don't have time!" Ray said. "You've got to get your mike on, and..." He watched as Sam nodded and then closed his eyes like he was going to fall asleep standing up. "Stay here!"

Ray rushed out of the bathroom and around the corner to the supply closet. He grabbed the first-aid kit and headed back for the bathroom. He saw Hugo emerging from the control room, looking shocked as the assistant director was trying to explain the problem.

Ray nearly plowed down the door as he went back in. Tearing into the box, he found the smelling salts. He cracked a package open and went back to Sam, shoving his hand under Sam's nose.

"Oh!" Sam shrieked, his eyes flying open. But Ray put an arm against Sam's chest, holding him against the stall wall as he pushed the smelling salts under his nose again. Sam struggled. His face lit up as if he were being electrocuted. Coherent enough to know he was being held against the wall, Sam fought off Ray's arms. Ray backed out of the stall and watched Sam shake his head. "Ah!" Sam complained.

"Sam, look at me," Ray demanded.

Sam blinked, then turned to Ray. "What?"

"You're on in six minutes. I'm on in about four minutes. We have to go."

Sam's eyes widened. The panicked look on Sam's face was a good thing.

Sam tore out of the stall and toward the bathroom door. Ray followed. As they rounded the corner out of the bathroom, they ran into Hugo.

"What are you two doing?" Hugo shouted. His face looked like a giant red blister. It seemed apparent that Hugo noticed the men had been in the women's room.

"Sam was sick," Ray said. "But he's going to make it through the broadcast. Aren't you, Sam?"

Hugo looked at Sam, who nodded. "I gotta get my…my thingy on…" Sam ran past Hugo. Hugo turned to watch him, then looked at Ray.

"Me too," Ray said, and hurried toward the spot in the newsroom they'd chosen for his backdrop. Ray ran the microphone up his shirt, clipped it on, and positioned himself to look casual as he leaned against the desk.

He'd been dreading this all day. His only option was to put together a touchy-feely piece, and now he was going to have to sit here and do a serious pitch for it. Viewers would love it, there was no doubt about that. They couldn't resist blow-by-blow accounts. But inside, Ray felt more disappointment than he could describe because, deep in his gut, he knew he didn't have the whole story.

They came out of commercial, and Ray could see Hayden at the news desk. "Tonight, sad news from the northeast side of town. A baby has been found dead…" Ray watched as Hayden paused and looked down at her notes. Tate looked like he didn't know what to do. Hayden looked back up at the camera. "Boy, this is a tough one." Her voice sounded like she might start crying. "A baby was found dead near the railroad tracks, and police believe the mother gave birth and then abandoned the baby, who…perished from exposure." Hayden looked down again then back up at the camera. Her eyes were shiny with tears. "It just seems like a hopeless time, doesn't it?" she asked. Tate looked like he didn't know whether or not to answer. Hayden smiled into the camera suddenly. "But it's not. There is good. And it will overcome." She looked at Tate, whose wide eyes managed to read the TelePrompTer.

"And now to our own Ray Duffey, who is recovering from quite an incident two days ago."

The red light on top of his camera came on, and it took everything in Ray to calm himself enough to look natural in front of the camera. He shoved thoughts of Sam, Hayden, and even his corny report out of his mind and drew upon his years of experience to get him through.

"It all started with a report on a backyard pigsty…"

Hugo's blue shirt collar was soaked with sweat as he stood next to Willis, studying the monitor that held Sam's image. The weatherman was standing by for his segment and…swaying?

"Is he going to pass out?" Hugo asked no one in particular. He grabbed the mike. "Sam, are you okay?"

"I'm fine," Sam answered, smiling with his eyes closed.

"You're on in thirty seconds. Are you going to be all right? We can go to commercial if we need to."

Sam didn't open his eyes. "I'll be fine."

He didn't look fine. He looked as pale as Gilda without her makeup.

Ray's piece was wrapping up, and on any ordinary day Hugo might've been concerned with it. It was pretty much Ray's retelling of the story everyone already knew from the night before, with added commentary about his feelings. It would pass, but Ray wasn't usually one to just pass. Anyway, Hugo had bigger problems this evening.

"Cut to camera two," Willis said, and the two anchors came up.

"Well," Tate said, practically chewing his way through his own over-done charm, "the snow sure took us by surprise."

Hayden added, "Sam, Mother Nature sure can be unpredictable, can't she?"

"Cut to camera three," Willis said, and Sam's pale mug filled the screen.

Sam looked angry. Very angry. Quite a contrast to Tate and Hayden's lighthearted banter. Was Sam taking Hayden's comment about the weather being unpredictable personally? Everyone stared at Sam as he tried to squeeze out a smile. It finally popped through, accompanied by quite a flush in his cheeks. Now he looked embarrassed. Or allergic.

"Well," Sam began, "she certainly can." He chuckled halfheartedly. "Even with all this fancy equipment back here, God can do whatever he wants and he does. I am, after all, a mere mortal." He gestured toward himself and smiled.

Hugo's eyebrows popped up. "Get ready to cut to commercial when I tell you to," he said to Willis.

"I'm the director," Willis complained.

Hugo glared at him. "This isn't about who is in charge, in case you haven't noticed!"

But as they both looked back to the screen, Sam managed to get into the actual weather part of his segment, discussing the snow totals for the state. He was talking very slowly, however, and Hugo was afraid he was going to run too long.

But before they knew it, Sam had left out the day's high temperatures and the night's lows and made his way to the anchor's desk to finish up with the seven-day forecast. It worked out well since they were falling behind on time, and Sam managed to get through only three of the seven days.

"Cut to camera two," Willis said, and a wide shot came up with Sam grinning at Tate and Hayden like they were a pile of money.

"Thanks, Sam," Tate said, trying to maintain his own smile in the awkward situation. "Sounds like we have a cold week in store."

Sam nodded and shifted his eyes to Hayden. "You look hot."

Everyone in the control room froze. "Did he just say she looks hot?" Willis whispered.

Hugo couldn't answer, because he was too worried about getting his heart to restart.

"I am," Hayden said pleasantly. "It's really stuffy in here. But sounds like all I need to do is step outside to cool off!" She engaged the camera with a wide smile then turned to camera three. "Stay with us. Sports is next."

"Go to commercial," Willis wheezed, throwing his head down on his desk.

Hugo was no longer feeling hot or anxious or worried. He was completely numb.

The control-room door flew open suddenly, causing everyone to jump. Roarke walked in, his eyes wide. "The phones are ringing off the hook, and our Web site is getting over a hundred hits a minute."

Hugo's heart sank.

Then Roarke added, "Hayden is a hit!"

Chapter 20

I t was almost eleven o'clock, and Ray couldn't remember feeling more exhausted. But thankfully, the week was over. He thought he might go home and try to get comatose. Watch ESPN for twenty-four hours straight. Maybe there would be a good celebrity poker tournament on. Or a Jack Hanna animal special. Something—anything—to get his mind off everything.

He walked out the back door of the station and was surprised to find Hayden standing against the wall in the exact place he'd seen her earlier in the day when he'd managed to thoroughly embarrass himself.

"Hayden," he said, and she looked up. "You were amazing tonight. Well done."

"Thanks, Ray. You really think so?"

"Haven't you heard? E-mails are pouring in! People loved you."

She laughed. "Well, they don't know me yet."

Self-deprecating humor? He didn't realize she had it in her. "I can't believe how well you were able to pull that off, never having done it before."

"I pictured my mom. Every time I looked in the camera, I pretended I was talking to my mom. It put me at ease."

"The way you handled Sam's asinine comment was…it was great." It occurred to Ray suddenly that perhaps Hayden wasn't aware of the meaning behind Sam's comment. She was, after all, more than a little naive. Ray was about to back-pedal, but Hayden's smile indicated she was fully aware.

"Sam didn't seem himself tonight," she said.

That's an understatement.

"But I think Sam's a nice fellow. I didn't want to embarrass him in front of his viewers."

Ray pressed his lips together because now, more than anything, he wanted to explain what kind of man Sam was—a man who moments before the newscast had been hanging over the toilet in the bathroom, and not because the flu was going around.

But something about Hayden made Ray want to rise above all of that. He realized in an instant that it wasn't that Hayden didn't know things. She was fully aware of what Sam had said on air. But she took the higher road. She put her own selfish needs aside, even to the point of not defending herself against his actions. She'd had every right to put Sam in his place tonight, but instead she made them both look good.

So Ray had a dirty little secret about Sam. He realized he had the same choice Hayden had. He could share the story of how he managed to get Sam on the air and make himself look good. Or he could follow Hayden's lead and keep his mouth shut.

"Well," Ray said, buttoning up his coat, "I hope you have a good weekend."

"I will. Thanks."

Ray walked toward the parking lot, spotting his snow-laden car near the exit. But with each step, a hunch turned into a suspicion, and the suspicion turned into a well-developed thought.

Sam had lied. Of course he had lied. It didn't make sense. First of all, Ray had never even seen Trent and Hayden say anything more than hello to one another. Second, he was pretty certain Hayden was not the kind of woman who would ask a guy out. He wasn't even sure if she would kiss before marriage, so it was hard to imagine her as an aggressive woman.

Ray turned around, and there she stood, under the dim light, leaning against the wall. He wondered why she liked to do that so much. It wasn't like she was coming out for a smoke. Maybe she was really coming out here to cool down because it was stuffy inside.

As if his feet were acting on their own, Ray headed back toward Hayden; she didn't seem to notice him until he was right up on her.

"Hi."

"Did you forget something?"

"No, um, listen. I just wanted to clear something up."

"What?"

"About this weekend…"

"Yes?"

"I know you said you were busy, and I totally respect that. But I just…" Ray couldn't believe his audacity. How desperate was he? "Look, Sam told me you were going out with Trent. Trent's nice and everything, but…are you really going out with Trent?"

Hayden laughed, studying him through jovial eyes. Then she shook her head. "You are persistent, aren't you? Maybe that's what makes you such a good reporter."

Ray smiled back. *Maybe.* He still wanted to know the scoop on Trent.

For the first time since he'd known her, Hayden looked coy. There was a flirtatious expression begging to emerge, but she seemed to keep it well restrained. "Why don't you join us?"

"Excuse me?"

"Are you busy tomorrow at six?"

"Busy? Uh, no…but…" Ray couldn't stop the suspicious eyebrow that popped up. Maybe he didn't know Hayden as well as he thought he did. "So you are going to be with Trent?"

"Meet us at Hattie's Seafood Grill. Six o'clock." She looked at him. "What, now you're bashful? Come on, it'll be fun."

"No…no, it's not that. It's just…I'm not sure…"

"It's at Yale and Second."

"Oh. Right. Yale and Second." He tried to smile. "That clears things up."

"I better get back inside and get my coat. I'm really exhausted."

"Me too."

"I'll see you tomorrow?"

"Sure." He opened the station door for her and then headed back to his car. What had he gotten himself into?

Sitting across from one another at a fast-food restaurant the next day, Roarke and Ray each prepared their tacos and bean burritos. It was barely eleven. Ray had just finished telling his story about his most recent mysterious encounter with Hayden.

"Well, you know what they say," Roarke said. "You can't make people love you, but you can stalk them until they give in."

"I'm not stalking her." Ray said.

"Dude, she turned you down and you went back." Roarke made a face that indicated disgust.

"I didn't go back to ask her out. I went back to clear things up."

"Yeah, and they're real clear now, aren't they?"

"Maybe she doesn't know the rules, of dating, you know?"

Roarke laughed. "Everybody knows the rules of dating. At least the basic ones."

"I don't know. She was homeschooled. I learned the rules by trial and error and a lot of observation. If she was sheltered, maybe she just doesn't know." Ray sighed, shoving his taco to the side. "I don't want to go on a date with Trent and Hayden. How humiliating."

"That would be awkward," Roarke agreed, "The very definition of 'the third wheel.'"

"If I'm going to be a wheel, then I'm going to be a steering wheel."

Roarke laughed. "Good one, man."

Ray watched Roarke doctor his burrito. "So I guess Gilda never read your note?"

"I took it out of her dressing room. I can't stop wondering if something bad has happened to her."

"I think she just got embarrassed about the Botox thing."

"But why? She chose to do it. So it was a little extreme. The Gilda I know is able to handle anything."

"How, um, well do you know her? I mean, she doesn't even know you have feelings for her."

"Look, you don't have to spend romantic dinners together to know a person. I've worked with Gilda. I know things about her, things other people don't know because they don't carefully observe her like I do."

"She's not a zoo animal."

"You know what I mean. Besides, I don't think you have a lot of room to talk. So far, you've managed to get yourself into quite the predicament."

"True," Ray sighed. "You've fallen for a vanishing act."

"And you've fallen for a religious fanatic."

"And they say there aren't any good women out there anymore," Ray said, smiling.

"Well, at least there's fast food."

Hugo hadn't felt this motivated in years, and he could hardly contain himself in the kitchen. He'd whipped up scrambled eggs, bacon, hash browns, toast, and even opened a package of sticky buns.

He'd yet to see his wife and daughter, as they'd been out at some football game and came home after he went to bed. But he was certain that the aroma of his late-morning creation would rouse them.

When it didn't, he clanged some pots and pans together until they finally came shuffling in.

"What's with you?" Jane asked, pulling her bathrobe closed like she thought they might be expecting company.

"Gross, Dad. Bacon? Do you know what's in that?"

Hugo hustled them to the table. "Come on, it's getting cold."

Jane's eyes grew wide. "Is it our anniversary?"

"No," Hugo said, eyeing her. "That's four months away, unless some-one changed the date and didn't tell me."

Jane looked relieved as she served herself some eggs. "Then what's the occasion?"

"I'm just in a good mood," he said, a little song in his voice. Kaylin and Jane exchanged glances.

"Why?" Kaylin asked.

Hugo joined them at the table. "I had a great night at work."

"We missed it, honey. We were out at the game."

"I know. But it was the most extraordinary thing. I can hardly describe it."

"Did Gilda's face go back to normal?" Kaylin said. "Everyone was talking about that at school."

Hugo tried not to let that dampen his mood, though he'd secretly hoped that nobody had noticed.

"No. In fact, Gilda didn't show up for work yesterday." He waited for one of them to ask what amazing thing he did about it. Both focused on their food. "Didn't call, just didn't show up."

Jane looked up. "That's strange."

"Yeah. And by some astronomical string of bad luck, there were no other female anchors available."

"Channel 10 sometimes has a male anchor by himself," Kaylin said.

"You watch Channel 10?"

"Just sometimes." Kaylin looked sheepishly at her food. "What? Patrick Buckley's hot."

Hugo sighed and grabbed a forkful of bacon. "*Anyway,* I had to find a female anchor. But there were none available. So you won't believe what I did."

Several moments of silence passed before either of them looked up, realizing he actually wanted them to ask. Jane pushed her food to one side of her mouth. "What did you do?"

"I used my assistant."

Jane nodded like she was doing her best to pay attention. Kaylin was examining her sticky bun.

"I used *my assistant*," Hugo said again, this time with a particular emphasis that indicated this was something out of the ordinary.

"Judith?"

"Honey, remember? Judith is on maternity leave."

"Oh."

"Hayden Hazard." Hugo laughed, thinking of how absurd it was. "I mean, no experience. Hardly able to talk without mentioning God. I took this amazing gamble, and it paid off! Everyone loved her."

"That's nice," Jane said. "Listen, I'm going to need you to go to the store today."

Hugo's revelry faded. "The grocery store?"

"Yes, Hugo, the grocery store." Jane looked annoyed. "If you want to eat this week."

He stabbed at his eggs with his fork. "I'm exhausted. I don't want to go to the store."

"You don't think I'm tired too?" Jane said, her eyes fiery. Hugo looked at Kaylin, who averted her eyes. "I work, too, if you haven't noticed. Kaylin has practice, and I'm in charge of bringing brownies. Would you like to stay home and bake brownies instead?"

"Are they instant?"

"Funny. As a matter of fact, they're boxed. You have to add eggs and water and oil. You wanna try it?"

"No," Hugo said. He rose from the table. He'd suddenly lost his appetite.

"Where are you going?" Jane asked.

"To get dressed."

"Fine." She gestured toward the table. "But remember. You cook, you clean."

By 5:30 p.m. Ray had nearly worked himself into a frenzy. He changed his mind every two or three minutes about whether or not he should meet Trent and Hayden for dinner. First of all, what would Trent think when Ray showed up on his date? Second, how pathetic would that be to show up on someone else's date? Third, why would she invite him on her date with Trent? Fourth, why did he care so much about what Trent thought? Fifth, did she really invite two men on one date? Sixth, if he didn't go, would he miss his only opportunity to make a good impression on Hayden? Maybe this was how they did it wherever she was raised. Maybe this was how they did it in the olden days…a suitor sort of thing. That would be awkward.

Not that things weren't already headed that direction.

Seventh, who exactly would be paying for the meal? Did dutch apply, except he and Trent would split Haydn's meal? Eighth, truth be told, Hayden's brand of evangelism, or whatever it was, made him uncomfortable. Ninth, why in the world was he considering this? He had his dignity, and he wasn't about to share a woman.

But tenth, what was he afraid of? A little competition? He could hold his own against Trent.

Ray spun to begin another pacing stretch across his apartment. But then he stopped.

"Duffey, make a decision."

For a solid five minutes, Ray stood in the middle of the apartment and did the only thing that seemed appropriate for his current circumstance. He prayed for wisdom while he doused himself in cologne.

Chapter 21

A t Hattie's Seafood Grill, disco music greeted Ray when he opened the door. To the right, he could see a deck with colorful umbrellas overlooking a parking lot. In the middle of the room, a line of waiters and waitresses did a little dance that they all looked like they loathed.

He was still wrestling with his thoughts. Eleventh, he wasn't a big seafood fan. But he would manage. There was always salad. Or chicken. The menu was the least of his concerns.

He was purposely five minutes late because he didn't want to be standing around waiting to see how this would all unfold.

As soon as he turned to his right, he saw Hayden. She noticed him too and smiled and waved. Ray waved back and immediately noticed Trent, who stood nearby, slumping, his hands stuffed in his pockets. He saw Ray and gave a little nod. At least he didn't look surprised. He did look terribly uncomfortable, however.

"Hey," Ray said, trying to play it cool, like there was nothing abnormal going on.

"Hey," Trent replied.

"Ray, I'm so glad you came." Hayden touched his arm. "We're just waiting to be seated."

"Ah." Ray couldn't help but look at Trent, but Trent was staring at a lobster hanging from the ceiling.

Ray really wanted to stuff his hands in his own pockets, but then he and Trent would probably look nearly identical, and the whole point of this, he assumed, was to stand out in the crowd. Trent seemed to be ignoring the ordeal all together, so Ray decided he could take advantage of the opportunity.

"I can't tell you how well you did last night," he said.

"That's nice of you to say, Ray. I did the best I could, and God blessed the effort."

Trent sighed heavily, and both Ray and Hayden glanced at him.

Hayden continued. "I learned some things. All those questions the anchors throw at the reporters after their segments are almost always scripted. I guess I really jarred Jill when I asked her a couple of questions after her segment!" Hayden laughed. Ray looked at Trent again. He wasn't laughing.

"What did you think of the newscast last night, Trent?" he asked.

Trent looked at them both. "Yeah, it was good. Hayden, you were really great." He looked like he could hardly muster a smile.

"So how long is the wait?" Ray asked.

"We should be seated pretty soon. But more time to talk, right?"

"Right," Ray smiled. And then he noticed a woman walking toward them from inside the restaurant, maneuvering around chairs. She looked remarkably like Hayden. In fact, she could've been Hayden's twin, except her hair was cut a little shorter and pulled back in a ponytail. She wore a sweatshirt, jeans, and sneakers.

And to Ray's surprise, she walked right up to them.

"Ray, I want you to meet my sister, Mackenzie. We call her Mack."

Mack smiled at Ray and extended her hand. She then shook Ray's with the might of an arm wrestler. "Pleased to meet you, Ray."

"Nice to meet you," Ray said. He felt like he was drowning in a sea of confusion.

"She's in from Las Vegas, where she works," Hayden said.

"Oh," Ray said, trying to keep up the pleasantries. "What do you do?"

"I'm a police officer."

"Oh. Good."

"My sister had quite a night last night, from what I hear," Mack said.

"Doesn't surprise me, though. I always knew she would do great things."

Hayden laughed, hugging her. "Mack has always believed in me, even when I didn't believe in myself."

"How nice," Ray said. "Excuse me. I need to use the rest room."

"Back there," Mack pointed. "But be careful. They just mopped the floors."

He made his way around the tables to the men's room, where all he did was stand inside the stall, buying himself time to figure it all out. So this wasn't a date? Just a get-together?

Ray wasn't sure how much time had passed, but he knew he had to get back out there. His deodorant, the one that advertised maximum effectiveness on big, sweaty men, was no match for an awkward dating experience. He stuck two paper towels into his pits, squeezed his arms down to his side, then dropped them out, and threw them in the trash.

"Just roll with it, Duffey," Ray whispered. He walked out and could see that they were already seated. Trent sat next to…Mack. And the seat next to Hayden was empty.

Ray joined them just in time to hear Hayden say, "And Trent, Mack loves movies too! We weren't allowed to see them when we were children, and we're still pretty picky about what we see now, but you will find Mack at the theater every Saturday!"

"It's true," Mack said with a smile and a shrug.

"Great," Trent said, but the word seemed aimed at the fact that Ray was back.

"They really have a lot in common," Hayden said to Ray, gesturing across the table where they sat. "That's one reason I thought they'd hit it off."

Ray looked at Trent, who was scouring the menu. *So this is a double date?* Ray laughed, causing everyone to look up. He tried to play it off by pointing to a dancing crab on the far wall, but he couldn't begin to express his relief. That's why Hayden had asked Trent out—she was setting him up with her sister, who was going to be in town. And then she'd decided to bring Ray along as *her* date. He laughed again.

Mack grinned. "You're right, Hayden. He does have a peculiar laugh."

Trent finally smiled.

Halfway through dinner, Ray realized how much he was enjoying himself. Mack and Hayden were cute together, and it was evident they were best friends. Ray sat and listened to them tell amusing stories of their youth, which included a lot of work with their parents' clown business. As entertaining as these two were, he had a hard time picturing either of them in clown makeup.

"I'm terrified of clowns," Hayden said, laughing. "Finally my parents let me work as the office manager."

"I still don't know what's so scary about clowns," Mack said. "They're fun and bright and cheerful."

"With weird-looking smiles and eyes," Hayden interjected.

"We tried everything to get her over it. We prayed for her, laid hands on her, took her to our pastor. Nothing worked."

"Finally my dad said it didn't have anything to do with the devil, it was just how I was made." Ray watched Hayden laugh at the memory, her nostrils flaring in just the right way to make his heart flutter.

"God made you unique, that's for sure!" Mack said as the laughter died down.

"So Mack," Ray said, "how long have you been a police officer?"

"Five years," she said, "I've been approached about doing undercover work."

Hayden frowned. "You have?"

"I told you that."

"Yes, but I thought we agreed it was too dangerous."

"No, you worried it was too dangerous, and I told you that God would bring me home when He was ready."

"Well, you don't have to help him out any, you know."

Mack looked at Ray. "*Anyway*, I've always wanted to do it. I've dropped hints here and there to my superiors. You don't really apply to get in. If they see potential, they'll approach you. We'll see how it all plays out."

"Good for you. Sounds like an interesting career."

"I like helping people. And I like to see justice served."

As they talked, Ray saw that Mack had always been the protective older sister, and though they looked very similar, with bright blue eyes, white blonde hair, and tan skin, Mack had more of an edge to her. She seemed more athletic, the tomboy type. They'd mentioned there were five other Hazard siblings. Ray couldn't imagine what the rest of them were like.

Yet even tough-as-nails Mack had a certain ingénue sense to her, and Ray was having a hard time seeing her in the middle of the grit and grime of the crime world. But at this point, he couldn't say he would be surprised by too much from them. Their "other world" sensibilities hadn't failed them yet, it seemed.

"You girls should go take a look from the deck," Trent said suddenly. "The view."

"Really?" Hayden asked.

Ray glanced out to the deck. What view?

"I heard there's a family of ducks out there. With little baby ones."

"Awww!" both girls said, clutching their chests.

"Come on!" Hayden said, and they stood.

Ray stood too, but Trent whispered, "Sit!"

He watched the girls walk off then looked at Trent. "What?"

"I've got to get out of here!"

"What? Why?"

"Are you kidding me? Sorry, man, but Mack isn't really my type. Hayden mentioned her sister was coming to town, and I dropped a billion hints that she should set us up on a blind date."

"Why would you do that?"

"Well, Hayden's really hot, but a little…you know…religious. So I thought maybe her sister was hot and not so religious. It was probably a rebound decision."

"Rebound? Didn't you break up with your girlfriend a year ago?"

"I'm about to go crazy sitting here."

"You can't make it through dinner?"

"Look, I've been on some weird dates before, but not once have I prayed on a date, and as far as I can remember, I've never talked about the devil before."

Ray winced. Earlier, after they'd ordered, Mack talked about how she'd believed the devil's lies about why she couldn't get dates. Along with their fondness for religion, the Hazard girls also didn't seem to have an earnest sensor. And "prayed on a date" referred to blessing their food.

"Trent, look, just give her a chance. You might like her the more you get to know her."

"Ray, I realize you're having fun here. I don't know why I'm surprised. You're a churchgoer and are probably familiar with the homeschool crowd. But I'm not into all this," he said, waving his hands in the air like he was trying to reproduce magic.

"Don't stereotype. Sure, they were homeschooled, and they're into their faith, but that doesn't mean they're not worth your time."

"Church doesn't bother me, okay, Ray? You go to church, and I've never once felt uncomfortable around you. You keep it to yourself, you know? I mean, Hayden's always blabbing on and on about God and sin and grace. The only grace I want to hear about is the one on TV that's attached to Will." Trent smiled at his own pathetic joke. Then he sighed.

"Why would I think her sister would be any different? All I know is that I've made a huge mistake and I have to get out of here."

Ray folded his arms together. "And how exactly do you plan on doing that?"

Trent grabbed his coat off the back of his chair and glanced toward the deck, where the two girls were still searching for the family of ducks. "By leaving."

"You don't think that's going to make for some awkward moments with Hayden at work?"

"It can't be any more awkward than it is now. Besides, maybe she'll keep her distance and stop trying to get me to come to church." He stood.

"Trent, wait. Man, don't do this. You're not this kind of guy."

"I'm not?" Trent laughed. "Tell them what kind of guy I am."

"You want me to make up an excuse for you?"

Trent took his keys out of his pocket. "Whatever. I don't care."

"Hey!" Ray said. "At least pay for your dinner."

Trent sighed and pulled fifteen dollars out of his pocket, throwing it on the table. "What are you, some kind of newly formed saint?" Then he whizzed out of the restaurant. Ray could hear the tires screeching just as Hayden and Mack returned to the table.

"Where's Trent?" Mack asked.

Ray looked down. He hadn't had an opportunity to figure out what he was going to say. He glanced up at Mack, who was staring at the money on the table.

"He, um, had to leave. Suddenly."

Hayden and Mack exchanged glances.

"The news business," Ray said. "Always on call, you know. He said he was sorry and—"

"Fifteen bucks?" Mack held up the money. "He just paid for himself. Which means..." She looked at Ray. "He bolted, didn't he?"

Ray glanced at Hayden, whose eyes glistened like she was about to cry. She seemed the more upset of the two. But he knew Mack was smart enough not to buy into any story he would make up. "Yeah."

"Mack, I'm so sorry," Hayden said. "This whole thing was probably a big mistake. I just thought Trent seemed kind of cool, like he really wanted to meet you."

Mack looked embarrassed, but not devastated. "It's because I'm a cop, isn't it? Guys are usually threatened by that."

Unsure if he should spill the beans on the real reason, Ray nodded slowly. He decided to change the subject.

"Look, let's forget about Trent. What do you say? I'm buying everyone's dinner tonight, and then we'll take Trent's lousy fifteen dollars and go get some ice cream!"

Hayden laughed. "Ray, that sounds perfect!"

"Who needs that loser anyway, right?" Ray asked, folding the money and putting on a cheerful face.

Hayden touched his arm, and with the kindest expression he'd ever seen, she leaned in and whispered, "Trent's not a loser. He's just misguided."

Chapter 22

I n a large circle of twenty-four people, Ray sat quietly, holding his Bible in one hand and his cup of coffee in the other. He kept stirring it, as if he might take a drink any second. Of course, he never did and nobody ever noticed. But he kept it by his side just in case he felt the need to get up and stretch his legs. His Sunday-school class tended to run long at times, and the only acceptable reason to get up was to refill your coffee. Even grabbing another doughnut was frowned upon, mostly because everyone thought you were a pig and you should throw more than a buck into the donations basket they passed around during the praise-and-prayer time.

Lydia, the self-proclaimed announcer for the singles class, was standing and speaking in a loud and clear voice, something she'd learned from Toastmasters. Every week she brought a new technique from that class to this class. One week, while giving details about the singles' hay ride, she made deliberate eye contact with every person in the class. And then there was the week that she learned to project, which came across as shouting.

This morning, she detailed plans for an evangelistic outreach they were putting together for the Christmas season. They would take fliers door to door in the surrounding neighborhoods, announcing their "crusade" would be held at a nearby park. People needed to bring blankets and lawn chairs, but hot cocoa, cider, and cookies would be provided. There would be live music, a message, and a skit.

Ray looked around while Lydia droned on and on. Half the class was listening; the other half was observing their doughnuts or their coffee or both.

Ray had hardly slept the night before. His date with Hayden and her sister after Trent bolted left him confused. How could he feel so at peace with a woman who continued to surprise him and put him on edge? She was never safe to be around. She continued to challenge his faith and the way he thought it was supposed to be done. The thing was, it wasn't like Hayden was thinking about it or trying to evangelize him or even make a point. It was just who she was. She never thought about the implications or the fallout. There was something refreshing and terrifying about that. On one hand, Ray knew exactly where Hayden stood, and he didn't have to worry about finding out about a hidden side to her. It was all out in the open. On the other hand, Ray knew that a certain part of him felt embarrassed to be around her, afraid of what she might say to him or to someone else. Yet he was certain he'd never met a nicer or more sincere person.

These thoughts kept him tossing and turning all night. And now, during doughnut, coffee, and announcement time, they kept him fidgety. He stood to get a new stirrer and pour himself a little more coffee. Most at the singles group knew him as Ray, the soft-spoken newsreporter, though no one could ever remember what station he worked for. Probably because nobody ever watched his station.

A few asked about the stitches across his forehead when he arrived and mentioned they'd heard something about a reporter getting attacked. But that was it.

He felt compelled to speak up. Why? Why couldn't he just sit here, uninvolved as usual?

Just keep quiet about it, he told himself. There was no reason to say anything. Why would he say anything? What would compel him to—

"I have a thought."

The entire room turned to look at him by the coffee and doughnut table, surprise on their faces. Lydia looked unsure as to what to do when someone interrupted her carefully planned speech. Her mouth hung open in midsentence.

"I'm just asking a question here. But maybe we're going about this wrong. I mean, we do these crusades, and we usually get about five home-less people and a few relatives."

"You have another idea?" asked Glen the class president.

Ray shrugged. "It's not so much an idea as a…a…" He set down his coffee. "Look, it's like this. This girl at my work, she's kind of—I don't know—radical I guess you could say. She holds nothing back. She just says it how it is, and she's compelled to tell everyone about her faith. In a way it's kind of obnoxious and unnerving." Ray laughed at some of his memories. "But at the same time, she's turning people on their heads. They don't know what to do with her, but they have to address her, you know? Or at least what she's saying to them. With no problem, she just looks at you and speaks the truth."

Glen said, "Where, exactly, did she learn this technique?"

Lydia said, "I bet she learned it from a Rick Warren book."

"It's not from a book," Ray said, but everyone started jumping in.

"Well, if it's not from Beth Moore, I'm just not sure that it's right for me," said Jenna. "I really connect with her teachings."

"Didn't Max Lucado write a book about that?" someone else asked.

"If you have to do it in forty days, I'm not in," added another. "A week works better with my schedule."

Ray waved his hands for everyone to stop. "People, there's not a manual for this. It's just who she is. She believes so deeply in what she's saying that she doesn't think it's strange to be saying it."

"Saying what?" Glen asked.

Ray tried to get his thoughts together so he would sound like he was making sense. "It's kind of hard to explain, but she's always talking about God to anyone who will listen, and she's always praying for people. She's concerned for people, even those who aren't concerned for her. She makes me feel…uncomfortable."

"Wait a minute," Glen said. "That doesn't sound like anything we'd be interested in. Remember, our whole objective is to connect to people.

That's why we go to their homes and leave door-hangers. We want them to understand *we're* coming to *them*."

"And what exactly does she do once she's offended them?" someone else asked.

"I don't know," Ray said. "I don't think she thinks about it."

"See, there's the problem," Glen said. "You can't just go up to someone, with no idea about their past, and start preaching to them."

"She doesn't really preach. It's more like—"

"At my work," Liza, a loan officer, began, "we're not allowed to have any religious symbols on our desk or our clothes. So I have to get really creative. One day I lined my sticky notes up in the form of a cross." She snickered. "Nobody caught on! I was sure I would get caught, but my boss walked right up to my desk and didn't even notice."

Glen said, "Look, Ray, if you make people feel uncomfortable, why would they want to come back? We have to show them how much we love and care for them, that we accept them, you know?"

Ray sighed. Why couldn't he explain this? It was like trying to capture the wind. Nobody got what he was trying to say.

"She's just made me think," he finally said. "Maybe we need to think about getting out of our comfort zone a little, that's all."

Glen smiled and started passing out fliers. "Exactly, Ray. That's why we offer this crusade every year. We are getting out of our comfort zone. Everyone knows how uncomfortable it is to go into neighborhoods alone."

"That's why we go in pairs," said Liza.

Ray grabbed a second doughnut and went back to his chair.

Pulling into his apartment complex, Ray saw Roarke waiting on the stairs for him. "What are you doing here?"

"Waiting for you, dude," he said, standing.

"How long have you been here?"

"Not long. I knew you were at church." He moved aside so Ray could climb the stairs and unlock his door.

"Come on in," he invited. "You want to order pizza?"

"I'm not hungry," Roarke said. "How was your date?"

Ray joined him on the couch. "It was nothing like what I expected."

"Is that a good thing?"

Ray laughed. "It ended up being a good thing. I met her sister."

"Really? There are more Hazards out there?"

"A lot more. Her sister's name is Mack, and they're like night and night."

"Huh." Roarke chuckled. "So, do you have chemistry?"

"I think so," Ray said. "I think I really like her. She's nothing like anyone I ever pictured myself with. But she challenges me, you know? Makes me reexamine everything I ever thought to be right and true."

"Plus, she's hot."

"But not in a 'this room's stuffy' sort of way."

Roarke laughed. "I wonder what got into Sam Friday night."

Ray shook his head, clamping his mouth shut. Then Ray noticed Roarke reaching into his back pocket. He pulled out four envelopes. "Here," he said, handing them to Ray.

"What are these?"

"I found them. I think they're from Mr. Green."

Ray looked at the unopened envelopes, then at Roarke. "Are these for real?"

"Look authentic to me. They're postmarked a few weeks apart from each other, sent to the station. First one about three months ago. There's no address, but in the corner it says 'P.G.'"

"Where did you find these?"

Roarke suddenly developed an interest in the television—which was off.

"Roarke?"

"In her condo," he mumbled. "This morning."

"You went to her condo this morning?"

"I was looking for her, okay? I'm worried. I think something has happened to her."

"You broke into her condo?"

"I didn't go crashing through the glass, if that's what you mean. I picked the lock on her deck door. Nearly killed myself trying to get over the wall there. But anyway, there's no sign of her. Her place looked like nobody had been there in days."

"Roarke, you can't just go snooping around someone's home!"

"I wasn't snooping. I came across those letters when I looked in her desk drawer."

"That's snooping."

"Snooping is when you're looking for something of someone's that you know they shouldn't have. I was looking for any evidence that Gilda might be okay."

Ray sighed and looked at the letters. "I don't know if I should open these."

"So you'd rather stick with interviewing yourself about how you got beaten up by this man?"

"I fell and hit my head."

"Whatever you say. It's your decision. Do whatever you want with them." Roarke rose from the couch and walked to the door. "Glad your date went well, man."

"Thanks." Ray couldn't tear his gaze from the envelopes.

"I'll see you tomorrow. Sweeps week, here we come," Roarke said. "I have a good feeling this time."

Ray glanced at him. "You do?"

"Yeah. Something tells me we're going to be the station to watch."

Roarke left and Ray clutched the envelopes. Then he opened the first letter.

Chapter 23

H ugo came in early Monday to gear up for sweeps week without their top anchor. He listened to his voice mail, and one of the messages was from Julia Richter, who called to let Hugo know that she'd gotten her teeth replaced and should be ready to go tonight.

But the rest of the voice mail messages, from viewers and station personnel alike, were about how much they liked Hayden Hazard. His e-mail in-box was full of the same. So what was he to do? Use Hayden all week? Part of the week? Bet his entire career that she didn't just get lucky Friday night?

His phone rang and he snatched it up to grab a break from the relentless thoughts that plowed through his mind. "Hello?"

"Hugo, what are you doing at work?" asked Jane.

"What do you mean?"

"You don't normally go in until noon or one."

"It's sweeps week, Jane. Everyone comes in early and works full days."

He could hear the huffiness in her voice. "Well, you were supposed to do laundry this morning. I called to tell you not to wash that green blouse, that I need to take it to the dry cleaner."

"I'll do laundry later. You know how important sweeps week is."

"I know." But her voice sounded distant.

Hugo blew a huge sigh into the phone. He hoped it sounded like rushing wind in her ear.

He glanced out his glass wall to make sure nobody lingered outside. "Jane, I don't think our little arrangement is working out all that well. Sure, there's a parent home for Kaylin at every waking moment, but what about us? We never see each other except on the weekends, when we're exhausted. And you know what? I don't like doing laundry. I *hate* doing laundry. When I have time off, you know what I want to do? Play golf! Or get a newspaper and read it on the couch. Not while I'm waiting for the dryer buzzer."

She gasped. "Hugo, what has gotten into you?"

"I'm simply telling you that I'm forty-six years old and I want to feel like a man, like I have some control over my household and that I have a wife who understands why I need that."

"Seriously, Hugo," she said, her tone low, "are you on something? Are you doing drugs?"

"I'm not on drugs..." Hugo glanced at the pill bottle in his half-open desk drawer. "Listen to me, just for a minute. Really."

"Fine," she said tartly.

"What if you quit your job?"

"What?"

"Listen!" Hugo barked, then tried a calmer voice. "Just listen."

"My husband's gone mad," he heard her whisper away from the phone, then she returned. "Fine, I'm listening."

"Jane, we're running our household like a corporation. We clock in and out, and we're so scheduled that we hardly resemble a family anymore. When was the last time we had a home-cooked meal?"

"Saturday morning."

Hugo rolled his eyes. Why was he even trying to explain? He took a deep breath and tried again. "Jane, maybe we can trade in the Suburban for a car. There's only three of us. We can make it on one income."

"How do you figure that?" she snapped. "We can barely pay our bills as it is."

"We just make cuts. We do without some things. We don't have to go to Hawaii every year. Why not go to the Ozarks, or stay around the city and go to the movies? Get rid of the digital cable that we hardly ever watch. Share a cell—"

"Hugo," she said, concern in her tone, "are you having a midlife crisis?"

"Maybe," he said. "I'm not saying any of this is your fault."

"This is not my fault!"

"That's what I just said."

"You just want me to quit my job and stay home and be your little housewife?"

"I'll quit my job then."

Hugo wasn't even sure if he'd said that out loud, but judging by the deep breathing he heard on the other end of the phone, it must've made its way out of his mouth.

"You'll quit your job? Is that what you said?"

Hugo wasn't sure he meant that exactly. Maybe he knew he'd be fired, so he was just beating Chad to the punch. But then again, why not take a lesser job? Why not go back to being a regular old producer instead of the executive producer? All he did was worry, all of the time, about everything. Why not be a stay-at-home dad and cook breakfast every morning?

"Hello?" Jane's voice crackled through the phone.

"I'm here."

"Is that what you said?"

Hugo's voice was soft. "Maybe we just need to rework some things, you know? Maybe I could take a less demanding job. Maybe you could work out of the house."

There was total silence on the phone now, and Hugo couldn't even hear Jane breathing or whispering to co-workers.

"Listen," he finally said, "let's just leave this up in the air right now. We can think about it, talk about it, maybe—"

Click.

Hugo held the receiver up against his ear, hoping she would come back, but the phone was still dead.

Then he heard another click, and his office door opened. It was Ray Duffey.

"I'll get back to you," Hugo said and hung up the phone. "Yes, Mr. Duffey?"

Ray closed the door and looked like something was bothering him. "Can we talk?"

Hugo gestured to the chair. "It's sweeps week, so this had better be important."

"It is, sir."

"All right. What's wrong?"

"It's about the water treatment plant explosion."

"What about it?"

"You've got Jill covering the story, sir, and I think that's a mistake."

"Why?"

"Because I don't think she's really getting to the bottom of it."

"She has two great eyewitness interviews. What's not good about that?"

"She had two other eyewitnesses. We don't need anymore eyewitnesses. We need the truth."

Ray paused. "A source at the police department told me that Howard Crumm was suspected but never convicted of embezzlement."

"Who is Howard Crumm?"

"The director of the sewage plant."

"I've never heard of him. We didn't get any interviews with him."

"That's because he had his deputy director answer all the media questions. Nobody thought much about it. Everyone was focused on casualties. But I think Crumm didn't want his name out there."

"When did you find this out?"

Ray hesitated, wanting to tell him that he'd tried to give Jill the info and she wouldn't take it. "After Jill ran her story. But if you give me the assignment, I'll run with it. I think there's a lot more to this story than meets the eye."

"So the director has a possible criminal history. What does that have to do with the explosion?" Hugo turned toward his computer, pretending to scan an important e-mail, but he couldn't get Jane off his mind. She had never—not once—hung up on him.

"Seemingly nothing, except…well, I've uncovered more evidence."

Hugo's phone rang again and he snatched it up, praying it was Jane.

"Hugo, it's Captain Wynn."

"Captain, what can I do for you?" Hugo asked. He couldn't ever remember the captain calling him before. Usually he dealt with the reporters.

"It's about Gilda Braun."

"What about her?"

"She hasn't turned up over the weekend, and I now believe there is foul play involved."

"What?" Hugo looked at Ray, who curiously listened. "Why do you say that?"

"I sent some men over there this morning to see if she was home. Someone had picked the lock to her back door."

"Someone went into her home this weekend?"

"It appears that way. The lock was intact Friday."

"So what are you saying?"

"I think we need to open this up as a criminal investigation."

"Okay…" Hugo's mind spun.

"You should probably send a reporter out here."

"Why?" Hugo asked.

"Don't you want first chance at the story?"

"What story?"

"You're the news guy. You don't think a local news anchor gone missing is a story?"

"Wait…wait a minute," Hugo said. "I don't want this thing to make the news. Why can't you do your investigation quietly and get back to me?"

"I can't promise that another station won't get wind of it."

Hugo stared at his desk. How could this be happening?

"Besides, you owe me."

"Excuse me?" Hugo asked.

"After how I was treated Friday, I think it's a good move on your part to make sure you show me, and my department, in a good light."

"What are you talking about? How were you treated?"

"Why don't you ask Ray Duffey about that?"

Hugo looked up at Ray, who stared at the carpet. At the pause, Ray looked up.

"I'll do that," Hugo said.

"We'll be designating the condo as a crime scene in about fifteen minutes."

"All right."

Hugo hung up the phone and looked at Ray. "What's going on?"

"Sir?"

"Captain Wynn is ticked off and says he was treated poorly."

A worried expression crossed Ray's face. "I…I had to cancel an interview with him Friday."

"Why?"

Ray fumbled his words. "Look, I decided there was more to the Green story than meets the eye. I was supposed to interview Captain Wynn about the investigation into Green's assault, but something told me…well, I went to Green's house."

"I know. I told you not to. Mr. Arbus indicated that Mr. Green is threatening to sue us."

"I know. And I'm sorry about that. But he said something very interesting."

"What?"

"He told me I should ask Gilda Braun why he was so angry."

"Gilda? What does she have to do with this?"

"That's what I wanted to find out, sir."

"Well, speaking of Gilda, that's who Captain Wynn was calling about. Apparently someone broke into her condo this weekend."

Ray's eyes widened.

"They think there may be foul play involved."

"Why?"

"Because someone broke into her condo."

"Well that doesn't mean anything."

"It apparently means something to Captain Wynn. He wants us to cover the story."

"He does?"

"He said we owe him. So get out there pronto." Hugo paused, trying to gather his thoughts. "Do we even want this to be a story?"

"Well...I was 'the story,' and all that happened to me was I banged my head."

"You got assaulted on live television. We didn't have a choice about coverage. This is *Gilda,* though." Hugo knew a certain level of fear permeated his tone.

"And with the captain calling already, it doesn't look like we have a choice in this case either."

Hugo stood and closed his eyes. Already, it was turning out to be another bad day.

"Where are you going?" Ray said.

"To talk to Mr. Arbus. Tell him what's going on."

"Oh."

Hugo walked past Ray and was almost out the door, when he stopped. "You mentioned you had more evidence about the wastewater treatment plant?"

Ray shook his head. "No. I mean, it's nothing important. It can wait."

Hugo walked out, his ear trained for his office phone, hoping it would ring and hoping it would be Jane.

"Roarke!" Ray said, scrambling toward him. Roarke looked up, his normally unexpressive face lighting up. "Roarke!"

"What?"

"Keep your voice down!" Ray hissed.

"My voice is down. What's with you?" Roarke said.

Ray looked around to make sure he hadn't drawn attention. Roarke looked around too. Then their eyes met.

"The police went to Gilda's condo this morning. They saw the picked lock on the deck door. They're calling it a crime scene! Hugo's sending me out to cover it right now!"

Roarke grew pale.

"You have to tell them, Roarke."

"Tell them! Why?"

"Because, they think it's a crime scene, and it's not."

"It might be," Roarke said. "*Something* has happened to Gilda. I'm glad the police are taking this seriously."

"Roarke—"

"If a picked lock makes them take a second look, then good. Maybe they'll find her. I'm telling you, Ray, I have a bad feeling about this."

"Roarke, you can't be serious!" Ray lowered his voice. "You have to tell them it was you!"

"No way, dude. Then they'll ask why I was there and I'll have to explain the love letters."

"But—"

"Besides, how are you going to explain those letters I gave you?"

Ray sighed.

"Did you read them?"

"Yeah," Ray said.

"What'd they say?"

Ray turned so his voice wouldn't drift into the newsroom. "They were unbelievable. Four letters signed P.G. about the sewage plant!"

"What? The sewage plant? How is Green involved?"

"According to the letters, this P.G. used to work for the sewage plant. He wrote Gilda four letters telling her that a chemical they had begun using was dangerous. His first letter told her how much he trusted her, because she looked like a nice woman and seemed to really care about the city. The second letter reiterated his admiration and explained again his concerns about the plant. He'd been fired, he says, because he protested the switching of the chemicals, said they were unsafe and weren't worth risking people's lives by saving money.

"By the third letter, he was clearly upset that no one had explored his story. He writes again about the dangers of the chemicals and says the station has an obligation to investigate.

"The fourth letter—well, let's just say it can be summed up by Mr. Green's left hook to my head."

Roarke looked dumbfounded.

"That's why he was so mad. It didn't have anything to do with the pigs. He hates our station because he felt like Gilda didn't do anything."

"That doesn't sound like Gilda," Roarke said. "Gilda would at least look into something like that."

"I agree. But Green is illiterate, or close to it. Most of the words were spelled wrong and written in large letters. Sometimes the letters were backward. The writing was in pencil, very heavy on the page, almost like a kid using a crayon. These letters could've easily come across to Gilda as from some crazed maniac."

Roarke shook his head. "I know Gilda. She wouldn't dismiss a letter like that just because of misspelled words."

"It sounds like she did, Roarke. I'm going to get to the bottom of this. There have to be answers." Ray looked at his watch. "I have to go. Hugo wants me shooting footage at the crime scene."

"You don't want to keep the captain waiting." As Ray turned to go, Roarke grabbed his arm. "Not a word about my being there."

"Roarke, just think—"

"Not a word."

Ray sighed and looked into his friend's eyes. Roarke never asked for much from their friendship. Ray could guess how humiliated Roarke would be if the police found out about his love letters. He nodded and turned, racing toward his desk for his notepad. Beaker was probably already in the van, waiting for him.

The shrill sound of the phone drew his hand toward it. *Don't answer it, Duffey.* He looked at his watch. He still had a few minutes to spare. And something told him this phone call was going to be important. *You don't have time…*

"Hello?"

"Ray Duffey?" The voice was digitally scrambled and sounded like that of a man who'd smoked eighteen packs a day. A chill tickled his spine and stood his hair on end.

"Yes?" Ray breathed.

"I have some important information for you."

Chapter 24

Hugo watched Chad Arbus's expression carefully, but to his surprise, Chad's face lacked any expression at all. The response was only silence as Chad folded his fingers together and placed his hands against his mouth, which propped his head up as he stared at his desk.

"Sir?" Hugo finally asked.

"I'm thinking, Hugo," he said. "Sometimes you have to think."

Hugo wanted to talk, not think. He wanted to talk this thing through, figure it out.

Finally Chad said, "Why not?"

"You're serious?" Hugo asked.

"Of course I'm serious. This is a story, Hugo. Surely you recognize a story when you see one."

"But we're talking about Gilda. How are we supposed to remain objective? I mean, it was one thing to cover Ray's story, but this could be serious. Something terrible could've happened to Gilda."

"And as our luck would have it, it happened during sweeps week." Chad glanced at Hugo. "It sounds cold, Hugo, but it's the news business. We can't pick and choose how the world decides to self-destruct and who goes with it. We can only offer pictures and commentary."

"Gilda wouldn't want us to do this," Hugo complained. "She has a reputation to think about. She is highly regarded in this community, and she would never approve."

"That might be true, but what can we do? She's not around to give her opinion, is she?"

"We don't even know if this is a real story yet. We don't know what has happened to her. We can't report on what we don't know."

As Chad unthreaded his fingers, a tolerant smile spread thinly across his face. "All right, Hugo, if that's the way you want to play it."

"Play what?"

"You're going to sit across from me and act like your conscience is bothering you."

Hugo looked away. Was his conscience bothering him? Shouldn't it be? He looked back at Chad, who now wore an amused expression. Hugo tried another angle. "Look, Ray may be on to something. He says there may be more to the sewage plant explosion."

"The sewage plant is an old story, Hugo. Surely you know that."

"Maybe it has run its course, maybe it hasn't. But there still hasn't been a good explanation for what caused the explosion. There may be more to the story. If anyone can find out, Ray Duffey can."

Chad shook his head. "No. Let it go." His eyes narrowed. "You don't have the guts to say it, but I do."

"Say what?"

Chad leaned forward. "Hugo, you and I both know this business is not about covering the best news. It's about sensationalizing the news you do cover."

Hugo felt embarrassed, for himself and for Chad. It wasn't what the news business used to be about. Not in the old days. It used to be about keeping viewers informed with real news they could use. Not car chases and people dangling off the sides of buildings.

Chad grinned. "We could cover an apple dropping from a tree, and with the right music, sad-looking people, and sound bites, we create an angle. And that's what it's all about. The angle. Something mundane becomes something sensational. And then it becomes news." Chad leaned back in his chair without taking his eyes off Hugo. "I'm still waiting for that independent analysis to come back, Hugo. And when it does, it will be interesting to see who the weak links are. Know what I mean? Somewhere there's a weak link."

Hugo stood.

"Where are you going?" Chad asked casually, apparently surprised that Hugo had actually stood without Chad's prompting.

"To work," Hugo said, making a dramatic gesture toward the door.

"Are you putting that girl back at the anchor's desk?"

"Her name is Hayden Hazard. And yes."

Chad nodded. "I think it's a good plan. She has the right look, seems to be able to connect with the audience. I'd like to see her in a blouse cut a bit lower. Gilda always liked to unbutton the top two. Not too much, but enough."

"Why don't we worry about getting through the newscast without imploding tonight, okay?" Hugo walked out, hoping Chad would threaten to fire him. If he were fired today, he doubted he would shed a tear.

Ray looked around the newsroom, then at his watch. He was going to be late to the scene if he didn't leave within a couple of minutes. He didn't want to risk ticking off the captain again, but as he clutched the phone to his ear, he also knew he couldn't just hang up. Not without asking a few questions.

"What kind of information?" Ray asked the heavy breather on the other end of the phone.

"Information that will put a few puzzle pieces in place."

Ray tried to find the in-control, cool-headed reporter that he knew lived somewhere inside of him. "You'll have to be more specific. We're solving several puzzles right now."

"I'm only interested in one." Ray heard a smile in the voice.

"Okay. What is it?"

"First of all, I need to know that I can trust you."

Ray blinked, glancing around the newsroom again. "How do I know I can trust you?"

"Well, Ray, I'm the one with the information, so you'll just have to risk it."

"You know my name," Ray said, starting to feel the thrill of it all surge through his veins. "What's yours?"

There was a pause. A long one.

"I...um...don't call me anything."

Ray lifted an eyebrow. "I need to know what to call you."

"Why?"

"It's just how it's done. The caller or informant always has a name they go by. Like...Deep Throat."

"That's no good. I don't want to be called anything associated with pornography."

"I understand." An awkward pause followed.

"I've got it," the voice said. "Call me the Midnight Cowboy."

"The Midnight Cowboy?"

"Yes. That sounds good. Shadowy."

"Are you talking about the movie with Dustin Hoffman and Jon Voight?"

"Never saw the movie, but yes."

Ray paused. "Well, um, that's about two gigolos in New York City."

"I thought it was about rodeos."

"You might be thinking about *Urban Cowboy.*" Ray offered.

"Urban Cowboy. That doesn't have as good a ring to it."

"It had Debra Winger in it. She's cool."

"I liked her in *Terms of Endearment* and *An Officer and a Gentleman.* That's it."

Ray stared at his desk. This call was getting more and more bizarre.

"What about Electric Horseman?" Ray offered. He was running out of ideas, time—and cowboy movies.

"How can I be dark and shadowy with an electric light suit on?"

"You won't actually be wearing an electric light suit. It's just the name I'll call you."

Another long pause. "All right. Electric Horseman it is."

"Great," Ray said, feeling exasperated. "Now, about the information."

"The director of the plant, Mr. Crumm, has been investigated for embezzlement schemes. Start there."

Ray had his pencil and notebook in hand, but he didn't write anything down. "I know that."

"You do?"

"Yeah. What else do you have?"

"Petey Green, who assaulted you, used to work at the wastewater treatment plant."

Ray sighed. "I know that too."

"How do you know that?"

"Look, Electric Horseman, I'm not about to divulge my sources here. But so far, you haven't given me anything I don't already know."

"I'm trying to help you. You're not being very grateful."

"You're not being very helpful." Ray looked at his watch. He had to leave now if he wanted any chance of the captain still being at Gilda's condo. "I've got to go, but why don't you call me back if you have anything else that's helpful."

He could hear an irritated sigh, or what he thought was a sigh. It was hard to tell with the voice scrambler. "One more. Did you know Mr. Crumm owns the company that makes the chemical that may be responsible for the explosion of the plant?"

Ray's grip tightened around the phone. He'd only heard about the embezzling. "I didn't know that."

"Tell no one of our conversation. You'll be hearing from me soon," said Electric Horseman, and the phone went dead.

Ray tore off the page in his notepad, stuffed it in his pocket, and raced toward the door, where he could see Beaker coming toward him. "I'm coming!" Ray said, and Beaker sneered and walked out. Ray walked as fast as he could toward the door. As he opened it, he ran right into a woman standing outside.

"I'm so sorry!" Ray said, reaching down to help her off the pavement. When she looked up at him, Ray was mortified to recognize Mack, Hayden's sister. "Oh…"

"Hi, Ray," she smiled, helping herself up. "Don't worry, I'm okay. It's stupid to stand in front of a door anyway."

"No, really, it was my fault," he said, trying his best to make a good impression while watching Beaker out of the corner of his eye throw up his arms in disgust. "How…how are you?"

"Fine. Just hanging around the station. I'm here for a week, so I thought it'd be fun to see what Hayden does."

"Oh. Good." Ray needed to bolt to the van, but how would that look? He'd nearly knocked her unconscious.

"What are you up to?"

Ray pitched a thumb toward the van, where Beaker stood with his arms crossed. "Just getting ready to cover a story. Crime scene," Ray added, hoping to make himself sound exciting, since he wasn't doing a good job of making any other kind of impression.

Mack's eyes lit up. "Really? A crime scene?"

"Yeah." Ray smiled. "I have to get going now. But I hope to see you again before you leave."

"Can I go with you?"

"What?"

"Just a ride-along? You know, like we do in the police department. I promise to stay out of your way."

Ray glanced at Beaker. Maybe having Mack along would keep the cameraman from griping. "Why not?" he said, smiling.

Chapter 25

H ugo waved Hayden in. "Ready for another exciting night?" he asked without much excitement in his voice. He knew Hayden would have enough for both of them.

"I am."

"I'll have a script ready for you in a little while." He put down his pen and papers to focus on her. "Hayden, not to put any unneeded stress on you, but you do realize that this is sweeps week, which is one of the four most important weeks in our year?"

"Yes, Mr. Talley."

"But I don't want you think about that," he said. "I just want it to be in the back of your mind. Sometimes knowing something like that can help you kick it up a notch."

"Or have a complete breakdown," Hayden said.

"Uh…"

"I'm teasing you, Mr. Talley. I'll be fine," Hayden said with a definitive wink. "I actually came to see how you were doing."

"Me?"

"I know Gilda is a friend of yours. You must be worried about her."

Hugo looked down. Was he worried? About her? Or how it affected the station? After all, her disappearance had solved numerous problems for him. He'd known Gilda for years, but he wasn't sure he would call her a friend. They'd shared a lot of laughs together, but also many arguments. The most social time they'd spent together was the annual Christmas party, which ended up being canceled three years ago because of the likelihood that someone would end up going on the air drunk.

"I'll tell you who I'm worried about," Hugo said. "Sam. I'm going to need him in here as soon as he arrives."

"Yes sir. I'll tell him. Now, back to you. Have you considered our discussion about your medication?"

Hugo stiffened. "Medication" sounded so…medical. He didn't think of it that way. He thought of it more like his anticoffee. Coffee stirred him up, and the Blue Pill calmed him down.

"Mr. Talley, you can do this. You're just going to have to start trusting God. When you trust God, there's nothing to fear. Not even death."

Not even death. He wasn't afraid of death, apparently, because Friday he'd prayed that by some miracle he would just drop dead. God must not have been handing out miracles that day.

She held out her hands like she was holding a baby bird. "Just like this," she said with a smile. "He will hold you in his hands. It's not that bad things won't happen. I had to learn that lesson when my parents died. He will take whatever happens and make you stronger, put you in places you never thought you'd be, and bring joy where there was none before."

Hugo's head was pounding, and he frantically rubbed at his temples, a cue most people would take that they were being annoying. But there Hayden stood, holding out her cupped hands, as if perhaps Hugo wasn't getting it.

"Right," he said, trying to smile and agree so she would go away. His doctor had told him that this particular pill had no side effects if he quit cold turkey. Maybe Hugo could take up smoking again instead. Except this was a smoke-free building, so he'd have to go outside all the time.

Hugo looked up at her wide eyes. "Hayden, I appreciate the sentiment. I really do. But I'm just not spiritual like you, okay? One person can burn incense and feel warm and fuzzy inside. I burn incense and just see smoke and smell funny things."

"I don't actually burn incense, Mr. Talley," Hayden laughed. "But I do read my Bible. Do you have a Bible? I will get you one if you don't."

Hugo held up his hand. "You know, Hayden," he said, trying to be gentle, "it's kind of an unspoken rule around here that we don't discuss our religious beliefs."

"Really? Why?"

"Well…" Hugo didn't really know why. It wasn't separation of church and state. Maybe it was separation of church and everything that wasn't church. "It makes people nervous."

"Why would it make you nervous?" Hayden blinked. She really seemed not to know.

"It's just kind of uncomfortable, you know? I mean, I don't really pray and go to church, so when you tell me that I should, it makes me feel weird. I mean, not me. People in general."

"That's because they know they should be going. If I came in here and told you to go see a movie tomorrow night, and you didn't want to, then you wouldn't go. You wouldn't feel uncomfortable about it, would you?"

She wasn't letting up, and he was a teapot ready to spew. He wasn't going to be spewing water, either.

"Hayden, I'm just going to have to be very clear about this, okay? You have to respect my personal beliefs. I appreciate your concern for me, but we're at work, and I don't want to have these discussions anymore. I've got work to do and more important things to worry about than my eternal destiny. I've got a ten o'clock newscast to put together, starring a woman who doesn't know the first thing about being an anchor." He gestured playfully toward her to try to take the sting out of it all. Strangely, she didn't look stung.

"Then Mr. Talley, I will be your friend. And I will still pray for you. Underneath, I know there's a man who wants to be happy. But you're right. I can't make you believe in God." She smiled warmly and left.

That was the weird thing. Despite what he said, she made him want to believe.

"Can you drive a little faster?" Ray asked Beaker. He never had to tell that to Jim, the live truck operator, when he was at the wheel.

Beaker scowled at him. "First of all, I'm ten over. Second of all, if I'm not mistaken, there's a cop in the back of the van."

Ray looked back at Mack and smiled sheepishly. "Sorry. It's the news business. It's all about getting there first."

"I've heard it a thousand times," she said. "And I always tell people you can't get there at all if you're dead."

As Ray checked his watch, he felt Beaker let off the gas. They were about six blocks away.

"So how long has your anchor been missing?" Mack asked from the back of the van.

"A few days. She didn't show up for work on Friday, the day after she'd gotten a Botox treatment that…didn't go well."

"And now they suspect foul play?"

Ray had to choose his words carefully. He figured police officers everywhere had some code or brotherhood or sisterhood or siblinghood. He wasn't sure how sensitive Mack might be to critical remarks, plus he didn't want to blow it with Hayden by ticking off her sister.

"The police captain's all about getting his mug on the tube," Beaker blurted out. "He likes to create stories when there aren't any, just so we can interview him. In exchange, he gives us the first interview on any real story. Yeah, there's an underbelly to the news business. Shocking."

Ray cut his eyes to Beaker, but he didn't have much time to react, because the condo complex was up ahead. As they pulled up, to Ray's relief he could see Captain Wynn walking out of Gilda's condo.

Ray jumped out of the van before it stopped and rushed toward the captain. When the captain spotted him, his face turned stern. Ray was going to have to grovel, and under the circumstances that was not going to be a problem.

"I am so sorry, Captain," Ray said, pulling out his pad and pencil. "We had a hang-up at the station. Beaker is getting the camera set up, and we'll be ready in less than five minutes."

"Sorry, Ray, my work's done here. I've got other things that need attention."

"Captain Wynn, please accept my apology. It's been a crazy day, and I had to take an important phone call right before we were set to leave. Can we please set up the camera and do a quick interview?"

"No."

"Then what about giving me some quotes?"

The captain laughed. "You're really desperate, aren't you, Ray?"

"Look, if you don't do it for me, then do it for Hugo Talley."

"I don't owe Talley any favors."

Ray was losing control of the situation quickly. He had to get *something*. "Can you just tell me what happened in there? What did you find?"

"You want to know what happened in there? Watch Channel 10. I granted them the interview ten minutes ago." Captain Wynn moved past Ray, got into his car, and drove off.

Beaker came around the side of the van, carrying all the equipment. "Where's Captain Wynn?"

Ray looked around. "Where's Mack?"

Beaker pointed to the condo. "There."

"Come on," Ray said, realizing the condo door was still open and a couple of officers were finishing up.

As they approached, Ray could hear Mack talking with one of them. "Hey, Ray, this is Officer Platt," Mack said. Ray shook his hand. "I was just talking with him about what they found."

"We're finishing up here," Platt said.

"Officer Platt," Ray said, "would you answer a few questions?"

Platt shuffled his feet. "I can't really do that. The captain does the interviews."

"Has he ever told you not to talk to reporters?"

"No, but he's never told me to talk to them either."

"See? I doubt it's a big deal. I just need a few basic quotes for the camera. Nothing big."

Platt looked uneasy. "I'm not sure."

"Come on. Wynn always gets his face on camera. It's not like he's the only one who does the work around here, right?" Ray hoped this angle would work.

"I have acne."

Ray looked at Mack for help. Mack smiled at Pratt. "That's understandable, Officer. But there's a woman missing, and any information the public could use to help find her could save her life."

Suddenly Pratt's acne didn't seem so important. He looked at Ray, who tried to communicate through intense eye contact that Pratt could be a hero in this situation. Pratt's startled eyes caused Ray to dial it back a notch and try to look as casual as Mack.

Pratt glanced into Gilda's condo. "Look, we're supposed to be wrapping it up here. So let's make this quick."

Ray nodded and waved Beaker over. It took them about four or five minutes to set up the tripod and get the microphone ready. Finally Ray asked, "You ready?"

"Yeah."

"Officer Pratt, what did you find when you entered Ms. Braun's condo?"

"We found a sliding-door lock around back that had been picked."

"Any evidence of a struggle?"

"No."

"Anything pointing to foul play other than the door?"

"No."

"What about inside of the condo? Any evidence that she left on her own accord?"

"It's hard to say. There don't seem to be clothes missing from her closet, and her house looks to be in order. That's all I can say at this time."

Ray said, "May we get a few shots from inside the condo?"

"Absolutely not. It's private property."

"Where does the investigation go from here?"

"You'll have to speak to Captain Wynn about that. Now, if you'll excuse me, we need to secure the scene and leave."

"Sure," Ray said, stepping aside as the officer went to his car to get something. He looked around. "Where's Mack?"

"She was standing right here a minute ago."

Ray peeked into the condo, but it was dark and he couldn't really see anything except light coming in through the drawn shades.

Beaker had turned and was capturing the officer by his car. He said, "Are you sure we have enough footage here? It doesn't seem like we have enough."

"We'll make it work," Ray sighed, still looking for Mack. Great. Now he'd lost Hayden's sister. He really knew how to win 'em over.

"Hey."

Ray turned to find her strolling out of the condo. "Get what you need?"

Ray nodded, glancing to make sure the other officer was still at his car. "What were you doing?" Ray whispered.

"Figuring out where your Gilda is."

Chapter 26

Roarke walked into the conference room, closing the door behind him. "What's going on?"

"You're not going to believe this."

"Why can't we meet in the break room? Someone brought cookies."

"Sit down," Ray said.

Roarke carefully sat down in his chair. "You look serious, dude."

"It's unreal." Ray lowered his voice and told him about the Electric Horseman.

"You think Green is the one calling in?" Roarke asked.

"I don't know. Whoever it is, he's using a voice scrambler."

"Really?" Roarke's mouth dropped open.

"I'm going to get to the bottom of it. The voice said to tell no one."

"You're telling me."

"I know." Ray paused. "And one more thing. Hayden's sister found out some interesting things about Gilda."

"What?"

"She went into the condo while we were interviewing the police officer. She checked around as quickly as she could. She noticed two things the police overlooked. One, all of Gilda's makeup and moisturizers were gone. Makeup is one thing a woman won't leave behind if she's got any time at all to plan." Roarke raised an eyebrow. "I'm just telling you what Mack said."

"What else?"

"The officers said no clothes were missing, but Mack noticed a sack at the top of Gilda's closet. She climbed on a step stool. The sack was labeled 'summer clothes,' but when Mack looked inside, there was nothing there."

"You're saying Gilda went on vacation? That's impossible! Nobody's allowed to go on vacation during sweeps weeks."

"I'm not saying anything. It just seems peculiar. And a little more planned. They did mention the back door being picked. You should talk to the police, Roarke, and tell them what you were doing. They'll understand. I can back you up."

"Forget it." Roarke stood and walked to the door. "Gilda wouldn't leave for vacation during sweeps week and not tell anyone. I know her better than that."

Ray sighed. Roarke seemed to think he knew Gilda better than anyone, and Ray didn't know how to tell him otherwise. But for now, he had to focus on the story. And the story was taking him back into the battlefield.

Jill Clark pushed the door open to Hugo's office. She caught him with his hand to his mouth and a pill bottle in the other hand.

Hugo swallowed and stared at Jill. "Yes?"

"You've still got me covering the sewage plant explosion. It's sweeps week. I want to do something bigger."

Hugo sighed. Jill was such a whiner. She was also very competitive, and Hugo knew every move she made was a move to get to the top. But Chad had said the sewage plant story was old news. Maybe give it to the anchors, cut the segment, and move on.

"What did you have in mind?" Hugo asked.

Jill smiled. "You know one of Gilda's stories investigated the diseases we can catch from animals."

"Yeah, well, Gilda's not here, Jill, in case you haven't noticed." And as far as Hugo was concerned, the disease series had just about run its course.

"Why don't I do it?" She tried using her innocent smile to cover the devilish twinkle in her eyes. "Why not? I mean, the segment is edited and ready to roll. They'd just have to take off Gilda's voice-over and put mine on. And I did help Gilda with the research. I hooked her up with my vet, who says you can catch the flu from your dog."

Hugo sighed. It would be one of their top sweeps stories, a week-long segment Gilda had thought up that everyone had really liked. And they had been advertising it last week. But still, just to hand it off to Jill? Something didn't seem right about it.

"We're working under extraordinary circumstances," Jill added. "Normally drastic measures wouldn't be necessary, but if we have any hope of saving sweeps week, we'll have to make some exceptions to the rules."

Hugo held his head in his hands. Something about the effect of the Blue Pill tended to keep him from feeling his "gut." It numbed his gut and any other emotion that might prompt him in the right direction.

"Sure, why not," Hugo said. "We'll hit the sewage plant in the highlights and reinsert the animal-and-disease segment."

"Thank you!" Jill said, clasping her hands together. "You won't regret this. I know we're going to be pulling in a lot of viewers tonight because of it. Shall I tell the promo department to go ahead and run a new teaser with me?"

"Sure."

"And one more thing, Mr. Talley, just to plant a bug in your ear. I've been thinking of a piece Ray and I could work on together."

"What are you talking about? You and Ray don't do pieces together."

"I know. But maybe next week we could. A co-reporting kind of thing."

Why is she talking about next week? Hugo wondered. They were barely getting through this one.

"I'll talk to you about it later." She smiled and left.

Then he saw Ray walk by. He looked in a hurry. Hugo jumped out of his chair, raced around his desk, and stuck his head out the door.

"Ray, come here."

Ray turned, looking guilty for some reason. He made an obvious effort to stroll. "Yes, Mr. Talley?"

"Where are you going?"

"Just doing some work."

"What kind of work?"

"You know, just getting things ready for tonight."

"You interviewed Wynn about Gilda's disappearance?"

Ray's face told an immediate tale, one that Hugo didn't like very much. "Uh…Wynn was leaving when I got there."

"You didn't get an interview with him?" Hugo felt his blood pressure rising.

"No. But I did interview an officer on the scene who gave us plenty of good quotes. They wouldn't let us inside the condo."

"What did they find out about Gilda?"

"Nothing conclusive."

"Wynn told me the back-door lock had been picked. That doesn't sound good."

"Nothing was disturbed. Didn't look like there had been a struggle."

Hugo sighed and leaned against the wall. "Better off anyway, I guess. Chad thinks we should run with this Gilda story, and I think it's a mistake." He looked at Ray. "Where are you going now?"

A sheepish expression crossed Ray's face. "Look, just don't ask me too many questions right now," he suddenly said.

Hugo stiffened. That wasn't what he was expecting. It was his job to ask questions.

"What's going on?" he demanded in a voice loud enough for people to turn their heads.

"Mr. Talley," Ray said quietly, "I can't tell you right now. And I can't tell you why. But I'm asking you to trust me. I think this lead is going to turn out to be very important for us."

Hugo didn't know what to say. If there was anyone he trusted, it was Ray. But lately, Ray had been unpredictable.

"Is this about the wastewater treatment plant?"

Ray's expression changed just enough that Hugo understood that it was.

"I just took Jill off that story," Hugo said, making himself sick at how much he sounded like Chad. "It's yesterday's news."

Ray's eyes begged Hugo for understanding and trust.

"You can't tell me?" Hugo asked again.

"It would be better if I followed this lead. I'll let you know if it turns up anything, though. I promise."

"Okay, fine," Hugo finally said. "Well, at least it'll keep you away from Mr. Green."

Captain Wynn sat in his office and nodded for Officer Pratt to close the door. The kid looked scared, as he should. "Tell me the rumor isn't true," Wynn said, glancing at Detective Martin, who stood next to him.

Pratt stared at the carpet. "It was a mistake, sir. I just got caught up in the moment. The reporter looked desperate."

"Reporters always look desperate, Pratt, when it serves their need. They'll do anything to get a quote. Don't you know that? You should see what I've had to put up with through the years. I've been on TV more times than Patrick Buckley. It's ridiculous." Wynn leaned forward, making Pratt engage him. "What did you tell them?"

"Nothing important, sir. I promise. I just gave the basics. Told him we didn't find clothes missing or anything that would indicate she'd left in a hurry. I also said they would need to talk to you for further information."

Wynn let out a deep sigh. "Fine. Good. You're dismissed. And Pratt, no more interviews. Got it?"

"Yes sir."

"Close the door behind you." Wynn watched the kid walk out and close the door, then he turned to Martin. "Let me see them."

The detective pulled out a paper sack and opened it on top of Wynn's desk. He handed him a stack of neatly folded paper tied up with a rubber band. "Nice, heavy-weight paper," Wynn observed.

"Yes."

He opened the note on top. "Handwritten."

The detective smiled.

Wynn read the first note. "So we obviously have someone who is obsessed with Gilda Braun. Writing her love letters. Looks like rather frequently too."

"And," the detective said, holding up another paper sack. "Inside is a paperweight, which we found on top of the letters. Inscribed on top are the words *You are lovely.*"

"How do we know it's from him?"

"Because he refers to it in his sixth letter. Apparently he liked to leave her little gifts, such as chocolates and flowers. And paperweights."

"Any leads?" Wynn asked, folding the note.

"If you read all the way through those notes, you'll find that the person leaving the notes most likely works with her. There's a hint here and there."

"Does he threaten her?"

"No. They're all letters expressing how much he likes her and how great she is."

Wynn huffed. "My wife could take a few lessons in that area." He gave the stack of notes back to the detective. "The fact that the back door lock was picked is significant. Let's get on this."

"I agree." Martin paused at the door. "There's going to be a media storm on this one, considering the subject."

"I know," Wynn said, shaking his head. "I'll handle it."

Martin left, and Wynn picked up the phone and dialed. "Yes, I need to make an appointment for a facial."

Like a fast spreading rash, a horrible hot itch caused Ray to claw at every exposed piece of skin as he stood on Petey Green's porch. He'd knocked. Well, tapped. Lightly. He was losing his nerve with every second that passed.

He could hear the pigs around the corner, rolling around in their mud, oblivious to their part in all this. He rubbed his head, feeling the prick of the stitches against his fingers. He was an idiot for coming back here. But something told him that this was what Green had wanted all along. Someone to—

The door flung open and there he stood in his overalls and dingy white shirt. But that's not what caught Ray's attention. It was the shotgun tucked under his arm like a newspaper.

"Uh…," Ray stammered.

"I knew it would be you!" Green spat. "What is wrong with you, boy?" He looked around, maybe for a camera. Then he looked back at Ray, curiosity replacing anger. "Why are you here?"

"I don't have a microphone or a recorder or anything," Ray said. "I came here by myself because I want to talk to you."

"'Bout what?"

"Howard Crumm and the sewage—wastewater treatment plant."

"It's a sewage plant, son. Call it what it is. Tell it like it is. That's what got me fired, you know."

"Because you knew the chemical being used was dangerous."

Green's eyes grew still, staring right at Ray. Then he glanced around and lowered his shotgun to his side. "Come in."

Ray entered the small house. He could see the kitchen straight ahead, which looked barely big enough to hold a refrigerator and stove. A narrow counter was cluttered with dishes. To the left was the living room, where two recliners with cushions held together by duct tape sat in front of an ancient television.

Petey Green looked unsure what to do with company. When Ray just stood there, he grunted and pointed to one of the recliners. Ray sat down in the one that looked the least used. It appeared he made a good choice.

"What do you know?" Mr. Green asked, lighting a cigarette.

"I know you tried to communicate with Gilda Braun about it. You signed your initials instead of your name."

"How do you know that?" Green snapped.

Ray tried to keep his calm. "Mr. Green, I'm an investigative journalist. You told me to go figure this thing out, so I did. And I'm starting to find out some things that appear, at least on the surface, very disturbing. For one, your old boss, Howard Crumm, owns the company that supplies the chemical in question."

Green nodded, putting his cigarette into a bowl. "I was a nobody at the plant, you understand. But I came to work every day and did my job. I noticed one day that one of the chemicals we used had changed. The smell was different, and the color was a darker shade of blue. So I went to my supervisor and asked a few questions. The more questions I asked about it, the more I was told to shut up. But I take my job seriously, you know. I knew the chemicals I handled could be dangerous. Finally I was told that they switched chemicals because the new one was cheaper and did the same job. I questioned its safety, I got fired. They said I was stirring up trouble. I tried everything I could, but I was just one man against...well, a lot of people who just wanted me to stop talking. So I decided the best way to get their attention and others' was to put the media on it. I watch your news channel. I thought Gilda Braun really cared about people. But when it came down to it, the truth came out. I watched every day for four months, and the plant was never mentioned on the news, not once. I was ignored, and look what happened."

Ray decided to try to steer the conversation away from the man's grudge. "Tell me how you discovered Crumm was involved."

"I decided to figure out where this chemical was coming from. This was after I was fired. When I went to get my stuff out of my locker, I wrote down everything from the bottom of the plastic barrel. It took me about six weeks, but I figured out who was at the end of the rope. A company called Betreal. Crumm owns it, like you said. It's covered up with a lot of other companies, so you can't just trace it back by looking up a few things. But if you keep digging, you find Crumm. Betreal owns companies that own companies that own companies, if you know what I mean."

"So Crumm would've benefited financially by switching chemicals."

"Yep. He used a cheaper chemical, so he probably was pocketing what he saved there, plus he was being paid for the use of the chemical."

Petey Green sounded a lot more educated in person than he did in his letters. "I'm going to get to the bottom of this, Mr. Green," Ray promised. He stood and offered a hand to shake. Green looked pleased as he shook it.

"Thank you. Thank you for believing me."

"I'll get back to you."

Ray walked to the door, and just as he was about to leave, Green said, "And listen, not that my opinion means anything, but that Hazard girl, she's one good anchor."

Chapter 27

H ugo had been watching Sam carefully all day. He seemed back to normal. Hugo had no idea what had gotten into him Friday, but he'd made several intentional trips to the weather center, and Sam seemed fine, though not apologetic. Hugo wasn't going to push it. He had a lot of ground to cover.

Hayden was working hard on her script, and so was Tate. Amazingly, this woman seemed to put everyone at ease. Though nothing would get rid of Tate's infamous smirk except a mouth transplant, he did seem more confident with Hayden by his side. So Hugo decided to give Tate a couple more serious stories.

Unfortunately, it was looking to be a dull news day. Almost always, Hugo could count on a car wreck, a shooting, a fire—something spectacular. But all was calm, so he sent Trent out to the mall to do a story on how many stores had Christmas decorations up before Thanksgiving. That wouldn't win any ratings points, but if Chad was right, Gilda's disappearance might.

Hugo went to the break room to get a glass of water, instead of using the pricey bottled water out of the fridge. He was an old dog. He knew it. But to his credit (and probably nobody would agree with him), he'd come a long way in changing with the times. Sure, there were things he still couldn't get past—like casual dress at the office or calling everyone by their first name—but he'd also conceded things too. He permitted personal calls when needed, and he had put in vending machines for those who couldn't manage to pack their own lunch.

He worried a lot about the next generation. It wasn't that he necessarily saw a lack of work ethic. Every kid he knew here worked like a horse. He supposed it was the sense of entitlement that concerned him, that if they made A and B happen, then C should be handed to them. He worried about their expectations, their spending habits, their ideals, and where they set their hopes and dreams.

Of course, who was he to talk? He was having a hard time managing his own life. He couldn't make it through the day without anxiety medication for an anxiety disorder he didn't have. And expectations? He had plenty to keep people in his life weary.

Maybe he was holding on too much to the past. He still remembered the days when his father would come home at 5:30 p.m. sharp, and dinner was always served at 6:30 p.m. sharp. They would watch television together for exactly one hour, and then his mother would help him get ready for bed. His father would always come upstairs and read him a story before bed, and then the three of them would sit on the edge of Hugo's bed and pray.

Those days were long gone, but they were comfortable, secure days. His father died of a brain aneurysm when Hugo was seventeen, and his mother passed away four years ago after living in a nursing home for nearly a decade.

What about this life was so worth all the effort? There were pockets of pleasure, days of peace, but most of the time, life was lousy. One could never keep up with anything or anybody. There was always more work to do, more people to please, more effort to give. And for what? Another day worse than the one before?

Hugo sipped his water and leaned against the wall. Maybe if he'd had a different disposition. He was kind of a negative guy. But he hadn't always been. He'd grown that way the older he'd become.

Now he had his own daughter to raise, and nobody could tell him he wasn't giving it his all. Every extra ounce of energy and money he had was spent raising that girl. And it was only lately that he'd begun to resent Jane's work. He just wanted her to be happy—maybe he just wanted to be his wife and daughter's champion. But maybe he was just a chump.

Ray walked in to the break room, straight toward Hugo, as if he expected him to be there, except this room didn't have glass walls.

"Mr. Talley, I've got a lot of information for you."

"A while ago you didn't want to give me any information."

"Just hear me out. Green found out that Howard Crumm, the plant director, was using a chemical...an unsafe chemical...brought in from a company that Crumm also owns."

"Green...the pig guy?"

"Yes. Crumm's company is hidden by a lot of different other front or shelter companies. But if you keep digging, you find a company called Betreal at the end of it all. Crumm is the CEO."

"This chemical—did Crumm know it was unsafe?"

"That's not clear, but Green said he tried several times to bring that possibility to his superiors' attention, and he was fired for it."

"So all we have are Green's charges? You have nothing else to corroborate this?"

Ray hesitated.

"Ray, what else?"

Ray sighed. "I got a phone call from someone calling himself Electric Horseman. He's the one who gave me the Crumm lead that Green verified."

"Electric Horseman?"

"I know the story sounds crazy. Comes complete with a voice scrambler."

"This is what you were keeping so hush-hush?"

"Look, whoever is calling wants us to know more about the plant explosion, but he's going to great lengths to make sure we don't identify him. He's probably scared the same thing is going to happen to him that happened to Green."

"So Green, the man at the center of the pig controversy, is now at the center of the plant explosion?"

"That's why he attacked me. He's been so mad at our station because he wrote several letters to Gilda and—"

"Letters to Gilda? How is Gilda involved in this?"

Ray paused. "I found letters that Green sent to Gilda about the plant."

"What kind of letters?"

"Green was trying to get our station to pay attention to this problem before it got out of hand."

"What?" Hugo could hardly believe what he was hearing. "We can't get involved in something like this."

"We can make things right, Mr. Talley. We didn't listen the first time. Now we have a second chance."

"I told you not to see Green!"

"I know you did. And I'm sorry. But I had to follow the story." Ray's expression looked stoic. "It's news, Mr. Talley. This is *real news,* news that affects people's lives. Isn't this what we do all this for? Isn't this what you always tell me the news world used to be like, before we began worshiping the gods of sensationalized video clips?"

Hugo looked away. He'd always thought of Ray as his protégé. Now look what he'd created. A kid with a conscience. Hugo wiped the moisture from his lip. Chad had insisted they not run with this story, but that was before they had this information. Chad really wanted the Gilda story to be the top news, but it was a publicity stunt to say the least. Maybe this story would persuade Chad to dial it back a notch where Gilda was concerned.

"Let me get a piece together for it," Ray said. "This is the story, Hugo. This is it! We're the only channel that has this information."

"I'll talk to Mr. Arbus. It's not definitive. Don't get your hopes up about it. And you better have something ready for the Gilda story that you were supposed to be working on."

"It's ready to go."

Hugo raised an eyebrow. "That was fast. Didn't have much to work with?"

"It's a developing story."

"I'll get back to you."

Hugo could see the contained excitement in Ray's face as he respectfully nodded and rushed out of the room. He guzzled down the rest of his water and headed to Chad's office.

But to his surprise, Chad wasn't there. And Hugo couldn't find him anywhere.

Ray was busy in editing bay three. Excitement continued to stir inside of him. There was nothing like the idea of bringing down a crook. He already had plans for tomorrow. He would start interviewing plant employees to see what they had heard. He imagined many of them would be reluctant to talk, especially if they had their suspicions about the chemical. But Ray felt sure he would be able to gather enough information to make Crumm very, very nervous. He hoped he would be watching tonight.

He'd covered all his tracks. He'd left a message for Crumm to call him back, knowing full well that Crumm wasn't returning phone calls from anybody in the media. Still, there was the off chance that the plant director might want to tell his side of the story. Ray was careful not to tip him off about the nature of the phone call.

He glanced up and noticed Jill in the doorway, her arms crossed. The room was so small that having someone stand in the doorway made Ray feel claustrophobic. "Jill," he acknowledged.

"Ray," she said, smiling. He pretended not to notice. Any time Jill smiled, it meant she was going to say something to make him feel small. "Did you hear?"

"Jill, I've been kind of busy," Ray said.

"I landed Gilda's week-long piece about diseases we can catch from animals."

Ray looked up at her, hoping that small amount of attention would make her go away. It didn't.

"Great, Jill. Good for you." *Nothing like stealing another person's hard work while they're inexplicably away.*

"It's part of the business, Ray. You've never understood that, you know? You're still the 'hold the door for everyone' kind of guy. You just can't seem to slam the door in other people's faces, can you?"

Ray swiveled in his chair to face her. "Jill, I'm busy. Do you mind?"

"I heard you're covering Gilda's case. Any idea where she went?"

"Why don't you watch tonight and find out?"

"My theory is that she just took off. She couldn't handle the pressure anymore, especially after her Botox disaster. Instead of facing up to it, I think she just bolted."

"Maybe." Ray sighed. "I need to get back to work."

"Right. Guess you only have time for office mingling with your girl-friend."

"Excuse me?"

"Please, Ray. It's no secret. Everyone knows you're hot for Hayden."

"What? No! I mean, who…why would you say that?"

An impish grin spread thin across her lips. "It's what separates a good reporter from a great reporter, right, Ray? You've always looked down on me. Don't you think I know that? You judge my work constantly. It's never good enough for you. Maybe it's not as good as yours, but at least I know how to conduct myself professionally, which means avoiding office romances."

"It's none of your business what I do with my free time."

"That's the whole point. It's not your free time. It's office time. And don't think that I haven't noticed how much you've wanted to ask me out."

"What?"

"Please, Ray. It's obvious we have chemistry, but you never did ask me out. Why? Because you knew I'd turn you down. We have to keep things professional between us."

At the same time, Ray and Jill glanced at Tim, the editor, sitting next to Ray. He looked away and went back to editing. Jill looked amused. Ray felt sick to his stomach.

"Jill," he said in a low tone, "I have no idea what you're talking about. I've never been attracted to you. You're nice and everything, and I'm sure many men would be happy to date you, but—"

"Say what you want, Ray. I know what I know."

"Jill, seriously—"

"It's not worth it, Ray. For either of us. And I don't think it's worth it for you to risk throwing away your job for someone like Hayden Hazard. I mean, the girl is cute, I'll give her that. But she's also from another planet, if you know what I mean."

Yeah. Planet Decent and Good.

Jill glanced at Tim, who was devoting an abnormal level of concentration on the screen in front of him. "It's just sad that we couldn't have met under different circumstances."

"Jill, for the last time, this isn't about professional conduct. It's about the fact that I'm not attracted to you."

"You keep up that act," she said with a wink.

As she walked off, Tim shook his head. "Who wouldn't want that chick?"

Ray had no idea if Tim was being facetious or not, but he had other

things to concentrate on for now, like getting this piece together and figuring out how he could ask Hayden out for another date.

It was seven minutes until nine when Hugo finally saw Chad walk into
the station, his stupid trench coat flaring behind him. The news director
smoothed out the sides of his ponytail and headed straight for his office,
oblivious to the death rays Hugo shot across the room at him.

He'd been trying to get ahold of Chad for hours. It was as if he'd disappeared off the planet. And now he came sauntering in at nearly nine
o'clock in the evening.

Hugo took the long way to his office, hoping to calm himself down
a little. This would be all Chad's fault. Hugo had to make the decision
without him, and after viewing Ray's piece, which was compelling and
put together very well, Hugo made the call to air it.

Now he was going to have to explain to Chad that they were following a story he told them not to.

The Blue Pill wasn't working as well anymore.

He rounded the corner, deep in thought, only to look up when he
saw two feet standing in his way. Two very familiar feet.

"Jane?"

"I've been trying to call you all afternoon. We need to talk."

"Now?" Hugo said.

Jane's eyes narrowed in a way that told Hugo that wasn't the right
response.

"We're on air in an hour, Jane."

"Well," she said in a very sour voice, "according to our last conversation, you were willing to quit work in order to become some modern-day
Quaker. So what's the hurry?"

"It's sweeps week, honey," Hugo said, trying to muster up that sooth-ing sound that oftentimes back-pedaled him out of a sticky situation. "Can't we talk about this when I get home?"

"You don't even know what 'this' is."

"I know." He touched her arm gently. "But I know we need to talk. I'll come home right after the news, I promise. Straight after the news."

"You always come home straight after the news. What's the differ-ence? Am I supposed to take that as some sort of sacrifice?"

Hugo glanced sideways. He could see Chad in his office. He hadn't taken off his coat, which made him wonder if he was here to stay or just stopping by for a second.

"Something more important you need to tend to?" Jane asked, notic-ing his eye's shift.

Hugo sighed. Loudly. He didn't know what else to do. He couldn't just drop everything and tend to Jane. Why did she need everything to be on her schedule? He tried one more time. "Jane, you are the most impor-tant thing to me. That's why I talked to you earlier about our jobs, our lives. I think some things need to change. But we're not going to be able to sort through it all in an hour. Let me come home, we'll sit in the liv-ing room, and talk this through, okay?"

"I came up here to tell you I want a divorce."

"What?"

"So maybe you can give that a good thinking over in the next hour. And you know what? Some people have to get up early and work in the morning, so staying up late to 'talk this through' isn't going to work for me."

She spun on her heel and walked out. Hugo looked up and Chad was walking toward him, still wearing his coat.

"Hugo, you look like you're in a trance. What's the matter with you?" Chad said, sounding irritated.

"Where have you been?" Hugo snapped back and would've gasped at his own remark had he been able to breathe.

Chad's face twisted into a mess of ugliness. "What did you say?"

"I've been looking for you all day."

"Since when do I report to you?"

"You don't. I report to you. Which is what I've been trying to do all day."

"You're an intelligent guy, Hugo," Chad said. "I'm sure you've been getting along fine without me."

"I made the call to run a story on the wastewater treatment plant."

"You what?"

"There's new information. I think it's going to be the big story."

"I thought we agreed we were going to cover Gilda's disappearance."

"We did. That was before Mr. Duffey came across information about the plant."

"What kind of information?" Chad actually took a step forward, but Hugo stood his ground.

"Important information," Hugo said. "Information that may implicate the plant director. He knowingly used subgrade and apparently dangerous chemicals and profited off of it."

Chad laughed. Hugo had no idea why. He didn't feel like laughing and wondered if he ever would again. The word "divorce" kept trailing behind his thoughts like the tail of a kite through the breeze in his head. Hugo Talley never in his life thought he would be divorced. The possibility never even occurred to him. He just wasn't the kind of guy that got divorced. He was the kind of guy who would live unhappily for four decades, but he wasn't a guy who would divorce his wife just to live happily.

"Talley, you don't even look like you've checked in," Chad said.

"I haven't checked in? I've been here all day!" Hugo roared, surprising himself, Chad, and everybody else within earshot.

Chad glanced around, offering a dirty look to anyone who wished to stare. Hugo kept his eyes fixated on Chad.

"You're not going to run that story," Chad said.

"What?"

"You heard me. I told you not to pursue it, and you deliberately disobeyed my orders."

"It wasn't deliberate. It's the news business. Things change hourly. And in case you haven't noticed, this has been a really slow news day, so a story like this could really put us on top."

"Where did you get your information?"

"Unnamed sources," Hugo said.

"You're going to bet an entire story on an unnamed source? Who are you—Bob Woodward?"

"Mr. Duffey found another source to corroborate the information. This could be the biggest story of the year, Mr. Arbus. You should rethink your position."

Chad stood still for a moment, his eyes transfixed ahead. Then he said, "It's your call, Hugo. You are, after all, the executive producer. I'm handing the responsibility to you." He paused, then added, *"All of it."*

"I'll go down with the ship. Happily. You're not even on the ship, Chad." Hugo used his first name, for the first time, and Chad took notice. Hugo realized, suddenly, that Chad Arbus didn't seem so threatening without the formal title and the respect that came with calling someone *mister*. Now he looked like a man going through a midlife crisis way too early, and he had the foolish earring and ponytail to prove it.

Chad turned and, without another word, walked out of the station. Hugo let out the breath he was holding. He wondered exactly how he would be handling this without the Blue Pill.

Speaking of his Blue Pill, it was time to take one. He walked past the anchor desk, where Hayden and Tate were both studying their scripts and going over the show's time line. The floor director gave Hugo the thumbs-up sign and nodded to Hayden, indicating he thought she was ready to roll. Ray was setting up to do a live shot from the newsroom to follow his edited segment on the wastewater treatment plant. Jill watched Ray. Why, he wondered? Maybe because all she had to do today was dub her voice over Gilda's. And Trent was somewhere at the mall counting Santa displays.

Hugo sat in his desk chair and slapped his hand over his mouth to keep a rather large moan from escaping. What was it about his life that invited such chaos? He closed his eyes, picturing Hayden Hazard's blissful face, free of any worry or anxiety. Well, Hayden had her religion, and Hugo had his Blue Pill.

He pulled out his desk drawer. His heart skipped a beat when he didn't see the pill bottle. He reached as far back as he could, but there was no pill bottle. He looked all around his desk, on the floor, in the wastebasket.

The pills were gone.

Chapter 28

H i, Hayden."
"Hi, Jill."

Jill had waited until Tate had left the set to powder his face. Now Hayden was completely alone. Jill forced herself to be nice to this little goody two-shoes. She was self-righteous and smugly virtuous.

"How's it coming?" she asked.

Hayden looked down at her script. "Okay. I'm a little more nervous than I was Friday. I guess because I know what to expect now. And maybe the sweeps-week thing is getting to me."

"A little trick of the trade," Jill said. "Sit on the bottom of your suit jacket. It will pull it taut across your shoulders and make you appear pulled together." Jill learned that trick from the movie *Broadcast News,* but Hayden didn't need to know that.

"Good advice. Thanks. "

"You know, I could've been an anchor. Mr. Talley has asked me several times to consider it."

"Why haven't you?"

"Oh, you know, I didn't want to be just a talking head. I'm a hard-core journalist."

"You do great work, Jill. I think it's really admirable. It takes a lot of guts to do the things you have to do."

"Not everyone has guts," she said, smiling. "Like Ray, for instance."

"Ray? He's one of the best reporters I've seen."

"True. But I'm not talking about his reporting skills. I'm talking about his Casanova skills."

Hayden laughed. "What?"

Jill kept the smile on her face. "He's had the biggest crush on me forever. I mean, big-time crush. He just can't get up the nerve to ask me out."

"Really?"

Hayden Hazard wasn't one for poker, Jill could see. There was no hiding the disappointment on her face.

"I think he's getting close, though. He's been flirting like crazy lately. We'll see. Anyway, I just wanted to come by and wish you the best for tonight. The anchor, after all, is the glue that holds it all together. And it's not every day somebody with your experience gets to anchor during sweeps week. Some people are saying you're taking advantage of Gilda's disappearance, but I say that you're bailing us out of a tough situation."

Hayden looked genuinely mortified. "I would never try to take Gilda's place. I'm just praying she comes back safely."

"We all are," Jill said soberly. "Good luck." As she walked off, she glanced back once and, as she suspected, Hayden was watching Ray, a bit of remorse on that smug face of hers.

Ray was starting to get a complex. Ever since Jill had made her feelings known—or rather, tried to make up Ray's feelings for her—she'd been transfixed on him. She seemed to be everywhere he was. From across the room, he could feel her staring at him. And every chance she got, she managed to be in his way.

It was the last thing he needed today. He had a big story, and he didn't want to be distracted, yet it seemed there were nothing but distractions in his way. When he wasn't thinking about everything he needed for his story, he was thinking about Hayden. He was falling hard for her. And the more he got to know her, the more he wanted to get inside her head. What made her tick? Was it possible to act the way she did in this day and age? It was almost like she'd stepped right out of a Norman Rockwell painting. Could she be for real?

And then there was the fact that he practically had one ear glued to his phone, waiting for the Electric Horseman to call. He'd set up a recorder to tape any additional calls that came in, but his phone had been eerily silent all day.

Ray tried to concentrate on his notes. He had a lot to say in a short amount of time. This was his shot at a really big, important story, and he didn't want to blow it. They had thirty minutes until they were on.

"Ray?"

Sam stood next to him. He hadn't even heard him walk up.

"Oh, hi, Sam."

"I know what you're thinking about me," Sam said. "I probably deserve it. But I wanted to thank you for not telling Mr. Talley about my, um, condition on Friday."

Ray nodded. He wasn't sure he'd made the best call, but it looked like Sam had his act together today. "I'm glad you're feeling better," he said with a smile, one that said he was genuinely happy but there was a better time to talk about it. Sam didn't get the hint.

"You know," Sam began, and it was the kind of "you know" that indicated someone was about to do some heavy reflecting. "I don't know why I did it. I guess I haven't been feeling really happy lately. And maybe I was a little bummed that I didn't get the girl. Hayden Hazard, I mean. That girl's a real winner, if you know what I mean. The kind of winner you'd want to take home to mom and dad, not the kind you end up going home with from the bar."

Ray nodded.

"And maybe I'm a little bummed that I'm not the kind of man my dad was. He was a real hero to this town, you know? People connected with him. I'm just a stupid weatherman with a stupid slogan. I don't draw people in like he did."

"Sam, I wouldn't say that. You're great…" Ray tried to think up words that affirmed Sam but didn't keep him sticking around.

"I don't know, man. I think there's more to life than this, you know? And more to me than the looks and the fashion sense. So I save thousands of lives a year. So I can make any tie work with any suit. What am I really doing with my life? What difference am I making to the common man?"

Poor Sam was dead serious.

Ray needed to excuse himself to get to his work when he heard shouting. Sam heard it too. They both turned, looking for the source. It came from the anchor desk.

"Where are they?" It was Hugo, flapping his arms, his face beet red.

The person on the receiving end of the shouting was…Hayden?

"I said, where are they?" Hugo shouted again.

Hayden's mouth hung open, and Tate looked back and forth between them both.

"I don't know… What are you…?"

"Give me a break!"

"Come on," Ray said to Sam, and they both rushed toward the set. "Mr. Talley," Ray said, still a few feet away. "Mr. Talley, what's going on?"

Hugo hardly seemed to notice them. His eyes were fixed on Hayden. She looked desperately at Ray.

"Mr. Talley." Ray said, his voice firm as he stepped beside him. Boldness swept over him. "What's going on?"

Hugo glanced at Ray, then at Sam, as if just now realizing he was making a scene. His posture stiffened, and he focused back on Hayden. "This is between Ms. Hazard and me."

"Mr. Talley, I have no idea what you're talking about," Hayden said. "What pills?"

"What pills?" Mr. Talley laughed. Everyone else gave nervous chuckles since nobody was used to seeing him do much emoting at all. "Please. Your innocent shtick might work with others, but I see right through you. You know good and well what pills I'm talking about. The pills you told me I needed to get off of. What did you decide to do? Take matters into your own hands and dump the pills yourself? Or were yours in short supply, so you decided to borrow mine?"

"You're talking about your anxiety medication?" Hayden asked.

The entire newsroom hushed. Hugo's face grew red with embarrassment. "That's just *great*. Announce it to the entire world!"

"I'm sorry! I didn't mean to…Mr. Talley. I'm so sorry, I just…" Hayden was dissolving to tears, and Ray knew if he didn't act quickly, there was a huge chance he would punch his boss.

He took Hugo's arm, which was in and of itself a bold move. Hugo didn't ever look like he wanted to be touched, under any circumstance. Then, to his own surprise, he said, "Mr. Talley, let's step over here."

Hugo yanked his arm away but followed Ray a few feet away and behind a camera.

"Are you okay?" Ray said when they were out of the hearing of others.

Hugo was visibly shaking. He seemed to be trying to calm down, taking deep breaths and closing his eyes. Ray was breathing deeply too, maybe to encourage it or maybe to keep himself from hyperventilating.

"Mr. Talley, I don't think Hayden is capable of stealing anything. I'm sure this is a misunderstanding."

Hugo could hardly look Ray in the eye. "I just need those pills."

"Can you get through the newscast without them?" Ray said, glancing at the wall clock.

"I'm not going to wig out, if that's what you mean," Hugo snapped. Then he sighed disconcertedly. "Stop looking at me like that."

Ray wasn't exactly sure what kind of expression he was wearing. Not that an expression was going to make or break things at this point, but he tried to comply. Hayden still looked miserably concerned.

"We're on the air in less than a half an hour, sir." He nodded in Hayden's direction. "Maybe you can do some damage control?"

Hugo glanced at her and then away. But then he shook his head. "I'm an idiot."

"Oh, no…no…don't say that…"

"Ray, shut up. You know it and I know it. We both know that girl wouldn't take anything. I just jumped to conclusions because she'd told me I didn't need to depend on those pills, and, well, I thought maybe she was trying to help me along. But it's fairly obvious that I'm the one who made the mistake." He left Ray and walked over to Hayden, who stood as he approached. "I'm sorry, Ms. Hazard. I shouldn't have jumped to conclusions."

"It's no big deal, Mr. Talley," Hayden said, touching his arm. "Are you okay?"

"I'm fine." He turned to the group. "We need to focus. Can everyone just forget this happened?"

The entire newsroom nodded eagerly. Ray smiled. That was one way to get everyone on the same page.

"Good. Now, from this point on, *no more distractions.* Okay?"

Ray's smile faded as he spotted Roarke, who was walking fast, pumping one arm while flailing the other. Ray stepped out from around the camera as Roarke approached the anchor desk.

"Roarke?" Hugo asked. "What's wrong?"

Roarke caught his breath and stood up. "I don't know what this means, but…but…"

Everyone waited impatiently as Roarke caught another breath.

He pointed toward the front door. "News Channel 10 just rolled up. And they're setting up a camera in front of our station."

Heather Lewis, Channel 10's ace reporter, famous for her loud attire and even louder voice, didn't look surprised to see Hugo walk out the front doors. In fact, she looked pleased to see him.

"Hello, Hugo," she said, offering a red-gloved hand.

"Ms. Lewis." Hugo tried to smile appropriately. "What exactly are you doing?"

"We're going with a live shot in front of your station," Heather said. "What does it look like?"

"And why would you do that?" Hugo asked.

Whether it was feigned or not, Heather looked surprised. "Our lead story is Gilda's disappearance."

"What?"

"You're surprised by that?"

"Well, I mean…yes, I suppose." Hugo tried to gather his thoughts and words. "It surprises me that you would give our station any unneeded attention."

Heather's carefully lined lips curved like a satisfied cat's. "It is the big story."

"It's not that big," Hugo said. "After all, there's no evidence that anything bad has happened to Gilda."

"Right. Sure."

"You know something?"

"Hugo, you must be insane if you think I'm going to divulge that kind of information. Besides, you are the station with the missing anchorwoman. Surely you have the scoop on it." A raised eyebrow showed she questioned her own statement.

"Morty must be desperate," Hugo said, referring to Channel 10's ten o'clock producer, who always made it a point to one-up Hugo at every awards banquet they attended. It didn't matter if it was the news or the brand of clothing he wore, Morty was one of the worst one-uppers Hugo had ever known. "Well, carry on. And be sure and get a nice shot of that seven right there."

Hugo walked back inside, chilled from the cold and hot from the conversation. He spotted Ray practicing. "You're sure you got all the pertinent information on Gilda's case?"

"I told you everything the police officer told me," Ray said.

"Because it's Channel 10's lead story, and we've got ours buried five minutes into the newscast."

Ray shrugged. "I don't know, Mr. Talley. The officer I talked to seemed unconcerned."

"You didn't speak to Wynn, though."

"No. Like I said, he was leaving."

Hugo rubbed his temples. They had fifteen minutes to go. "Maybe we should move this up to our lead story."

"With what? A few quotes from an officer about nothing? Mr. Talley, with all due respect, I really think the sewage plant is the big story."

"Of course you do," Hugo said. "I've got to go to my office and think." Hugo walked into his office and closed the door. This was a total judgment call. Maybe Heather was bluffing, but it sounded like they had enough of a scoop to make this story tantalizing. All Channel 7 had was enough to sound like they were exploiting themselves. And if Ray was right, and this sewage story unfolded like they thought it would, the tables could turn, and Channel 7 could be on top.

He was going to have to go with his gut.

His gut.

It was strange, but all those emotions that the Blue Pill canceled out, when working properly, seemed like the very thing that might lead him in the right direction. Yes, he was full of angst, which stood in front of a long line of other emotions that wanted his attention. But maybe that was a good thing. Maybe he needed to *feel* again.

His mind instantly turned to Jane and her declaration of divorce. Did he really want to feel that? What good would that do? Still, something told him that he needed to feel even that. Maybe then, and only then, he would begin to understand it.

But how could he think about it all now? He had a newscast to run and a job on the line. He had to make the call. And he had to make it now.

Chapter 29

The electricity hovered over everyone in the newsroom. Even in the silence, there was a soft hum of energy. Hugo had never seen the newsroom so focused. Why weren't they this alive all the time?

With his pills gone, Hugo nearly trembled inside, but he decided to embrace it rather than fear it. He'd been numb far too long. Everyone had already found out he was an above-average emotional guy. There was nothing left to hide now. And it felt good to feel a little fear again. It felt good to have his heart flutter with anticipation.

He decided not to focus on Channel 10. It was unnerving to have a rival television station outside, and there was nothing more he wanted to do than stand out there and see what they said. But he had a news show to run. So he assigned the task to Roarke, who tuned one of his televisions to Channel 10.

He'd made the call to run the wastewater treatment plant story. If Ray had his information right, they were going to break one of the biggest stories of the year. Of course, if Ray was wrong, they were going to get flushed.

With two minutes until airtime, Hugo decided to give the anchors a pep talk. "Hayden," he said through her IFB.

"Yes, Mr. Talley?"

"Tate, can you hear me too?"

"Yes."

"Listen, I know there's a lot going on. We're all curious about why Channel 10 is out there. But we need to put that aside right now. I want you both to be upbeat, okay? We don't want to show any signs that we're stressed over the fact that another news station has decided to make us its focus. So I want to see smiles—not smirks, Tate—and complete professionalism. As you know, we're going to touch on Gilda's story, but we're not going to linger on it. So report it as you would any other story. The emphasis tonight is going to be on the wastewater treatment plant, as you know. All right, then. Let's do our best. Everyone up for the challenge?"

They both nodded, and Hayden shot her thumbs-up. Hugo smiled. That girl was something else.

Willis was counting down. "And we've got seven…six…five…four…"

Hugo held his breath.

"Good evening. I'm Tate Franklin."

"And I'm Hayden Hazard. Thanks for joining us. Breaking news tonight in the investigation into the wastewater treatment plant explosion last week. News Channel 7's Ray Duffey has uncovered new and disturbing information. Ray?"

"That's right, Hayden," Ray said, sitting tall on the edge of a desk with the newsroom as his back drop. He looked determined and focused. Hugo smiled, remembering a time when he, too, tackled every news story with that kind of zeal. And then he let out a breath, because he knew Ray was going to handle it. He'd viewed the tape Ray put together, and it gave a lot of information without making broad statements they couldn't back up with proof or sources.

Ray continued. "Though no one was seriously injured in the explosion last week, questions remain about the cause of the explosion. Plant spokesman Ron Griffith attributed the blast to human error, but our investigation uncovered an unlikely error: greed."

"Roll tape," Willis said.

And then the control-room phone rang. An assistant in the back answered it and announced, "Mr. Talley, it's Trent."

"Trent?" Hugo rushed to the phone. "Trent, what's wrong? Your segment's up in eight minutes."

"I know…sir, there's been a shooting at the mall, and I wasn't sure if I should—"

Hugo looked up and the control-room door opened. Roarke stood in the doorway, and Hugo had never seen that shade of gray on a human being before. "Roarke?"

"No sir, it's Trent. I'm at the mall and there's—"

"Cover it if you've got enough info," Hugo said into the phone.

"But sir, I'm not sure how to—if I should talk about the Christmas decorations and—I've never done something like this with so little time—"

"Handle it," Hugo said, and he hung up the phone. He glanced at the monitor as he rushed toward Roarke. Ray's piece was still running. "Roarke? Are you okay?"

Roarke went from gray to white, and his eyes seemed unfocused.

"Roarke? Talk to me. What's wrong?"

"Can you step outside?" Roarke whispered.

Hugo glanced at Willis, whose focus had left the monitors. Hugo gestured for him to pay attention to his job and then stepped outside the control room. "What is it?"

"Channel 10 just finished their lead story."

"About Gilda, right?"

"Yeah."

"So what'd they say?"

Roarke blinked slowly, and for a moment Hugo thought he might pass out. "What's wrong? What'd they say?"

"Well, it pretty much went down like this. They reported that the police went to Gilda's condo after they received a complaint that she had been missing for several days and had not reported into work as she normally would."

"And?"

"They found that the back-door lock had been picked, but the condo seemed relatively undisturbed, and no clothes or suitcases appeared to be missing. Everything seemed in order and there were no signs of a struggle."

Hugo smiled. "And that's what they led with? We're running a story about how the wastewater treatment plant's director has an embezzlement history and that he owns the company that supplied the chemical that may have caused the explosion, and that's all they've got? Beautiful!" Hugo slapped his hands together. His gut was paying off.

"Uh…"

"What?"

"There's a little bit more."

"Okay." Hugo couldn't imagine anything that would trump his sewage plant card.

"They, um, well, they also found something else. A small thing, really. I mean, I think they're blowing it way out of proportion. You know how Channel 10 always embellishes to make things sound more dramatic than they—"

"Roarke, what did they report?"

"Something about some letters."

"Some letters? What letters?"

Roarke started turning gray again. "Love letters."

Love letters? Hugo was trying hard to understand, but none of this was making sense. "What are you saying?"

"The police found some love letters from someone to Gilda. And according to the police, they're focusing their investigation on whoever might've sent them."

Hugo rolled his eyes. "For crying out loud. They're going to make this into some lurid love triangle? What nonsense! What, did they quote some anonymous source?"

"They quoted Captain Wynn."

"How did that happen? We were supposed to get the quote from Captain Wynn!"

Roarke looked unable to breathe, let alone answer.

"That's it! I'm calling Channel 10 this instant! This is ridiculous! I am not going to put up with their attempts to smear us during sweeps week!"

"Uh…you don't have to call. They're still outside, and they don't look like they're going anywhere fast."

"What do you mean?"

"They're not packing up. They still have their camera set up and they're just standing out there."

Hugo walked in circles, unsure of what to do. The door to the control room opened and an assistant said, "Willis needs you. Now."

Hugo walked in to find Willis gesturing toward a monitor that showed Trent. "What is he doing?" Willis asked.

"What do you mean?"

"Listen."

"…in front of Sneaker Sneaker, next to a large display of Santa and eight tiny reindeer. The manager of the store said he didn't…um"—Trent looked down at his notes—"didn't hear anything, but that he…saw people…they were running…screams…well, one lady screamed…and then…okay, let's see what happened here. One lady screamed, and then, yes, then some people snuck behind the Santa into Sneaker Sneaker, thinking they were going to—well, I can't say what they were thinking because I wasn't there, but I am coming to you live now…anyway, with the account from the…"

"Tell Dale to have him wrap up!" Hugo barked, and Willis ordered the cameraman to give Trent his signal. Trent, however, wasn't even looking at the camera. He was flipping through his notes.

"…anyway, so they all came into the store, and not to buy sneakers, allegedly, I mean…and…"

"Tell Dale to give him the signal again!"

Willis ordered it, but Trent had yet to look up at the camera. The crowd now gathered behind Trent, however, noticed it and they were all staring at the cameraman, probably wondering what he was doing with his finger over his head.

"...and the manager tells me that there was a lot of chaos and that people were screaming...well, again, it was the one lady, but she sounded like several people...and so then, it turns out, what they thought was a gun sound was just a blow-up snow globe that popped. Incidentally, that snow globe was erected on November 15."

Trent finally looked up at the camera, saw Dale's signal, and with wide eyes said, "Uh, back to you."

Willis cut to Tate, and for the first time ever, that stupid little smirk looked appropriate. Tate seemed at a loss for what to say. Willis cut to the wide shot, and Hayden stepped in to fill in the silence. "All right. Thank you, Trent. We're so glad everyone's okay. They sound like they had quite a scare. Is the woman who screamed okay?"

"No! Not back to Trent!" Hugo lamented. But Willis had no choice, and he cut to Trent. "I told Hayden to stop asking reporters questions!"

"She's fine," Trent managed, doing his best to look calm and collected.

"All right. Trent, thanks for that report." She turned to Tate. "And sounds like we've got some more cold weather moving into the state tomorrow."

"That's what I hear," Tate said. "How about it, Sam?"

Hugo walked outside the control room, gulping air. His chest felt like it was going to explode. He went to the bathroom and splashed water on his face. His mind was spinning with one scenario after another. Thoughts bounced around the walls of his brain like a handful of small rubber balls.

Back in the hallway, he glanced out a window and saw the back end of Channel 10's van still sitting there. *Why in the world were they sticking around?*

Hugo's stomach cramped and he moaned as he backed himself against the wall. There was something to be said for numbness.

Ray finished his segment. It had gone really well. He'd never felt so good about anything he'd ever done. He was covering real news with a real impact on people's lives. Suddenly the eight stitches in his head seemed worth it.

He'd decided to watch the rest of the news on the floor, and during a commercial had given Hayden a big thumbs-up, hoping to encourage her. She seemed a little nervous but was handling herself well.

During the break after the weather segment she'd said, "Am I looking upbeat enough?"

Ray laughed. He wasn't sure she was capable of looking downbeat.

"You're doing wonderfully," he said, gleeful enough for a couple of the cameramen to exchange glances and laugh. Ray didn't care if they laughed at him. She was great enough for him to endure it.

As sports came on, he felt a tap on his shoulder. He turned to find Roarke, who immediately pulled him away. Ray followed him into the break room, and to his surprise, Roarke locked the door. Ray didn't even know you could lock the break room door.

"What's the matter?"

"They found the letters!"

"What letters?"

"The love letters! They found them!"

"Who?"

"The police, Ray! The police!"

"Okay, calm down. Tell me what's going on—"

"What's going on is that this will be a huge story! Channel 10 just reported it and said the police are focusing their attention on the writer of those letters." Roarke's face turned red. "This is your fault!"

"My fault?"

"You're the one who had to know if Gilda was connected to Petey Green."

"I never asked you to go to Gilda's house."

"You knew I would!"

"I did not! It didn't even cross my mind!"

"You have no idea how bad this is. They're going to figure out it's me, and I'm going to get the chair!"

"Roarke, calm down, man. Seriously, I think you're overreacting. First of all, how are they going to link the letters to you?"

"They're all handwritten!"

"But you didn't sign your name."

"No."

"So why would they suspect you?"

"I didn't leave behind any fingerprints in her condo. I wore gloves when I was inside."

"See…"

"But all those gifts I left her! They have my fingerprints all over them!"

"Roarke, calm down. You're getting yourself worked up over something that hasn't even happened yet. This is reality, not one of those television crime dramas. And there's no indication whatsoever that the police are looking for you. Or that they've called in forensics." Ray paused, letting his friend catch his breath. "I suspect your conscience is bothering you, and you're better off going to the police and explaining why you went to her condo."

"Are you crazy? Why would I do something like that? They're going to take one look at this big, fat guy and make the assumption that I was desperate for her affections and decided to kidnap and kill her."

"Why would they assume that?"

"People assume a lot of things about fat people, Ray. You should try walking in my shoes for a day."

"Look, first of all, I can back up everything you tell the police."

"Oh yeah? You want me to tell them I was breaking into her condo to gather evidence on your sewage plant story?"

"I never asked you to do that."

"Well, that's why I was there."

"I thought you were there to check on her."

"That too."

Ray sighed. "Okay, let's just lay low about this, okay? Chances are nothing will happen and Gilda will turn up, and it will all be over."

"Since when did you become an optimist? That Hazard chick has done a number on you."

Beneath his remarks Ray knew Roarke was scared. "Let's go to my apartment, watch the shows I TiVoed like we always do, and relax."

Roarke sighed. "Maybe you're right. I've watched those cop shows for too long."

Ray smiled. "Maybe we should start watching reality TV shows."

"Dude, this is no time for jokes." Roarke breathed in deeply and let it out. "I saw all those letters when I was in her condo, you know. They were in a drawer in her kitchen, bundled up with a rubber band around a paper weight I gave her. She'd kept all of them. That says something, right, Ray? That means she took them seriously, that they meant something to her."

"I think so, buddy. She could've just as easily trashed them."

Roarke grinned and slapped Ray on the back. "My place tonight. Supreme or sausage?"

"You pick, my friend."

Roarke unlocked the door and walked out, stopping midstride. Ray ran right into his back, bounced off, and nearly fell to the ground.

"Roarke, what are you—" Ray stepped to the side to see why Roarke had stopped in his tracks.

Four uniformed police officers and two detectives were walking into the news station, followed by Heather Lewis and a Channel 10 camera.

Chapter 30

H ugo gathered up his belongings in his office. Things were such a mess that he hardly knew where to begin. But maybe that was a good thing, because he couldn't do anything about it tonight. He turned off his cell phone. He knew Chad would be calling to complain, and Hugo thought there was a real possibility that he might get fired.

But before that, he had to go home to see if he was getting divorced. He'd promised his wife he would be home after work, and lucky for her, the last place he wanted to be was work, so it was a no-brainer.

Of course, he was starting to feel the same way about home.

He'd searched his desk drawer one more time for his pills, but they were nowhere to be found. Well, why not just go with it? What did he have to lose, really?

He put his coat on and snapped his briefcase closed. He stacked all his folders together and put his pencils away. A sadness engulfed him as he tidied up. He could remember a day, not long ago, when he loved work and work loved him. But it was also just work, and it brought home a paycheck to feed and diaper his daughter. Now it had become a part of him, like an extra organ or extremity. What if it was cut off? How would he survive?

He flipped off the lights and closed the door, making mental notes about what he was going to have to do tomorrow. First, he'd have to talk to Trent, who made a complete fool of himself and the station due to apparent inexperience. Then he had to say something to Hayden, who in an enthusiastic attempt to end things upbeat, decided to tell everyone how happy she was that her sister was visiting. Tate still couldn't master an appropriate expression for any kind of story that had an element of tragedy.

Sam looked bored with his own weather predictions. Jill's pathetic attempt to hijack Gilda's animal disease story caused her to overdo her own commentary before and after the segment. Ray's story was the only hope they had of salvaging the newscast. And these were the least of his concerns.

Another station had the scoop on Gilda's disappearance. Channel 7 would have to spin it as a deliberate attempt to guard Gilda's privacy, but at the end of the day, they'd lost out on information, and information gave power to the ratings engine.

The bouncing rubber balls in his brain had now morphed into one gigantic bowling ball, rolling heavily from one side of his head to the other, sending sharp pain splintering through his skull. Something told him a couple of Advil wouldn't help.

A shadow crossed in front of him, and Hugo looked up. It was Captain Wynn.

"What are you doing here?" Hugo asked.

"I'm investigating a crime."

"What crime?"

"In case you haven't noticed, you have an anchor missing."

"What makes you think it's a crime? Your officer told our reporter today that besides a picked lock you didn't find anything that indicated foul play."

"My officer was instructed to leave the divulging of details to me."

Hugo shook his head. "So you gave it to Channel 10. Terrific."

"I waited for your reporter, Hugo. Nobody showed up. Channel 10 was there. What can I say? Time wasn't on your side."

"So why are you here?"

"We have reason to believe that Ms. Braun had a stalker."

"A stalker?"

"We found several notes from someone who seemed to have a great deal of interest in Ms. Braun. The content of the notes is highly disturbing."

Hugo set his briefcase down. "In what way?"

"The man claims Gilda is the most beautiful woman he's ever seen. He uses words like 'lovely' and 'adoring.' There are several references to a 'soul connection' that he believes they share."

Hugo frowned. If that was stalking, he wished someone would stalk him. Like his wife. "What else?"

"I'm not going to give you the entire content of the letters, Hugo."

"Is there some reference to this person wanting to harm her?"

"No."

"Any indication that she was frightened by them?"

"We're investigating that. Which leads us here. We believe the person who wrote these notes worked with Gilda."

"That's ridiculous."

"Is it? Several letters contain information that could only be known by someone who works with her."

Hugo crossed his arms. "So you're here because...?"

"We have a warrant. We're going to be asking some people some questions. And for those who would like to offer up their DNA and fingerprints, we'd be more than happy to take those."

"You're going to do *what*?" Hugo couldn't contain himself any longer. Captain Wynn looked happy to have provoked some emotion. And then Hugo saw her for the first time. He couldn't believe he hadn't seen her before.

Heather Lewis stood a few feet away, clutching her microphone, with a cameraman standing nearby, taping the entire thing. "What are you doing here?" Hugo raged, stomping toward her.

Heather's eyes grew big, but she stood her ground. "Mr. Talley, we just wanted to ask you a few questions about Gilda Braun's disappearance—"

"Who let them in?" Hugo shouted. "Who let them in?"

Captain Wynn stepped up. "You need to calm down."

"Turn off that camera!" Hugo pointed his finger directly at it. Captain Wynn stepped up and put his hand on Hugo's chest. Hugo ripped it away.

"You're going to have to calm down," Wynn said collectedly—and loudly, Hugo noticed. Loud enough for the microphone.

Hugo stepped away from Wynn and glared at Heather. "You have crossed the line."

"We're simply covering the news," Heather said.

Hugo was sure the camera was zoomed in close enough to see his pores. He took a deep breath and then said, "I want you out of our news station. Now."

"We just wanted to ask you a few questions," Heather said, her voice dripping with innocence.

"I would be happy to answer questions at a more appropriate time," Hugo said. "For now, I've got more important things to deal with. Turn off the camera and leave."

Heather motioned to the cameraman, who lowered his camera. He heard her whisper, "I think we've got plenty." They were escorted out by the station's security guard, who must've been napping when they walked in. How could this have happened?

Hugo would look like an idiot in the morning, if not earlier. He could just see Morty running this as late-breaking news.

"This is voluntary," Captain Wynn said. "Please let your employees know that. But we have a warrant to search Gilda's computer and work area."

"Voluntary," Hugo sneered. "So if they refuse, then they suddenly become suspects."

"There's no reason for anyone who isn't involved in this to be alarmed," Captain Wynn said mildly.

Then why was Hugo's heart about to explode with distress? Probably because he'd just created Channel 10's lead story for an entire week.

Roarke shoved Ray back into the break room. He was hyperventilating and looked like he was going to pass out. "Ah! AHHH!"

"Roarke, calm down. It's going to be okay."

"This! This from a man who told me I was o…o…"

"Overreacting."

"I have to get out of here," he wheezed. But there was only one way out of the break room. "This is horrible. My face is going to be all over the news. I'm going to be disgraced, not to mention incarcerated."

"You need to sit down," Ray said.

"I need to get out of here." He looked at Ray. "You're going to have to distract them while I slip out the back."

"Where will you go?"

"Home, I guess."

"Roarke, my guess is that they're just here to see if they can find any clues to Gilda's disappearance. So they have a few notes. It doesn't mean anything."

"Don't you watch *Dateline,* dude?" Roarke said loudly. "That's how they tell it too. At first it's just a few innocent notes, but forty-five minutes into the program, you learn they weren't so innocent after all."

"This isn't *Dateline.* If you would just go out there and tell them the truth, I think you would feel more at ease."

"I'm getting out of here. Do something to distract them." Roarke cracked open the door and peered out. "They're at her desk now. And one detective is questioning a couple of people."

"What do you want me to do?"

"Think of something." Roarke pushed Ray in front of him and out the break-room door. Roarke slipped out behind him and down the hall toward the back door. Ray kept his eyes attentive but tried to act as casual as possible as he made his way to his desk. He glanced back just as Roarke was rounding the corner. He had about fifteen feet to walk, and then he would be out the back door. A detective noticed Ray and started walking toward him. "You're Ray Duffey?"

"Yes."

"Mind if we ask you a few questions about Gilda Braun's disappearance?"

"I don't know much."

"Any detail you can give us might lead to something."

"Sure."

"Did you speak to Gilda after the last broadcast she made on Thursday?"

"No."

"Did she give you any indication that she was planning on leaving or taking a vacation?"

"Vacations are prohibited during sweeps week. Nobody gets to go."

"Do you know of anyone here at work who had a problem with Gilda, who would want to harm her?"

"Absolutely not."

"What about a crush?"

Ray could feel the color drain from his face. "Um…"

"Yes?"

Suddenly, from a few feet away, Ray could hear his phone ring. There would be a lot of buzz about the sewage plant story. But it could also be the Electric Horseman, who he suspected was also watching tonight.

"I need to get that," Ray said, and hurried toward his desk. He snatched up the phone. "Duffey here."

"I'm disappointed," said the voice. It was the Electric Horseman. He would've recognized that scrambled voice anywhere. Ray glanced up to see that the detective had decided to stand by and wait. Ray put his focus back on the phone conversation.

"Why?"

"Why? You hardly did any investigating. I gave you great information, and you turned up nothing more than empty facts."

"That's not true. I…" Ray looked at the detective, who made no effort to hide his eavesdropping. "I reported on the fact that—"

"I watched it, I know. But you didn't dig deep, Ray. I was counting on you to dig deep."

"How deep?"

"There are two more Greens out there."

Ray paused, trying to process what was being said. "You mean, two more people who knew what Green knew."

"And who lost their jobs for it."

"Okay. What else?"

"I'm not going to spoon-feed you the story, Ray. A real reporter goes out and finds the cold, hard facts. That's what you need. Not a bunch of speculation. You're working against the clock. The other stations are on to the story now too. This is information you needed to get this morning, not tomorrow."

"I'll do what I can," Ray said.

"Do better than that. You're not going to let Channel 10 get the best of you, are you? Let this Gilda Braun story take over? Your own news station is being exploited for headlines, Ray. They're playing up theories as fact. You've got to get the bigger story. The real story. Don't miss the opportunity."

"I don't have much time," Ray said. "Give me a tip, tell me where to start looking."

"Someone you work with knows more than they're saying." The line went dead.

Ray hung up, and the detective pulled out his pad again. Ray didn't have time for this. And he also didn't want to have to lie to the police about Roarke. He was in a bit of a pickle, as his grandfather used to say.

Think fast.

"You know," Ray said, before the detective could ask any more questions, "I remember seeing a suspicious e-mail on Gilda's computer one day when I borrowed hers because mine was down."

"Suspicious how?"

"I don't really remember much about it, except it had a—" *Don't overplay it.* "—strange tone to it."

"Who was it from?"

"I can't remember, but if I got on her computer, I could probably find it."

The detective glanced at Gilda's desk, where another detective was sitting. "What makes you think you can find it?"

"Gilda's a meticulous filer. She taught me everything I know about clearing out my in-box. Give me ten minutes, and I bet I can locate it."

"You don't remember anything else about this e-mail?"

"I just remember thinking that Gilda should be careful."

The detective didn't look like he was completely buying it, but he called the other detective over. After they quietly discussed it, Ray was given access to Gilda's computer. He couldn't believe it! Going by what the Electric Horseman told him, someone at the station knew more about this case. Roarke hadn't found anything suspicious, but maybe Ray could find something.

The two detectives were breathing down his neck. "Fellas, can you give me some space?" Ray asked, and they took a few steps back and began talking. Ray plowed through the various e-mail folders, trying to find something, anything, that would give him a clue about the Electric Horseman's hints.

Minutes ticked by, and Ray felt like he was looking for a diamond in the ocean. There were thousands of e-mails. How would he find anything significant?

He located a folder three folders under her main "Office Memos" folder. It read simply "For reference." That folder opened up to twenty or more folders, one for every person in the office whom Gilda dealt with.

"How's it going?" one of the detectives asked.

"Give me a few more minutes," Ray said. "I'm making progress."

He glanced up and noticed one of the detectives heading toward Tate and Hayden, who were still on the newsroom floor.

He scrolled down to see if any name caught his eye. There were so many, all people he knew, including himself. He decided to check out Hugo's folder. He'd been reluctant to run the story at first. Maybe there was a reason.

Nearly five hundred e-mails filled the folder. Ray groaned. There was no time to go through them all. He scrolled down, hoping something significant would hit him. But each folder contained multiple e-mails. There was no time.

Then he saw Chad Arbus's folder. It felt a little strange to peek, since he was the big boss man and there was bound to be some information in there that no one but Gilda should look at.

That twinge of guilt didn't stop him, though. He clicked on it, and to his surprise, the folder was completely empty. How could that be? There were no fewer than twenty e-mails in every folder, and most of them contained hundreds.

Ray stared at the white space in front of him. Something was wrong. This folder should not be empty. Ray knew he had received at least forty or fifty e-mails from Arbus in the last couple of months, and Gilda was the lead anchor.

"Anything?" the detective behind him asked. He was starting to sound agitated.

Ray clicked on another folder quickly, scanning each e-mail to make it look like he was doing something. "I'm not finding it," Ray said, trying to sound disgruntled even though he felt rather optimistic.

The other detective approached. "Let's go. We've got a lead."

Ray's ears perked up as he turned. "What lead?"

"Thanks for your help," the detective said, and within a minute, the police were gone. Ray glanced around and saw Jill staring at him from her desk across the newsroom. She smiled.

Ray didn't smile back. Instead, he decided to leave. He had to do some heavy thinking, and Jill wasn't helping him concentrate. Ray switched off his computer, grabbed his keys, and turned around to find Sam right in his path.

"Hey," Sam said, his voice heavy. He slumped a little.

"Hey, Sam."

"Nuts, isn't it? Tonight, I mean."

"Yeah. Crazy. Well, have a good night."

"What are you doing right now?" Sam asked. "I mean, you got a hot date or anything?"

"Uh, no."

"Yeah, me either. You want to go hang out? Maybe go to a sports bar, get some nachos?"

The Ray that attended church on a regular basis knew this was an opportunity to "minister." Sam was lonely, looking for a connection. He'd been clear about how disgruntled he was. And now he was asking for Ray's attention.

This was exactly how they described the "searcher" in the book they were studying in their Sunday-school class. And the five steps to converting the searcher included spending quality time with the person. Sharing nachos qualified.

"I'm beat," he said carefully. Dejection smothered Sam's expression. Ray wanted to kick himself—one, for caring so much and, two, for being a schmuck and not caring enough.

Ray glanced away and saw Jill, still watching him. How could he have been so clueless about Jill's feelings for him all this time? Maybe it had been buried in the competitive nature of their business. Whatever the case, Jill was definitely not his kind of woman. But...

"Hey, Sam?"

"Yeah?"

"Listen, you may not have noticed, but I think Jill is interested in you."

Sam's eyebrows popped up. "Jill Clark?"

"It's just a feeling," Ray said. "But look, she can't take her eyes off us." Sam slowly looked over. Jill smiled. "Maybe you should go over and chat with her. You know how women are. They play hard to get, but it's worth a try."

Sam grinned widely. "She's hot."

"And has such a great personality," Ray said with a straight face. Well, what could he do? He wasn't a saint. Sam charged off, and Ray rushed toward the side door and out into the cold night air.

He fumbled with his keys while taking long strides toward his car. His mind was racing in a thousand directions, but each thought orbited a single source: Chad Arbus.

What was he getting himself into?

He unlocked his car door, and as he heard it click, he also heard someone behind him.

Chapter 31

Ray's heart had finally slowed to a normal pace after he arrived at Hayden's apartment, only to start beating abnormally fast again when he realized he would be near her outside of work.

Mack had stopped him in the parking lot and told him to meet them at Hayden's apartment in half an hour. She handed him a piece of paper with the address and walked away. The whole affair had a quasi-cloak-and-dagger feel to it, so once again Ray was confused about the intent of the gathering. He didn't want to assume it was a date, but if it was, he wanted to be fully prepared, so he stopped at Walgreens and bought some cheap cologne and hair gel. He'd gone on air without looking his best, but reporters weren't known for their glamour. He'd been focusing so hard on the story, he'd forgotten to check on his hair. It looked a little funky, and Ray wasn't sure hair gel was going to do much to help, but he blobbed some on anyway.

He found the apartment. The lights were on. That was good. Ray didn't want to be loitering awkwardly at the front door. Hayden answered his knock quickly and greeted him with a large smile. She was still dressed in the suit she'd worn on air, and she looked as radiant as if it were nine in the morning.

"Come in!" she said.

"Thanks." Ray stepped in and took in the decor. A Yankee candle aroma filled his nostrils. The drapes were blue and matched the chambray couch. A small television sat on a small table next to a large, old-looking trunk. The kitchen was tidy, as was the breakfast table that sat next to it.

"Nice place," he said.

"Sit down," she said. "I know it's late, but I'm glad you could come over."

"Me too." Her enthusiasm was contagious. The rule was that you were supposed to play it cool when you were around someone you liked, but part of Ray wanted to gush. And gushing could not be inserted in any way into the definition of "cool." But Hayden wouldn't stop smiling, so Ray could only return the favor.

"You found the place okay?"

"Yes." He glanced down the hallway. "Is Mack here?"

"She'll be right back. She had to run an errand. I'm baking brownies."

"Great. I love brownies." Ray watched her wrap an apron around her waist and pull on two oven mitts. Could she possibly be any more adorable?

"Crazy night, huh?" Ray said, strolling to a bookcase on the far wall of her apartment. He studied some of the titles. There were a lot of older books that looked like they might fall apart if touched, so he kept his hands off of them.

The front door opened and Mack walked in, carrying some groceries. "Hi, Ray," she said.

"Hi."

He wondered if Trent had been invited. But he didn't have to wonder long. Mack said, "Okay, we have a lot to talk about. I've been investigating your anchor's disappearance."

Ray joined them at the kitchen table. "Really?"

"Yeah. As you know, her makeup was missing, and I'm speculating that some summer clothes were taken as well. That tells me the woman left and had enough time to think through what to pack. It also tells me her plan was to go somewhere warm."

"I just can't see Gilda, at least in her right mind, packing up and leaving without telling anyone."

"Exactly. I thought it was also odd that Gilda's suitcases were still sitting in the middle of her closet. The first thing I noticed was that her apartment was very neat and organized. It seemed to me that the suitcases were left out intentionally, so the first reaction would be to rule out the fact that she'd gone somewhere. And then there's the fact that the back-door lock was picked."

Ray nodded. Mack seemed pretty perceptive, and he didn't want to spill Roarke's secrets. He averted his eyes, which he was sure made him look spectacularly uncorrupted.

"I checked flights and rental cars, but nothing came up with her name on it. I also checked her credit cards, which haven't been used, and her bank account, which has had no money withdrawn from it for over a week. Something's not right about it. If she'd decided to leave intentionally, she would've used money. But if she left by force, why would she take the time to pack summer clothes and her makeup?"

"Hayden told you about her embarrassing Botox incident?" he asked.

"Yes," Hayden said. "I thought she might've just wanted to get away from it all."

"But you have the back-door lock that has been picked. I looked at it, and it was picked recently. Some traces of metal shavings were on the concrete. Whoever picked the lock had no idea what he was doing. It was definitely amateurish. In fact, I think whoever opened the door finally just got fed up with it and yanked it open, which isn't hard to do if you don't have a safety bar, which this sliding door did not." She glanced at Hayden. "Please tell me you have a safety bar."

"Of course."

"Good." Mack sighed. "So I'm really at a loss, but something tells me that there's someone else involved."

Ray stared at the table, trying to decide how much information he should divulge. Sharing that Roarke had picked the lock would be helpful, but it would also spill Roarke's secret, which he had sworn he wouldn't do. Instead, he decided to tell Mack and Hayden what he knew.

"I found something odd today," Ray began, as Hayden stood to cut the brownies.

"About Gilda?"

"I think so." He didn't know where to begin, but he started by telling them about the Electric Horseman and the information he'd given concerning the plant explosion. He ended by explaining what he'd found on Gilda's computer in Chad Arbus's file.

"Strange," Mack said, scratching her temple.

Ray looked back and forth between the two sisters. They were both walking clichés, in a sense, and yet had no idea they should be concerned about it. How could they be clichéd and genuine all at the same time?

He tried to focus on the problem at hand. "You know," he said, "before the police left, one of the detectives said they'd gotten a new lead. What do you suppose they found?"

Mack shrugged. "I don't know. I did notice they left quickly."

"Me too," Hayden said. "In fact, they were kind of rude about it."

"What do you mean?" Mack asked.

"Well, they were right in the middle of asking Tate and me questions, and then suddenly the detective snapped his notebook shut and walked away. He didn't even say thank you," Hayden recalled. She looked at Mack. "I know you would've at least thanked us for the time."

Mack, however, didn't seem too hung up on the thank-you portion. "Tell me what the detectives asked you."

Hayden stirred her second bowl of brownie batter. "Gosh, there were so many questions. Tate answered most of them, I think. Things like, when was the last time we'd seen Gilda, was she acting strangely? I mentioned the Botox incident, but they already knew about that."

"When did the detective close his notepad?" Mack asked. Ray was beginning to think Mack would make a good investigative reporter. She asked all his questions.

Hayden stopped stirring and thought for a moment. She seemed to be running through a list in her head. Then she said, "I know."

"What?" Mack asked, leaning forward just like Ray.

"Hold on." She held up a finger. "I've got to pour this batter into a pan."

Ray could only laugh, and as he glanced at Mack, she smiled too, and gave Ray a knowing glance. They watched Hayden carefully pour the batter and smooth out the top. Ray whispered to Mack, "Is Hayden always this laid back?"

Mack nodded. "Most of the time. I've only seen her really uptight once."

"Really? When?"

"It was shortly after our parents died, and our brother, Mitch, announced that he was selling the family business. Hayden was devastated." Mack looked toward the kitchen as Hayden prepared to stick the pan in the oven. "And look at her now. Our parents would be so proud. I always knew she would be something big, but she never believed in herself. She always felt second-best because of her clown phobia."

"She's a really special woman," Ray said, glancing at Mack before bowing his head in embarrassment. This woman turned him into a gusher! If Roarke had witnessed this, he would've stuck Ray in front of a television and made him watch an ultimate fighter marathon.

Roarke! He'd forgotten that he'd promised Roarke he would come over after the show. Ray slapped his hand to his forehead. Not only was he a gusher, but he was now officially a loser friend.

Mack took notice of his distress and was about to say something when Hayden finally replied, "Okay, got the brownies going. Now, the detective asked both of us if we knew of anybody at the office who had taken a sudden interest in Gilda. Tate said he hadn't noticed."

"And what did you say?" Ray asked.

She grinned. "Well, isn't it a little obvious?"

Ray and Mack exchanged glances.

"Obvious? What's obvious?"

Hayden took off her oven mitts and came to the table. "Anyone want milk with their brownies?"

"Who did you say was interested in Gilda?" Ray said, trying to get her focused.

Hayden sat down. "You don't know, Ray? Maybe it's because I'm a woman, but it seemed fairly obvious to me."

"Who, Hayden?" Mack asked, and Ray was relieved he wasn't the one to have to push her along.

"Roarke, of course!" She giggled. "I noticed it when I first came to the station. He has a huge crush on her. He's always watching her like she's the most adorable thing he's ever seen." She smiled, but it lessened as she looked at Ray. "What's the matter?"

Ray had a hard time getting any words out. "You told them Roarke had a crush on Gilda?"

"It wasn't a big deal. I figured they were just trying to find out who liked Gilda and who hated her. Obviously, Roarke likes her."

Ray stood, making a small circle near the table as he tried to think. "I need to use your phone."

"What's the matter?" Hayden asked, handing it to him.

Ray dialed Roarke's home phone number as Mack explained why the police might suddenly be interested in Roarke. As the ringing started, he heard Mack having to explain it further. Obviously Hayden had never seen any kind of crime drama on television. Roarke's voice mail picked up, and Ray hung up the phone. He dialed Roarke's cell but got his voice mail too. As he was trying to think of what to do next, he heard Hayden ask Mack, "So you think they went to Roarke's home to question him?"

Ray turned away. Her naiveté wasn't quite so charming anymore. He decided to check his messages at home, if he could remember how to access them. As he dialed the number, Hayden was by his side, grasping his arm. "Ray, I am so sorry. I had no idea that this would make Roarke a suspect."

Ray tried to smile and nod, but he could only think of Roarke right now. He punched in what he hoped was his four-digit password. He held his breath, hoping and praying he would have a message from Roarke.

The rigid female voice announced plainly, "You have eighteen messages."

Hugo entered a completely dark house. Normally Jane left a living-room light on and sometimes even the television, muted. But there was no sound nor sight in his home. He felt for the light switch in the kitchen and flipped it on. He'd lost his appetite, especially when he realized he wouldn't be able to come home right after the show like he'd promised, but he peeked in the fridge for his dinner plate anyway.

To his surprise, there was nothing there. They'd had a lot of fights over the years, but Jane had never thrown his food in the garbage. Come to think of it, the kitchen didn't have the normal, lingering smell of dinner in the air. Maybe Jane and Kaylin went out. But even then, she always ordered him something to leave in the fridge.

Hugo sighed. If he ate, it would only be to get his mind off his troubles. So maybe he should figure out how to get out of his troubles so meals could be meals instead of distractions.

He laid his things on the table then decided to scoop them up and take them upstairs like Jane liked for him to do. She had this pet peeve about things left on the table, but most nights Hugo was too tired to organize. He never understood why he couldn't do it the next day.

He climbed the stairs, another reminder of their differences. Hugo had wanted a house without stairs, while Jane had insisted on two stories.

He normally checked on Kaylin, but he wanted to talk to Jane, even if he had to wake her up. This couldn't wait until morning, and he could only pray that she would understand what kind of night he had had.

That's the sad thing, he thought as he plodded down the hallway toward his bedroom. He needed someone to talk to about tonight. Hugo had awakened Jane on only a few occasions, but she'd always listened, even with her eyelids halfway drawn.

Yet even the dilemmas at work paled in comparison to the state of his marriage. Something told him he could save it if he would just listen to her, try to figure out where things had gone wrong. Maybe it was as simple as leaving socks on the floor. Or maybe it was more complex, since he knew he'd seemed distant the past few months. But Hugo knew every problem had a solution. It was just a matter of finding it.

He walked quietly across the dark bedroom toward the bathroom, his eyes barely adjusting to the darkness. He had always wanted a night-light so he could see better coming home, but Jane had a list of criteria that had to be met for her to sleep soundly, and one of those was a pitch-black room.

In the bathroom, he quietly closed the door, flipped on the light, and set down his things. As he undid his tie, he thought about all the feelings swirling inside. Something could be said for pain.

Alongside the pain, he also felt hope. He would do anything to save his marriage. He loved Jane. But it was true that ever since he'd taken the executive producer's job, which made him the ten o'clock show's producer, their relationship had grown distant. They'd sat down one day and charted out each of their schedules, and both had been ecstatic when they realized, with careful planning, they could make both of their schedules work.

But what hadn't been on that chart was the emotional distance they would eventually develop from running in separate directions. Jane had been elated at the increase in salary, and Hugo had finally landed his dream job. So why was this so hard? Weren't all the fringe benefits enough to sustain them?

He decided to give his teeth a quick brush. He was stalling, but he figured his chances of starting out the conversation on a good note vastly improved if his breath was decent.

Then there was nothing else to do but go in there. He opened the door and decided to keep the bathroom light on. There was nothing that woke Jane up faster than light, which was why they had hung shades heavy enough to cloak the sun.

"Jane?"

Hugo stared at the bed, which was neatly made and empty. As if turning on another light would help, he rushed to the bedside table and turned on the lamp. Jane was gone. In her place was a white envelope, blank on the outside.

Hugo left it there and rushed to Kaylin's room. He pushed open the door, and her bed was empty too. He ran back to his room and tore open the envelope.

In her sloppy handwriting it read, "We're at my mother's. I will call you next week."

Hugo sat down on the bed and read the note over and over. She hadn't even known he was late. She hadn't even waited for him to come home. She had packed her things after she'd come to the station. *Maybe before.*

Hugo threw the note across the bed and kicked off his shoes. He slammed his hand against the lamp, causing it to crash to the ground. A sliver of bathroom light sliced across the bed just to his left, but everything else was dark.

"Fine!" Hugo yelled at the top of his lungs. "Fine!" he said again as he galloped downstairs. He turned on every light he could find. The entire house looked alive enough to throw a party.

In the kitchen, he opened a can of SpaghettiOs and grabbed a spoon. He turned on the television, burrowed into the couch, and put his feet on the coffee table, just like Jane hated.

Chapter 32

A s big as Roarke was, he seemed small sitting behind the bars at the county jail. When he looked up and saw Ray, he looked betrayed. "I'm sorry," Ray said, clutching the metal bars. "I should've been there for you."

"If you'd been there," Roarke said, choking up, "they would've believed me. I was so nervous trying to explain the letters and the break-in that I ended up sounding like Hannibal Lecter's crazy brother. It didn't help that I pretended I wasn't home for the first half hour while the police were knocking."

Ray smiled through his own tears. Roarke could always make him laugh. Roarke hadn't been fully processed yet, but thanks to some connections he had at the jail, Ray was able to visit him in the holding cell at this late hour. It looked like a slow night. Only three other people were in there, too drunk or too high to care about what was happening around them. The stench was horrible.

Roarke finally stood, holding his back from sitting on the hard, metal bench.

"Tell me what happened," Ray said quietly.

"I have no idea how they figured out I wrote the letters. But why am I surprised? We watch *CSI* enough to know they can figure out practically anything, you know?"

Ray nodded and swallowed. Now was not the right time to tell him Hayden had given him up.

"Anyway, it didn't take much, you know. They asked a couple of questions, and then I broke down and told them everything…about my crush, the letters, breaking into her condo." He looked up. "I didn't mention you." He looked back down. "Anyway, I was nervous, you know? And even as I was talking, I thought to myself that I sounded like a raging lunatic. But I couldn't stop, and I couldn't collect my thoughts to make any of it sound reasonable."

Ray shook his head. "I don't know that they have enough evidence to hold you, Roarke. I mean, you confessed to the letters and the break-in, and you gave them the reason why. Beyond that, they don't really know what happened to Gilda."

"They're holding me on unpaid parking tickets," Roarke sighed.

"How can they do that? Hold you in jail for a few unpaid tickets?"

"Twenty-nine."

"Oh."

"But it won't be long until they bring other charges against me, Ray. You have to get me out of this."

"I'll do everything I can. You know I will."

"And you've got to keep this off the news. Keep me out of the news. I couldn't bear for this to get out, for my name to be attached to this, and for everyone to know I wrote those letters to Gilda."

Ray struggled to keep his composure. He knew he couldn't make any promises. He had no idea how to keep this out of the media. "Were any news crews around when you got arrested?"

"Only the news copter up above, circling like a stupid vulture."

"What channel?"

"Ours." Roarke looked up. "I'm going to become the laughingstock of the city, aren't I?"

"I won't let that happen."

Roarke couldn't hold in the tears in any longer. "You know, Ray, I've been fat since I was born. I was a fat toddler, a fat kid, a fat teenager, and now I'm a fat adult. One year we moved right before I went into junior high. I decided I was going to change my name, since my parents gave me a name that seemed to rhyme with every word that meant fat. So I thought long and hard and decided to go by my middle name, Roarke. I told my parents that would be my new name and not to call me anything else. But you know what? We don't give mean kids enough credit. They're pretty creative. At my new school, I acquired two new nicknames. Roarke the Fork and Roarke the Pork."

Ray couldn't look at Roarke any longer. It was breaking his heart to see his friend in such distress.

"But my parents always taught me to do the right thing. They told me that people could call me all the names they wanted, but if I did the right thing, they could never destroy my dignity. And that's what has always kept me going, Ray. My dignity. Now I don't even have that."

"That's not true," Ray said, clutching his friend's hand through the bars. "We're going to clear your name, buddy. I promise. We're going to find out what happened to Gilda, and you'll have your dignity again." The word *promise* felt so heavy on Ray's tongue. He didn't know what he could do, but he had to try, and he had to give his friend hope. "I'm on it right now. We're going to figure this thing out, okay?"

Roarke nodded, and Ray could see a flicker of hope on his face. Ray squeezed his hand and turned to leave.

"What are you doing to do?"

"Trust me, my friend," Ray said as he walked toward the door. He had no idea what he was going to do.

It wasn't hard to find Hugo's house in the middle of the night. It glowed like a lighthouse. Ray pulled into the driveway with his lights off and shut his car door quietly. He'd been to Hugo's house once, back when the station used to do Christmas parties.

On the front porch, Ray hesitated before he knocked. What was he going to say? Why was he even here? He didn't know, really. But in the parking lot of the jail, he sat in his car and prayed like he hadn't prayed in years. If he'd been able, he would've gotten on his knees. He had never felt more desperate, and he knew one thing for sure: God had the answers they all needed.

Ray knocked, and to his surprise, the door flew open almost immediately. Hugo looked like he was about to say something when his face registered it was Ray. Ray wasn't sure who he had been expecting, but it wasn't him. Hugo's shirt was half untucked and his hair looked like his hand had run through it about a hundred times.

"Ray?" Hugo squeaked.

"I'm sorry to bother you at this time of night," Ray said. "I hope I didn't wake up your family."

"What do you need?"

"It's about Roarke. They arrested him tonight for parking tickets, but that's just an excuse to hold him until they can find more evidence linking him to Gilda's disappearance."

Hugo blinked as if the sun had suddenly popped into the sky unannounced. "They think Roarke has something to do with Gilda?"

"It's a long story," Ray said. "May I come in?"

Hugo opened the door wider and glanced outside a time or two before closing the door. Hugo said, "I've just been up working."

"Oh." Ray also noticed the can of SpaghettiOs on the living-room table with a spoon sticking out the top.

Hugo shook his head and laughed, but it wasn't the kind of laugh you give after a good joke. It had a sardonic feel to it. Ray didn't know where to begin. "The notes they found were from Roarke. I just recently found out myself that Roarke has had a crush on Gilda. Apparently he's had one for a while."

"Roarke and Gilda," Hugo said, leading Ray into the living room. He gestured for him to sit down. "Who would've thought? Well, who knows? Maybe they'd make a great couple. You just don't know about people. You think two people are matched up perfectly…they have a lot in common, have similar life goals, are good friends. But it can all go away, you know? There doesn't seem to be one thing that can keep a couple together. If you could say, make sure to have A or B, that would make it a lot easier. But there is no A or B. In fact, there's nothing in the alphabet that can give you any hope."

Ray nodded, trying to follow, but he had no clue what Hugo was trying to say. Ray was about to continue on the subject of Roarke's plight, but Hugo started talking again.

"You want to get drunk?"

"Excuse me?" Ray asked.

"Drunk."

"I…uh…"

"I don't drink much, you know. Maybe some wine now and then or a beer at my uncle's. Things like that. But this just seems like a good time to get drunk. Everything's falling apart. I tried some deep breathing exercises, but that didn't really do it for me, although I was distracted for a while when I figured out I could suck my nostrils shut."

Ray lowered his head. Hugo already sounded drunk.

"I'm sorry," Hugo said. "I'm making you feel uncomfortable. I forgot, you're a Christian."

Ray sighed. A lot of people seemed to be forgetting that.

Hugo suddenly rose, went to the fridge, and opened the door. It was going to be an uncomfortable moment, but Ray was going to have to stand his ground and tell Hugo he had no plans to get drunk with him. Hugo returned with two brown-glass bottles and handed Ray one.

"Sir," Ray said. "I'm sorry, I just can't drink this."

Hugo fell into the couch and said, "You don't like root beer? We've got Coke, I think."

Ray looked down at the bottle. Root beer. Embarrassment flushed his cheeks, and he took a swig. "Root beer's fine, sir."

"You know," Hugo continued, "you're single, Ray. You have the whole world in front of you. You should think about not settling down. Maybe you already have, and that's why you're the age you are and aren't married."

Ray tried to smile.

"Anyway, if you do find that special someone, you might want to talk through your whole life together. Come up with every scenario possible, and then see what the other person would do. That's a good way to spend a date actually."

Ray really wanted to get on with how to help Roarke, but he was in this man's house at an obscene hour. He figured he should afford Hugo the courtesy of listening to him ruminate. Hugo waggled his finger toward a bookcase like it might be listening. "You tell that Roarke that as mismatched as he and Gilda are, I think they have a future. And tell him not to bother with premarital counseling." Hugo took a breath and then a swig of his root beer. "This isn't really doing it for me."

"Doing what for you, sir?"

"Ray, I'm going to let you in on a little secret."

Ray didn't want to be let in on anymore secrets.

"Did you know that I'm a high-strung kind of fella?"

"You?" Ray laughed a little. "I would never think of you as high strung. Jill Clark, yes. You, no."

"I'm high-strunger than Jill," Hugo said, and Ray had to glance down at the bottle in his hand to make sure it was root beer. "You see, I'm on the Blue Pill. It's real tiny. Smaller than an aspirin. It makes me calm."

"Do you…take it regularly?" Ray asked, wondering if he might need to get it for him now. Hayden had already spilled the beans on his antianxiety medication, but Hugo looked like he needed to explain.

"Twice a day. My doctor is very strict about it. She won't write me a prescription for anything above what I'm on. She thinks I don't need it. She thinks the problem might be that my life, not my chemicals, are unbalanced."

Ray started to feel like he might need to come up with an excuse to leave.

"I'm talking about the chemicals in my brain," Hugo continued, pointing to his skull.

"I see," Ray said. He didn't.

"And there is something to be said for not feeling all numbed up. Going with your gut, you know? My gut made the decision to run your story, for example." He patted his slightly bulging belly. Then he sighed into the silence. "I'm not the person everyone thinks I am."

Ray laughed a little. "Well, sir, I am the person *nobody* thinks I am."

Hugo scratched his head and laughed. "Okay. You're going to have explain that one."

"I don't know. People think of me as soft-spoken. I guess I am a little. But you know, I used to be more outspoken about my faith. In the past few years, I guess I started taking it for granted, you know? I stopped talking about it, stopped applying it to my everyday life."

"For heaven's sake, Ray, that's what I like about you. Do you know what it's like to work with Hayden Hazard? She's always wanting to pray for me and encourage me. And even when I'm mean to her, she's nice to me. It's annoying. Nothing gets her worried. I think there's a mental condition or something that causes some people not to worry. I can't remember the name of it. Anyway..." Hugo sighed. "But she is nice."

"What made you decide to put her in the anchor chair with no experience?" Ray asked.

"The woman has nerves of steel. Nothing gets to her. I saw her showing Tate how to look into the camera, and I realized she was going to be a natural. I have a good sense for talent."

Ray settled into the couch. He wasn't going anywhere anytime soon, and maybe during Hugo's erratic rants, he might come up with a solution on how to get Roarke out of jail.

For the next forty-five minutes, Ray contemplated whether or not he should tell Hugo about the strange disappearance of every e-mail from Chad Arbus to Gilda while Hugo detailed his theory about what makes the Purple Pill better than the Blue Pill.

Chapter 33

R ay awoke and looked around, trying to figure out where he was. His head snapped to the left, and there was Hugo next to him. They were both sitting on the couch, and Hugo's head had fallen backward. He was snoring loudly. Ray rubbed his eyes and sat up. Outside the sun was just warming the dark sky. Ray had never felt more embarrassed in his life. He looked toward the staircase, wondering if Mrs. Talley had come down to discover him on the couch.

He promptly stood up, waking Hugo. He glanced at Ray, as if not surprised to see him standing in his living room, then grabbed the remote to the television. He checked his watch as he turned the TV on.

"Sit down, Ray," he ordered. Ray slowly obeyed, sitting on the edge of the couch and resisting the urge to ask if there was any coffee. He really needed an excuse to pace.

That familiar and hated News Channel 10 jingle filled the quiet around them. Ray could feel the tension build in the air as they both waited for the news to start. Their morning anchors' normal cheery faces were replaced with serious expressions. Hugo shook his head and looked at Ray. "This isn't good."

"Good morning," the woman anchor said. "Breaking news this morning concerning the disappearance of News Channel 7 anchor Gilda Braun." Pictures flashed up of their news station, and both men groaned. Then a small insert showed Gilda's picture, and Ray was pretty sure it was the most unflattering picture he'd ever seen of her. Her mouth looked contorted and her hair unkempt. "Last night, police conducted a search of the News Channel 7 station…"

The visuals now told the story as the screen showed a shot of the inside of their offices. As the camera turned, so did a lot of faces, right toward it, with expressions of bewilderment, despondence, and fright. The anchor's voice smoothly added words to the pictures, as if they didn't tell their own story. But in this case, they didn't want the pictures to tell the story, they wanted the story to tell the pictures.

"...in connection with the disappearance of Gilda Braun. And late last night, police tell us they arrested a man they're calling a 'person of interest.'"

"Oh no," Ray groaned.

"They have not released his name yet," the anchor continued, and Ray let out a huge sigh, "but they do tell us that he wrote love letters to the anchor and that he is a News Channel 7 employee. He is being held on unrelated charges.

"Meanwhile, executive producer Hugo Talley had no comment on the situation..." Hugo winced as they showed him putting his hand up and yelling at the reporter to get out of the station.

Hugo punched the remote, turning off the television. "This is going to make the national news."

"What do you want me to do?" Ray asked. He'd never seen his boss look so desperate.

"I don't know. I've got to get into the office, figure out if there is any way we can spin this thing. We're going to have to report the story or we'll look like fools." Hugo cut his eyes sideways to Ray. "The police aren't saying who they have in custody. We can have the one-up by breaking that part of the story wide open."

"No!" Ray said. He turned, wanting to reach grab Hugo by his shoulders. "No, Hugo. We can't do that to Roarke. He's innocent. We know that. We can't exploit him like that."

"If we don't, they will soon enough. If we get it out there first, we'll have control over the story instead of lagging behind and trying to play catch up. We spin it first, and we have control over the story."

Ray put his hands over his face, trying to get a grip. "Then let me take the story. I want to report it."

Hugo shook his head. "No, Ray. You have to follow up on the sewage plant explosion. We've got to have another story to draw upon. You break that story wide open, and Gilda's disappearance will take a backseat."

Ray sighed, and his shoulders felt the burden of the task that could save his friend from eternal embarrassment. "Who are you going to put on Gilda's story?"

"Jill, of course."

"Hugo, Jill doesn't have the sensitivity needed to cover this story."

"You're suggesting Trent?"

Ray ran his hands through his hair. "I don't know. Trent is too inexperienced."

"I'm going with Jill. But I'll micromanage the story. Ray, I know what's at stake, okay?"

Ray nodded then looked at his watch. "I'd better be going." He looked at the staircase again, surprised that he hadn't seen Hugo's wife come down. He thought she had to leave for work pretty early.

"Make certain you are at the afternoon meeting. We'll have a lot to discuss."

"I know." Ray went to the front door. He wanted to say something, anything, that might give some hope to the situation, but nothing came to him, so he gave Hugo a nod and walked to his car. He heard the door close behind him just as his cell phone rang.

"Hello?"

"Ray, it's Mack. What are you doing right now?"

"Uh..."

"Good. Meet me at the corner of Eighth and Vessel in ten minutes."

"But—"

"We're going to find out what the news director of a station with a missing anchor does with his morning."

Ray slid into a maroon Pontiac, keeping his sunglasses on. Mack smiled, and Ray noticed her glasses were even darker than his. In one sense, Ray felt ridiculous. He had a huge news story to cover, with the two leads the Electric Horseman had suggested, and here he was hiding out in the rental car of the sister of the woman on whom he had a crush. But in another sense, he trusted Mack. She'd already found out valuable information on Gilda, and maybe she could help him put together the puzzle pieces.

She handed him a steaming foam cup. "Here. Hayden said you liked coffee."

"Oh. Thanks."

"That's his house up ahead," she said, pointing to a huge, colonial-style mansion that seemed out of place in the neighborhood.

"So we're going to break in and look for information?" Ray asked.

"That would be illegal," Mack said. "We're going to wait until he leaves, and then we're going to follow him."

Ray sighed. "Mack, I appreciate your involvement, I really do. But I've got a huge story to follow, and I can't waste time sitting around waiting for Chad Arbus to drive to what will probably be his office."

Mack smiled a little. "A hundred bucks says he doesn't go to work."

"Why do you say that?"

"Deal or no deal?"

Ray sighed. "Let's go for ten. Anything over that does make one wonder about gambling tendencies, doesn't it?"

She laughed. "Fine. Ten bucks."

"Why do you think he won't go to the station?"

"Because Hayden said that Mr. Talley has had a hard time reaching him, that he's not answering his phone, and that he's not keeping his usual hours."

"Not surprising," Ray said, "considering the circumstances."

"You have to use your imagination, Ray," she said. "And when I imagine what I would be doing in Mr. Arbus's shoes, I imagine I'd be at the station and in everyone's business."

Ray stared down at his coffee. He really could use the caffeine, but he'd hate to gag in front of Hayden's sister.

"Where's Hayden?" he asked.

"She went in early, just to see how she could help Mr. Talley, if he needed it. She was up all night praying for Roarke. She feels horrible." Mack adjusted her glasses and stared forward as she said, "You know if you hurt my sister in any way, you'll pay. And I'm not talking in the gambling sense."

Ray's jaw would've dropped had it not been clenched shut with shock. "What?"

"I like you, Ray. I really do. And I have a feeling you know how to treat a woman—particularly a woman like my sister—with respect and decency. But if you for some reason decide not to, you'll really be sorry. I've been known to make grown men cry, and not in the 'happy tears' sense."

Ray swallowed, squeezing the cup in his hand.

"I like to pray, Ray. I pray a lot. In fact, while I was waiting for you, I prayed that we would find out the truth about this whole situation. And I believe God is going to answer that prayer. I pray for a lot of things and a lot of people. But nobody wants me praying for them when I'm angry, you know what I mean?"

Ray nodded a little. Though her voice was calm and even a little cheerful, the words and the threat weren't lost on him.

"I think you two would make a great couple," she continued, still keeping her focus ahead. "You're really cute together. And Hayden likes you a lot. She talks about you all the time."

"Oh…good…," he tried to pull off casually.

"So it perplexes me as to why you would also be interested in another reporter. I think her name is Jill."

"Jill?" Ray nearly shouted. "I'm not interested in Jill! I hate Jill!" Ray cleared his throat. "I mean, I dislike Jill. I very dislike Jill."

"That's not what Jill said," Mack said, finally looking at him. She pulled her glasses down to the tip of her nose.

"Jill said what?"

"That you two were an item."

Ray bit his lip, trying to keep a string of profanity from traipsing out of his mouth and making a really bad impression. "I just learned that Jill has feelings for me, but the feelings are not mutual," he said eagerly. "I can't stand Jill, and I can only imagine that her intentions were to ambush my relationship with Hayden."

Mack studied him for a moment. "I believe you."

Ray's head throbbed with stress and sleep deprivation. And he noticed, for the first time, that Mack's gun was barely visible beneath her sweater.

Mack smiled again. "Glad we got that cleared up."

"Yeah…"

At the same time they noticed the large iron gate in front of Chad's home slowly swinging open. Ray couldn't deny how uncomfortable he felt spying on his boss. But then again, he couldn't explain those missing e-mails either.

"Here we go," Mack said as Chad's silver Jaguar turned onto the street. "Let's see where Mr. Arbus takes us."

Ray nodded and slid down a little in his seat. It was going to be a long day.

They followed Chad for fifteen minutes on the highway. Mack was concentrating hard, and Ray didn't want to break that, but he also wanted to clear up a few things.

"Mack," he said gently, "I want you to know that I really like Hayden. She's not like anyone I've ever known. But I don't know if she's the right person for me, either. I'm just getting to know her."

Mack didn't glance over but nodded. "I know, Ray. You can't just jump in without getting to know a person."

"Okay, just so we're clear." Ray couldn't take his eyes off her gun. "You carry that weapon with you all the time?"

"Yes," she said.

"You know, I thought you and Hayden were a lot alike when I first met you, but now I'm realizing you two are pretty different."

"We are," Mack said. "And it doesn't surprise me you're drawn to Hayden's innocence. She's been like that her whole life. Some people mistake it for stupidity, but she's not stupid. Naive, yes. But that seems to get her from one place to another. And sometimes I wish I had a little more of that, you know?"

Ray smiled. Yes, he knew. "Some people just seem to be born with good hearts."

Mack nodded. "Yeah."

"So let me ask you a question. Where did you all get your names? Being from a conservative family, it seems you'd all be named after people from the Bible or something."

"We were all born during an unfortunate time in my mother's life when she was addicted to soap operas."

Ray laughed. "Really?"

"Yes. We're all named after soap-opera characters. Finally my dad made my mother stop watching them."

"I had a different picture of your family. I can't really see your mother watching soap operas."

"My mother was a saint. She homeschooled all of us. I think soap operas were an escape for her during the day. I remember her up in her bedroom, huddled around an old black-and-white television. None of us were allowed to disturb her between 2:00 and 3:00 p.m."

"Wow. Who would've thought?"

"I hate my name. Mackenzie. It sounds so…"

"Soap opera-ish?"

"Exactly. That's why I go by Mack." She suddenly sat up taller and pointed. "Look, he's getting off the highway."

She slowed down a little and followed carefully as Chad made two right turns and then a left into a mall parking garage.

"He's doing a little shopping?" Ray asked.

"Yeah, except the mall isn't open yet." Mack pulled the car onto the first level of the garage and watched Arbus go up. "Come on. We're going to have to follow on foot."

Chad checked his rearview mirror as he headed to the top story of the parking garage. The morning light was getting brighter, but he'd made a good choice to meet him here. The mall employees were coming in, and there were several cars around so as to not draw attention to his.

He slowed down and found a parking spot. Rolling down his window, he looked around cautiously for a tan Oldsmobile. He spotted it a few cars away from his. Through the dark tint he could see a shadowy figure inside. As calmly as possible, he got out of his car and walked to the other car. He didn't flinch as the Oldsmobile's car door opened. Howard Crumm's oily hair stayed stuck to his head even in the morning breeze. He didn't look happy and didn't mind showing it. Chad watched carefully as Crumm pulled out a briefcase and met Chad a few feet away.

"Don't look so surprised," Howard said. "You knew I would come."

"Your past speaks for itself," Chad replied.

Crumm kept a steady expression as he handed over the suitcase. "Count it if you'd like."

"Sure. I'll open up a suitcase full of money right here in the middle of a parking lot. Nobody will notice."

"There's a security camera up there," Crumm said, without averting his eyes toward it.

"I know," Chad said. "That's just in case you decided to do something crazy, like kill me."

"But if I don't do anything, then nobody has any reason to look at those tapes."

"Exactly."

"In return for this," Crumm said, "you will stop the investigation into the explosion."

"Yes."

"Enough damage has been done, but I can handle it as long as nothing else leaks out."

"I'm sure you can," Chad said. "You're a capable businessman."

"Save the compliments," Crumm said. "I have your assurances there will be no more of the story aired, and that you will retract what you've already said?"

"We'll smooth it over," Chad said. "We'll make a reference to our sources as untrustworthy, something like that."

"It'd better look authentic."

"Believe me, it won't take much. The big story around town is our anchor's disappearance. We'll have no problem distracting our viewers."

"And this reporter, Duffey, isn't going to be a problem any longer?"

"I can assure you I will take care of him. Personally."

Crumm's face turned sour as he looked at the briefcase. "I'll be on my way. I'd better never see you again."

Chad smiled and turned toward his car. It was time he went back to the office and earned his money.

Mack kept a hand on Ray's shoulder as they stayed in the shadow of the stairwell.

Ray was speechless. They'd watched the two men exchange a briefcase and a few words, though they couldn't quite hear what was being said. What in the world was Chad Arbus doing meeting with Howard Crumm? And what was in the briefcase?

"We have to get closer!" Ray had whispered as they watched the two men. "I can't hear anything they're saying."

But Mack kept her hand against Ray. "A picture speaks a thousand words, my friend."

"What's in the briefcase?" Ray asked.

"I don't know," Mack said. "But we're one step closer to explaining why those e-mails disappeared."

They watched both cars drive off and then walked back to Mack's car. "Gilda knew something," Mack considered, thinking out loud. "But what? What would Gilda know that Chad Arbus wouldn't want anybody else to know?"

"Or vice versa," Ray said. "Who knows who erased those e-mails? Maybe it was Gilda, maybe it was someone else."

"True," said Mack. "We're going to have to get back on Gilda's computer somehow."

Chapter 34

P lease tell me you have more to the story," Hugo said, his eyes full of desperation. "Because right now, I can't figure out how to spin Gilda's thing in a positive way. We've got to have something big on the sewage plant."

"Mr. Talley, I've got a huge break in the story," Ray answered, then paused. "I think. But I'm going to need access to Gilda's computer."

Hugo grumbled. "Why?"

Ray quietly closed Hugo's door. "Mr. Talley, I don't know how to tell you this, and right now I think it's best if I give you as little information as possible."

"Me too," Hugo said, looking like he might just start crying.

"We know that Petey Green tried to contact Gilda concerning the plant and the chemical. But there may be more. And"—Ray took a deep breath—"this may go up into management."

"Management."

"Yeah."

"Are you talking about—what are you talking about?"

"Chad Arbus."

"How could he be involved in the plant explosion?"

"I don't know exactly. But I do know that Mr. Arbus and Howard Crumm met this morning in a parking garage."

"How do you know *that*?"

"I'm an investigative reporter, sir."

"You're spying on our boss?"

"What legitimate reason could Mr. Arbus have for meeting with Howard Crumm?"

"I don't know, but there are always two sides to a story. We can't just go around making assumptions, Ray. I need cold, hard facts."

"I know, sir. That's why I need Gilda's computer. I happen to know that a bunch of e-mails between Gilda and Arbus are missing. I checked this morning with the IT department, and the techs said they'd also been erased from the backup system."

"Ray, you've always been gutsy. That's one thing that I like about you. But you've gone too far. Implying that—well, whatever you're implying could get us all in a lot of trouble."

"You know me well enough to know that I don't chase rabbits. If I didn't think there was anything significant to this, I wouldn't ask. Sir, not only is sweeps week on the line here, but so is the integrity of our station. You've got to at least let me check this out. If I don't find anything, I'll back off." Ray took a step closer as Hugo contemplated this. "Let me take a look at her computer."

"Yeah, well, good luck with that. The police confiscated it this morning."

Captain Wynn stood to shake the young woman's hand, which was so soft it made his entire body tingle. He stretched a delighted grin across his face. "Captain Tony Wynn."

"Mack Jones." The woman flashed a badge, but Wynn was too busy looking at her to take notice of it. "Las Vegas Police."

Captain Wynn nodded. "Someone from your office called earlier to say you'd be by."

"May we speak in private?" the woman asked, and Captain Wynn rose to shut his door. There weren't too many women in law enforcement that Wynn found attractive. Maybe it was because he had to work with them. But this woman he could definitely look at all day.

And she looked a little familiar. He wondered if he'd seen her on TV. Maybe during the Las Vegas bank robbery that made national news last February.

"What can I do for you?"

"As my supervisor mentioned, we're interested in Roarke Keegan."

"She didn't say why," Wynn said, opening his hands. "And as you may know, I'm a curious person."

"Of course," the woman said, smiling, and there was a lot of flirt in that smile. "I understand you have the computer of the woman who disappeared."

"Yes."

"May I take a look-see?"

Look-see. Cute. He hadn't heard that word in a while. It reminded him of his grandmother. "You want to tell me why?"

"This may sound strange, but we've got an egregious and assailable situation involving an eidetic individual who is indubitable in her report of an arcane robbery in south Las Vegas. Now, I'm not convinced. At one point, she abjured her written statement, which then caused us to have to retract our avouchment. And you know how embarrassing that can be." Wynn nodded a little. "So as you can see, the situation is precipitating, but if our theory holds together, you and I are going to have one stupefying story for the media."

Media. Now that word he understood.

Her face twisted into an apologetic expression. "I'm sorry. Am I talking over your head? I tend to do that sometimes."

"No…"

"Great. So you understand why I need to look at that computer. Chances are we'll find no connection, but if we do, you could find yourself on the cover of *People* magazine."

"Right this way."

Ray was coming up empty. Without Gilda's computer, he had no way to clarify her relationship with Chad. Without a reason as to why those e-mails disappeared, his story was at a dead end. He needed more time. Mack had said she was going to investigate, but he hadn't heard from her all afternoon.

It didn't help that Hayden had come by his desk and told him how much she appreciated him. He needed to be focused, but part of him just wanted to run off into the sunset with this woman and leave all his troubles behind.

Unfortunately, that would mean leaving Roarke behind, and he couldn't do that. He'd talked to his friend by phone, assuring him they were making progress. But he knew he didn't sound very hopeful, and Roarke didn't sound like he believed him.

Ray's stomach felt woozy as he realized it was time for the afternoon meeting. He gathered his notes, and then he noticed Chad come out of his office for the first time all day. He'd seen Hugo go in a couple of times but had yet to see Chad since witnessing him accept the briefcase from Crumm. It was going to feel strange sitting at a table opposite him, but Ray was going to have to deal with it and hope that Hugo had kept the information to himself.

Strangely, Chad had energy in his step, and there wasn't an ounce of concern on his face. A few others made their way to the conference room. Ray decided there was nothing he could do but join them.

Hugo called the meeting to order fairly quickly, and he spent the first ten minutes detailing what the other stations had reported. Then he finished by explaining that they were going ahead with the report on the sewage plant as their lead story.

"Ray, what do you have new?"

Ray glanced around the room and said, "I'm still working on some leads."

"What leads?" Chad asked.

"Well, um, there seem to be a lot of missing pieces to the story. And"—Ray held his breath for a moment—"Gilda's disappearance may be a part of it."

The mood of the room indicated both surprise and skepticism. "I know it sounds crazy," Ray said, attempting to speak over the alarmed voices and nervous laughter. He avoided Chad's eyes. "But we do know that Gilda was contacted by Petey Green, and maybe she had too much information."

"What do you have other than those letters to prove that?" Chad asked.

"I'm working on it," Ray said.

"Look," Chad said, "I know we all want to know what happened to Gilda, but right now we've got to set our emotions aside and realize that we've got a news station to run. And the top story right now is Gilda's disappearance. Jill, you've got quite a few good sound bites, don't you?"

"Yes," Jill smiled, "including one eyewitness who swears she saw Gilda on the south side of town."

"The other stations have been covering this all day, but we're the station with the missing anchor. People are going to tune in to us to see the personal side of the story," Chad said. "I think we should do some in-house interviews, talk to some of the staff, see how they're feeling."

"What?" Ray could hardly believe what he was hearing.

"It's human drama, Ray," Chad said. "One of our own is missing, and one of our own is suspected in her disappearance. I want interviews with people who worked closely with Roarke. How are they feeling? Did they ever suspect anything? What odd behaviors did he have to indicate he might be a stalker?"

Ray jumped to his feet, slapping his hand against the table. "No! I won't stand for this! We all know Roarke, and we know this is just a huge misunderstanding. They haven't even charged him yet!"

"But they are calling him a person of interest," Jill said smoothly, smiling at Chad.

"How can you all even think of doing this to him?"

"Ray, you're letting your emotions get the best of you," Chad chided. "And you know one of the top rules of the news business is to leave your emotions out of it. We're simply reporting a story here, and it is certainly a sad turn of events. But are we going to censor ourselves and keep the public in the dark simply because we want to protect one of our own?"

"This is ridiculous!" Ray shouted. "You and I both know that this is being spun for ratings purposes at the expense of Roarke's integrity."

Chad said, "Hey, I'm not the one who wrote love letters to her."

Ray was seconds away from springing across the table and punching the daylights out of Chad. But he caught a glimpse of Hayden and her wide, scared eyes. He took a breath to get himself together.

Chad glanced at Hayden and deliberately ran his eyes from the top of her head downward. Then he looked back at Ray, grinning. "We're cutting the wastewater treatment plant all together."

"What?" This time it was Hugo. Ray didn't have any breath left. Anger and shock rippled through him.

"Come on, gentlemen. Aren't we just stabbing in the dark here? Yeah, it has some compelling pieces to it, but that's like covering a wildfire while a hurricane strikes. The wildfire is interesting until something bigger and more threatening comes along. Scandal and embezzling can go a long way, but it's no match for kidnapping, murder, and one man's obsession for a woman." Chad smiled at everyone like he'd just announced bonuses.

"You're saying cut the whole story?" Hugo asked, bewilderment evident on his face. He didn't look angry, just confused.

"That's what I'm saying. Folks, I've been in this business a while now, and I know what makes good news. We're going with Gilda's disappearance, and I want it covered from every angle. Jill, get interviews with the staff. Trent, I want you live from in front of the jail. See if we can get some good sound bites from the police. And Ray…" He paused and locked eyes with him. "Why don't you go out and see what the public thinks about it? Go to some nursing homes and see what the elderly are feeling and thinking. They must be devastated."

"You're making a huge mistake," Ray said. "You know this sewage story is big. You just don't want…" Ray paused, wondering if he should show all his cards. He could expose Chad right now, but was that the smart move? And would Ray just look like he was desperate? Who would believe him without evidence?

"Yes, Ray?" Chad asked, looking as if he wanted Ray to make a spectacle of himself.

"Nothing," Ray mumbled and sat down, shooting Hugo a look.

Hugo didn't make eye contact but instead said, "All right, everyone. You have your assignments. Let's make sure we're at the top of our game today, okay?" Hugo looked at Ray and tried to give him a reassuring nod.

The first one out of the meeting, Ray couldn't begin to disguise his disgust. He went to his desk and shuffled papers in an effort to keep himself from going off on a certain someone. Chad walked out of the meeting and smiled at Ray as he passed.

But no matter how many papers Ray shuffled, he couldn't stop the imaginary conversation in his head in which he told off Chad Arbus and, more important, told Chad Arbus that he knew his dirty little secret too. What that dirty little secret meant, he didn't know, but he was going to find out. Right after he went to the nursing home.

"Hey."

Ray looked up. Hayden was smiling at him. He couldn't smile back. The time of faking his own serenity was over. The fact of the matter was he was a flawed human being, and he couldn't see the rainbow after every storm like Hayden. He just didn't have a faith like hers, and he was done pretending he did.

"Ray," she said calmly, "it's going to be okay. I know you're worried about Roarke. We all are. But God knows what he's doing. It's all going to work out for those who love God and are called according to his purpose. For everyone else, I can't say. But there is a reason behind all this, and we just have to trust him."

Things were messed up right now. And his friend was suffering in jail because of it. Injustice was rearing its ugly head, burning everyone with fire, and Ray was supposed to believe this all had purpose? That God was in control?

Ray looked down and wished Hayden would go away. But she didn't. She started to say something, but he cut her off. "Look, Hayden, you're an extraordinary person, okay? I recognize that, and so do half the people here at the station. You live your faith. You believe God, you take him at his Word. I'm not like you, though, okay? I have doubts. Lots of them. Almost all of the time. Yes, I pray and go to church and read my Bible. But sometimes I shake my fist at God. It's not the picture of peace, I realize, and I certainly make no claims of wearing the armor of God. I'm lucky if I can get the underwear of decency on, all right? All I care about right now is getting my friend out of jail. Of all people, Roarke doesn't deserve to be in there, and he certainly doesn't deserve to be exploited so we can conquer sweeps week." Ray's voice cracked, and he could feel his eyes tearing up. "So go ahead, say whatever you were going to say. But don't expect me to smile and agree, okay?"

He finally looked up at her, and more than anything, she looked concerned. But he also saw hurt in her eyes. Ray felt horrible. Of all the people who could have hurt Hayden, he was the one to do it. Shame swept over him, and he wanted to crawl under his desk.

"I'm sorry," he said softly.

Hayden rushed around his desk and took his hand. "Don't apologize, Ray. And don't think more highly of me than you should. We all have our doubts. I have many, just like you."

Ray looked at her. He had a hard time believing she had doubts. He was also having a hard time swallowing the fact that he'd mentioned his underwear.

"What were you going to say?" Ray asked. "I probably need to hear it, even if I don't want to."

She smiled and took his hand. "I wanted to tell you that I heard from Mack. She told me to tell you she thinks she's figured it out. She wants you to call her from a secure location."

Chapter 35

M ack pulled the car up in front of a hotel. Ray could only imagine that the occupants inside were as sleazy as the outside. It looked greasy, from the roof to the sidewalk below. They were on the south side of town, a place Beaker absolutely refused to go. Ray hadn't been here much either.

He looked up at the neon sign. In pink cursive it read *The Laguna.* "Are you sure?"

"No," Mack said. "But I have a good hunch."

On the way over, Mack had explained what she'd found on Gilda's computer. It was not in her e-mail, but in her Word documents, notes containing information Gilda had found confirming Crumm's shell corporation scandal and the fact that the chemical being used at the plant was unsafe. Mack said there were ten pages of notes in all, including testimony from two other plant employees, neither of whom were Petey Green.

"The two people the Electric Horseman mentioned," Ray said. "So Gilda knew. Then why didn't she go forward with the story? That's not like Gilda. She lives for stories like this."

"That's what we have to find out," Mack said, opening her door.

Ray got out too, jittery with anticipation.

As they walked toward the dimly lit front desk, he asked, "Why do you think she's here?"

"I don't know for certain that she is. But when I got access to her computer, I saw that she had been on the Internet late Thursday night, and she had done a lot of searches for 'Laguna Beach.'"

"Which would explain the summer clothes."

"Yeah."

"So why do you think she's here? Just because the sign says Laguna?"

"There were many signs."

Ray sighed heavily. "From God? He told you to come here?"

Mack stopped and turned to him. "Yes, Ray, complete with a boom-ing voice and fire on the mountain." She continued walking, and Ray fol-lowed behind, kicking himself for being such a moron. "I checked to see if she had been on MapQuest. She had, and this was the address that came up. There were signs in her Internet search that showed that at some point Gilda realized she wasn't going to California."

Mack approached the man at the front desk and flashed her badge. He didn't look impressed or surprised.

"Have you ever seen this woman?" She held up a publicity photo of Gilda she printed off the Internet.

"I'm not very observant," he said with a thin smile.

"How many occupants do you have that have been here for five days?"

The man sighed. "You know, in my business, people rely on me to be discreet." He pulled out a dingy looking piece of paper and eyeballed it. "Three."

"How many female?"

"One."

"Room number?"

"Forty-two."

"Key?"

The man grumbled and handed it over. "Stay here," Mack instructed the man. "We'll let you know if we need anything."

"Just don't go shooting holes in my walls, okay? I just got four suites repaired."

"Suites," Mack said. "Right."

The Laguna was a hotel, not a motel, with five stories. The elevator's creaky doors opened halfway. "Come on," Mack urged then grinned. "I'll catch you if we drop."

"Funny."

Mack pushed the button for the fourth floor, and the elevator crept upward like it was carrying an extra seven tons. Ray and Mack stood with their backs against the wall. Ray was pretty sure he could hear his own heartbeat.

"So how'd you get access to Gilda's computer at the police station?"

"I have my ways. The toughest part was leaving. Captain Wynn apparently likes blondes with guns. Hayden tipped me off to the fact that he also likes to see himself on television. I worked that to my advantage, needless to say. Then I had to make him believe it was all a misunderstanding and that I didn't find anything useful on the computer."

"How'd you do it?"

"I told him I thought I saw a network reporter out front. It was like magic."

Ray laughed. "Good one."

"Thanks."

They were only at the second floor. The ride seemed to be taking hours.

The silence was too much for Ray. "I yelled at your sister today and mentioned my underwear. I'm truly sorry."

Mack didn't look pleased. "In what regard did you mention your underwear?"

Ray swallowed. "In a…metaphorical sense."

Mack raised an eyebrow. "Did my sister cry?"

"She almost made me cry, actually."

Mack nodded like that pleased her. "Let's keep your undergarments out of the relationship. Understood?"

"Yes."

"Good. Now let's go find Gilda."

There were many things Hugo should've been doing, and to anyone observing him outside his glass wall, he would have seemed to be in a feverish work mode. Instead, he was writing a lengthy e-mail to his wife. He knew better than to write something so personal on company e-mail. One employee had gotten burned when he thought he was passing a dirty joke along to a friend. Turned out it went to the entire station.

But he'd tried to call her and hadn't had any luck. On a normal day, Hugo lived for this kind of news. The fact that his station was in the middle of it made it a bit more complicated, but still, he would've approached it with effort and fervor.

Instead, he was typing a letter to his wife.

Jill Clark opened his door, interrupting his thoughts. "I need to talk to you."

"I'm busy," Hugo said without looking at her. Then he heard the sound of a shaking pill bottle.

"I stole them," she said, placing them on his desk. "I'm sorry."

"Why?"

"I've seen you taking them," she said. "I didn't realize it was anxiety medication. I thought it was for a social phobia."

"A social phobia?"

Jill looked embarrassed. "I thought it might help me approach this guy I like. I have trouble telling people how I really feel. I act one way but feel another. I don't really know if it worked. It definitely made me feel calmer. But I felt bad for taking them."

"You thought I had a social disorder?"

"Well, you are really calm. I mistook that for social problems. I'm sorry." And she walked out.

Hugo looked at the e-mail. He had just been explaining to Jane about the missing pills. Before, he had known in his head how much she meant to him, but he couldn't feel it in his heart, and, he admitted, perhaps he'd become a little robotic in their relationship.

Hugo assured her that if she wanted him to keep his job, he would, but he begged her to tell him what it was she wanted, to give him another chance.

He closed by telling her that for a while he'd had his ideals about what his family should be like, where his wife should be and when. He'd been misguided to think that it was the modern world around him that was to blame for his discontentment. He'd realized, in fact, that he had to find contentment and peace with himself and the world in which he lived before he could make anybody else happy.

He ended it with a few simple phrases. "I'm praying for us. I'm praying for you. Pray for me."

It's what Hayden always told him, and it had sounded so foolish for so long. Now it seemed all he had to hang on to was prayer and divine intervention. He finished the e-mail and saw Hayden walk by. He rushed to his office door and called her in.

"Yes, Mr. Talley?" she asked. He shut the door and told her to sit down.

"Hayden, my marriage is falling apart."

"Mr. Talley, I'm so sorry," she said, reaching for his hand. He took it and squeezed it. He didn't care who saw or what office protocol he was breaking. He just wanted hope.

"My marriage is the only thing I have left of who I was," Hugo said. "It might shock you to know that I wasn't always like this. I had ideals and convictions, you know. But after a while, you give in a little, and then you give in a little more, and the next thing you know, you can watch an entire family being brought out of a house in body bags with complete indifference. All you care about is getting it on the news first and making sure you've got the best pictures. I don't need a stupid pill to numb me. I've been numb for a long time." He wiped his tears. "Will you pray for me?"

"Of course I will. I will pray for you as often as the Lord brings you to my heart."

"Will you pray for me now?"

He could tell that surprised her. "It's time I felt a little discomfort," Hugo said.

"Gilda?" Ray could hardly believe the sight in front of him. She stood in the doorway of her hotel room, decked out in a white bathrobe, her hair pulled back by a barrette.

"How did you find me?" she whispered, then noticed Mack. "And who is this?"

"We need to come in," Ray said.

Gilda looked reluctant. She opened the door and said, "The cleanest place to sit is the window sill."

Ray walked into the darkened room, lit with a single lamp. There was a crusty-looking bathroom and the lingering smell of pot that overflowed from the other rooms. A laundry bag sat on the chair next to the bed, and Ray could see the edge of what looked like a Hawaiian shirt poking out. The television was on, turned down low, and a few books were scattered across a filthy, but neatly made bed.

"Are you okay?" Ray asked, turning to her.

She nodded as tears flowed from her eyes. "You weren't supposed to find me. What tipped you off?" she asked. Ray was about to explain everything when she said, "It was my accent, wasn't it?"

"What?"

"I tried to hide it, but it's hard to hide a southern accent."

Ray's jaw dropped. "*You're* the Electric Horseman?"

"Isn't that how you found me?"

He shook his head, almost laughing. "It's a little more complicated than that."

"I bought the cheapest voice scrambler they had. I thought that's what did me in." She looked at Mack. "You look a little familiar."

"This is Hayden's sister, Mack. She's a police officer."

Gilda looked down. "Are you arresting me?"

"I have no jurisdiction here, ma'am, though don't tell anybody that. I faked my way into finding you."

Gilda looked at her. "Your sister, she's got real talent. I've watched her every night she's been on. She's a natural. And really beautiful."

Ray leaned against the window sill on Gilda's advice. "Tell me why you're here. What led to all of this? Was it the incident Thursday?"

Gilda scowled. "That's what it was made to look like." She sighed and threw up her hands. "I might as well tell you the entire thing. At this point, I don't care if I go to jail."

"Roarke's in jail," Ray said.

"Roarke?" Gilda looked astonished. "Roarke is the person of interest? Roarke is the one who's been sending me the love letters?"

"He didn't mean any harm," Ray quickly explained. "You know Roarke. He's not weird. He just didn't know how to tell you how much he liked you." Ray felt his throat swell a little. "Let him off easy, will you?"

"Easy? I'm not letting him off anything. That man owes me dinner and a bouquet of roses." She smiled. "I'm glad it was Roarke. I thought it might be Tate or Sam, and that was really starting to worry me." She shrugged. "You're right, Roarke's not really my type. But maybe that's because I didn't know what a romantic he could be."

Ray smiled, but Mack didn't look as engaged. "Ms. Braun, we need to know how you ended up in this hotel. There are a lot of people who want to know where you are."

The joy in the room faded and Gilda slowly sat on the bed. "It started with someone sending me anonymous letters over the last two months about the wastewater treatment plant. I began investigating the claims and found two employees who had been fired. They worked in different parts of the plant and didn't know one another. Both of them had been 'laid off' due to budget cuts, but they both suspected that it was because of what they knew. One was in accounting and had raised questions about the exchange of money between the two companies. The other worked as a safety coordinator. Neither one of them, however, was the real whistle-blower."

"I read all your notes in a file called 'Funny Forwards,'" Mack said. "You didn't seem like the kind of person who would collect forwarded e-mails into a file."

"Actually, I like them. Roarke was always sending me the funniest—anyway, the file was originally named 'Wastewater Notes.' Then things got complicated."

"How so?" Ray asked.

"I was floored at what I discovered. But all I had was personal accounts. I couldn't pin down any hard facts. Still, I was pretty sure I had a story building, especially when I discovered Howard Crumm's background. I put together what I had and asked to meet with Chad. I wanted to begin putting an investigative piece together. It had been years since I'd done anything like it, but I wanted everyone to see that I was a real news-woman, not just a talking head. If I couldn't be beautiful like the other anchors, at least I would be smart. And make a difference. I went straight to Chad because I wanted the story to myself and I knew it would prob-ably be reassigned if I brought it up in the meeting."

"What happened?"

"Chad shot it down immediately. He told me it was ludicrous and then asked me what exactly I thought I'd be accomplishing by suggesting that there was a bit of scandal inside a sewage plant. He said, and I quote, 'If it's not sexy, lurid, horrific, or dramatic, there's no need to waste airtime.

There's nothing sexy about sewage.' And then he added that his sewage bill was down five dollars a month, so what did he have to complain about?"

"When did this happen?" Ray asked.

"A week before the plant exploded. The day it happened, I was furious. I sent Chad an e-mail and reamed him up one side and down the other. And that's when it happened."

"What?"

"He blackmailed me."

"How?"

"Chad made the connection as to who P.G. was before I did, but when I told him we needed to go public with our information, he told me Green planned on suing our station and that I, personally, along with the station, was named in the lawsuit."

"He had to have made that up," Ray said. "I visited Green, and he never mentioned it."

"Chad said that not only was my job on the line, but so was everyone else's, and that if this lawsuit happened, he would make sure everyone blamed me for it. I was powerless. I didn't know what to do. The conversation I'd had with Chad was in person, so I had no documentation proving he'd made the original call not to pursue the story."

"So he made you come here?"

"He told me he wanted me to disappear for a week. One week. He said he would make all the arrangements and that I was to leave no evidence that I'd left in a planned manner. He just wanted it to appear that I'd vanished. After the week was up, I was to explain that I'd had a nervous breakdown and had gone to seek help."

"Let me guess," Mack said. "You were under the impression that the boss was sending you to some resort in California."

Gilda nodded. "I thought I was going somewhere nice. And you have to understand what kind of mental state I was in. I wasn't thinking clearly.

After Chad rejected my story, I felt useless. That's when I went to get the Botox, and we all know how that went. So I thought it might be good for me to take a nice little vacation."

"Why did you think Chad concocted this plan?"

"At first I thought he just wanted me out of there, to lay low, so to speak, and let it all pass over. But then I realized he'd planned all along for this to be a big story. He saw an opportunity to create buzz for sweeps week at my expense, and now, unfortunately, at the expense of others."

"So he was going to ride the wave of publicity through sweeps week," Mack said, "then use you and your supposed mental breakdown as a scapegoat. Who cares how the story ends, right? As long as it was after sweeps week."

"Exactly," Gilda sighed. "I've been sitting in this dungeon, hating myself for what I've done. But I couldn't bear to show my face either. Watching your sister made me realize maybe it's time for me to step down." She glanced at the books on the bed. "I've been reading a lot of Dr. Phil."

Mack stood. "Well, Gilda, there's a new story to tell, and it's time you told it, starting with the police. There's an innocent man behind bars who would probably stay there if he thought it would help you in any way."

Gilda's lip trembled. "I'll go to the police. But first, I want to settle a score. Let's go pay Chad Arbus a little visit, shall we?" She walked to the door. "I'm glad I have my frown back."

Chapter 36

M r. Talley?"
Hugo stopped clicking the Send-Receive button, which he'd been hitting every minute for the last hour, and waved Tate Franklin in. Still no reply from Jane. He had so much to do—scripts to write, loose ends to tie up—but he was waiting for a single e-mail.

"Look, Tate, I'm working on the script. I'll get it to you as soon as I can. I realize everyone's really stressed, and I can appreciate your concern, but we're just going to have to be a little flexible. Okay?"

Tate sat down in the chair across from his desk. "The thing is, Mr. Talley, I don't think this is for me."

"What isn't?" Hugo asked, reaching over to hit the Send-Receive button again. Nothing. His heart sank.

"I just need something more, I think. I'm not really sure." His hands opened up like he was searching for words, and Hugo tugged his attention away from his computer.

Hugo wasn't really following. "Tate, you're going to have to be more specific. You need more airtime? More lighting? What?"

"No," Tate said, laughing a little. "I'm talking about my life, Mr. Talley. This whole TV thing; it was cool for a while, you know. I mean, who doesn't want to be on television every day and have your face really big on a billboard? But I'm kind of"—Tate drew his eyes upward, then back to Hugo—"bored, I guess."

"I hate to break it to you, but this is about as exciting as it gets around here. We don't often get to cover our own news." *And thank goodness for that.*

Tate smiled awkwardly. Smiled, not smirked. Where had that been all this time? "I'm saying that I think I'm done."

"What does that mean?"

Tate glanced down like he was embarrassed. "I'm sorry. If my mother heard me say, 'I'm done,' she would pinch my cheek and tell me I'm not a roast. What I meant to say is, I'm finished."

Hugo's hands moved around his desk for no reason, except to find some sort of sharp object. He kept his eyes locked on Tate. "You're finished."

"I think so. It's been fun. Really. You've been great, and everyone here is amazing. But last night, during the broadcast, I was thinking about how much I miss skydiving, and I thought maybe I'd go out to New Mexico and start a skydiving company."

That would come in handy for him when Hugo pushed him off a cliff. Hugo stood, pacing behind his desk. "Tate, that is the most immature thing I've ever heard. First of all, why would you be thinking about that *during* the broadcast? Shouldn't you be thinking about *the broadcast?*" He sucked in a breath and a few choice words that nearly escaped. "Second, do you know how many people would give their right arm for your position? Son, I don't think you know how good you have it."

Tate looked humble but unashamed. "I know, Mr. Talley. And that's another reason I think my time's over. There are a lot of people who want to do this, but I don't. So why not move on?"

"In case you haven't noticed," Hugo said, "we're in the middle of sweeps week! This isn't really a good time to be talking about this! Not to mention your contract—have you looked at that lately? You can't just drop everything and walk out."

"I don't think I have another show in me."

Hugo marched around his desk and grabbed Tate by the shirt, pulling him to his feet, pushing his face within inches of Tate's. "What do you mean by that?" Hugo realized how nice it felt to be able to do this. He wondered how red his face was. This felt really, really good. Had he not been so angry, he would have smiled about it.

Tate's eyes flew wide open. "Mr. Talley, you're hurting me."

"I'm hurting your fancy shirt, Tate, not you." Hugo let go of him and he fell back into his chair. "Are you saying that you're quitting? Right now?"

Tate barely nodded.

"How can you do that? Don't you feel any sense of responsibility? Don't you understand the consequences of your actions? That's the problem with your generation! It's all about you, isn't it?" The tension in Hugo's voice climbed with every word. "Your mother didn't spank you, did she? This is what has happened to the entire generation of children who weren't spanked."

Tate's eyes widened. "Are you going to spank me?"

Hugo laughed, and then started laughing harder. He couldn't stop himself. He knew this was the kind of laugh that probably echoed through the corridors of every mental hospital in the country, but he didn't care. Tate felt like quitting? Hugo felt like laughing.

Tate smiled a little. "It's kind of freeing, you know."

Hugo teared up with laughter now.

"To be able to just walk away from something."

"My wife knows exactly what you mean," Hugo said. The laughter settled a little, and Hugo wiped the tears from his eyes.

Tate stood and stuck out his hand like he was some kind of gentleman. "I want to thank you for the honor, sir."

Hugo's smile had yet to fade. "It's three hours before we go on air. You don't see anything wrong with this picture?"

Tate kept his arm stuck straight out and pressed his lips firmly together.

And then Hugo saw her through his glass wall. She was walking across the newsroom, her stride swift, determined. Tate's arm was still sticking out when Hugo maneuvered around it and out the door of his office. Hugo thought he was seeing things, because upon first glance it looked like she was wrapped in a white, heavenly light. But then he realized she was wearing a white bathrobe. Hugo stood with his mouth open, watching her petite figure beeline toward Chad's office.

"Gilda?" he whispered, his voice hoarse with shock. He glanced around, hoping everyone else was taking notice, that he wasn't just seeing things. Everyone saw it. A few people stood. One person was clapping. Most everyone else was frozen. A few feet behind her, Ray followed. He looked at Hugo and smiled a little, then gave him a thumbs-up. Hugo had no idea what that meant, but it had to be good.

Of course it was good. Gilda was back.

Hugo raced forward and fell behind Gilda's quick stride and next to Ray, who said, "You're not going to believe this."

Gilda carried herself clear across the newsroom in a way that would not indicate she had any problems being seen in her bathrobe. It made Hugo wonder why, with that kind of confidence, she ever considered Botox. But that thought could wait.

"What's going on?" Hugo whispered.

But before Ray could answer, Gilda was in Chad's office, and Ray and Hugo were right behind her. The newsroom fell into complete silence.

Judging by Chad's expression, he wasn't expecting to see Gilda either. And then suddenly, he opened his arms and cried, "Gilda! You're back!"

"Give it up," Gilda said calmly. "Nobody's going to be fooled."

"Fooled?" Chad asked.

"I'm going to tell the entire story," she said. "On air."

Chad tried to hide his shocked expression with an uneasy smile. "Oh really."

"Yes."

"And what story would that be?"

"That you made a mistake telling me that my investigation into the wastewater treatment plant wasn't relevant, when, in fact, a week later the plant exploded. Then, to cover up your mistake, you blackmailed me, first by stealing all the e-mails detailing our discussion on the matter, and second, by claiming that I would take the fall if the station were sued. So you convinced me I should leave for a week until all this blew over and then come back claiming some sort of nervous breakdown. You said you would pay for it all, and that it was the best thing for everyone involved."

Chad glanced at Hugo, then at Ray, then back at Gilda. He looked speechless.

"But instead of letting it blow over, you decided to use it to your advantage by making it look like I disappeared. And besides that, you're a cheapskate. You could've afforded to send me to some nice resort. You sent me to a ratty old hotel!"

Chad now looked amused. "Gilda, who is going to believe a has-been like you?"

"I will," Ray said.

"Me too," Hugo said.

The rest of the newsroom agreed.

Chad didn't look deterred. "You're going to bring the entire news station down, Gilda. Don't you get it? Look around at all these people," he said, gesturing toward his office door. "You're sure you want to put their jobs in jeopardy too?" Chad walked around his desk and out the door, causing Gilda, Ray, and Hugo to step aside. Gilda's arms remained crossed and her face determined as she watched Chad walk by. "Our ratings are at an all-time high, people," Chad said, addressing the entire crowd. "Everyone wants to know where Gilda is and what has happened to her. We ride this one more day, and we have sweeps week sealed. Not only that, we'll take our rightful place as the number-one news station in the city. What we've all worked for. You're not going to let one woman's foolish accusations take that away from you, are you?"

Hugo stepped forward. "What, exactly, are you suggesting?"

"We're going to spin this thing."

"Spin what?" Hugo asked. "Pretend Gilda didn't show up?"

Chad smiled. "Now, Hugo, that would be misleading, wouldn't it?"

He stuck his hands in his pockets. "I'm simply suggesting we air some video of Gilda standing here in her…her bathrobe. Maybe we can gather some footage off the security camera of her walking into the station. We call it 'breaking news' and there you have it."

"You mean, don't tell the whole story," Ray said. "That's misleading."

"Suddenly everyone has a conscience, do they? Well, let me offer a little refresher course for you people. Every time you air a story, you're giving the story you want to give. You pick a sound bite here, a sound bite there, show an image here, show an image there. And what do you have? A story exactly the way you want to tell it. Everyone in this room knows how to do it. We know what image to show and when. We know what music to play under what sound bite. Give me a break!" Chad was nearly shouting now. "You expect me to believe that you're suddenly worried you're not telling the entire side of the story?" Chad gestured to Ray. "Correct me if I'm wrong, Ray, but wasn't it last year that you covered that drunk-driving story? Where the quarterback of the football team struck and killed an eighty-six-year-old woman?"

Ray nodded.

"And did you not interview his mother, his father, and all his friends? Did you not show pictures of him winning awards and making touchdowns and being crowned homecoming king?"

Ray nodded again.

"In fact, you gained special access to the prison and interviewed the young man yourself, didn't you?"

"Yes."

"If I remember, we ran that story for an entire week. And how much footage did we show of the woman's family or her funeral or that her three poodles wondered where she was?"

"What's your point?" Ray asked.

"Okay. I'll answer for you. Thirty-eight seconds. That's how much coverage that old lady got. Our quarterback, however, came across looking like a young man who had a lot going for him but made a terrible mistake. All because of airtime, visuals, and sound bites."

"We both know."

"Know what?" Chad asked.

"There's fact, and then there's truth. You can report the facts all you want, but it doesn't always tell the truth. The truth is the story I told, and it was supported by fact."

Chad smiled slightly. "But you didn't tell the whole truth, did you?" Chad looked at Hugo. "And Hugo, you and I both know that we had three hours of footage on that old woman, from interviews with her children to the sunset burial. You made the call how to air it. It sort of tugged at your heart, didn't it? You could see your own daughter, in a few years, possibly making the same kind of mistake."

"That was the story," Hugo said firmly. "The story behind the story was that a young man's life, and countless others', was forever changed by one mistake. We aired it the way we did hoping that it would have an impact on other kids and maybe they wouldn't make the same kind of mistake."

"Fair enough," Chad said mildly. "If you want to paint it as a noble endeavor, go ahead. But you didn't tell *the* story, you told *a* story, and it was a story that fit the need of the viewers and the station. Period." He paused for a moment. "Don't you see? It's bits and pieces, and following the same formula, we can save our station. I've got a report due on my desk any day now. And it's going to assess the weaknesses of this station. What's it going to tell me? Who's gutsy? Who's willing to take a risk, to lay it all on the line for success? This is your moment, people, to prove you've got what it takes to be in this business. To prove you're more than glorified tattletales. Gilda, this is your moment to prove you're a team player. That it's not all about you. You can talk all you want about justice and the right thing to do, but at the end of the day, we're all working our butts off to keep our heads above water because of you. You should've stepped down a long time ago, but instead, you just keep on keeping on. Well, it's cost us a lot. Now it's time to pay me and all these nice people back by giving us three more hours."

Hugo looked at Ray, and Ray looked at Gilda. That pink flush she had to her cheeks had vanished, and now she looked small and delicate. Tears welled in her eyes as she looked around the room.

"I won't do it," came a voice, soft and from somewhere nearby. Hugo turned but couldn't identify who said it. Then Hayden stepped forward and around another person in her way. "I won't lie on the air, or tell a half truth, or whatever it is you want us to do."

Chad smirked. "Not a problem. Go back to being an assistant, Hayden. It's what you do best. Besides, tomorrow, Gilda's back, and your job is over. Tate. Where's Tate? Now that's who my money is on. That kid's got a future. Tate?"

Hugo couldn't stop the smile. "Tate quit about fifteen minutes ago."

Chad glanced around. "Fine. We'll put Trent in. Or Jill. Even Sam—not much is going on with weather. Why don't you do it?" Chad's tone was sarcastic, but his expression flickered with desperation.

"No," Hugo said. "We're putting Gilda back on the air. Tonight." He looked at her and smiled. "Along with Hayden."

Chad growled out a laugh.

"Why not?" Hugo asked. "Tate's gone, Hayden's capable, and Gilda's an icon, especially this week. It'll bring the generations together." Hugo smiled back at everyone who was nodding in agreement. And everyone was nodding except Chad.

"That's the stupidest thing I've ever heard," Chad said. "These two are going to look ridiculous together. Gilda's old enough to be her mother. And Hugo, in case you haven't noticed, same-sex anchors, no matter what their age, look really awkward together."

"It's going to work," Hugo said, and he couldn't contain his enthusiasm. "It's going to work! We'll break new ground here, everyone. Why not?

I mean, what do we possibly have to lose here?" He looked at Gilda. "And Gilda, you've been in this business a long time. I'll leave it up to you how much you want to say on air tonight. This story is about you. You tell it."

Tears streamed down Gilda's face. "Hugo, this story is about so much more than me. Look how many lives it has affected. There are so many sides to it, so much beneath the hard-core facts." She took a deep breath and gathered herself. "But I will do my best to tell it."

Hugo slapped his hands together. "All right, folks. We've got a news story to cover, and we're on the air in three hours. Gilda, your first order is to call the police. Then I want you to get to your dressing room."

Everyone laughed, and for the first time in a long time, Hugo felt like laughing too. Really laughing. "Someone get in touch with Jill and Trent, and tell them to call me immediately. Ray, you and Beaker get out to the jail and get set up. I want a shot of Roarke walking out of jail. We are going to run breaking news in thirty minutes, before this thing leaks. Hayden, you're going to do it. We'll have complete details at ten." He looked at Chad, who suddenly didn't seem to be anybody important. "And by complete details, Chad, I mean *complete* details. You might want to start by packing up your office."

Hugo watched Chad turn and walk into his office, slamming the door shut. Somewhere in the back of his mind, he thought he remembered something in the Bible about the first being last and the last being first. He watched Hayden take Gilda's arm as they walked together toward her dressing room. He watched Ray talk to Beaker with excitement. He watched the newsroom come alive.

This was how it was supposed to be. This was news. This was human drama. And this was going to make at least one day in his life right again.

Chapter 37

Good evening. I'm Hayden Hazard, and this is News Channel 7. This evening, we are covering one of the most extraordinary stories in the history of our station. As you know, our own anchor, Gilda Braun, has been missing for several days now. Today, she was found alive and with an unprecedented story to tell. Tonight, Gilda is back in the anchor's chair, and we're so glad to have her here, alive and safe. Gilda, I know you're eager to tell your viewers where you've been and what is behind your disappearance."

"Thank you, Hayden." Gilda looked at the young woman next to her and smiled. In those tender, young eyes she saw authenticity and even wisdom. "First of all, I would like to commend Hayden for the wonderful job she has done in my absence." Gilda took a breath and could feel a nervous energy threaten to destroy her calm. She turned toward camera two and looked into the lens, knowing thousands of eyes were staring back at her. "I know there are many questions to be answered, many rumors to address, and there have been many misguided attempts to explain my situation. I know everyone is anxious for the scoop." Gilda smiled slightly. She swore she would never use that word on air, but it had to be said. And it did make her sound about two decades younger. "But before we get into details, I think something more is at stake here. I've been in the news business longer than many of you have been alive. I knew I wanted to do broadcast journalism the first day I watched Edward R. Murrow. I wanted my voice to have that deep, authoritative quality to it. I wanted to make a difference with the news I covered. Over the years, I've grown older, and life has been whizzing by me like a bullet train. Today I sit in a chair and stare out at a generation whose idol has become the instant visual.

"I, for my part, have contributed to the worship of that idol. We live in a culture that does not have time to know, nor does it care to know, all the facts. That refusal invades our need for entertainment, these lengthy descriptions, extended reports, in-depth investigations. News has become entertainment, and I am deeply grieved for it. There was a time when news made a difference. But it is rare now that news is anything more than a puffed-up, self-important sideshow. Who doesn't gather around the television, watching to see if all 183 passengers on an airplane with its nose gear stuck will survive or die in a fiery crash? We see images come through our television every day…but we've all become so numb that we've forgotten how very real the people behind those images are.

"In due time, the real story behind my ordeal will emerge. You will see images and interviews and plenty of commentary. But tonight, suffice it to say, I must resign my post." Gilda paused, hoping to keep her voice steady and professional. She blinked once and averted her eyes for a moment, but she quickly recovered and sat tall as she looked into the lens. "It has been an honor and a great pleasure serving you over the many years you have invited me into your homes. I never took that for granted. But I did lose myself. I forgot what was important to me. And I forgot that I was more than an image and a talking head. I've found myself now, and the person I am knows that for many reasons I must say good-bye."

Gilda smiled warmly, though she imagined her eyes glistened with tears of regret. She stood and walked away from the news desk. On the monitor, she could see the camera zooming in slowly on the empty chair in which she once sat. She stood to the side and watched. She'd never known so much silence to go by. Then the floor director cued Hayden, and her voice carried over the picture of the empty chair. "We'll be back after this."

Gilda turned and walked to her dressing room. She wouldn't be back on air, but Gilda Braun *was back*.

"Mr. Keegan, do you have any comment?"

"What do you plan to do?"

"Do you have anything to say to Gilda Braun?"

"Were those letters really from you, Mr. Keegan?"

"Can you give us any idea what it was like for you in jail?"

The questions shattered the quiet night air. Ray stood clustered with all the other reporters, punching his microphone toward the man walking down the front steps of the city jail.

Roarke looked tired but happy. He eyed the cameras not with surprise but with suspicion. He tried to go one way, but the horde blocked him. He held up his hand and said, "Please, let me be."

But nobody was letting him off the hook.

"Just a few questions, Mr. Keegan!" one reporter shouted. "Don't you want to vindicate yourself?"

Ray stumbled, nearly tripping Beaker, who was trying to hold the camera steady as they followed Roarke toward a cab that was parked twenty yards away.

"Please, just leave me alone," Roarke said, and the frustration on his face grew as he tried to make his way to the cab.

Ray jammed the microphone under Beaker's arm. "What are you doing?" Beaker whispered.

Without answering, Ray shoved his way through the crowd and grabbed his big friend by the arm. Ray turned to the reporters and stuck a hand out. "Leave him alone! He asked to be left alone!" Ray's voice echoed against the concrete, and the reporters hushed and whispered. "Come on, my friend," Ray said to Roarke and ushered him toward the car.

He opened the door, and Roarke laughed. "You just made a spectacle of yourself."

"What are friends for?"

Roarke lowered himself into the cab. "How's Gilda?"

"She's fine."

"Did she…mention…?"

Ray closed the door, hurrying around to the other side of the cab and hopping in. "Let's get out of here," he told the driver. He turned to Roarke. "You okay?"

"Fine. Hungry. Really hungry. We on tonight for pizza and TV?"

Ray laughed. "Yeah, unless you have a hot date."

Roarke looked down. "You're just saying that."

"No, I think you have a real shot."

"You do?"

"Yeah."

Roarke stared forward, looking bemused. Ray took a breath and tried to calm himself from all the excitement. He looked out the back window to cameras lingering in the night's darkness.

"Roarke," Ray said after a moment, "I want to…I want to apologize."

Roarke looked at him. "For what? You didn't do this to me."

"I know. I'm not talking about this. I'm talking about…I don't know. I just feel like maybe I haven't been very…" Ray searched for the words. They were hard to come by.

"Yeah?"

"I haven't really been open about my faith. We're really good friends, you know, and I don't talk about God much with you. Being around Hayden has made me understand how important it is to me, and since you're my good friend, I want you to know that about me."

Roarke laughed, and Ray felt a little self-conscious. "Dude," he said, "don't worry about it. I already know that about you."

"I know you know it, but I don't really—"

"Look, dude, you don't order salads, okay?"

"What?" Ray asked.

"It's like this. I used to hang around this guy, and every time we'd go out to eat, he'd order a salad and water. Then he would sit there and talk about the health benefits of salad and water. He was always trying to get his point across, you know? I felt like he was my friend because he thought he could change me. I'm perfectly aware of the health benefits of salad and water. I saw him once at a restaurant with another friend, and he was eating cheese fries. You're my friend because you like me. And you don't care about embarrassing yourself with me when we go places. I've never once felt like my weight was an issue. Ray, Hayden's cool and everything. I really like her. But you're cool too, and you don't have to talk about it all the time. It shows in everything you do. You know I started reading the Bible last year?"

"You did?"

"Yep. And when I go home to visit my folks, I attend church with them."

"You do."

Roarke nodded. "And you know what? I'm going to start eating more salad and drinking more water."

"You are?"

"Well, there's nothing like seeing yourself on television to get the message. They say the camera adds ten pounds, not a hundred."

"Hmm. TV-and-salad night. Has a nice ring to it."

"Whatever. I'll eat salad the rest of the time. We're sticking to pizza for TV night."

Ray laughed. "What do you say we swing by the station?"

"I hear there's a couple of hot chicks there. Maybe it's time we both burped the Tupperware."

"First, my friend, we gotta go by Walgreens. We could use some cologne."

The newsroom had finally settled down. Hugo loosened his tie and walked out of his office after checking his e-mail one more time. What a night. He'd had such an adrenaline rush he was having a hard time winding down. He wanted to do something, go out and celebrate, but everyone had gone their separate ways. Oh well. He'd pick up an Icee on the way home. He didn't want to go home and face an empty house. He wanted to go home and tell someone about his night, but there was no one to tell.

Hugo observed Chad's office. The lights were off. Chad had slithered out some time during the newscast, when everyone was distracted, reportedly carrying a couple boxes. He was never so glad to see anyone go in his life, and the fact that he had to go shamefully was all the better. The D.A.'s office had called Hugo the minute the newscast was over, and a criminal investigation had already been launched.

"Hi, Mr. Talley," Hayden said as she approached.

"Great job tonight," Hugo said, embracing her with a hug. "You really held your own. This was not an easy night to cover. Especially by yourself."

"Thank you, sir. How are you doing?"

"I'm…okay," Hugo said. He couldn't feign a smile. And he knew he didn't have to for Hayden. "I booted the Blue Pills."

"That's good news!"

"Yeah. It's nice to get some feeling back in my soul."

"It's nothing to be ashamed of, sir. The prophets in the Bible, they were some of the saddest people you ever saw. It's okay to feel deep pain. It makes joy that much nicer."

Hugo patted her on the back. "I'll see you tomorrow."

Hugo decided to go to Chad's office and see if he'd left anything behind. Turning the light on, he was surprised to see the desktop emptied of all of Chad's beloved bragging pieces and the bookcases cleaned out. The office felt cold, like nobody had opened the door in years. Dust rings

marked where memorabilia used to sit. Hugo eyed the leather chair. He'd
have to swap his out. He'd always coveted that chair.

A stapled stack of paper caught Hugo's eye. It sat in the center of
Chad's desk like it was something important. Hugo glanced around and
then nonchalantly made his way around the huge desk. He put a finger
on top of the stack and drew it near the edge of the desk. Sitting down,
he read the top page. There were a lot of fancy words, but the one that
caught Hugo's eye was "Evaluation."

"The report!" Hugo said to himself. He flipped through the pages,
which contained a lot of graphs, numbers, and charts, until he came to
the last page which simply read: "Summary." And to his disbelief, the
summary was only few, small sentences long.

Data indicates that poor ratings are due to the network programming.

"Programming?" Hugo laughed. *Programming?* The reason they were
last in the ratings was because their network had bad programming?

Reports indicate that the majority of viewers do not change
channels after viewing television shows. The network is last in
five out of seven days of its prime-time programming, which
includes three police dramas, two reality shows, and two court-
room dramas. The viewership is down for the network, there-
fore it is down for the news segments following the
above-mentioned programming.

Hugo could hardly believe it! *That* was the problem? Bad television
dramas?

"That sounded like you've had a heavy day."

Hugo looked up.

"Hi," Jane said, standing in the doorway. She was holding two boxes of Chinese food. "Thought you might be hungry."

"I'm starving," Hugo said, though barely, because he thought he might start crying. He stood and motioned for her to come in. "Pull up a chair."

"We can eat in here?" she asked.

"It's presently unoccupied," Hugo said with a smile. He reached out for the Chinese box but instead grabbed her hand. She looked up at him. "You got my e-mail?"

"Me and about thirty other ladies." She grinned. "It was the nicest thing I'd ever read. I had to share it with the girls." She set down her food. "I moved back in tonight. I'm sorry I moved out. That was a stupid thing to do."

"We have a lot to talk about."

She nodded. "There's going to have to be some changes. From both of us."

"I'm thinking about taking an eight-to-five job," Hugo said. He looked around the vacant office. "In fact, there's a nine-to-six here that just became available."

She smiled and opened up the Chinese box for him. "I ordered your favorite. Happy Family."

"We've got to stop meeting like this," Ray said as Hayden came out the back door of the station. He'd left Roarke to visit with Gilda, and things looked like they were going well.

"Hi." She grinned.

"Where's your sister?"

"She's exhausted. I sent her home a couple hours ago. You would think she was the chief of police or something around here. I had to remind her she's on *vacation*."

"You two probably have plans tomorrow."

"Nothing that can't include you."

Against his better judgment, Ray took her hand. She looked up at him, surprised but also, if his radar was working correctly, delighted. "I guess it's no surprise anymore. I kind of like you."

"Kind of?" she teased. Good, she could tease. That was a relief. He hadn't quite found her complete range. He was pretty sure she wasn't capable of sarcasm, but that was fine. The world could use fewer sarcastic people.

"I've never met anyone like you," Ray said. "You're extraordinary in every way. Assistant one day, superstar anchor the next. How do you do it?"

Hayden laughed. "Well, I do come from a long line of people who've had very colorful occupations."

At that moment, with her hair lit by the moon and her eyes shining from the gleam that must've been bouncing off of what he hoped was a million-watt smile, Ray wanted to kiss her. But considering the home-schooling background and her sister's occupation, he decided it could wait. Instead, he held her hand and watched Sam and Jill making out in the far corner of the parking lot.

Things had a way of working out.

Chapter 38

T here," Hayden said, pointing to the two-story home where she'd
spent most of her life. It still looked warm and inviting, with pris-
tine white paint and a dark red door. After their parents' death, Mitch and
Claire had moved into the old house and renovated it. So much of the
inside looked different. The room Hayden had shared with Mack was
now their four-year-old niece's bedroom, and it was decorated with Dis-
ney characters. But the outside was the same, with that red door she loved
so much. The four old rocking chairs that her grandfather had made lined
the long front porch, and dark green ivy still climbed the outside walls.

"This is a beautiful house," Ray said as he pulled behind the crowd
of cars in the driveway.

Hayden couldn't stop smiling. So much had changed in her life.
Coming home for Christmas made everything seem right. She looked at
Ray, and he was staring at the large bay window that framed the crowd
inside.

"Are you okay?" she asked.

Ray glanced at her. "Just a little nervous. I want to make a good
impression." He paused. "And I have to say I'm curious about meeting the
rest of the Hazard clan."

"Well, looks like we're the last ones to arrive, so you'll get to meet
everyone at once." She patted his hand. "They're eager to meet you. I've
told them all about you."

She'd been dating Ray for about a month, but things had turned serious pretty quickly. When he'd suggested he wanted to spend the holidays
with her, Hayden didn't hesitate. There was something special and unique
about Ray Duffey. She saw him as her flashlight, lighting a path for her

in a dark world she didn't always understand. He reminded her of her father, a sensitive man but with direction and instinct. He made her feel safe.

Ray turned off the ignition of the rental car and looked at her. "Here we are."

Hayden pointed to the window, where all her siblings peered out and waved.

"Oh my," he said, timidly waving back.

"I promise they won't eat you alive." Hayden laughed. "Come on!" She jumped out of the car. The day had clouded over, and light snowflakes had begun to fall. Mitch had put up Christmas lights on the house, and Claire had hung Mom's favorite wreath on the front door. Hayden took Ray's hand and guided him toward the front door, which Mitch opened before they were even at the porch.

Every year that passed, Mitch looked more and more mature. He stuck his hands in his pockets casually, and though he was smiling, Hayden could tell he was sizing Ray up. She caught his eyes and gave him a reassuring nod.

Mitch held out his hand to Ray. "Mitch Hazard."

"Ray Duffey."

Mitch turned to Hayden and grabbed her, pulling her into a bear hug. "Come in, come in!" he said, nearly pushing them both through the door. "Everyone's here!"

Hayden hugged each of her siblings and her two nieces. Then she introduced Ray. "Everyone, this is Ray. Ray, these are…the Hazards."

She watched Ray smile and blush a little, giving a short wave. "I'm sure I'll get all your names down before the end of the day!"

Everyone laughed and Hayden let out a little sigh. She watched as Cassie and Claire ushered Ray into the kitchen, both declaring he was, indeed, hungry and that they had plenty of food to go around. Ray glanced back once and smiled, then he disappeared through the doorway.

Hank stood nearby and Hayden walked over to him. "How are you doing?"

"Fine," he said softly and smiled, his two small dimples piercing his skin. "He seems nice."

"Yeah," Hayden said. "He's terrific."

"Mack's been showing us your tapes."

"What tapes?"

"Of your news show."

"What? She taped it?"

"When she was in town visiting you, I guess. You're really good. Wish Mom and Dad could see it."

"Thanks, Hank," she said, touching his arm. In his eyes, she could see that a lot of sadness lingered there. Christmases were hard, even with them all together. "I don't know what God has me doing there, but I guess I'll just have to trust him."

"I'm sure he has his reasons," Hank said.

Mack walked out of the kitchen and made a beeline toward Hayden. "Hey, sis," she said, pulling her into a hug and slapping her back like one of the guys.

"Tell her your news," Hank said.

"What news?" Hayden asked.

Mack smiled a little. "I got the call. They want me to go into the undercover program."

Hayden felt her heart thump.

"You don't look happy," Mack said.

"I just don't want anything to happen to you."

"I'll be fine." Mack elbowed her. "It's got to be easier than the dating scene." She looked toward the kitchen. "Ray's one great guy. Just be cautious. Don't rush into anything."

"You're one to lecture me on caution," Hayden said, swinging her arm around Mack's neck.

Mitch announced above the noise, "Time to eat!"

They all made their way into the dining room. The long table that had been handed down through four generations of Hazards was decorated with candles and garland, and their mom's china was set at each place, looking as new as the day their dad had bought it for her.

"Wow," Ray said, walking up beside her. "This is some kind of setup!"

"Claire did all this. She's a really good hostess."

Claire, pregnant to the point of looking like she was carrying a turkey inside her, walked out with a final platter. Mitch took the seat at the head of the table and everyone quieted.

"And now we will thank God for all the blessings he has given each of us throughout the year. Let's bow our heads."

Hayden closed her eyes and reached to her side. This year she had one extra blessing for which to be thankful.

Acknowledgments

The conception of this idea happened one day when I realized how fascinating people's occupations are. I recognized how much I enjoy hearing about what other people do, the culture, so to speak, of their occupations. I love exploring the perception of an occupation versus what it is really like. This birthed the Occupational Hazards series.

To say that I relied on people's expertise is a real understatement. Two people in particular helped me grasp the reality of their lives and occupations. Angi Bruss and Chris Kalinski were so gracious with their time and knowledge. This novel would not be what it is without their help. I had so much fun interviewing them.

I'd also like to thank my editor and friend, Shannon Hill, who brought so much insight and a ton of hard work into the project, as well as Jamie Cain and Laura Wright, for their input. Also, special thanks to Dudley Delffs, who continues to support my work in every way. And to everyone at WaterBrook Press, who work tirelessly in jobs that are often behind the scenes but critical to the success of any book—thanks to all of you!

Last but certainly not least, thanks to my agent, Janet Kobobel Grant; my church home, the Flock That Rocks; my ChiLibris friends; and my wonderful family, Sean, John Caleb, and Cate. I love you!

About the Author

R ENE GUTTERIDGE is the author of nine novels, including *Ghost Writer, Troubled Waters,* and the Boo series. She worked as a church playwright and drama director, writing over five hundred short sketches, before publishing her first novel and deciding to stay home with her first child.

Rene is married to Sean, a musician, and enjoys raising their two children while writing full time. She also enjoys helping new writers and teaching at writers' conferences. She and her family make their home in Oklahoma.

Please visit her Web site at www.renegutteridge.com.

GOD WORKS IN MYSTERIOUS WAYS—
ESPECIALLY IN SKARY

Available in bookstores and from online retailers.

WATERBROOK PRESS

www.waterbrookpress.com